a daring escape from the
enslavement of the evil
ferret King Agarnu
and his daughter
Princess Kurda…

T. HOWELL: 02

'Twixt leaning ash and poison gold,
Trisscar Swordmaid, look, behold,
What is sought by everyone.
Now! Ere high noon light moves on.

Praise for *Triss*

"The fifteenth saga in the Redwall series continues the satisfying formula in which the separate paths of valorous companions and brutal villains eventually converge. Expected humor is plentiful . . . And also present are the familiar feasts, all regaled in delicious detail. Of course, Jacques doesn't skimp on violent, gory battles . . . The myriad Redwall fans will relish this." —*Booklist*

"[The Redwall books are] tales of good and evil, clear and unambiguous moral stories that a parent can read and enjoy." —*Arkansas Democrat-Gazette*

"Chaos and mystery ensue, but eventually the good beasts prevail." —*The Des Moines Register*

Redwall
The book that inspired a legend—the first novel in the bestselling saga of Redwall! The epic story of a bumbling young mouse who rises up, fights back . . . and becomes a legend himself . . .

Mossflower
Brave mouse Martin and quick-talking mousethief Gonff unite to end the tyrannical reign of Tsarmina—who has set out to rule all of Mossflower Woods with an iron paw . . .

Mattimeo
Slagar the fox embarks on a terrible quest for vengeance against the fearless mouse warrior Matthias, cunningly stealing away what he most cherishes: his headstrong son Mattimeo . . .

Mariel of Redwall
After she and her father were tossed overboard by pirates, the mousemaid Mariel seeks revenge against searat Gabool the Wild . . .

Salamandastron
When the mountain stronghold of Salamandastron comes under attack, only the bold badger Lord Urthstripe stands able to protect the creatures of Redwall . . .

Martin the Warrior
The triumphant saga of a young mouse destined to become Redwall's most glorious hero . . .

The Bellmaker
The epic quest of Joseph the Bellmaker to join his daughter, Mariel the Warriormouse, in a heroic battle against a vicious Foxwolf . . .

Also look for *Castaways of the Flying Dutchman*— a thrilling adventure from Brian Jacques!

TRISS

Brian Jacques

2003
50TH
ANNIVERSARY

ACE BOOKS, NEW YORK

TRISS

An Ace Book / published by arrangement with
The Redwall Abbey Company, Ltd.

PRINTING HISTORY
Philomel hardcover edition / September 2002
Ace mass-market edition / September 2003

ISBN: 0-441-01095-4

ACE®
Ace Books are published by The Berkley Publishing Group,
a division of Penguin Group (USA) Inc.,
375 Hudson Street, New York, New York 10014.
ACE and the "A" design
are trademarks belonging to Penguin Group (USA) Inc.

PRINTED IN THE UNITED STATES OF AMERICA

10 9 8 7 6 5 4 3 2 1

PEACE
ISLAND

THE GREAT SEA

STOPDOG

RAURA'S CAVE

DUNES

MIGOOCH
TRIBE

SALAMANDASTRON

SEARATS' HUT

DUNES

FLATLANDS

Routes Taken by Vessels on Great Sea

○○ Stopdog's Route

•• Triss's Route

□□ Seascab's Route

□–□ Seascab with Vessel in Tow

NORTH
PATH

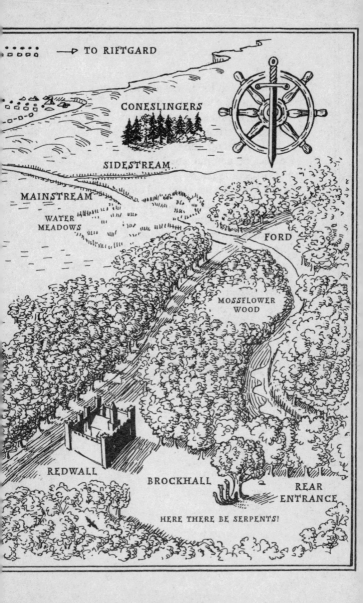

TO RIFTGARD

CONESLINGERS

SIDESTREAM

MAINSTREAM

WATER
MEADOWS

FORD

MOSSFLOWER
WOOD

REDWALL

BROCKHALL

REAR
ENTRANCE

HERE THERE BE SERPENTS!

Were days that long, was grass so green,
In seasons of youthful desire,
Roaming o'er seas of aquamarine,
Where westering suns drown in fire?
'Cross mountain, forest and river,
I'd wander, carefree and bold,
Never heeding the days to come,
When I'd wake up, slow and old.
Oh, how the silent summer noon,
Warms dusty memories,
In an orchard, midst my dreams,
'Neath verdant, shadeful trees.
Come visit me, you little ones,
Hear stories, songs and rhymes,
A roving warrior's saga,
Of far-gone, golden times.

—Kroova's Song

BOOK ONE

A Season of Runaways

1

Princess Kurda was considered by all to be a highly skilled swordbeast, the best blade at Riftgard since her grandsire, great King Sarengo. She was a Pure Ferret, as were all of the royal blood, creamy white from tailtip to nose, with coral pink eyes. Kurda worked hard at being the best. Every morning from breakfast to lunch she could be found practising in her weapon chamber. This particular morning was no exception.

Rows of turnips hung by strings from the rafters. Two squirrel slaves, one a young maid, the other an old grizzled male, stood by, awaiting her commands. The Princess donned a single long-sleeved glove of ecru linen. Pulling it tight on her paw, she nodded at the long rack of swords, her voice curt and imperious. "De heavy sabre, yarr!"

Triss the squirrelmaid hastily wrapped an oiled rag about her paws and lifted the heavy sabre from the rack by its blade, carefully avoiding getting oil on the leather-bound hilt. Kurda flexed her limbs gracefully. Without even a glance at Triss, she grabbed the sword, drawing the blade so swift and hard from the squirrelmaid's grasp that it sliced through the oiled rag and nicked her paw. Triss

3

leaped smartly out of the way, her teeth clenched in pain as the ferret Princess went slashing at the turnips. With deadly accuracy the heavy sabre made the air thrum, chopping through the solid vegetables. Halves of turnip flew everywhere, striking both slaves, bouncing off the floor and caroming from the walls until there was nothing left but straggled roots dangling from the strings. Kurda wiped a scrap of turnip from her cheek with the linen glove, panting slightly. Holding the sabre point forward to Triss, the ferret grated, "Clean diss good, I try rapier now, yarr, de rapier."

Triss hurried to select the rapier Kurda had indicated.

The old male squirrel, Drufo, scrambled to clear the floor of turnip pieces, careful to wipe any wet spots, lest the Princess should slip. It would go badly for both slaves if she did, as they knew from bitter experience.

Fixing her paw firmly in the basket hilt of the rapier, Kurda whipped the keen flexible blade back and forth, enjoying the sound it made. Triss signalled Drufo with her eyes; he skirted the walls furtively until he arrived behind his young friend. Diligently cleaning the sabre blade upon her oiled rag, Triss watched Kurda work with the rapier. Poising herself like a dancer, with one paw outstretched, she attacked the root stems on the string ends.

Snick! Whip! Zip!

The blade struck with swift snakelike movements, snicking the roots off at the string, though the last two strikes missed the roots, severing the strings. Kurda snorted with anger. Dropping the sword carelessly, she rapped out more commands.

"Get me der straight sword, middle size! You get ready to throw ven I say. Move yourselves!"

Drufo ran and picked up two of the larger chunks of cut turnip. Triss grabbed the rapier and selected a long, medium-weight straight sword, with a cross-hilt and fine-honed double blade.

The ferret Princess snatched it impatiently from her, whirling the blade and shouting at Drufo, "Trow! Trow!"

Throwing both pieces of turnip upward, Drufo covered

his head with both paws, jumping out of the way. Kurda slashed up, then sideways, in two speedy movements. She cut one piece, but the other thudded to the ground untouched.

Kurda's pink eyes blazed with anger at her error. Drufo was bending to pick up the pieces when she whipped the flat of the blade viciously across his back.

"Stupid oaf! Ven I say trow, you trow dem proper. Trow high, vot do you tink I am? You t'ick mudbrain bunglepaws!"

Drufo stayed bent over, still protecting his head with both paws as the ferret vented her spleen on him with the flat of the swordblade. Knowing her old friend was in danger of losing his life, Triss yelled as she began throwing turnip chunks in the air with all the haste she could muster.

"Princess, I can throw better than that old fool, look. Hup! Hup! I can send them higher, too. Ready, throw!"

The ploy diverted Kurda's attention. She turned and chopped both chunks as they came down. The squirrelmaid, who was ready with two more, made sure she tossed them high and slow. The sword cut through the chunks easily. Kurda was out of breath, but her temper had improved. She leaned on the sword, nodding and panting. "You t'row good, dat's de vay to t'row turnips, yarr!"

The door opened and another Pure Ferret ambled in. He was bigger than his sister and had a silly grin all over his face.

Kurda addressed her brother contemptuously, "Vot do you vant, Bladd bootnose?"

Bladd was used to his sister's insulting manner. His droopy oversized gut wobbled as he chuckled. "Huh huh huh huh, you make a better cook than a swordbeast, yar. You still choppin' turnips for der stew, liddle sister. Huh huh!"

She raised the sword, advancing on him. "One day I chop you for der stew, lard barrel. Yarr, I chop you good. Vy you come here, eh?"

Bladd shuffled to the door and held it half open, creating a shield between them. He poked his tongue childishly at Kurda. "King vant to see you, yarr, he mad about der herrinks. He say come now, quick, or he put a big lock on his door."

Kurda pointed at him with the sword, her bad mood renewed. "Sneaknose, you been tellink tales to King about me!"

Bladd took off downstairs, laughing idiotically, with his sister hard on his heels.

Triss helped Drufo up as the door slammed behind the two Pure Ferrets. She steadied the old squirrel.

"Are you all right, Drufo? She didn't cut you, did she?"

He smiled, rubbing his back ruefully. "Thanks t'you, she didn't, missie, thanks t'you. Huh, swordbeast? That white streak o' slime ain't half the swordbeast yore dad was. White streak o' slime!"

Triss chuckled silently at the way her old friend often repeated phrases. She set about gathering up the cut turnips. "Lend a paw with these, you old grumbler, let's get them out to the others. Every bit helps."

The squirrelmaid poked her head over the sill of the high chamber window and imitated the harsh skrike of a seagull. Far below a gang of creatures were working, laying a path of pine logs to make a walkway between the sloping grass hill and the rocky shore of the river. It would run from the gates of Riftgard fortress, along its edge, to the jetty. Moored at the pier's end, facing downriver to the sea, was a ship. It was small, with one square purple sail, a very pretty little craft, skilfully built and wonderfully ornamented.

The workers, an assortment of squirrels, mice, hedgehogs and otters, looked upward at the window. A slim, pretty sea ottermaid named Sleeve murmured, "Stan' aside, mates, 'ere comes supper, thanks to miz Triss."

As they dropped the turnips down, Triss questioned Drufo about her father, whom she had never known.

"Do you remember my father? What was he like, Drufo?"

The old squirrel shook his head fondly. "Like no other, young 'un, like no other! There was never a swordbeast born could cross blades with Rocc Arrem, an' I knows, 'cos I fought alongside him. We was like brothers."

Triss heaved more turnips over the sill to her friends below. "But despite all that, he was slain."

Drufo paused for a moment, his face grim. "Brought him down with arrows, more'n a score o' those dirty Riftgard rats. I remembers it t'this day, but Rocc, yore pa, went down fightin', snapped his blade an' hurled it in their faces. Rocc Arrem wasn't never one to surrender, never!"

Triss sighed as she swept the last vegetables up from the floor. "Wish I'd have been old enough to fight, they'd have never got him. We'd have still been free, living in the mountains upriver, all of us."

Drufo watched those below gathering the last of the turnips. He looked to the high mountains on either side of the river, thick pinewoods sweeping down their sides to the rocky banks, still patched with last winter's heavy snows.

The old squirrel voiced his thoughts. "Ah, 'tis a cold hard place to live, this northland, I tell ye, an' a harder place to be enslaved in than any I know."

Keeping her voice low, the squirrelmaid drew close to Drufo. "Once we've got the boat built, it'll be downriver and the open seas for us. We'll find a better life in those lands beyond the great sea."

Drufo grabbed her paw anxiously. "Triss, don't be foolish, nobeast ever escaped from Riftgard an' lived to tell of it. You've got to ferget those mad ideas!"

Triss pulled her paw from his grasp. "Four more days, that's all it'll take, Drufo. I'm not missing a chance of freedom by being fainthearted. Shogg the otter and Welfo the hedgehog have been helping me. Our boat should be ready soon. You can escape with us, there's room for one more!"

Drufo looked at Triss anxiously, keeping his voice low. "You three don't know the danger yore in, missy. Y'just don't know. Stealin' wood from the King's new walkway, pilin' up vittles, an' tackin' t'gether rags for a sail, 'tis too risky. I want no part of it, no part, d'ye hear me? I ain't goin' t'be responsible for the death o' young creatures!"

Triss cocked an ear to a sound outside on the stairway. She muttered swiftly under her breath, "Stow it, somebeast's coming!"

The door was wrenched suddenly open. Captain Riftun and four of his rats marched into the chamber. Triss and Drufo fell upon all fours, making a pretence of cleaning the floor. Riftun was a mean-natured rat; cruelty was stamped on his narrow face. He leaned on his spear and placed a footpaw hard on the back of Triss's neck.

"So tell me, wot are slaves doin' alone an' unattended in a roomful o' weapons, eh?"

Drufo kept his tone humble as he explained. "Princess Kurda gave us permission, Cap'n. We been attendin' her at sword practice. Me'n'Triss is just cleanin' up. We're near done, Cap'n."

The rat Captain glanced round the chamber. "Looks clean enough t'me, eh, lads?"

The four rat guards nodded their agreement eagerly. "Aye, Cap'n!"

Riftun lashed out with his spearhaft, knocking Drufo flat. "Don't ever let me catch yer alone in here again. Get down t'the walkway an' report for work. On the double!"

Drufo scrambled up and made for the door. Triss was about to rise and go with him, when Riftun brought his spearpoint down to rest at the base of her skull.

"Not you. I've had you watched, missy. Yore goin' down in the cages t'keep yore two liddle pals, the otter an' the spikepig, company. Bet you thought I didn't know you was makin' an escape boat. Take 'er, guards!"

Two rat guards grabbed Triss's paws whilst the other two menaced her with their spears. Drufo tried to intercede.

"But, Cap'n, it couldn't have been 'er, she's been with me all the time fer days now. Triss ain't done nothin', I swear it!"

Riftun gave him a kick that sent him staggering awkwardly down the stairs. He winked at the four guards. "Show me a slave an' I'll show yer a liar. Take 'er to the cages, she'll sing like a lark when I'm done with 'er!"

Triss was hauled off downstairs, tight-lipped but struggling. She glimpsed Drufo's pitiful, frightened face as they dragged her off to the punishment cages.

2

Beyond the trackless seas, far from the fjords and mountains of Riftgard, the late-spring afternoon was mellow as butter and blue as a periwinkle. Great Abbot Apodemus and his old companion Malbun Grimp sat dozing peacefully on the sunwarmed ramparts of Redwall Abbey's northeast wall. Somewhere over the treetops of Mossflower a blackbird warbled its rich, fruity aria to the season. There was hardly a breeze to be felt. Down below, the Abbey grounds basked still and silent in serene noontide.

Malbun was a wood mouse who held the position of Healer and Recorder of Redwall. She was drifting off into a slumber, both eyelids drooping as her chin dropped toward her chest. An admiral butterfly ventured to perch on Malbun's nose. She banished it with a twitch of her snout and opened one eye.

"Any sign of them coming back yet, Ap?"

Apodemus had his eyes closed, but he was not yet asleep. "I dunno. Why don't you go and look, Mal?"

Malbun opened her other eye, turning her gaze upon the yellow-necked mouse who was Father Abbot of all

Redwall. "'Cos I'm only a lowly beast around here. You're the Abbot, they're your responsibility."

Apodemus kept his eyes closed, relishing the warmth of the sun upon his ears. "'Tis a powerful position, being Abbot of Redwall Abbey."

Malbun considered this statement before replying. "Aye, so it is."

A slow smile broke the repose of Apodemus's features. "Well, I'm glad you realise that, Mal. I order you to go and look to see if the whortleberry gathering party are returning!"

With a sigh, the Healer Recorder pushed herself upright, smiling as she shuffled to the battlements. "That's a flagrant abuse of power, Father Abbot. I'll do your bidding, but I'd like it noted, I'm doing it under protest."

The Abbot opened his eyes and winked at his companion. "Protest noted. Now go and look, will you?"

Turning her back, Malbun leaned against the battlement. "Don't have to look, I can hear 'em. . . . Listen!"

Carrying over the still air, voices could be heard raised in song, young and old alike.

> "All in the days of spring,
> When flowers do bloom about,
> We merrily go and sing ho ho,
> Whortleberries come out.
>
> Whortleberry, blaeberry, bilberry, too,
> They taste so good to me, my friend,
> As they must do to you,
> And yet I say to you now,
> Oh what is in a name,
> For whortle bil or blae sir,
> The berry's all the same.
>
> We range the forest far, for,
> There's nobeast will deny,
> Nought is half so good, ho ho,
> As a whortleberry pie.

Bil whortle blae, blae whortle bil,
All around the woodlands,
Field or valley or hill,
Get ready good old cook, marm,
Stoke up your oven's fire,
A whortleberry pie this eve,
Is my dear heart's desire!"

Apodemus rose and stretched lazily. "We'd best go
down and open the gate if we want any pie for supper.
C'mon, I'll race you!"

Malbun Grimp's huge middle shook with laughter.
"Are you talking to me or that snail just by your footpaw?
Race me indeed, we'll soon need a hoist to get us up and
down the wallstairs!"

The Abbot gazed ruefully at his considerable stomach.
"Oh, for the days when we were Dibbuns."

The two old friends linked paws and shuffled off down
the broad, red sandstone wallsteps, chunnering away to
one another.

"I'll wager that snail would've beaten you easily."

"Aye, you're right, Mal, we're built for comfort, not
speed."

"Right, and we've got the dignity of our positions to
consider. Wouldn't look right, a Father Abbot and a
Healer Recorder, charging about like two frantic frogs."

Wandering between vegetable patches and around
through the orchard, they came out onto the front lawns.
Late daffodils, blue milkwort, buttercup and pink speed-
well bordered the soft green grass. Behind them, as they
made their way down the gravelled path to the main gate,
Redwall Abbey reared high in dusty rose-hued splendour.
Arches, buttresses, bell tower, carved gables and long
stained-glass windows sat square in the centre of Abbey
grounds and stout outer walls. Apodemus stopped a moment, turning to cast a fond eye over the ancient structure,
then gripped his friend's paw a little firmer and sighed. "I
love our Abbey, Mal. Sometimes I get up early just to

look at it in dawn's light. There's no place like it, is there?"

Malbun patted his paw fondly. "No place at all, Ap. We're lucky to be living here, very lucky!"

Between them the two mice lifted the wooden gatelock bar amid ribald calls outside from the Redwallers.

"Open up or we'll scoff all these berries!"

"Quick, afore we starve t'death!"

"Hurr you'm never starven t'death with ee gurt stummick loike that on ee, zurr!"

"Huh, take a look at y'self, ole fatty chops!"

The huge oaken doors swung open. Apodemus and Malbun jumped smartly aside as the Abbey creatures poured in: squirrels, mice, moles, hedgehogs, some shrews, three otters, even a large old female hare. All of them carried some form of basket, pail or trug, laden with ripe whortleberries. Abbeybabes, or Dibbuns as they were called, had their paws and faces liberally stained with the purplish blue juice. The Abbot shook his head in mock severity at a molechild who was stained from top to tail.

"Dearie me, master Ruggum. You look as if you've had a busy day."

Ruggum explained in curious molespeech. "Oi wurr doin' gurtly well, zurr. 'Til ee rascal Bikkle pushed oi into ee barsket o' berries, but oi etted moi way out'n 'em!"

Bikkle, a tiny squirrel with a huge bushy tail, tried hard to look the picture of innocence as she defended herself. "Farver h'Abbot, Ruggum pulled me tail, so I chased 'im an' 'e falled into the berries hisself by askident!"

Apodemus could not hide a smile as he replied. "By askident? Goodness me, that Ruggum's always having askidents. What d'you say, Memm Flackery?"

The fat old female hare, who was nurse to all the Dibbuns, pulled off her poke bonnet and fanned her whiskers with it. "Fiends, marauders, all of 'em, wot! Into the tub with the bloomin' lot of you, that's what I jolly well say!"

Yells of dismay arose from the Dibbuns.

"Waaah! Not more tubs, Memm. Us on'y got baffed last night!"

"Oi'll be scrubbed to ee shadow if'n you'm put oi in ee tub again, marm. B'aint that roight, Turfee?"

Turfee the mousebabe scowled darkly. "They scrubs likkle ones t'death in this h'Abbey."

Gurdle Sprink, the hedgehog Cellarkeeper, eyed Turfee sternly. "You mind yore manners, young 'un. A bath'll do ye the world o' good, then off t'bed with the lot of ye!"

A horrified silence fell over the Dibbun contingent, then Ruggum raised a small clenched paw and shouted. "Dab!"

Immediately the little creatures scattered, all yelling, "Dab! Dab! Dab!"

Memm Flackery grabbed the two nearest her to stop them escaping. "I say, somebeast close the flippin' gates, sharpish!"

Skipper of otters was lithe and brawny. He swiftly closed the gates and dropped the gatelock shut. Catching a hogbabe by her apron strings, he shook his rudderlike tail in puzzlement. "Dab? Wot's Dab s'pposed t'mean, mate?"

Crikulus, the ancient shrew Gatekeeper, explained. "It's those liddle scamps' latest secret society. Dibbuns Against Bedtime, that's wot Dab means. They don't like bein' sent off t'the dormitories early. Huh, I'll never join 'em, I loves my bed. I'd stay there all season if'n I could."

After a deal of chasing, the Dibbuns were rounded up and herded inside the Abbey. Memm and Friar Gooch, the Abbey squirrel cook, followed them in.

"Hmm, think I'll preserve some o' those berries in honey."

Memm tried not to look crestfallen. "Not all of 'em, Friar, you are goin' t'cook some tonight?"

Friar Gooch patted her paw. "Don't fret yoreself, marm, I've planned some whortleberry sponge puddens with cream'n'crumble toppin'."

The fat Harenurse's eyes lit up greedily. "Oh my aunt's whiskers, you're a bloomin' toff, Gooch, an absobally-lutely first-rate grubslinger, wot wot!"

* * *

Beyond the locked Abbey gates, Ruggum the molebabe and Bikkle the little squirrel sat on the path giggling. They had evaded capture by nipping out a second before Skipper shut the doors.

"Hurr hurr hurr, ee Skipper a'most chopped moi tail offen in yon doors. Oi bee's most speedy furr a mole-choild, hurr hurr!"

Bikkle whirled her bushy tail in delight. "Us won't get baffed an' sended to bed early no no more!"

Ruggum sucked juice from a berry he found on the path. "Burr, Bikk, we'm shore t'get catchered if'n uz be a stoppen owt yurr. Ee Memm bee's orful farst furr a gurt fatty beast."

Bikkle did not hesitate. She grabbed her friend's paw resolutely. "Cummon, us run 'way an' live inna woods, Ruggs!"

Ruggum brightened up at the thought of this capital scheme. "You'm roight, Bikk. They'm b'aint goin' to keep baffin uz an' senden uz oop t'bed urrly til we'm old an' dead and buried!"

Paw in paw, the two Dibbuns trundled off north up the path, cutting off east into Mossflower woodlands and making plans for the marvellous life that lay ahead of them.

"We live up inna tree an' eat h'apples, an', an' . . . anyfink!"

"Boi 'okey uz will, an' never get ee baff, or even ee likkle wash!"

"Us jus' play an' play, all day an' all night long. Hee-hee!"

"Burr, they'm big uns be vurry sad us'n's gonned."

"Tchah! Now they 'ave to baff each other an' all go to beds early. That teach 'em a lessing, heeheehee!"

Spring eventide threaded crimson gold and lavender rays through the leafy woodland canopy. Day's last long shadows darkened Redwall's lawns, shading the grass to a rich emerald carpet. Single notes and trills of nightingales echoed from the Abbey orchard, serenading the coming darkness.

Gooch and his trusty assistant cook, a young molemaid named Furrel, checked the rows of earthenware basins as they loaded up trolleys in the kitchens. Both were satisfied that the whortleberry puddings were perfect in every respect. Foremole, Redwall's traditional mole leader, stood by his trolley, button nose aquiver at the delicious aroma from the basins. Furrel chuckled at the look of bliss upon his face.

"Yurr, h'uncle, oi'll 'elp ee load yon trolley, afore yore snout be a fallen off in deloight."

Foremole patted his niece's paw fondly. "You'm a gudd an' koindly mole, Furrel, thankee gurtly moi deary."

Redwall had two dining rooms, the Great Hall, which was used for large feasts or special occasions, and Cavern Hole, a smaller, more comfortable chamber. Abbot Apodemus took his seat in Cavern Hole, alongside Gurdle Sprink.

Rubbing his paws in anticipation, the Cellarhog remarked, "I wager in less'n a score o'days 'twill be light and warm enough to take our evenin' meals out in the orchard."

Apodemus watched Redwallers seating themselves. "Aye, summer will soon be upon us, Gurdle. Oh, look out, here comes trouble, but don't they look nice and clean!"

Straight from the bathtubs, a horde of Dibbuns in clean smocks came dashing in to claim their favourite places at table. Memm, Sister Vernal, and Malbun shepherded them in, issuing cautions as they tried to keep order.

"Don't run! What've you been told about running, eh? Walk nice and slowly now. That includes you, Turfee!"

"I say, go around the table, you little rip, don't you dare try to climb over the Father Abbot!"

"Come here, Toobles; there's still soap in your ears. Gotcha!"

The tiny hedgehog squealed outrageously as Malbun cleaned out the soap with her apron corner. "Waaah! I bein' slayed, 'elp me!"

Old Crikulus the Gatekeeper covered both ears and closed his eyes tightly, until peace was restored and the

Dibbuns seated. Abbot Apodemus rose from his chair to recite a grace.

> "Be thankful for the season,
> And happy for the day,
> Be grateful for the bounty,
> Which comes to us this way.
> Good food from the earth is grown,
> And brought unto our table,
> By honest toil and labour,
> Let's eat, whilst we are able!"

The silence was broken by Turfee the mousebabe, banging his spoon upon the table and roaring, "Where are me pudden?"

Gurdle Sprink glared severely at the rowdy Dibbun for a moment. Then he called out, "Aye, where's that child's pudden? Bring it right away!"

Amid hoots of laughter the puddings were served.

Halfway through the meal, Skipper of otters was pouring out dandelion cordial for some of the little ones, when he glanced around and scratched his rudder.

"Where's liddle Ruggum an' Bikkle, anybeast seen 'em?"

Sister Vernal looked at Memm. "I can't recall bathing them, can you, Memm?"

"Not really. I say, Malbun old thing, did you scrub those two rascals, wot?"

Malbun tapped a paw against her chin thoughtfully. "No, marm, but I recall we had two clean smocks left over when we dressed the Dibbuns. I just thought they were extras."

The Abbot addressed the other Dibbuns, who were spooning in whortleberry pudding and swigging cordial as if they had survived a seven-season famine.

"Did any of you see Ruggum or Bikkle this evening?"

Foremole murmured into the Abbot's ear, "No use arskin' they'm h'infants, they'm busy h'eatin' puddens."

Memm Flackery chuckled drily. "Indeed they are, old scout. You'd get more sense out o' the puddens than those ravenous scoundrels. Just look at 'em eat!"

Gooch and Furrel went and took a quick look around the kitchens. The two missing Dibbuns were nowhere to be seen.

Old Crikulus shrugged his narrow shoulders. "They've prob'ly pinched a couple of puddens for themselves and gone off to eat 'em without gettin' bathed first."

Apodemus was inclined to agree with him. "That's right, they'll turn up sooner or later. I wager they're snoozing in some quiet corner. If anybeast should find them, I'd be grateful if you'd bring them both up to my room. I intend to have a severe word or two with the master Ruggum and miss Bikkle!"

Out in Mossflower Woods darkness had descended. Moonshadows and shifting breezes created an eerie pattern through the leafy tree canopy. Somewhere an owl hooted and a nightjar's churring staccato rent the woodlands. Ruggum and Bikkle huddled together in the shelter of a fallen beech tree. Both were cold, hungry and frightened little creatures.

"Yurr Bikk, oi'm a thinken et bee's toime t'go 'ome."

Bikkle was of the same mind as her molefriend. "Me wanna go 'ome too, but Memm be shoutin' at us an' send us to beds wiv no puddens. Me still wanna go 'ome, though."

"Yurr, then us'ns go roight now, and you be knowen ee way, Bikk?"

"I not know. You said you knowed."

"Hoo urr, you'm gurt fibber, oi never said oi knowed ee way."

They sat looking at one another, then chorused aloud, "Waaaaaah, we's lost!"

3

Nightdark waves lapped softly upon the western shores, like a black velvet cloak, endlessly unfolding. A full honey-dipped moon shed its light over the scene below, softening the rugged formation of the mountain fortress known as Salamandastron. Four creatures, two badgers and two hares, leaned on a smooth, wide windowledge, about halfway up the mountain. Watching the activity of two young creatures below, they conversed in hushed tones.

Lord Hightor, the great badger ruler, heaved a sigh of resignation. "Oh well, if he's got to go, then I suppose 'tis inevitable. Maybe out there Sagaxus will learn a bit of sense. I can't take much more of that young rip. It's probably all for the best. If he stays here disobeying me, we're bound to meet head-on before long. I still have my doubts about it, though!"

Hightor's wife, the Lady Merola, stroked his paw soothingly. "It didn't do you much harm when you ran off for a few seasons as a young badger, you told me so yourself. Two male badgers on the same mountain, 'twould never work, even I can see that. Poor Sagaxus, he's a born rebel. I can't help worrying about him, he's got a lot of

19

hard lessons to learn out there. I do hope he'll be all right."

Colonel Whippscut of the Long Patrol was a hare of the old school. Twirling his waxed moustached whiskers, he puffed out his medal-clad chest and murmured confidently, "All right, m'Lady, h'rumph! Why shouldn't they be jolly well all right, wot wot? Your son an' my son leavin' home for a bloomin' good adventure or two, do 'em a bit o' good, I say. Keep the blighters out of our fur for a while. D'you know, it's flippin' hard t'tell who's the worst rascal between 'em, young Sagaxus or that Bescarum o' mine. Rogues! Rogues 'n' bounders, the pair of 'em! H'rumph, they won't come t'much harm, believe me."

The Colonel's wife, Dunfreda, interrupted him sharply. "I should say they won't come t'much harm, Whippy, 'cos you'll be out there followin' 'em. Every pawstep of the way!"

The Colonel looked slightly deflated. He began blustering, "I say, steady on there, old gel. Me, followin' those two rips for a couple o' seasons? What d'you think I am, a bloomin' stalkin' duck? H'rumph! Out o' the question, I'm afraid. I've got my command to attend to here, wot wot?"

That did it. Dunfreda whipped out a small kerchief and commenced weeping inconsolably. "Whoohoohoo, you heartless hare, waaaaah, my poor little Bescarum an' Merola's only son, wanderin' round the world willy-nilly like two homeless waifs. Whoohoowahaaah!"

Whippscut raised his eyes in despair, apologising to Lord Hightor, as Lady Merola comforted Dunfreda. "Beg pardon, sah, the good lady wife can't resist a jolly good blubber now'n'again, wot. Here y'are, old gel, take my kerchief. That'n won't be enough t'stop the tide comin' in, wot!"

Lord Hightor placed a paw about his friend's shoulders. "Dunfreda's right, you'd best follow them. Keep an eye on that pair. It'll only be for a season or two, but it will put all our minds at rest. I'll look after the mountain."

Colonel Whippscut was flabbergasted. "Wot, wot, wot? Harrrumph! Y-y-you don't really mean that."

"O' course he means it, you waxy whiskered clot. Go on, follow the two poor dears, right now, this very instant. Go!"

Hightor peered out of the window at Sagaxus and Bescarum on the beach far below. Both were starting to head north, carrying massive backpacks of food, purloined from Salamandastron's kitchens. The Badger Lord could not resist a chuckle.

"Look at that lot they're carrying, 'tis enough to keep a regiment going for a full season. No need to hurry, Whippscut. At the rate they're travelling, you'll pick up their trail quite easily after breakfast tomorrow morning. Huh, that's if they've left enough vittles in the kitchens for the cooks to make a meal."

Bescarum tried to set the pack more evenly between his shoulderblades, grunting with exertion. "Wait f'me, Sagax old lad. Me blinkin' paws are sinkin' in the sand with this confounded heavy pack!"

Sagaxus, who liked to be called Sagax, was by far the stronger of the pair, though even he was staggering a little as he called back over his shoulder to Bescarum, who preferred the name Scarum.

"Good job we don't have to walk far, then, Scarum. Just round the cove to the rocks at the north spur. Wait'll Kroova sees all the grub we've brought along, eh?"

Scarum caught up with his badger pal. "Indeed. If we're runnin' off t'sea then we need the proper scoff, wot? Yukko! I don't mind livin' off the land, but that idea of Kroova's of livin' off the sea: raw fish'n'seaweed! Huh, I should jolly well say not!"

They edged down below the tideline to where the sand was firmer underpaw. It made the going easier.

Sagax was smiling happily. "No more being sentenced to washing the pots!"

Scarum grinned like a demented rabbit. "Or scrubbin' the bloomin' Mess Hall out!"

"Or weeding the rock gardens all day!"

"Or polishing spears'n'shields in the dratted armoury!"

Sagax did a fair imitation of his father: "I can understand Bescarum, he's a hare. But you, Sagaxus, you're supposed to be the son of a Badger Lord! Why your mother even named you Sagaxus I'll never know. She said you were supposed to be like that old Badger Lord she'd read of, Russano the Wise, her fifth great-grandsire. So she called you Sagaxus, that's supposed to mean wise also. Huh, now this is your last chance, d'you hear me?"

Scarum did an even better impersonation of his father: "H'rumph! You're a rip, sah, an utter flippin' rip, wot! Y'see these grey hairs ruinin' me best moustache, eh? Well, you put 'em there. H'rumph, if y'were one o' my patrol I'd clap you in the bally dungeons, wot wot?"

Kroova heard them coming. Making the bowline fast to a nubby rock, he leaped down onto the sand. "C'mon, mateys, stir yore stumps or we'll miss the tide!"

His boat was a double-sailed ketch, which he had stolen from three searats a season ago. It was a trim-lined little vessel, with fore and aft sails, the latter being set slightly in front of the rudder. Kroova gasped as he helped them heave their packs on board. He loosed the bowline as they skipped aboard.

"Stamp me rudder, are y'tryin' to sink us wid vittles?"

Scarum wrinkled his nose at the sea otter. "You carry on scoffin' seaweed'n'sprats. Leave this to us, pal."

Kroova caught the breeze just right and sent the ketch skimming on a northwesterly tack, his hearty laugh ringing out. "Haharr, me old mateys, welcome aboard the *Stopdog*!"

Sagax looked at him questioningly. "The *Stopdog*?"

Kroova winked and gave him a roguish grin. "Aye, that's the last thing I 'eard those three searats hollerin' after me. 'Stop, dog!' So that's wot I called 'er, the *Stopdog*!"

Scarum tried to rise gingerly from a sitting position.

"Shouldn't we be doin' something, paddling or tugging on ropes to make this boat go?"

Kroova had the foresail fixed and the sternsail controlled in one paw as he held the tiller with the other. "Bless yer 'eart, no, mate. This 'un goes by 'erself, though it needs a h'expert's paw like mine t'keep 'er on course."

Sagax watched the skilful otter intently. "How did you learn to sail like that? Did your parents teach you?"

Kroova shrugged. "I never 'ad no parents, mate, least-ways none that I knows about. Out 'ere on the briny, it's learn fast or perish, an' I wasn't about ready to perish!"

Scarum began opening one of the backpacks. "Talkin' about parents, I'll bet my old pa's whiskers will really curl when he finds I've hopped it. As for Mum, she'll probably blubber till there ain't a dry kerchief on the flip-pin' mountain. Loves a good blubber, though it drives Pa scatty, wot."

Sagax felt his conscience twinging guiltily. "Let's stop talking about parents. 'Tisn't as though we'll never see 'em again. We'll prob'ly drift back to the mountain in a season or two, when we're too grown up for them to push and shove us around. Huh, bet they'll be glad to see us then. Come on, Kroova, you old seadog, give us one of your ditties."

Immediately the cheerful sea otter obliged. He had a good voice.

"Ho I was born in a storm one winter's morn,
When I was fat an' tiny,
With the wind for me pa, an' the sea for a ma,
Way out upon the briny.
Let the codfish sing with a dingaling,
An' the crabs dance wid the shark,
Hey ho again for the rollin' main,
I'm 'appy as a lark!

Ho my first ship was a cockleshell,
I painted it bright red,

Away I'd judder, wid me tail as a rudder,
Far o'er the waves I sped,
Then a nice ole whale made me a sail
That helped me to go faster,
So I voyaged free on the deep blue sea,
Wid nobeast for a master!"

The little ketch was soon lost in a world of silver-flecked water, scudding out north northwest over moonlit realms, like a willow leaf on a huge immeasurable pond.

By midnoon of the following day, Colonel Whippscut was back at Salamandastron, making his report to Lord Hightor after a fruitless search of the shoreline.

"H'rumph, I, er, lost 'em, sah!"

Hightor's brows beetled low over his fierce dark eyes. "Lost them, Colonel! How in the name of scut and stripes could you lose two younguns carrying great heavy backpacks? Surely their trail must have been clear enough!"

Whippscut shook his head, scratching his waxed moustache until it became like tattered string. "H'rumph! Well, had m'breakfast as usual an hour after dawn, took a stroll down t'the blinkin' beach, an' there were the tracks, plain as the ears on me bonce, wot. Had followed 'em for only a short while, when they bloomin' well vanished."

Controlling his temper, the Badger Lord stared at his colonel. "Where exactly did you lose sight of the trail?"

Whippscut gestured back over his shoulder. "Round those rocks at the north spur, sah, where the tide washes over at flood. Not a sign o' the scoundrels. I've got a search patrol north along the coast. They'll find the villains if anybeast can. Did all I could, sah, 'pologies!"

Hightor placed a huge paw on his friend's shoulder. "No need for apologies, Whipp. You did your best."

A knock sounded on the chamber door. Hightor called briskly, "Come!"

Sergeant Widepaw, a fine big capable veteran hare, entered. With him was a runner, an extremely bright and pretty haremaid. Both saluted with their lances, then Widepaw spoke, keeping his eyes to the front.

"Colonel, sah, M'Lud, no sight o' the runaways whatso h'ever! H'I did find this, 'owever, on the north spur. Sah!" He produced a quadrant braided cord of red and green.

The Colonel inspected it, nodding. "Bescarum's paw bracelet, made it for him m'self. What'n the name o' scut'n'ears would that be doin' there, wot?"

Sergeant Widepaw nodded for the haremaid to step forward. "Sah, Mindel 'as somethin' t'say. Carry on, gel."

The haremaid runner bobbed a brief curtsy. "I was on afternoon second run yesterday, sah. Spotted a little sailboat near the north spur. There was an otter on board. He didn't see me, sah, so I carried on, thought nothing more about it, sah. He looked like most sea otters, friendly type."

Lord Hightor and the Colonel exchanged glances. The badger waited until Whippscut had dismissed both hares.

When they had gone, the Colonel banged a clenched paw on the tabletop. "Kroova Wavedog, I might have bally well known!"

The hackles rose on Hightor's broad shoulders. "That pirate! How many times have I warned Sagaxus to stay away from him? Kroova is nought but trouble. I wish I had that young sea otter in front of me now, I'd make that rudder of his sting. He wouldn't sit down for a season!"

The realisation of what had happened hit Whippscut. "O lack a bally day an' a half! They've run off t'sea with him. No wonder I lost the confounded trail!"

Hightor sat at the table, placing his striped head between both paws, his voice weary with resignation. "Better not breathe a word to Merola or Dunfreda. No use worrying them further. Just say you lost the tracks over some rocks and shifting sands. I tell you, Whipp, those two have really done it now!"

The Colonel twirled his moustache fiercely, tidying it up. "You're right, old friend, the worryin' will be up to us from now on, wot!"

4

Agarnu, King of Riftgard, hated the sea. Just the smell of it could make him queasy. He loathed sailing and detested boats or ships of any kind. He had been this way even when he embarked on that final ill-fated voyage with his father, Sarengo. Agarnu was quite content to rule his kingdom of fjords, mountains, pine forests and pebble beaches from the comfort of his father's throne.

Only Pure Ferrets could rule Riftgard. Agarnu was a true Pure Ferret, snow white with pink, glittering eyes. Slumping down on the purple cushions of his shell-ornamented throne, he glared out over his gross stomach, which extended right up to his many chins. A false leg, carved from the white bone of some great fish, clicked against the floor, a dreadful reminder of that last voyage. Agarnu had been the only creature to make it back to Riftgard alive.

The peace of his throne room was shattered when Prince Bladd came hurtling in yelling and wailing, "Dadda, stop Kurda, she come after me vit der sword!"

He scrambled behind the throne as Princess Kurda bounded in, swinging her sword.

Agarnu nodded swiftly to his Ratguards. Six of them penned her in, grasping their spearhafts to form a barrier around the irate Princess. Agarnu glared at her.

"Stop dis fightink, you 'ear me, Kurda. Now, vot you got to say for youself, eh?"

The Princess strode forward with the Ratguards still penning her, but moving along with her as she went. She sighted her brother cowering behind the throne and pointed the sword at him.

"Dat fat toad, he been tellink tales again, yarr!"

Her father's pink eyes continued glaring at her. "Tales? T'ree barrels of herrink iz not tales. Dey's food, not practice for der swordplayink, you no do dat vit food!"

Kurda curled a contemptuous lip at her father and made some slashing motions in the air with her sword. "Tchak! Der be plenty more fishes in der sea."

Agarnu stamped his carved-bone paw irately on the floor. "Nodd if you keep choppink dem up for sword practice der von't. But I not called you two here to talk about dat. Guards, leave us now. Bladd, gedd out from be'ind dat chair. Listen, I haff somet'ink important to talk about vit you both."

As the guards left, Captain Riftun strode in. Agarnu eyed him quizzically.

"Yarr, Riftun, vot is it?"

The Captain saluted with his spear. "I've caught the creatures who were stealin' the walkway wood, yer majesty. Three of em, a squirrel, an otter an' a 'edgehog. They was buildin' an escape boat, stockin' it up with vittles, too. Turnips, carrots an' chopped 'errings. Wot d'yer want doin' with em? I've got all three locked up in the punishment cages."

Agarnu snorted and shrugged moodily. "Vy tell me all dis? You de Cap'n, do vat you vant, don't bodder me. A king have udder t'ings to do. Drown dem!"

Kurda interrupted. "No, I'll deal wid dem. Live prisoners are good for der sword practice, 'specially thiefs an' escapers!"

Agarnu shook his head, regarding his daughter with dis-

taste. "Jus' like you gran'father. Yarr, you a cruel one, Kurda.
So be it. Save spoilin' more barrels of herrink, eh, eh?" The
King's stomach shook as he laughed at his little joke.

Kurda pawed her sword edge with anticipation.

Triss and her two friends shuddered with cold. The punishment cage was half submerged in the cold shallows of
the fjord, which were fed by icy water from the mountains.

Welfo the hogmaid laughed bitterly. "Brrr! Can't stop
me spikes from rattlin'!"

Shogg the otter stared gloomily through the boards.
"Yore spikes'll soon stop rattlin' fer good, marm, Cap'n
Riftun will see to that. It's the death sentence fer us,
mates, I'll wager anythin' on it!"

Triss gritted through her chattering teeth, "Stop that
kind of talk, Shogg, we're not dead yet. Let's see what we
can do about breaking out of this cage. We've got nothing
to lose now."

The rest of the slaves labouring on the walkway cast
sympathetic glances at the three creatures in the punishment cage. A guard flicked his whip out across their
backs.

"Get workin', ye idle scum, lest yer wanna join yore
pals in the cage. C'mon now, get that wood laid,
straighten that ground, keep those logs tight'n'even there,
ye lazy lot!"

Badly fed and poorly clad, the slaves toiled on, unable
to stop and remove long pine splinters from their paws,
or bandage scuffed, stone-scarred limbs with tufts of
moss and grass. They were terrified to stop, lest they too
end up in the dreaded cages, where they would face death
from exposure, or execution at the sadistic whim of Captain Riftun.

Only when darkness fell were the workers allowed to
halt in their chores. Whips cracked as they were led off to
the slave quarters beneath Riftgard. There they would be
fed on a single bowl of grain porridge, some vegetable
roots and a pail of water between every group of ten.

Beneath the waning moon, cold night winds swept over the deserted worksite. Activity in the cage, which had begun furiously, had now slackened, owing to the intense cold eating into the bones of the three captives. They had groped around through the floor bars and collected rocks from the riverbed. First they had tried wedging them between the bars to see if the metal could be bent enough for them to squeeze through. Then Shogg the otter, who was the strongest and most resistant to cold, battered away at the big well-greased padlock on the door grille. Neither method proved successful. Their limbs were growing slower and stiffer as the night advanced.

Welfo began to weep softly. Triss threw a paw about her shoulders and tried to comfort the hogmaid. "Hush now, friend. Don't cry. Keep your chin up, you wouldn't want to give those vermin the satisfaction of seeing your tears now, would you? We'll go down fighting to the last if we have to."

Shogg let his rock sink to the cage floor, whispering urgently, "Quiet, mates, somebeast's comin'!"

It was Flith, Captain Riftun's lieutenant. He stood watching them closely. Ceasing their activities, the three prisoners grasped the bars and stared dumbly back at the impassive rat.

Flith poked his spear out and rattled the bars. He tested the padlock by prodding it. "Don't worry, you three. We won't let yer freeze t'death in there. We ain't that cold-'earted, are we, 'edgepig?"

Welfo wiped tears from her eyes hopefully. "No, Lieutenant."

Flith leaned on his spear and chuckled. "Course we ain't. Not one of us Riftgard rats is goin' to lay a paw on ye. Princess Kurda is, though. She's got somethin' special planned fer yew three. Goodnight an' sleep well, now . . . if ye can. Heeheeheehee!"

Flith padded off, sniggering happily at his own joke. Triss felt her stomach turn over at the thought of Princess Kurda's unimaginable designs for their fate.

No sooner had the lieutenant gone than another figure appeared from behind a stack of pine logs on the bank. "Triss, miss Trissy, are ye all right?"

The young squirrelmaid pushed her face to the bars, trying to keep the eagerness in her voice down. "Drufo, I kept hoping you'd come. Good old Drufo!"

The aged squirrel waded into the water, holding an earthenware jug above his head. He brought it close to the bars, but it would not go through.

"Come t'the bars, Welfo. You too, Shogg. I'll hold this while ye sup it. 'Tis some 'ot veggible soup we made out o' bits of this'n'that. 'Tain't much, but it'll keep the life in ye."

Heads up, mouths open, they stood side by side whilst Drufo shared the soup out, pouring it, still hot, straight into their mouths. It was meagre stuff, cobbled together with a few pawfuls of grain, turnip, carrot and some wild onion.

Triss had never tasted anything so delicious. They held their mouths open like young fledglings being fed by a mother bird, until the last precious drop had gone.

"Sorry that's all I could manage for ye," Drufo apologised.

Triss felt new life coursing through her. "What's happening inside Riftgard? What've you heard, Drufo?"

The old squirrel pulled himself to the river side of the cage, so that he could not be seen from the bank. "I follered Cap'n Riftun up t'the throne room an' got me ear close to the door. Good'n'close, Triss. Agarnu was talkin' to Kurda an' Bladd, an' Riftun, too. So, 'ere's the gist of it. We've got t'get you out o' this cage, one way or another, quick! 'Cos instead o' turnips, Kurda plans on usin' you three for 'er sword practice. I don't like t'bring bad news, but that's 'ow 'tis goin' t'be!"

Shogg began shaking the cage bars. "Then wot're ye waitin' for, Drufo? Get us out of 'ere, now!"

Welfo clasped Triss's paw anxiously. "But what'll we do then? They've prob'ly smashed our escape boat up. We've got no food, no weapons, an' no place to hide. Riggan the slavecatcher will hunt us down. We'll be dragged back here for Kurda to slice up with her swords!"

Triss had to stifle her friend's mouth with a paw before she started to get hysterical. "Hush now, I'm sure Drufo has a plan. Panicking will get us nowhere. Er, you have got a plan, haven't you, Drufo?"

The old squirrel bit his lip and shrugged. "It ain't much of an idea, but 'tis yore only 'ope."

He fumbled an object through the bars to Triss. It was a file, rusted, broken and old, with a piece of rag where the handle once was.

"I risked me life gettin' that. My old bones won't take this icy water much longer, but 'ere's wot you must do. Once you've filed through the bars, yore only 'ope is to steal the King's new boat an' sail away to someplace they'll never find ye. I'm sorry I couldn't do more for ye, Trissy, but that's it."

"You did all you could, old friend. We'll manage. Now get yourself out of this fjord and back inside before you freeze to death."

Drufo took her paw and clasped it fervently. "Yore the model of yore dad, missy. Good luck an' fortune be with ye!"

5

Far from the Northlands and Riftgard, beyond the great seas, dew glinted off the leaves as a warm spring day dawned over Mossflower Wood. Bikkle was still asleep, curled up beneath the beech trunk, covered by last autumn's dead leaves. Ruggum, however, was up and about, as the molebabe's confidence had returned with the advent of daylight and sunshine. He dug up coltsfoot roots and found more whortleberries and young dandelion buds. Trundling back to the fallen tree trunk, he wakened his little squirrel friend by tickling her nose with a stem of hedge mustard plant.

"Yurr, waken ee oop, gurt dozeychops, oi finded brekkist!"

Bikkle rubbed her eyes with grubby paws, sat up and scratched her bushy tail. "H'I'm firsty!"

Ruggum reached up and grabbed a low-hanging wych hazel branch. Shaking it, he drenched Bikkle's head with dew, chortling, "Hurr hurr, you'm 'ave a gudd drink, moi dearie!"

Bikkle seized another branch and sprinkled him back. They giggled and chuckled, splashing one another with dew and rolling in the dead leaves.

The breakfast was not a roaring success. Bikkle lost no time in telling her friend, "I still hung'y, that not nice brekkist, me like warm pasties an' strawbee juice. When are us goin' back to the H'Abbey?"

Ruggum lay on his back, gently kicking the wych hazel twigs and catching the water in his open mouth. "We'm losted. Dunno ee way back to H'Abbey. Oi 'speck they'm come a looken furr us'n's afore long. Whichaways de ee thinken Red'all bee's, Bikk?"

The Dibbun squirrel pointed with her tail. "West norf h'east, dat way . . . me fink."

They set off in the direction she had indicated, neither of the two babes feeling very confident.

But it was a warm bright day, almost summerlike, and the anxiety they were causing did not occur to their infant minds. Along the way they found other things to eat and a small stream, where they drank their fill and had a good old paddle.

Gurdle Sprink had discarded his heavy apron and climbed the cellar stairs for the third time that morning. Puffing and panting, the Cellarhog made his way out into the orchard, where he sat down on an upturned wheelbarrow, next to Malbun.

"That's the fourth time I've searched those cellars o' mine. Still not a whisker of those two rogues t'be seen."

The Healer Recorder beat dust from her faded green habit. "I've been scouring the gatehouse since the crack o' dawn without any luck whatsoever. Where can they be?"

Crikulus, the ancient shrew Gatekeeper, approached. "Move up there, Gurdle, my old paws are weary from rootin' round the dormitories, an' me back is broken in ten places from crawlin' round under beds. What a pair o' pickles those Dibbuns are. Ho there, Memm Flackery, anythin' new?" The fat Harenurse dug a few warm almond scones from her apron pocket and munched on them worriedly.

"Nope, 'fraid not, old lad. That rotten Gooch won't jolly well let me search his kitchens anymore! Huh, cooks are like that, ain't they? Heard the Abbot tellin' Skipper to round up his otters for a woodland search, though I can't think for the bally life o'me how the little scoundrels slipped out, wot?"

Abbot Apodemus stood at the gate, calling advice to Skipper and two stalwart young otters as they set off north up the path. "Find a stream if you can. See if there are any Guosim shrews about, they may have seen our Dibbuns."

Skipper waved his javelin in the air, acknowledging Apodemus. "Right y'are, Father Abbot, though if'n shrews 'ad found 'em, they'd prob'ly brought 'em back 'ere long since. 'Tis worth a try, though. Don't fret yoreself, mate. We'll find Ruggum'n'Bikkle if'n they're out there. Go in, an' keep those gates closed now."

The sunny day clouded slowly. It was late afternoon when the two little runaways decided they were even more lost than they had been. All around them the silent vastness of Mossflower seemed to be closing in. Ruggum was making plans for the oncoming darkness.

"Hurr, Bikk, us'ns b'aint a-getten caught out in ee open when it bee's dark, burr, nay marm. We'm lukk abowt furr ee cumfy likkle den an' camp in thurr, all safe an' cozy loike."

Bikkle was forced to agree. She pointed off to the sky eastward. "Lookit dem clouds, might rain by dark."

Even though they were only Dibbuns, the tiny creatures had instinctive feelings about weather conditions. Wandering farther into the woodland, Ruggum held up a pudgy digging claw.

"Oi'm thinken ee bee's roight, Bikk, breezes starten to move ee treetops. Us'n's best foind ee gudd cover, hurr, by 'okey aye!"

As often happens with springtide weather, the change was sudden. Low breezes gathered force, scurrying through the random ranked trunks of oak, beech, alder, sycamore, elm and other forest giants. The tree canopy began swaying, creating a forceful rustling of twig, branch and leaf. Paw in paw, the two little ones ran through the gusting woods, afraid of being outside the Abbey walls, which represented safety, peace and home. Late noontide darkened as lowering clouds raced to cloak the previously bright day. After an all-too-brief spit-spot of damp, the rains came sweeping in, thick and heavy, driven by the gale, slanting through the leafy canopy and drenching the loamy ground.

Breathless and fearful, the Dibbuns took temporary refuge against the massive trunk of an ancient spreading oak. Still clutching one another's paws, they stood with their backs against the rough bark. Ruggum cast an angry glance at the skies, resentful of the trick played on him by the elements. Bikkle, scared out of her wits by the stormy event, began to whimper.

"Me not like alla this, ho no, not one likkle bit!"

Ruggum pulled her around to what appeared to be the lee side of the oak. She gave a sudden squeak. "Yeek!"

The Dibbun mole blew a sigh of frustration. "Worra matta now, marm? B'aint so windy this yurr soide."

Bikkle turned to face the tree. "Likkle door wiv words on it, see?"

It was a door, let into the broad oak trunk low down.

Ruggum traced the word carved on it with his digging claw. "Oi wonders wot ee wurd do say, Bikk?"

Bikkle shrugged. "I non't know. Open a door afore uz gets soaked an' drowned."

Moss, soil and dead vegetation had built up under the door. Ruggum found a stout stick and levered at it whilst Bikkle shoved hard. The door scrunched against the ground as it gave way, fraction by fraction, opening inward. Groaning rusty hinges popped free and the whole thing heeled crazily. This left a space through which they could both enter.

Some Guosim shrews, who had been on their way to visit Redwall, met up with Skipper and his two otters as they entered the fringes of Mossflower.

Spiky-furred little creatures with coloured headbands and short kilts, they all carried rapiers in their broad belts.

Guosim were known by the initials of their kind, Guerilla Union of Shrews in Mossflower, and they were traditional friends and allies of Redwall Abbey. Their Chieftain held the title Log a Log. He was always the toughest and wisest of the shrews.

Skipper saluted them cheerily, hugging the leader affectionately. "Haharr, Log a Log Groo, you ole streamwhomper. Yore just the laddo we're lookin' for. I bring ye a message from the Abbot."

Groo and his twenty shrews listened as Skipper told them of the two lost Dibbuns. They agreed to help with the search, one of them piping up from the back, "We'll find the liddle snips, an' old Gooch the Cook'll reward us with double 'elpings of everything. Yum yum!"

Log a Log Groo cast a severe eye over the speaker. "I'll reward ye with a pair o' boxed ears, m'laddo. We don't need no rewards fer helpin' friends. That ain't the Guosim way."

Skipper chuckled. "No offence, mate, I know wot yore pal meant. We'll all get double 'elpings if'n we find the Dibbuns. Come on."

They struck off into the woods and soon picked up a trail.

Ruggum and Bikkle stayed in the entranceway of the hole from which an old flight of steps ran down into the darkness beyond. Neither felt brave enough to venture any further. They stood in the doorway, where it was sheltered from the rain. Again, the little mole traced the lettering on the door. He was unable to read or write.

"Oi wonder wot thiz yurr place be called?"

Bikkle stared at the lettering, blinked and yawned. Sleep was beginning to overcome her. The word on the door was written thus: "Brockhall."

She pretended that she could read and translated. "I can read words better'n you, Rugg. It say, hide in 'ere from d'rain."

"Burr, you'm makin' et oop!"

"No I not!"

"Yuss you bee's!"

Bikkle was tired and not prepared to continue the argument, so she changed the subject. "Wonder wot down dose steps?"

The molebabe ventured to the top step and peered downward into the gloom. "Sumthin' shoiny!"

Bikkle scoffed. "You not see'd sumthin' shiny down d'steps."

Ruggum was a molebabe born to argue. "Ho, yuss oi did!"

Bikkle sat down. Leaning against the wall, she closed her eyes, not wanting to get into another debate with her stubborn friend. "Well, if it bee's nice'n'shiny, you go an' gerrit f'me."

Ruggum needed no second bidding, he was overcome with curiosity. "Roight, then, oi'll goo an' gerrit to show ee oi speaked true!"

Nerving himself up, he descended the steps, hugging the side wall closely.

Bikkle dozed off amid visions of Cavern Hole and a wonderful meal of hot plum pudding with creamy almond sauce, and a beaker of strawberry cordial. She was very partial to anything with the flavour of strawberries. But she was instantly brought back to reality by the sound of a gruff mole shriek, as Ruggum came out of the gloom like a dark-furred cannonball, a shiny golden object gripped in one paw. He grabbed Bikkle with his free paw and pulled her along, out into the rain and wind.

"Whooooaaarrr! Coom on! Quick loike!"

Bikkle dug her footpaws in, reluctant to be out in the weather. However, the look of shock and dumb terror on Ruggum's face and the fearful glance he shot over his shoulder at the dark hole behind them soon decided her. Wordlessly she ran headlong beside him, out into the darkness of the storm-torn woodlands.

Brambles snagged their smocks, sodden shrubbery made them stumble, rain beat in their faces. Both Dibbuns fled as though a pack of foxes were after them.

"Over here, I see 'em, there they go!"

The strange gruff-sounding voice sent them scurrying even faster, hearts pounding fearfully, sobbing for breath. Suddenly they were seized in a grip of iron. Their tiny footpaws left the ground as they were whirled high into the air.

"Haharr, gotcher, me liddle beauties!"

6

Skipper of otters held the two limp figures close to him. Log a Log Groo took a swift look at them, shaking his head reprovingly at the otter Chieftain.

"Wot were ye thinkin' of, y'great riverdog? You gone an' scared the liddle 'uns right out their senses. Pouncin' on 'em like that, shame on ye!"

Skipper's face was such a picture of dismay that Log a Log was forced to smile. He clapped his friend's back. "No real harm done, Skip. They're safe enough now. Let's get 'em back to Redwall. Memm Flackery an' ole Malbun'll soon 'ave the rascals as right as rain!"

Skipper covered the unconscious pair with his cloak. "Ain't nothin' right about rain, matey. Don't tell Memm or Malbun this, or they'll 'ave me rudder for rugstrings!"

Gurdle Sprink and old Crikulus were keeping watch on the northeast wall battlements. Peering out into the rain-swept night, they held their lanterns high.

The Cellarhog was first to hear Skipper's powerful shout. "Ahoy the Abbey, anybeast 'ome? We're comin' in!"

Crikulus swung his lantern to and fro as Gurdle yelled, "Come in by the northeast wicker gate, Skip me ole mate!"

Hurrying down the wallstairs, the Gatekeeper and the Cellarhog withdrew the bolts on a small gate in the centre of the rampart wall. He held up his lantern.

"Over 'ere, Skip! Hah, I see you got some Guosim with ye. Welcome, friends, get in 'ere outta the weather. Well well, ye found the Dibbuns. Good trackin', pals!"

Blankets were laid near the hearth in front of the fire at Cavern Hole. Abbot Apodemus watched anxiously as Malbun Grimp tended to the little ones' bruises and scratches. Skipper warmed his paws by the blaze.

"Groo spotted 'em east an' a touch north in the woodlands. I'm surprised two babes could've gotten that far alone."

Memm Flackery held a small camphor vial under the Dibbuns' noses. Screwing their faces, they coughed and whined as they began to come around. The Harenurse spoke without looking up. "Huh, I'm never surprised at anythin' flippin' Dibbuns can get up to, wot. Especially these two fiends, wot wot? I say, Groo old lad, what's that thing you've got there?"

Log a Log Groo passed the shining object over to the Abbot. "It fell from the molebabe's paw when Skipper grabb . . . er, picked 'im up. 'Tis 'eavy enough, I tell ye."

Apodemus inspected the object, holding it near to the firelight. It was bright yellow metal, a thick oblong band, smooth to the touch. On either curve of the oblong a jet black stone twinkled. Sculpted at the centre of the band was a curious inset design.

The good Father Abbot passed the stone on to Crikulus. "I can't make head nor tail of it. You take a look, old one."

Nodding his head, the ancient shrew Gatekeeper spoke. "Hmm, 'tis a pawring, meant to fit over the broadest part of somebeast's paw. Very nicely crafted too, from the finest gold. You see these two black stones? They are true jet, rare precious gems. But as for the markings on it, I'm afraid I haven't the slightest idea what they mean."

Ruggum and Bikkle were sufficiently recovered to sit up. They looked at their elders sheepishly. "Hurr, zurrs, we'm gotten losted."

Bikkle nodded vigorous agreement, then decided to blame Memm and Skipper. She pointed an accusing paw at them. "Youse locked d'gate on us, we was shutted out. Us knock an' knock, but nobeast 'ear us. So we go for a walk inna woodses."

The Harenurse muttered under her breath. "Locked 'em out? Fibbin' little wretches, wot wot!"

Foremole Urrm, the traditional leader of all Redwall moles, came trundling in. Urrm had brought supper for the runaways. "Yurr, oi saved ee summ workleberry pudden an' a beaker of strawbee corjul apiece. Tho' you'm b'aint deservin' of et. You'm a roight pair o' scallywaggers, hurr aye!"

The Dibbuns hugged Foremole Urrm, then set about eating like ravenous beasts.

Apodemus whispered to the Foremole. "Baby Bikkle is a dreadful liar, we won't get the truth out of her. See if you can coax Ruggum to tell you what happened."

Urrm wrinkled his jolly face as he winked both eyes at the Abbot. "You'm leave et to oi, zurr. Oi'll foind out ee trooth!"

Dibbuns liked and trusted the Foremole, and Urrm soon had the molebabe telling all. Licking pudding from his wooden spoon, Ruggum related his story:

"Yurr now, let oi think. Ho yuss, we'm was losted in ee furrest, summwhurrs east norf south. Et wurr a comen on to rain, us'n's run round an' round looken furr shelter. Ee skoi went all darkened an' wind blowed an' rain falled. Et wurr turrible, zurr, jus' turrible! H'all of ee sudding we foinded a gurt h'oak tree, burr ay, wi' a likkle door in et. So uzz opinged ee dor an' getted in owt ee rainwet."

As if not wanting to explain further, the molebabe went silent and began licking his pudding bowl out. Foremole Urrm took the bowl from him and shoved the pawring under Ruggum's nose.

"Tell ee zurr H'Abbot 'ow ee gotted this yurr h'object."

Ruggum babbled out a veritable deluge of words. "Oi falled down ee gurt 'ole wi' stairs on et an' grabbed ee h'objeck. Thurr wurr ee gurt monister surrpint an' ee snowy whoite giant, oi runned away vurry farst afore they eated oi!" Ruggum threw himself facedown on the blanket, wrapping it round his head, an indication that he would speak no more to anybeast.

Foremole Urrm took Bikkle upon his lap. "Yurr, ee'm a silly ole feller, bain't ee. You'm a gudd choild, tell oi abowt ee likkle door in ee h'oak tree."

Bikkle dipped her paw in the strawberrry cordial and did a scrawl upon the floor near the hearth. "Me fink dat was writted onna door."

The squirrelbabe's markings were hard to decipher. *B o k a l.* The gaps in between the letters were filled in with Bikkle's fanciful swirls. Urrm studied it, scratching his chin.

"Lukks loike ee wurm wriggle to oi."

Malbun, however, grew quite excited. She turned to Crikulus. "Can you see what it looks like?"

The ancient shrew peered at it and shrugged. "I'm afraid not. Should I know?"

Without replying, Malbun took a charred twig from the hearth and wrote underneath Bikkle's attempt the word *Brockhall.*

She compared the word to the letters the Dibbun had made.

"See, there's the *B,* an *o,* a *k,* an *a* and one of the *l*'s. It's Brockhall, sure as the fur on your face, they've found Brockhall!"

Memm Flackery busied herself wrapping both Dibbuns in their blankets, ready to be carried up to the dormitories. "What'n the name of my aunt's pinafore is Brockhall, wot?"

Malbun explained patiently. "Brockhall was once the home of badgers, but it was used by Redwallers before the Abbey was ever built. It was so long ago that the exact location of the place has been lost. Crikulus and I read of it in some old gatehouse records. We've been researching it, trying to find out more about Brockhall. It's a vitally important part of our Abbey's early history. Now the Dibbuns have stumbled upon it purely by accident. Who knows what we might find inside that ancient place?"

Memm twitched her long ears fussily. "Indeed. Great monster serpents an' snowy white giants, if Ruggum's to be believed, wot?"

Foremole Urrm brandished the jet-studded gold pawring. "Hurr, an' gurt wunnerful treasures loike this'n, may'ap!"

All eyes were fixed on the pawring. It glinted in the firelight.

Gooch the squirrelcook gave voice to what they were all thinking. "A store of 'idden jewels'n'gold. 'Twould be a treasure hunt!"

Sister Vernal, normally a shy, austere mouse, leapt up, crying, "A treasure hunt! That's for me! When do we start?"

7

The ketch *Stopdog* plowed her way merrily northward, westering a slight touch. Kroova, having shown Sagax the rudiments of tiller, ropes and sail, was taking a nap beneath the broad seat in the bows, which served well as a tiny cabin. Like a fish to water, the young badger had taken to the seafaring life. He enjoyed the freedom of wind and wave.

Scarum turned his back upon Sagax. Sitting on the bowseat, he began rummaging in the knapsacks, muttering to himself, "Nutbread an' cheese an' apples, wot wot. That's the stuff t'put the twinkle in a chap's eyes. I say, what bounder's gone an' scoffed all the blinkin' apples, eh, wot?"

Keeping the ketch on a level keel, Sagax answered the hare. "You have, you great stomach on legs. What're you doing rummaging in those packs again?"

Scarum looked up indignantly. "Doin'? What'n the name o' perishin' barnacles d'you think I'm doin', eh? I'm makin' a meal t'keep jolly old body'n'fur together. A chap can't survive on fresh air, y'know!"

Sagax stared severely at his gluttonous friend. "That'll

44

be your fourth meal today, and it's barely noon. Go easy
on those supplies—they're all we've got."

Scarum held up a wedge of thick yellow cheese. "Oh,
right, well, I'll just have a smidgeon of this to tide me
over until dinner. Hawhaw! Tide me over, wot. Now,
there's a nautical expression for you, me ole heartie, me
old seadog, me old barnacle bottom, eh, eh, hawhawhaw!"

Sagax quickly lashed the tiller arm to a sailrope.
Bounding for'ard, he grabbed the cheese from Scarum's
paw and dropped it back into the knapsack. Then, taking
both packs, he made his way aft and stowed them under
the stern seat.

"You've eaten quite enough for one day, mate. I'll take
charge of the supplies. You can just wait until dinner this
evening, like me and Kroova."

The hare glared at him and flopped his ears indignantly.
"You, sah, are a flippin' grubswiper, a pirate! Huh, de-
privin' a poor young 'un like me of vittles. You'll stunt my
growth. I'm warning you, if I die, it'll be your rotten
fault!"

His friend chuckled. "If you can stay alive until dinner,
there's hope for you. But just put one thieving paw near
these rations and I'll bite it!"

Scarum scuffed the deck dolefully. "Does this mean
I'm goin' to starve t'death?"

The badger hardened his expression. "Aye!"

The hare's mood changed in an instant. He became
tough and resolute. Grabbing a coil of rope, he declaimed
aloud, "Right then, so bloomin' well be it! I'll fish for me
food, that's what I'll jolly well do. Oh yes, us old sailin'
beasts can get along spiffingly on the bounty provided by
the briny. Fish, that's the ticket, whoppin' great fat tasty
fish, wot!"

Tying an oversized hook onto the rope, Scarum
searched about and came up with two apple cores, which
he stuck on the hook. Whirling the lot around his head, he
cast it out into the sea. "Right ho, come on, little fishies.
No, on second thoughts, come on, big fishies, you little
chaps stay put. Well, come on, you big chaps, take the

blinkin' bait. I can't sit around here starvin', y'know, so get a flippin' move on!"

Wakened by the disturbance, Kroova came out on deck. Rubbing sleep from his eyes, he took over the tiller from Sagax. "Wot's ole Scarum up to now, matey?"

"Oh, him, he's got to catch a fish before he dies of starvation."

"Haharr, him die of starvation, that's a good 'un. He ate more brekkist than both of us, an' he's scoffed two more meals since then. . . ."

"Three," Sagax corrected the sea otter.

Scarum cast a jaundiced eye over their smiling faces. "Go on, laugh, you curmudgeons, but when I catch a whoppin' great fish, you ain't gettin' any. Not a confounded morsel, so there!"

Kroova's keen eye caught a large dorsal fin homing in on the line. He leaped up, yelling, "Pull that line in, quick! Heave it in, matey!"

Scarum defiantly tied the line to the bowsprit. "Shan't! No point in gettin' jealous an' shoutin' at me."

He fell over backward as the line was snapped taut and the ketch took off like an arrow, with Kroova roaring, "Shark! We've been caught by a shark!"

Whipping out a small knife, Sagax dashed to the bow. He raised it to chop at the rope, but Scarum struck his paw aside. The knife dropped into the sea and sank.

Kroova came running. He grabbed the hare by his tunic front. "Ye blitherin' fool, didn't you 'ear wot I said? That's a shark towin' us, a full-growed shark, too, by the rate we're goin'."

Sagax dashed water from his eyes as the ketch set up a bow wave. "Aye, and the only weapon we've got aboard you just knocked out of my paw!"

Scarum fought free of the sea otter's grip and sat down amidships. "Good old mister shark, wot, givin' us a fine ride, ain't he? I vote we let him tow us along for a league or two, wot. When he gets tired and packs in pullin' us, we'll heave him aboard an' cook him up into a good big scoff. Super idea, wot?"

Bumping up and down, the ketch skimmed over the waves. It was difficult to stand. Kroova crouched close to the triumphantly grinning hare and berated him.

"Belay, ye flop-eared, pot-bellied, wire-whiskered buffoon! Yore trouble is that y'don't realise we've caught a big savage beast 'ere, or rather it's got us. We're ridin' the whirlwind an' yore sittin' there smilin'. You can't see the danger we're in! Ye don't even know wot a shark looks like!"

Scarum twanged the taut line with a carefree paw. "Oh, don't get your rudder in an uproar, old chap. I expect the jolly old shark's enjoyin' this as much as I am, wot? Huh, you two are just jealous I was the one who jolly well caught the fish. Anyhow, I bet we get to where we're goin' a blinkin' sight faster'n we would twiddlin' the tiller an' tweakin' those sail ropes. Our friend the shark'll get worn out, you'll see. Then all we do is pop the blighter aboard for dinner!"

Sagax clung to the stern seat, blinking spray from his eyes. Though he hated to admit it, he was actually enjoying the sensation of speed, never having travelled at such a rate in all his life. The young badger tried to calm his otter friend.

"Maybe Scarum's right. No real need to panic, is there?"

Kroova's head banged the for'ard mastpole as they shot sideways onto a choppy wave. Ignoring the pain, he yelled furiously, "I'm surprised at you, mate! That shark could turn any moment an' smash this vessel to splinters, or it could suddenly dive an' pull us all down with it. Hah, wait'll it gets tired, then pop it aboard fer dinner? Don't lissen t'that fool. If'n we pulled a live shark aboard without a weapon atween us, we'd be the dinner! It'd eat us alive!"

The danger they were in suddenly hit Scarum. His jaw dropped. "Oh corks, we're in a bit of a bloomin' fix, wot. S'all your fault, Sagax. Y'should've let me have a snack instead of makin' me fish for it. What do we do now, chaps?"

The shark made the decision for them by slacking off for a moment, then going into a dive. The *Stopdog*'s stern began to lift clear of the water. Kroova had surmised right. They were beginning to be pulled under.

"Eulaliiiaaaaaa!"

Scarum made a dive for the rope, which was attached to the great seabeast. Frantically he bared his teeth and savagely tore at the rope fibres like some sort of mad creature. Sagax and Kroova could only sit flabbergasted at the sight of their friend, suddenly gone wild, roaring as he chomped away.

"Grrmph grrmph! Y'flippin' foul fish! Chompchompchomp! You ain't pullin' us down t'the blinkin' bottom! Gratch gratch! Can't have my ma blubbin' herself t'death! Grrmph! Chomp! Grumff! Grratch! Go an' find your own dratted dinner! Grripp!"

Curling and twirling, the rope strands began to part. Scarum's jaws began going fifty to the dozen, his large, white buck teeth moving like a blur as he attacked the fraying fibres. Finally there was a loud twang as the rope snapped. All three were thrown flat. The *Stopdog* splashed down onto an even keel.

Kroova was first up. He dashed over to Scarum, who was lying facedown on the bow seat, and pounded his back delightedly. "Haharr, ye did it, shipmate! Stiffen me rudder, I never seen anythin' like that afore. 'Twas tremendous!"

Still with his head hard against seat timbers, face down, the young hare called out in a strange language, "Gow! Geggoff! Gon't goo gakk!"

Sagax placed his head flat on the seat, level with his friend. Trying hard not to burst out laughing, he explained Scarum's predicament to Kroova. "You'll never believe this, but he's got his front teeth stuck in the wood. Scarum must have been biting so hard that when the rope snapped and our vessel slapped down into the water, he was still open-mouthed. His teeth stuck right into the seat!"

The hare wailed, "Git's nog gunny, an' it gurts!"

Sagax patted Scarum gently. "I know it's not funny and

it hurts. Keep quite still now, mate. Let's see if I can get you loose. Kroova, hold his shoulders."

The sea otter braced Scarum's shoulders. Sagax went to work with his powerful blunt claws. Loosening odd splinters carefully and pulling away the larger fragments, he freed the hare's teeth. Scarum sat up and clapped a paw across his numbed mouth.

"Hanks'agax . . . mummff! My teemff hurth!"

He had to repeat the phrase until the badger understood.

"Oh right, you said, 'Thanks, Sagax, my teeth hurt,' correct?"

Scarum nodded his head gingerly and retired beneath the bow seat, where he lay nursing his sore mouth. Kroova was sympathetic.

"Never mind, messmate. Yore gob'll prob'ly be painin' ye for a while. But you'll soon be shipshape."

The remainder of the day passed uneventfully, with the otter and the badger tip-pawing quietly about, so as not to disturb Scarum at his rest. In the early evening, Kroova put tinder to flint and made a small fire with charcoal in a deep stone bowl. Sagax rummaged through the rations and came up with wheat and barley flour, a jar of preserved damsons in honey and a few other ingredients.

Mixing them together with some water from their little water keg, he asked Kroova, "Ever had skilly'n'duff, mate?"

His friend's eyes lit up with anticipation. "Ho arr, skilly'n'duff, ain't nothin' tastier. A sea otter's favourite vittles, I'd say!"

Sagax baked the mixture to a soft doughy pudding, using the damson juice and honey as a sauce. It smelled delicious.

Kroova made his way for'ard and shook Scarum awake. "Grub's up, matey. Guess wot Sagax made fer us: skilly'n'duff. Nice'n 'ot, with damson juice an' honey sauce poured over it."

The young hare crawled from beneath the seat and sat

up with his head in both paws. He had turned a peculiar
unhealthy shade. "Boat's been goin' up an' down, up an'
flamin' well down, all day. Ooh, my mouth hurts like the
blazes. I don't think I'll be takin' any supper this evenin',
thank you. Just leave me alone here so I can die quietly,
wot."

Kroova went back to the stern seat and accepted a bowl
of supper from Sagax whilst he explained, "Ole Scarum
don't want no supper."

The young badger was taken aback by the news.
"Doesn't want any supper? Is his mouth still paining
him?"

Kroova spoke through a mouthful of the hot skilly'
n'duff. "Aye, but I knows the real reason. That creature's
seasick."

In the gathering twilight, Sagax found it difficult to see
Scarum's face. He served himself a portion of supper.
"Seasick, how d'you know?"

The sea otter chuckled mischievously. "'Cos he's gone
the colour of a toad's tummy. There's one sure way t'tell,
though. Watch this."

He called out in a jolly voice to the hare. "Feelin' better, me ole mate? If the duff doesn't suit ye, I'll make ye
up a tonic. Some cold water an' oatmeal with a wild onion
chopped in it, mixed up with a touch of beeswax tallow
from a candle. That'll put y'right, wot ye say?"

A moan escaped Scarum as he staggered to the side
of the ketch and leaned over, retching and heaving.
"Great rotten fat ruddered cad, that's what you are. I'd
sooner be scoffed by the shark than eat your foul concoction, wot!"

Kroova grinned at Sagax and helped himself to more
supper. "Aye, our ole mate's seasick sure enough!"

Sagax sipped at his beaker of water. "Poor Scarum.
But with all the food he put away and that excitement today, plus getting his teeth caught fast, he has only himself
to blame, really.

"While he's laying around the deck like that, why
don't you go and give a good check round under the bow

seat? I'll search back here. There must be some sort of weapon, a knife, anything. I'd feel much safer if we had something better than a few wooden spoons in case of trouble. It's important that we have at least one weapon."

They lit two small lanterns from the fire bowl and set about their task. Scarum gradually moaned himself back to sleep again as night shades set in over the trackless deeps of the seas. In a corner beneath the stern seat, Sagax found a sling and some stones wrapped in a roll of old barkcloth. He was unwrapping them when Kroova returned carrying various objects.

"Lookit wot I found under a ledge by the forepeak—a sword, a dagger, an' this old bow. Pity it ain't got a string or arrers."

The badger inspected the sword. "This is a typical searat blade, curved, with a cross hilt. My father has a collection of them in the armoury. Rusty blade, with a few nicks in the edge. Sharp, though. I'll clean it up a bit and it'll look just fine. Let's take a look at the dagger there, mate."

The otter tossed the knife in the air, catching it deftly by the blade tip. He turned it this way and that. "Good ole apple slicer, this 'un. Ain't a mark on it. No, wait. . . . Aharr, this 'ere pattern burned into the 'andle 'tis the same as the signs marked on the stern o' this vessel. Must've belonged to one o' those searats I borrowed ole *Stopdog* from. Cast yore eyes over that, matey."

Sagax took the blade. Holding the lantern close, he inspected the brand.

"Hmm, wonder what it means. Some sort of lucky charm, mayhaps?"

The otter shrugged as he tested the wood of the unstrung bow. "This ain't much use. Nice bit o' yew wood, though, 'twill do for a walkin' staff. Wot was in yore barkcloth?"

Sagax indicated the sling and pebbles. "Nothing much, but look at this barkcloth. There's more funny markings on it, not writings or a pattern."

Kroova brightened up as he inspected the thing. "A map, me 'eartie, that's wot it is! I reckernize this coast-line, up north an' east of 'ere, well beyond yore father's mountain—that ain't marked on it. But see, I know these bays an' inlets from long ago. Take this 'un. If'n we was to sail due east at dawn, we'd prob'ly run right into it."

Sagax held the lantern closer as he inspected the map. "There's an arrow marked here, straight up a river that runs out over the beach from these tree shapes and dunes. Any idea where that would take us, if we were to find it?"

Kroova pondered. "Could be that wood's called Moss-flower, prob'ly, though I ain't never been up that far."

The young badger's eyes lit up. "Mossflower! My dad and mum are always talking about it, most of the older Long Patrol hares, too. The Abbey of Redwall is supposed to be somewhere in Mossflower area. Have you ever heard of Redwall Abbey, Kroova?"

"Hah, who ain't? Redwall Abbey's supposed t'be a wondrous place, peaceful, 'appy, an' I 'ear they've got the most marvellous vittles there. Expert cooks an' the best of grub."

Sagax rolled the cloth up carefully, though his paw was shaking slightly with excitement. "Then let's make it the destination of the voyage. There's a river runs across the shore into the woods, it says so on the map. Why don't we sail up that way and pay Redwall a visit?"

Kroova grinned from ear to ear as he shook his friend's paw. "Aye, shipmate, why not? I don't think Scarum'll object, d'you?"

The badger cast an eye over his friend's sleeping fig-ure. "The only way he'd object to a voyage was if there was no scoff at the other end. Once he's feeling better he'll jump at the idea. How far do you think this river is?"

Scratching his rudder, the sea otter estimated. " 'Tis 'ard to say. We got dragged off course by the shark today.

We're a bit far west'ard. But I'll tack 'er east an' north. Then we'll see where we are a few days from now."

Sagax could not help shuddering with delight. "I've heard about that Abbey all my life, but now I'm going there to see it all for myself. Redwall, here we come!"

8

It was Shogg who did most of the hard work, with Triss helping him and Welfo keeping lookout. All through the night the otter and the squirrelmaid toiled valiantly, disregarding the water's icy temperature. With nought but a broken old rusty file between them, they laboured away in a veritable fever of anxiety, racing against dawn's light, when the Ratguards would be back outside on duty. Shogg selected one bar at the end of the cage nearest the jetty where the ship lay moored. He crouched, half submerged, whilst Triss perched upon his shoulders and filed at the top of the round iron bar.

Welfo kept shivering and calling out false alarms. "Wait, stop, I think somebeast's coming! Sorry, Triss, it was only a moonshadow on the path. You can carry on."

Shogg shifted position to stop his limbs stiffening. "Stone me, I wish that 'ogmaid would make up 'er mind. That's the sixth time she's said that in the last hour!"

Gritting her teeth as she attacked the solid iron with the file, Triss murmured down to Shogg, "Poor Welfo, she's terrified we'll be caught. It doesn't take much to set her nerves on edge, she's just plain scared."

The otter took hold of the bars to steady himself. "Huh, I don't know why she's afeared. They can't kill us twice. How's it goin' up there, matey?"

Triss clamped her jaws resolutely, ignoring the skrike and screech of metal against metal. "Slowly, that's how 'tis going. Once I got a decent bite on this iron, the file keeps sticking. Cutting the top of the bar'll take the best part of the night. Owch! I've gone and filed my paw. Stop disturbing me, Shogg, it's hard enough trying to work in this darkness."

Slightly less than two hours before dawn, Triss managed to file through the bar. "Ahah! Good news, mates, I've done it! My paws are in a terrible mess, though, but I'm so cold I can't feel them."

Welfo helped her down, jabbering agitatedly. "The guards'll see it, I know they will. You can see the iron shining silver where you've been filing, it sticks out like a cherry on a cake. We'll all be caught, I'm certain of it!"

Brushing iron filings from between his ears, Shogg took hold of Welfo and pressed her face to the bars in lookout position. "Give yore gob a rest, missy, an' keep yore eyes peeled. Leave the bar to us. A bit o' riverbed mud plastered on the shiny bits'll disguise 'em, trust me."

He was right. Once the cut bar was smeared with mud it looked quite normal and unbroken. Shogg leaned all his strength against the bar, trying to bend it outward. He pushed until his eyes bulged. "Phaw! It ain't budgin' at all, Triss. Right, I'll 'ave to start on the bottom. Gimme that there file!"

The otter could hold his breath for an incredible amount of time. Triss was of little use in such circumstances, so she joined Welfo on lookout. Totally submerged, Shogg filed away underwater in complete silence. It was very heavy going.

Dawn rose mistily. The fjord looked as if it had pale smoke floating upon it. Ratguards herded the main body of slaves out for the final few hours they would need to complete the walkway. The day for the launch ceremony of Agarnu's ship had finally arrived. Lieutenant Flith peered suspiciously at Triss and Welfo, gesturing with his spear.

"Hoi there, you two, where's yer mate, the otter?"

Triss kicked Welfo's footpaw underwater to keep her silent, taking it on herself to answer the lieutenant. "Shogg's not feeling too good, sir. He's sleeping underwater. Comes up whenever he needs air."

At that moment, the otter broke the surface smoothly. He gave Triss a swift wink before facing up to Flith. "Down there's the only place I can get a bit o' peace'n'quiet. That's unless ye'd like to smuggle me in a big ole feather bed."

Flith sneered at the captive's cheeky remark. "You'll get all the peace'n'quiet yer need at noon, riverdog. I 'eard Princess Kurda sharpenin' 'er best sabre, just to lull ye t'sleep with it. Ain't that nice of 'er, eh?"

Shogg liked baiting Flith. He winked insolently at the rat.

"Don't go sittin' on yore spear, vermin, or you'll damage yore brains. Haharrharr!"

Flith had no ready answer. He turned away, his face livid.

Shogg whispered to his companions. "Noon, eh? I'll just 'ave to try an' break through before then!" He vanished beneath the water noiselessly.

Triss murmured to Welfo, "One good thing, mate, the noise of the bar and the file can't be heard underwater. It deadens the sound."

As Drufo laid logs with the slaves, he muttered instructions to them under his breath. "If we're still 'ere when they breaks outta that cage, we've got to 'elp 'em, see. Create a diversion, get in the way o' the guards, shout, yell, make it look like we're tryin' to escape."

The message was passed on from one to another. Hope for the condemned prisoners was widespread. Though they themselves had no chance of escaping, the prospect

of three slaves not only avoiding death, but getting clean
away from Riftgard, had fired the imagination of all the
slaves.

Captain Riftun came out of the fortress to watch the com-
pletion of the path to the jetty. He stood beside Lieutenant
Flith, bringing him up to date on what was to happen.

Flith listened intently to his captain. "King Agarnu
ain't goin' anywhere on that new ship, not 'im; 'e's scared
witless o' the sea. It'll be Princess Kurda an' that oaf
Prince Bladd who'll be sailin'. I'll be goin', too."

This news surprised Flith. "Yore goin' with 'em,
Cap'n? 'Ow long'll ye be gone?"

Riftun was not one to give away valuable information.
"For as long as it takes. That's all you need t'know. Now
lissen, you'll be in charge 'ere while I'm gone, so I want
to find things in good order on my return. Got that?"

Flith saluted. "Aye, Cap'n, ye can rely on me. But there
ain't no reason fer you to go off sailin', none I can see."

Riftun leaned closer, dropping his voice so the slaves
could not eavesdrop on what he was about to say. "I'm
goin' to let ye in on a liddle secret, Flith, so keep it to yerself. Agarnu is only King by blood. 'E's a Pure Ferret, but
the law of Riftgard sez that a proper king must not only be
of the blood, but that 'e must possess an' wear the crown
an' pawring which is the symbol of 'is office."

Flith raised his eyebrows. "I never knew that! So wot
yer sayin' is, since he's got no crown an' pawring, Agarnu
ain't a real king, just a sort o' deputy?"

Riftun leaned on his spear and nodded. "Right! I
served under Sarengo, the old king. Now 'e was a proper
ruler. But then 'e went off on that voyage with Agarnu.
Hah, I recall well the day Sarengo told Agarnu 'e was
takin' 'im along. The fat useless fool wept like a baby. But
Sarengo wanted to toughen Agarnu up, said 'e'd either
come back 'ere as a king or not at all. They was off to
plunder some place called Redwall—it's supposed t'be
full o' treasure—but they never found it. Agarnu was the
only one to make it back to Riftgard alive. Nobeast

knows, except Agarnu 'imself, wot 'appened beyond the
seas in that other land called Mossflower. An' he ain't
never said a word of wot went wrong, or 'ow 'e lost a leg.
Think of it, a king, his crown an' pawring, fifty good Ratguards an' a great ship, all lost. Agarnu was close to
death's door when 'e crawled ashore off an 'alf-wrecked
ship's longboat."

Flith nodded. "I recall that. I was only a young Ratguard meself at the time. Ye can't blame Agarnu fer not
wantin' t'go back t'sea."

Riftun sniggered humourlessly. "No, that's why 'e's
sendin' Kurda an' Bladd. They've got to find out if King
Sarengo's still alive. If it turns out Sarengo's dead,
they've got to bring back 'is crown an' pawring. Then
Agarnu'll be a real king, an' so will whichever of 'is two
brats follows in succession."

Flith thought about this, then scratched his tail. "But
why d'you 'ave t'go, Cap'n?"

Riftun puffed out his narrow chest importantly. "'Cos
I'm the 'ighest-rankin' rat in Riftgard. I've got t'see that
the Prince an' Princess don't try to murder one another.
Kurda's got nothin' but hatred for Bladd, an' young Bladd
ain't as stupid as 'e looks. I bet 'e'd put a knife twixt 'is
sister's ribs as soon as look at 'er. So I'm bein' sent along
with a squad o' Ratguards, in command of everythin'. At
noon Agarnu'll come down t'the new ship with Kurda and
Bladd, to formally give the vessel to them. Aye, an'
Kurda's goin' to be allowed to execute those three prisoners in the punishment cage, just t'keep the other slaves
from gettin' fancy ideas. Then they're *all* goin' back t'the
fortress for a farewell feast. While that's goin' on, the
ship'll be provisioned, ready to sail at eventide. So I'm
warnin' ye, Flith, keep things runnin' smooth while I'm
away, or you'll be the one in the punishment cage when I
get back. Is that clear, Lieutenant?"

Flith kept his eyes on the ground. "Aye, Cap'n, crystal
clear!"

Riftun stalked off, back to the fortress. Flith watched

him go, then turned his attention to the Ratguards who were overseeing the path construction.

Flith tried out his new authority. "Youse lot, call yer-self Ratguards! I'd 'ave had this job finished three days back if 'twas left t'me. Get those slaves movin', I want to 'ear yer whips crackin' louder. You lot are in for it if this path doesn't reach the jetty in two hours. Wot d'ye expect, the King an' 'is family t'get muddy paws? The Prince an' Princess 'avin' t'walk over slushy ground? I'll see this path finished if I 'ave to use the carcasses of both guards an' slaves fer the royal party t'walk over. Get movin'!"

Shogg came up for air. "Nearly through now, though I'd take me oath these bars are thicker at the bottom than at the top!"

Triss cast a sympathetic glance at her friend. "Do you want to take a rest and let me have a go at it?"

The otter shook his head, chuckling. "No, no, matey, you couldn't 'old yore breath long enough underwater. There's only me who can do this. You keep watch."

Taking a deep breath, he submerged himself once more.

Princess Kurda put the final touches to her blade on an oiled stone and tested it on her paw. "Yarr, der heavy sabre be best for der choppink!" Swishing and slashing at imaginary victims, she prowled into the throne room.

Agarnu eyed the sabre distastefully. "Stop wavin' dat t'ing about. You like Sarengo wit mace'n'chain!"

Prince Bladd positioned himself behind Captain Riftun. "I not goin' on dat boat if she be takin' swords vit her!"

Agarnu banged his false leg on the floor decisively. "I say you go, den you go! Riftun be dere to proteck you, take some swords you'self if you vant, yarr."

Bladd tried to tough it out in front of his sister. "Yarr, I take mace'n'chain, like dey say mine granpa had!"

Kurda could not resist baiting him. "Mace und chain, yarr, you could not even lift von, fool!"

Bladd stuck out his tongue and made a rude noise. "Den I tell Riftun to stick his big spear in you!"

Kurda's pink eyes shone wickedly. "Nobeast's spear stop dis sword. Spears, tchah!"

Agarnu roared at them both, "Stop der fightink, you two!"

However, Kurda was bound to have the last word. "You watch der vay I deal wid dose slaves, den you try an' sleep tonight!"

The last logs had been laid, completing the walkway to the new ship at the jetty's end. Flith made his guards herd the slaves to one side.

Shogg popped his head up, dismayed. "The file's snapped, just when I was nearly through!"

Welfo sobbed nervously. "I can hear the gates being unlocked. They're coming! Can't we do something?"

The otter set his jaw grimly. "I'll try bashin' the bar with a rock!"

Diving beneath the surface, he located a hefty boulder, which they had previously been using to try to bend the bars. All caution was thrown aside now. The noise of Shogg's efforts could be heard clearly, echoing round the fjord banks: *Thook! Drrongg! Thook! Brrungg!*

Lieutenant Flith ran toward the quivering cage. "Wot in the name o' fangs is goin' on there?"

Drufo pushed a Ratguard in the back, sending him sprawling as he yelled to the other slaves, "Now, mates, now!"

They broke loose, hustling and jostling the guards. Flith was knocked flying into the water. Slaves were roaring and yelling as they grabbed whips from their surprised captors. The bar broke under the pounding from Shogg's rock. He grabbed it to use as a weapon, wading out of the cage into the fjord, calling to his two friends:

"Move yoreselves, mates, this is the only chance we'll get!"

*   *   *

Agarnu and his party froze as they emerged from the fortress. Riftun grabbed one of the twelve honour guards accompanying them. "Quick, run an' get the other guards, bring the archers! The prisoners have broke out o' the cage!"

Triss had a tight hold on Welfo's paw as she raced along behind Shogg. They splashed through the shallows, avoiding being caught in the melee on the walkway.

Drufo was waving Flith's spear, cheering them on from the midst of the chaos. "Freedom, Triss! You an' yore pals, go for freedom!"

A Ratguard who was close to the ship came running at the three with his whip raised. Shogg struck him down with the cage bar, while Triss and Welfo loosed the mooring ropes from their bollards and climbed aboard.

Shogg followed them and tossed the bar aside. "Get the oars, shove 'er out, the tide's beginnin' to turn!"

Kurda led the reinforcement guards. Charging into the massed slaves, she hacked left and right with her heavy sabre. The slaves wilted under the menace of shafts upon drawn bows and long pikes being thrust at them.

Drufo still had Flith's spear. He stood at the jetty end, anxiously glancing from the slow-moving ship to the on-coming guards.

Triss yelled hoarsely at her father's old companion-in-arms. "Drufo! Sling that spear away, swim for the ship! Come on, we'll pull you aboard! Throw the spear away!"

The old squirrel stood firm, watching Kurda coming toward him. He called back over his shoulder to the young squirrelmaid.

"Get away from 'ere, Trissy. Get away! I ain't goin' nowhere! This is as good a day to die as any. Remember me, remember yore father. You'll be back to free the slaves one day, I know ye will. Now go, don't waste the chance we gave ye!"

Drufo had time for no more words. Kurda was upon him. Chopping the spearhaft in half with a few vicious strokes, she ran Drufo through with her sabre.

Triss saw it all. It was burned into her memory like a red-hot iron. Shogg shoved her roughly.

"You 'eard 'im, Triss, use that oar! I'll loose the sail. Move yoreself quicker, or we'll all die 'ere. You, too, Welfo!"

Kurda waded into the fjord until it was above her waist. Then she was forced to duck as Bladd shouted at the archers, "Shoot dem vit arrows, cut dem down! Fire!"

A hail of barbed shafts thudded into the vessel's stern, some of them falling short into the water, narrowly missing Kurda.

The Princess dashed from the water, quivering with rage, her silken robes sopping wet. "Fools! Idiots! I could haff gotten aboard der ship!"

As she pointed back at the vessel with her sabre, a healthy breeze caught the single purple sail, billowing it out and sending the ship smoothly seaward down the fjord. Riftun seized the shamefaced Flith and rapped out orders.

"They ain't made it t'the sea yet. Git yore archers an' spear throwers on the mountainside, chase alongside 'em. Pour in arrers an' spears, rocks, anythin', but stop those slaves makin' it out to sea. Get goin', ye useless slob!"

Triss wiped blood from an arrow graze on her cheek as she watched the Ratguards mount the rocky slopes in pursuit. It was still quite a way to open water. "Looks like they're coming after us, Shogg. Best steer her over to the far shore or they'll pick us off easily."

The otter adjusted the tiller, judging the fjord cannily. "Can't take 'er too close, t'other bankside is very rocky. Keep those oars pullin', luck's on our side so far. I 'ope the tide's not run out altogether, otherwise we'll get stuck on sandbars at the estuary mouth."

The Ratguards were shooting arrows now. Their range was too far for spears, so the spearbeasts used their slings to hurl stones. Triss and Welfo could see the missiles coming, so it was not hard to row and avoid arrows or stones. Welfo felt a new confidence flooding through her, and the hogmaid winked at Triss. "We'll make it, she's

got the wind behind her pretty good now. Not far to go
and head for the open sea—*Unff!*"

Welfo had been looking up at the sail as she spoke,
when a big solid pebble from a Ratguard's sling struck
her hard on the side of the head. She collapsed unconscious to the deck.

Shogg was at her side immediately. "Stow yore oar,
Triss, tend to our mate. She ain't bad 'urt. I got to look after the tiller an' not let the bow drift too far over."

Flith stumbled and staggered over sharp rocks and snag-
ging shrubs, exhorting the guards. "Pour it into 'em,
we've taken care o' the 'edgepig. You front lot, get ahead
o' me, down to the estuary! The river mouth narrows
there. That'll be our best chance. We might even get 'em
stuck on a sandbank if the tide's run out enough!"

Shogg raised himself from the tiller, staring anxiously
ahead. "Triss, get Welfo down to the cabin out o' the way.
Tide's still ebbin' up yonder, I don't like it. Got to take 'er
out into midstream now, so keep yore 'ead down, matey!"

Flith's advance guard had reached the high peak at the
inlet when he joined them. The ship swung out into midstream, heading for the gap. The searat sniggered joyfully.
"I kin see the bottom from 'ere, 'tis runnin' shallow. Ha-
hah! Look, the ship's draggin', she's runnin' 'er bow onto
a sandbar. Now let em 'ave it! I want those other two
lookin' like pincushions! Fill 'em full of arrers!

"Split inter two groups, you lot. Stay up 'ere, keep
firin' arrers. The rest, foller me an' bring yore spears.
We'll wade out an' rip 'em t'ribbons! It ain't deep there,
we'll do it easy!"

The vessel ground to a shuddering halt. Shogg yelled
down the cabin hatch, "Up 'ere, Triss, quick, she's run
aground!"

The squirrelmaid came bounding up on deck. "What
do we do?"

Her otter friend outlined his desperate plan. "Leave
two lines runnin' over the stern so we can get back
aboard. Me 'n' you's got to lever 'er off this bank with the

oars. Come on, we ain't got much time. Flith's comin'
down after us!"

Shogg vaulted over the stern with two oars, while Triss
hung out the two lines, then joined him. They dug the oars
into the sandy bottom under the stern and placed the oar-
poles over their shoulders.

Shogg gave the word. "One, two an' push! One, two
an' push! That's the way, keep goin', I can feel 'er movin'
along. One, two an' push! Push!"

Flith came splashing through the shallows, brandishing a spear he had borrowed. He was not more than a
boat's length from his quarry when the ship cleared the
sandbar, gliding smoothly into the sea to catch the ebbing
tide.

Shogg patted Triss's back. "Good job, shipmate. Up
y'go, sharpish now!"

Flith hurled himself, spearpoint forward, at the otter.
Shogg turned just in time. He dodged the weapon and
swung out mightily with the big ship's oar. Once, twice he
cracked it down on the rat, as hard as he could, then, seizing the line, he shinned up aboard the vessel, helped by
Triss from above.

Open sea lay deep and blue in front of them, with a
good wind scudding the ship out onto the main. Welfo
staggered out on deck, holding a damp rag to the side of
her throbbing head. She managed a weak smile.

"We made it!"

Shogg glanced back over the stern, where he saw
Flith's limp form sink beneath the waves as it was pulled
out in their wake.

"Aye, we made it, friends, we're safe. Sit awhile an'
rest now." Welfo went back down below as Shogg took
the tiller. He watched sadly as Triss sat on the deck and
wept bitter tears for old Drufo, the last remaining link
with her family.

Prince Bladd was secretly glad that he did not have to go
sailing on a long voyage after all. He shrugged happily.
"Vell, dat's dat, ain't got no ship now, yarr!"

There had been no vessels moored in the fjord since Agarnu's ill-fated trip with his father. The stolen vessel had been specially built for Kurda and Bladd.

Now Kurda eyed her father contemptuously. "Yarr, only der fool who rules a kingdom by der sea would have no ships!"

Agarnu knew she was right. He flinched at the scorn in Kurda's voice. Wheeling about on his fishbone leg, he stumped back to the stronghold, blustering, "Tchah! No need for der ships. Vy us needs ships? Got everyt'ink else, kingdom, stronghold, yarr! Light der beacon, Freebooters see it. Dey got ships, let dem do der job for us. Jarr!"

Kurda gripped her sabre tighter. This was the best idea her father had ever come up with.

She grinned wickedly at Riftun. "Jarr, Freebooters! Get dose Ratguards to fix up de beacon, now!"

Eventide shades slid from crimson to slatey purple over the sea. On the high rocky point at the estuary a massive pile of pine logs, branches, foliage and dead moss had been erected by the weary Ratguards. Barrels of fish and vegetable oil stood close by. Kurda watched Captain Riftun set light to the beacon fire: it would burn red and gold by night and the oil would make it send up a column of dark smoke by day. Freebooters, vermin pirates and corsairs sailing anywhere in the region would see the signal and come to investigate.

Kurda pointed her sabre blade directly at Riftun. "Keep dis burnin', night an' day, and you stay 'ere! Let me know ven de Freebooters be sighted, yarr?"

Firelight reflected off the Captain's spearblade as he saluted. "Yarr, Princess, 'twill be as ye command!"

Kurda stared out over the restless deeps of wave and water. She spoke her thoughts aloud. "No slave escapes Riftgard. I'll find dem. Ven I do, dey be sorry dey was ever borned. Diss I vow!"

9

Dawn had always been the time that Skipper of otters
loved best. Rising silently at the first song of larks on the
western flatlands beyond the Abbey, he would pad gently
out of the dormitory for his morning exercise. This usually took the form of a good brisk swim in the Abbey
pond, after which he ran several times around the outer
walltops. Then he practised with javelin, club and sling.
The big sturdy otter was not a beast to let fat grow about
his middle. With his appetite sharpened, Skipper slipped
quietly into the kitchens. Friar Gooch the squirrelcook
and his assistant, the molemaid Furrel, were preparing
breakfast. Knowing Skipper was not a great talker first
thing in the morning, they left a tray out for him. With a
nod of thanks, he took his food: warm oat scones, a small
bowl of shrimp and hotroot soup (a special favourite with
otters), and a large beaker of mint and pennycress cordial.
Wordlessly, he left and went to seek someplace quiet,
where he could eat and meditate before joining the bustle
of Redwall's daily life.

Skipper dearly loved the Abbey, having lived on and
off there through his young seasons, often leaving to live

for a time with boisterous river otters and wild sea otters. But he always returned to Redwall, where he could trace his forebears right back to the famous otter Warrior, the one they had called Taggerung. Abbot Apodemus had tried to press onto Skipper the honour of being Redwall's Warrior, though he refused on the grounds that he had never felt himself to be the Chosen One. Skipper did, however, take on the role of Master at Arms to the Abbey, training others in weaponry and warskills, though there had never been the need for anything like that in living memory. Redwall's seasons of peace and plenty stretched back many, many seasons. But the big otter had chosen to stay in case he was ever needed.

Great Hall was an island of serenity when it was not being used for feasting. Rising sunlight cast soft strips of multicoloured light from the stained-glass windows onto the smoothworn stone floor. Skipper took his tray and settled down with his back against the base of a sandstone column. From there he could view the ancient tapestry depicting Martin the Warrior, the Abbey's first Champion. Foxes, rats, stoats, weasels and all manner of vermin could be seen fleeing from the armoured mouse who formed the centre of the picture. Martin had a face anybeast could trust: strong, smiling, kindly, yet with raw danger shining in his resolute eyes, which warned any evildoer to beware. He leaned upon a sword. Over the tapestry, on two silver spikes, the real one rested. Such a blade! It had a red pommel stone and a black bound handle with a cross-hilt. Like any warrior's weapon, it was proficient, plain and simple. But the blade, double-edged shining steel, had a point like an ice needle. Legend said that it had been forged by a Badger Lord in the fires of Salamandastron, from the metal of a fallen star. With such a sword in his grasp, a warrior could face any odds.

Eating in leisurely fashion, Skipper continued staring at Martin and the blade which rested above the skilfully woven tapestry. For some unknown reason, his eyelids began feeling heavy; and he had put aside the breakfast tray, when a sudden flash of sunlight shimmered on the swordblade. Skipper blinked at the spots of gold and silver dancing across his vision. Martin seemed to be staring at him from the tapestry. A voice, warm and distant, echoed around the room; the otter was not sure whether it was actually a real sound, or something inside his mind.

"Look to the summer,
Watch for the maid,
A young running slave
Who will hold my blade."

Time stood still for Skipper. The sunspots diminished and mist swirled slowly before his eyes.

"Hello there, big fellow. Not like you to be taking a nap this early in the day."

Skipper shook his head, coming back to reality at the sight of Abbot Apodemus standing over him.

"Er, wot? Er, er, g'mornin', Father Abbot. . . ."

Apodemus looked around at Great Hall. "Wonderfully calm in here, isn't it? I'd join you, only 'tis too much effort sitting down there and having to heave oneself up again. Pity I'm not as fit as you, Skip."

The otter rubbed his eyes and stood up, respectfully allowing the Abbot to lean on his paw. He supported the old mouse as they walked toward the door, listening to what the good creature had to say.

"Cavern Hole's like a battleground at breakfast time, far too noisy, between Dibbuns squeaking and scrambling about, and every otherbeast shouting about going on a treasure hunt. Oh dear, it was all too much for me. Let's take a stroll down to the gatehouse. Malbun and Crikulus are taking their breakfast quietly there, sensible creatures."

Skipper walked along in silence with the Abbot, trying hard to remember what it was he had wanted to tell him. But the otter's mind was a blank for the present.

Shining dust motes, like tiny slow-motion fireflies, swirled gracefully around the piled-up mass of parchments, scrolls and old volumes on the desk inside the gatehouse. Malbun Grimp and Crikulus the Gatekeeper both had quill pens behind their ears. The quaint pair munched on warm damson scones and sipped elder-bark tea as they sorted through the jumble. Crikulus moved a pile of scrolls from an armchair and allowed Skipper to plump the Abbot down in it, causing more dust to rise.

The ancient shrew peered over his rock crystal spectacles at them both. "A good mornin' to ye both. What brings ye here to this dusty dungeon on such a fine day, eh?"

Apodemus placed both paws in his wide habit sleeves. "This so-called treasure hunt. I want your opinion and advice as to such a fanciful venture."

Malbun, a normally placid mouse, became quite animated. She waved her paws about in excitement. "Oh, it's a must, we've just got to go, can't you see, treasure or no! Brockhall must be rediscovered. You've no idea how important it is to our Abbey archives!"

Malbun's outstretched paw hit a stack of heavy volumes, which toppled to the floor, causing a veritable eruption of dust. The Healer Recorder went into a fit of sneezing. Assisting the Abbot from his armchair, Skipper shepherded all three creatures out into the sunlight. Malbun stifled her face in a blue spotted kerchief.

"Achoo! Achoo! Ah . . . Ah . . . Achoooooh! Whew, pardon me!"

They sat on the wallsteps together. Raising his eyebrows in resignation, the Abbot sighed. "Oh well, if it's that vital I suppose we'll have to organise the whole thing and do it properly. Skipper, would you like to be in charge of things?"

The otter waved his rudder respectfully. "My pleasure, Abbot."

Apodemus leaned back, closing his eyes at the bright sun.

"Thank you, my friend, I know I can rely on you. Mmm, it's nice and warm here. Summer'll soon be upon us."

Skipper began to remember what it was he had been

going to say. Unfortunately his thoughts were interrupted by Memm Flackery, leading a pack of dancing Dibbuns toward them, each one of the little creatures singing uproariously.

"Summer summer summer sun,
Rumpetty dumpetty dumpetty dum,
See birds a-chirpin' in the air
An' bees a-buzzin' everywhere.
With sun to shine an' warm my fur,
Oh how could I have a care, a care,
Oh how could I have a care?

Summer summer summer sun,
That's the time for havin' fun,
Grasshoppers whirr an' hop around,
Flowers come shootin' out the ground,
Butterflies pass without a sound,
As bright long days abound, abound,
As bright long days abound!

Summer summer summer sun,
Can't catch me 'cos off I'll run,
I'll dash into the stawb'rry patch
An' every one I see I'll snatch.
Gobble it up, right down the hatch,
A fine tummyache I'll catch, I'll catch,
A fine tummyache I'll catch!"

Panting and blowing, Memm Flackery plumped down on the wallsteps, mopping her brow with an apron corner. "Whoo, I'm gettin' too blinkin' old for this lark, wot! Just lookit those little fiends, each one of 'em could scoff enough breakfast to sink a ship and then sing like a pack of wolves an' dance the bloomin' paws from under you!"

The Dibbuns swarmed over Abbot Apodemus, sitting on his lap, leaning on his shoulder and clambering on his back.

"Goo' mornin', Farver H'Abbot, lubberly day izzenit!"

Apodemus groaned under the weight of Abbeybabes,

chuckling. "So, what do you villains want from your Abbot, eh?"

Turfee the mousebabe tugged on the Abbot's whiskers. "Us wanna go onna treasure 'unt with you, h'all of us!"

Skipper scooped tiny bodies off Apodemus.

"Ahoy there, mates, we can't take you all. There's far too many in yore crew, you'd be gettin' lost all over Mossflower. Ruggum'n'Bikkle's the only two we need."

The Dibbuns, who could shed bitter tears at a moment's notice, set up a heartrending chorus of wails. "Waaaaahahawaaaaaaahwannagooooo!"

The Harenurse tweaked Skipper's rudder severely. "Y' great heartless beast, sah, fancy upsettin' my babes like that. S'pose I'll jolly well have to make the peace." She pulled a tiny mole out of the pack and wiped his eyes. "Listen up, young stumptail, I want y'to go and find Foremole. Tell him that Memm will be baking blackberry cream tarts today. Oh, an' ask him if he can find some jolly helpful creatures t'lend a paw to make 'em. Run along now, wot!"

As if by magic the wailing and weeping ceased. Dibbuns bounced up and down like mad frogs, waving their paws and shouting at the Harenurse. "Me! Me! I 'elp you, Memm! Me, me, I wanna 'elp!"

Memm shook her head, as if doubtful. "Tut tut, I never heard anybeast sayin' please."

One of the Dibbuns shouted "Please!"

Memm scratched her ears, turning to Skipper. "What d'you say, old lad, d'you think they look like good helpers for makin' blackberry cream tarts, wot?"

Skipper nodded vigorously, watching the hopeful infants. "Ho aye, marm, I don't think ye could 'ave a better crew in yore kitchens. They looks big'n'strong enough t'me."

There was no time for Memm to reply, as she was grabbed by her apron strings and tugged away to the kitchens by the Dibbuns, all of them yelling and shouting.

"Cummon, Memm, where our aprons?"

"I the bes' berrycream tart baker inna world!"

"Yurr, uz make lots'n'lots'n'lots, gurt 'eaps of em!"

"Looka, me paws be clean, me don't 'ave to wash 'em!"

Malbun was laughing as she nudged Skipper. "Hee-hee! You'd best go an' rescue Ruggum'n'Bikkle, they've gone off with the rest!"

The big otter dashed after the baking party. "Ahoy there, you two, get back 'ere. Yore needed by us treasure 'unters. Come back 'ere, I say!"

The Abbot rose stiffly, patting Malbun's paw. "Well, I see you're off to a good start. I wish you luck with your enterprise, old friend!"

10

By midmorning the searchers were leaving Redwall Abbey with Skipper and his two stalwart otter mates acting as guards. The party was composed mainly of grownup creatures, with Ruggum and Bikkle hemmed neatly in the middle of the shrews, still protesting at being excused from their tart-baking duties. Apodemus locked the main gates behind them and climbed up to the north ramparts. He stood watching his creatures trudge away up the path until they cut off at an angle into Mossflower Wood.

The going was fair, as they kept up a leisurely pace through the woodlands. Log a Log Groo and the Guosim shrews knew the exact location where they had found the two Dibbuns. This took a lot of guesswork out of the route.

Crikulus tramped alongside the shrew leader. "D'you happen to know that old Guosim song, 'Footlecum Durr,' I think it was called? I heard one of your beasts singin' it when you visited the Abbey last winter. I like it."

Log a Log Groo kept his eyes on the path ahead. "Even if I did, I couldn't sing it, old 'un. I'm more of a dancer than a singer. Hoi, Burrl, you know that'n, don't ye, 'Footlecum Durr'? Sing it out good'n'loud for us."

Burrl was a smallish, skinny-looking shrew, but he had a voice like a foghorn. He sang out loud and clear:

"Young Footlecum Durr, I do declare,
Was a fanciful little shrew.
With waxy grease he curled his fur
An' wore a greatcoat o' blue.
His ma was ever so fond of him,
That lest his paws should bruise
She made for him from aspen skin
A brand-new pair of shoes.

Well, pickle my fur, I tell you, sir,
Do you believe the news?
O what to do, a Guosim shrew,
Clompin' about in shoes!
With laces green, the best you've seen,
An' silver bells each end,
He strutted here an' swaggered there,
An' jigged about no end
'Til Footlecum took off his shoes,
An' paddlin' went one day.
Then a big old owl, the thievin' fowl,
Swooped down an' stole 'em away.
So now in the night, if you wake in a fright
At a strange sound in the air,
'Tis only that bird that you have heard
In the shoes of Footlecum Durr.
Too whit too woo, a ding dong clomp,
He's dancin' round out there,
Pursued by a shrew, cryin' out 'Hey you,
They're the shoes of Footlecum Durr!' "

Ruggum thought the song was hilarious and shook Burrl's paw. "Gurtly singed, zurr. Fooklum Gurr, ee'm wurr a sillybeast!"

It was sometime before midnoon when Log a Log called a halt. "This is about where we found the liddle 'uns. Let's 'ave lunch an' see if'n they can tell us which ways they went from 'ere to find that big ole tree with the door in it."

Malbun and Crikulus doled out barley farls, soft white cheese and flasks of pale cider. Both were glad to be rid of the extra weight they had been carrying. Skipper split his farl and packed it with cheese. Before he took a bite, he called the two Dibbuns to his side and questioned them. "Well, me ole mates, d'ye know where the old oak is from 'ere?"

Bikkle gestured in a wide arc nonchalantly. "H'east norfwest, or souf I fink!"

Crikulus could not help wagging a stern paw at her. "East northwest and south, that's a great help. Well, what have you got to say for yourself, Ruggum, eh?"

The little mole clapped his paws together and chortled. "Hurr hurr, oi did loike ee song bowt Fooklum Gurr, zurr!"

Malbun stroked the molebabe's velvet-soft head. "Crikulus means do you know the way to the oak tree where you and Bikkle sheltered from the storm?"

Ruggum answered candidly. "Oi carn't be sayin', marm, et wurr dark an' gurtly rainy ee see. 'Tain't gudd furr foinden ee way abowt in darkly rainy weathers, burr no!"

Sister Vernal's murmur was audible. "They'd have been more useful in the kitchens baking tarts!"

Malbun was about to say something when she was knocked suddenly backwards by a big dark bird, which had zoomed down without warning. She clutched her chin and cried out, "Aargh, what was that?"

Another one followed like lightning, pecking the cheese from Gurdle Sprink's paw. He swiped at it and missed. The bird swooped away into the trees amid a chorus of harsh cawing.

Skipper roared to his two otters and the shrews, "Crows, a whole gang o' the villains! Protect those two babes, mates. I ain't got a sling! Anybeast carryin' sling an' stones with 'em?"

Log a Log drew his rapier, casting an eye at the tree-tops. The big, dark-feathered scavengers were massing in the branches, watching the Redwallers menacingly. The Guosim leader kept his voice low and spoke calmly.

"My shrews never brought slings along, not that chuckin' stones'd do much good. There's too many of 'em. It looks like we're in real trouble, mates!"

Gurdle rubbed at the deep scratches on his paw. "Those birds are after our vittles! 'Tis the food they want. What d'ye think, Skip?"

The otter nodded, forming a plan in his mind as he spoke. "Aye, I think yore right, mate. We can't stand an' fight, they've got us outnumbered. Best thing we can do is to get out of 'ere safe an' sound. Log a Log, you an' yore shrews will be up front when we go. Keep the two Dibbuns, old Crikulus an' Sister Vernal with ye. Malbun, Gurdle, an' the rest, you stay close be'ind 'em. Me 'n' my two ottercrew'll cover yore backs."

Skipper sidled casually over to where the two food-packs were lying. Sliding his javelin through the handles, he lifted them cautiously off the ground.

The crows began crying out with renewed harshness. Skipper warded off two of them with a swipe of his rudder. They perched boldly on a raised tree root nearby. Hopping along the high branches, the rest of the crows dropped down to lower boughs threateningly. Skipper's keen eyes flicked from side to side, assessing the situation fully. He spoke gently to his friends.

"Lissen now, you start movin' out, slowly does it. But when you 'ears me shout Redwall, then go as fast as yore paws'll carry ye. Log a Log, get out o' the woods an' onto the path as quick as ye can. Now, get goin', easy-like."

As soon as the party tried to shuffle off quietly, the crows dropped even lower, cawing agitatedly. Skipper distracted the birds' attention by grabbing the food packs and laughing loudly.

"Haharrhar, ye winged vermin, is this wot ye want?

Fresh bread an' good soft cheese? I wager there's a few liddle cakes in these packs, too, let's take a look, eh!"

Loosening the straps on the two small knapsacks, he swung them in the opposite direction from the retreating Redwallers. There were cakes, some candied chestnuts, too; the whole lot, together with bread, cheese and cider flask, scattered wholesale, bouncing off treetrunks and spilling into the shrubbery. Squawking and pecking at one another, the scavenging crows fought among themselves as they pounced on the food. Skipper threw back his head and roared,

"Redwaaaaaalllllll!"

Stunning the birds in his path with thwacks from his javelin, he took off after the main party, who were now plunging headlong through the woodlands. Ruggum and Bikkle had not been scared since the crows' first appearance, surrounded by big, grown-up Redwallers. They felt perfectly safe. Bikkle was swept along, two shrews holding her paws. Lifting both footpaws from the ground, she was carried onward, giggling as she dangled in the air. It was good fun. Ruggum ran on his own for a while, then stumbled and fell. Before he could be alarmed at the main body passing him by, he was swept up onto Skipper's powerful shoulders. Grabbing the otter's ears, the molebabe hung on, gurgling, "Hurrhurrhurr, ee bee's a gurt game, can ee goo farster, zurr Skip?"

By the sound of the crows behind him, Skipper could tell they had decimated the foodpacks. Keeping his eyes on the path ahead, he assured the incorrigible molebabe, "Aye, mate, we'd best step the pace up. Those birds'll be comin' after us soon. Move on up there, mates, faster!"

Some of the older creatures were panting hard, so Skipper's two ottercrew mates and the Guosim shrews gallantly lent helping paws to speed them on to the safety of the path. Now the crows were on their trail, their raucous cawing echoing louder as they approached. Gurdle Sprink slowed his pace, allowing Skipper to catch up with him.

The Cellarhog glanced over his shoulder, puffing and panting. "Can't go on much further, Skip. You go on, I'll stay 'ere an' make a stand for us. Should 'old em off awhile."

Skipper shoved an end of his javelin into the hedgehog's paws. "No such thing, mate. Who'd be left t'brew good ale an' cordials for the Abbey? See, there's the path up yonder. Grab ahold of this javelin with me, we'll run together!"

Ruggum reached over and patted Gurdle's spiked head. "Yurr, coom on, zurr, us'n's won't leaven ee behoind!"

Log a Log was first onto the path. He shouted to his shrews as they hurried out of the woodlands, "Grab some stones, Guosim, we'll show those scurvy scum!"

More Redwallers poured out onto the open path, as they took the shrew's advice and gathered pawfuls of rough stones. A big crow was flying up behind Skipper, homing in on the back of Ruggum's neck, when a stone struck it square on the beak. Other crows found themselves pelted with a lively salvo of large pebbles and chunks of rock.

Skipper was last, but finally he made it to the path. Lifting Ruggum down, he picked up stones and began whizzing them off at the angry crows with amazing accuracy, chuckling wolfishly. "Haharr, buckoes, come an' chew on some o' this!"

But the crows would not leave the tree cover, knowing they would be at a disadvantage on open ground. They took to the branches, hopping awkwardly about and cawing harsh disapproval of their would-be quarry's tactics.

Old Crikulus was a surprisingly good rock thrower. He knocked a crow clean out of its tree with his first try. "You great filthy cowards, how d'ye like some of your own medicine, eh, eh? Here, try this'n for size!"

The unexpected retaliation was too much for the crows, and they quickly retreated back into the safety of the woods. Skipper hooked his rudder under Ruggum's smock cord, hauling him back as the molebabe went to chase after the crows with a rock he could scarcely carry.

"Cease fire, me ole mate, we've sent 'em packin'."

Ruggum rolled his rock off among the trees and dusted his paws. He shouted after the distantly cawing birds.

"Yurr, an' doant ee cum back or oi'll give ee billyoh, you'm gurt villyun rarscals!"

The remainder of the journey was uneventful. Skipper and his party reached the Abbey in time for afternoon tea. Abbot Apodemus opened the gates for them.

"Great seasons, you lot look as if you've been through some sort of adventure. What happened, my friends, tell me?"

Skipper made his report as they strolled across the lawns to the Abbey.

The Father Abbot reflected on the story. "No treasures found today—but some lessons learnt. Ah well, no great harm done. You're all back safe and sound, just in time for afternoon tea, I might add."

Sister Vernal smiled eagerly, for teatime was her special favourite. "Oh good, blackberry cream tarts!"

Apodemus shook his head woefully as they entered the Abbey. "Please, sister, don't even mention blackberry cream tarts to me. They'll haunt my dreams for seasons to come."

Malbun stifled a smile. "What happened? Did something go wrong with the Dibbuns' tart baking?"

The Abbot was still shaking his head with despair. "Did anything go right? It was the Dab organisation, you remember: Dibbuns Against Bedtime. On some pretext or other they got Memm and Foremole out of the kitchens, then the rascals ran back and bolted themselves in. Come and see."

When they arrived at the kitchens the door was off its hinges. Gooch the cook and his assistant, Furrel, were sorting through a selection of damaged tools they had borrowed from the wine cellars to unscrew the door hinges.

Gurdle Sprink clapped his paw to his brow. "Oh corks, is that my best bungspike? Looks more like a confounded corkscrew!"

Memm Flackery emerged from the kitchens, spattered from ears to tail with blackberry preserve and meadow-cream. "Steady on, old lad. Don't blame poor Gooch, 'twas me who borrowed your gear. 'Fraid we had to, wot! Those little cads locked us out! We had to break back in, or the jolly old kitchens would've never been the same again!"

Crikulus peered in at the chaos that had been caused. "Hmm, looks like they took to decoratin' the place with flour, preserve an' cream. Where are the Dibbuns now?"

Foremole Urrm wiped flour from his snout. "Oi got 'em all locked oop in ee veggible store, zurr. Tukk moi loife in moi paws doin' et. They'm was fierce h'infants!"

Skipper called on his two ottercrew to support him as guards. "Right, shipmates, let's parade these fierce h'infants out an' see wot they got to say for 'emselves!"

Some of the Dibbuns were so coated with baking ingredients that they were unrecognisable. Malbun pointed to one, who looked like he could be a mole.

"You there, stand up straight and take your paws out of that apron pocket. What's your name? Speak up!"

The Dibbun licked cream from his chin. "Oi'm Roobil, marm."

Friar Gooch pointed accusingly at him. "Roobil, that's him. He was the ringleader!"

Malbun Grimp stared at the line of bespattered babes. "You know where you are going now, don't you?"

A small voice murmured regretfully, "H'up to bed, marm."

Memm eyed Roobil. "Tell him he's jolly well wrong. Explain to him where you wretches are going first, wot wot wot?"

Roobil scuffed a footpaw across the floor, leaving a smear of blackberry preserve as he did. "Burr, straight in ee barff oi apposes."

The Harenurse waggled a paw under his snout. "Correct, sah, straight into the blinkin' bath, an' one whimper out of anybeast an' I'll bathe you twice!"

Sister Vernal lectured the miscreants severely. "Look at

you, look at these kitchens! Shame on you. Rogues! Right, it's bath, bed and no supper for the lot of you!"

Roobil rubbed his small but bulging stomach ruefully. "Us'n's couldn't manage no more vikkles to be eaten, marm."

Friar Gooch stamped a paw on the floor. "Don't dare talk back, you dreadful Dibbuns. You should be ashamed o' yoreselves. Away with you and get bathed. That's unless you have anything to add, Father Abbot?"

Apodemus used his sternest tone. "I'll see you all in Great Hall tomorrow before breakfast. That's when I'll decide what must be done. You're all on Abbot's Report!"

The Dibbuns exchanged shocked glances as they were led off, dumbstruck: Abbot's Report was a very serious matter.

It was only when they were safely out of earshot that Skipper broke down laughing. "Aharrharrharr! Did y'see the liddle faces on 'em, harr harr!"

Memm Flackery sniffed at the otter's remark. "I fail t'see anythin' funny at all, sah!"

The Abbot tried hard to keep a straight face, but failed. "That Roobil, hahaha! We could've stood him on the table as an ornament at a feast. Hohoho! I've never seen anybeast with that much preserve and cream on him. He, hahaha, he looked like a little statue!"

Suddenly they were all laughing, even Memm. "Hawhawhaw! That mousebabe Turfee, he will turn into a bloomin' statue if all that flour'n'water dries on him, wot!"

Everybeast had forgotten about Ruggum and Bikkle, who were still present. Both were quite peeved at having missed all the fun.

Ruggum viewed the matter sternly. "Hurr, they'm surrpintly vurry naughty beasts. If'n oi wurr ee, zurr h'Abbot, oi'd choppen thurr tails off, burr aye!"

With a swift paw gesture the Abbot warned the others to cease their merriment.

"Quite right, Ruggum. I hope you and Bikkle never behave as badly as they have. Better go and wash your paws for tea."

Bikkle looked as though butter would not melt in her mouth. "Ho no, Farver, we's very good likkle beasts, not never like those naughty Dibbuns, never ever!"

When they had gone, Apodemus turned to the elders. "Thank you for not laughing, friends. We've got to show an example to the young 'uns. Friar Gooch, would it be possible for you and Furrel to try and arrange some tea for us? Anything will do."

Gooch bobbed a small bow to the Abbot. "I'll see wot we can do, sir. Per'aps you'd all like to take tea in the orchard? 'Tis still a fine day."

Apodemus patted the Friar's paw. "Splendid idea. Thank you, my friend."

Tea in the orchard was extremely pleasant. Gooch provided them with some of his seedcake, thin cucumber sandwiches and hot mint tea. Memm sat next to Malbun Grimp, listening to the account of the crow attack.

The Harenurse poured tea for them both. "Crow attack, eh? Doesn't sound half as blinkin' bad as the Dibbun attack we put up with back here, little rotters! Oh well, I s'pose that's put paid to your hopes of rediscoverin' that old badger place, what was the name of it, Brockhall? 'Spect you'll never find it now, wot?"

Malbun blew on her tea to cool it. "I'm not givin' up that easy, and neither is Crikulus. Never fear, I'm thinking up a new plan already. Crows don't fly at night. The two Dibbuns weren't bothered by them when they were lost and alone at night in the woodlands."

Crikulus, who was seated nearby, brightened up. "Of course, that's when we'll return to search the area!"

Memm helped herself to an extra-large slice of seedcake. "Huh, wouldn't be me, old lad, indeed not. Trampin' all over Mossflower hopin' t'find some old ruin, wot!"

Gurdle supped tea noisily. "But yore fergettin' the pawring those Dibbuns found. I'll wager there's treasure aplenty t'be found at Brock'all. That's somethin' worth goin' t'look for, ain't it?"

The Abbot had been listening to the conversation.

Folding both paws into his wide sleeves, he leaned back against a pear tree and let the sun warm his old whiskers. "Perhaps next time you could take the Dibbuns along with you. Armed with blackberry cream tarts. I wager there's not a crow alive wouldn't turn tail at the sight of that."

Foremole shook his head gravely. "You'm roight thurr, zurr!"

11

Dawn was scarce an hour old when Sagax was wakened by an enormous belch and the sound of Scarum's voice.

"Whoops, I say, 'scuse me!"

The noise woke Kroova also, and being closest, he dived upon the gluttonous hare, who was in the process of raiding their food supplies. Sagax helped the sea otter to restrain Scarum, managing to get him in a headlock, whilst Kroova grabbed the hare's paws and shook them roughly.

"Leggo those vittles, ye longeared bandit. We thought you was seasick an' had sore teeth!"

As Scarum strained to reach his mouth with a honeyed oatcake, Kroova knocked it from his grasp. The ever-hungry hare protested volubly.

"Gerroff me, you rotters. Can't y'see I'm jolly well well again? Ain't a chap allowed t'make a recovery with some bally dignity, wot? Release my starvin' young body, I say!"

Sagax kicked the ration packs out of Scarum's reach, then he and Kroova got the culprit down and sat on him. The young badger looked at the slack knapsacks with horror.

"You thieving flopeared foodbag, don't tell me you've eaten all those vittles while we were asleep?"

Scarum became quite moody and self-righteous. "Serves y'right for laughin' at me. I mean, what's a chap t'do, eh? I made a flippin' miraculous recovery, no thanks to you two, snorin' an' wheezin', there, after stuffin' yourselves with skilly'n'duff. So I came t'the conclusion that I'd have to put m'self on the road to recovery with just a measly nibble or two, so there!"

Kroova was aghast at the amount of food the hare had bolted. "Measly nibble or two, d'ye say? Y'great lollopin' grub swiper, you've near eaten us out o'keel an' cabin!"

Scarum stared up at them pleadingly. "I say, messmates, d'you mind not sittin' on me? It's makin' me feel quite ill again, wot."

They released him. Kroova went back and unlashed the tiller, taking up his position as steersbeast. Sagax repacked scraps of food into the depleted packs while Scarum sat in the bow, sulking as his badger friend tried remonstrating with him.

"Really, Scarum, you make me ashamed to be in your company. Fancy sitting up half the night stuffing yourself with the ship's supplies. You're not the only creature aboard, there's me and Kroova, too, you know. Well, what have you got to say for yourself, eh?"

The hare nibbled crumbs from his paws moodily. "Huh, don't know what you two're gettin' y'selves in such a blue funk about. There must be absolutely loads of scoff an' scads o' vittles over that way."

He gestured to starboard. Kroova looked perplexed. "Where?"

Scarum pointed again, explaining his logic. "Over there, of course! That's where the land's supposed t'be, ain't it? You jolly well said so when y'took a look at that map. Matter o' fact, you were the chap who said he knew exactly where we were. So, if there's land over that way, there must be scoff of some kind. Huh, even a duffer could figure that out, wot wot!"

Sagax exchanged glances with the sea otter and

shrugged. "He's right, of course. We're not in any great hurry. Why don't we sail over that way and take a look, no harm done?"

Kroova shaded his eyes, peering at the watery horizon. "I never said I knowed exactly where we were, I'm just makin' a rough guess. But the coast is to our starboard side. I'm game to take a chance if'n you are, mates."

Scarum immediately began spouting nautical nonsense. "Belay then, me hearties, an' all that sort o' bilge scuttle. Lower your jolly old main wotsits an' turn that thingeeyo handle. Trim up those sail doodlemidads an' set course for dry land an' boatloads o' scoff, wot!"

After an hour of heading due east, they were rewarded by the sight of a thin grey strip on the horizon. Sagax was first to see it. "You were right, Kroova, looks like land to me. Do you have any idea what part of the coast it is?"

Studying the chart, the otter shook his head. "Don't see any hills stickin' up, or clear landmarks. Could be any-wheres, but like you say, mate, 'tis land!"

After a deal of tacking against an outgoing tide, they felt the *Stopdog*'s keel scrape sand. It was early noon. Sagax leaped over, landing waist deep in the sea. Throwing the bowrope over his shoulder, he began pulling the vessel closer to shore. Kroova jumped in to assist him, but Scarum went aft and sat playing with the tiller.

"No need for three of us t'get our paws soakin' wet, wot? You chaps are doin' a splendid job there. I'll stay back here an' keep the jolly old mast straight."

Kroova smiled as he called back. "'T'aint a mast, that's a tiller, an' 'twill look after itself. Now git yore paws wet, seawater's good for 'em!"

Scarum's reply was punctuated by a snort of derision. "An' get eaten by some hungry shark? Tchah, sah, my parents didn't rear this charmin' creature to have him end up as a fish's dinner. Indeed not!" He waited until they were level with the beach before making a sprightly hop onto the sand, pulling a face. "Yukk! Pretty damp around here, ain't it? Have t'watch I don't catch a chill. Righty ho, lead on, shore-party chaps!"

Kroova found a broken spar of driftwood on the tideline. Taking a sea-smoothed boulder, he drove the wood
deep into the sand on the lee side of the tideline and tied
the rope to it. "That should 'old 'er 'til we return. Right,
let's take the lay o' the land an' see wot's wot!"

They had landed on a broad beach of grey sand, dotted
with areas of shingle. Beyond that lay a shallow rise to
scrubby grassland, steepening to flat-topped dunes scattered with small gnarled trees. Kroova had armed himself
with the old cutlass they found on board. Scarum had the
dagger tucked in the back of his belt, while Sagax held the
old unstrung bow like a staff. He pointed up to the dunes
with it and began trudging through the sand. "That could
be a likely place. Come on."

They came across meagre bits of food, some wild
onions, sweet young dandelion roots and a patch of drop-
water parsley. Sagax took charge of it before Scarum
could start stuffing himself. The young badger stowed it
in one of the knapsacks, which he had emptied and
fetched along.

The hare pouted a bit. "Fresh vegetation's supposed
t'be good for scurvy. We should chew on a bit of that stuff
after our voyage, wot!"

Kroova whacked him lightly with his rudder. "Y'ain't
been long enough at sea t'smell salty, let alone git scurvy."

There was not much else edible to be found. Although one of the trees was a hazel, the nuts were still
green and solid. Nonetheless Sagax began picking the
biggest ones.

"Anything's better than nothing. We might find some
way of cooking these up that'll make 'em taste all right.
Where's that nuisance Scarum got to, can you see him?"

Kroova immediately spotted the hare. He was racing
along the dunetops like a madbeast, holding in his paw a
withered chunk of honeycomb, pursued by a small number of bees.

"Yeeehooooo! Gerroff, you rotters, I saw it first! Ow-
chyowch! Help, chaps, heeeeelp!"

There was a crashing noise and Scarum vanished in a

dip amid the dunes. Sagax started to run toward it, but
Kroova held him back.

"No 'urry, matey, let 'im get shut o' those bees first.
There's only a few of 'em, ole potbelly won't come t'much
'arm."

They strolled across the dunes, the sea otter pointed
out a stunted bush with the remains of a hive in it. "It's an
old 'un. Those are prob'ly the last few bees movin' away.
Their queen must've died." He loaded bits of broken honeycomb into the knapsack. "Nice of ole Scarum t'find it
for us, though!"

On reaching the dip, they found themselves staring
down into a ruined dwelling. It looked as if it had been
some form of hideout. The walls were made of stones and
driftwood, shored up by sand, and the roof was a lattice of
woven broad-stemmed grass and dried rushes. There was
a large hole torn through the roof. A few ancient bees
buzzed slowly out into the daylight, followed by Scarum's
complaining shouts.

"Go on, away, you miserable insects, be off with you.
Bee off? Oh I say, that's a good 'un. Yaaaaagh! What's
that?"

The hare sounded so frightened and urgent that the two
friends felt bound to investigate. Sliding down the sunwarmed sand into the hollow, they found the door, a crude
affair of cordage and rushes. Sagax pulled it to one side,
allowing noontide sunlight to stream in.

The petrified hare was lying flat on his back, flanked
either side by two skeletons clad in mouldering rags.
Scarum lay there, his eyes the only part of him that
moved. He rolled them beseechingly at the badger and the
otter.

"Pull me out of here quick! Quickquickquick!"

They reached inside and dragged him out by his footpaws. Scarum began stuffing his piece of honeycomb into
his mouth. "Good for shock, somethin' sweet. That's what
my old auntie used t'say. Good old auntie, mmff, grrmff,
s'good!"

Sagax sat down outside the ruined dwelling, peering in. "They look like the remains of rats to me. What d'you think?"

Kroova went inside and squatted by the grisly things to inspect them carefully. "I'd say you was right. This is wot's left o' a couple of searats. Lookit this."

He held up two brass earrings, now tarnished to green. Rummaging about in the sand, he came across some carved bone bracelets and a fish-skin eyepatch.

"Aye, they're searats sure enough, lookit those rags of clothin'. Typical searat gear. Wonder 'ow they came to perish in this forsaken place?"

Sagax pointed with his unstrung bow. "Well, look around for yourself. There doesn't appear to be any signs of upset, a battle or a struggle. I think these two rats just starved to death. They seem to be lying there peacefully enough."

The sea otter sifted his paws through the sand around both wretched skeletons. "Aye, yore right, mate. Ain't no traces of vittles, not even fishbones or empty water flagons. 'Twas starvation finished off these two, all right!"

Scarum, who had remained steadfastly outside, peered over Sagax's shoulder, a look of mixed horror and sympathy on his face. He shook his head sadly.

"I say, what an absolutely awful way t'go. Poor blighters. Fancy perishin' from lack of tuck and a measly drop t'drink. Good grief, it boggles the blinkin' imagination, wot. I'd jolly well die before I'd let that happen t'me!"

Sagax ignored the hare's inane comments. "Kroova, what's that thing sticking up out of the sand, there, just by your left footpaw?"

Digging his paws into the shifting sand, the sea otter pulled forth a smooth, shiny yellow cylinder. "Wot, y'mean this? Beats me, mate, I ain't never seen nothin' like it afore. 'Ere, catch!"

He tossed the object to Sagax. The young badger had no trouble in identifying it. "It's called bamboo. My father has a piece of it in his collection of searat stuff. He said it comes from the hot lands beyond the ocean. Look, it has a wooden keg-stopper knocked into one end of it!"

Sagax tried to dislodge the stopper, but it was fitted so tightly that it would not budge. Kroova emerged from the ruined dwelling. He gazed back inside at the dark, empty, eyeless sockets of the two searat skulls, fixed forever in the eerie grin of death.

"That bamboo must've belonged to one of 'em. Let's see if I can open it. There's prob'ly somethin' inside."

Kroova spent some time wrestling unsuccessfully with the stopper of the tubby yellow cylinder. He gave up after a while and looked at Sagax. "Wot's up, mate?"

The young badger sat still and tense. He spoke softly. "Listen to what I say, you two, especially you, Scarum. Whatever you do, don't look up. We're being watched. There's quite a few of 'em up there, I can tell by the way the grass is moving. Listen, can you hear hissing?"

Scarum started to look upward to the crater rim. Kroova tugged the hare's tail sharply. "You 'eard wot Sagax said. Keep yore 'ead down!"

Scarum obeyed reluctantly. "Hissing, you mean hissing like snakes?"

From the corner of his eye, Sagax caught a swift glimpse of a narrow reptilian head, peering down at them from the grassy fringe.

"Might be snakes. When I say 'now,' get inside that hut as fast as you can. Ready . . . now!"

Scarum streaked inside, regardless of the skeletons. In practically the same instant he was followed by his friends. Kroova flattened himself, stomach down, peering upward.

"Lizards, that's wot's watchin' us. Lizards, a lot of 'em!"

Rat bones clacked as Scarum scrambled to the otter's side. Sagax joined him to take a proper look at the lizards.

The reptiles were crowding around the crater's edge, many black and green-spotted males and light brown mottled females. They stood gazing unwinkingly at the new-comers to their territory, mouths opening and closing, dark snakelike tongues flickering in and out.

Scarum tried buoying his confidence as he watched more lizards pack in round the edge. "Ugly blighters, ain't they? Not as bad as sharks, though. Huh, one of those chaps isn't big enough to eat me, wot!"

Kroova pawed at his cutlass edge, remarking drily, "Mebbe not, but there's more'n a hundred o' those things waitin' fer us t'make a move. Little they might be, but they're predators all right, take my word fer it, mate."

Sagax surveyed the sides of the crater. "The question is, how do we get out in a hurry? Those sides are soft sand and pretty steep. I'd say we're in trouble. They're waiting on us to make a move, sure enough."

As he was speaking, a female leaned out too far and overbalanced. She came sliding and scrabbling down the slope, landing next to the dwelling entrance. The lizard stood rigid, as if hoping she had not been noticed.

Scarum chuckled nervously and addressed the reptile. "How d'ye do, old thing? Just dropped in for a visit, wot?"

The lizard backed off, raising first one front leg and then the other, opening her mouth and hissing. Scarum ventured a paw toward her, but she hissed even louder.

The hare waggled his ears severely. "Tch tch! Doesn't seem to speak a word of sense. Must be jolly difficult, not bein' able to say 'Pass the soup,' or 'Can I have another portion of pudden, please.' Tell y'wot, I'll send her back to her pals, ignorant lot. That'll show 'em we don't mean any harm. Like t'go back up to your family, marm, wot wot?"

Before Sagax or Kroova could stop him, the hare swept the sand lizard up in both paws and hurled it up among the other lizards. He could not avoid throwing up a certain amount of sand with the reptile. The lizards backed off speedily. Scarum smiled brightly.

"I say, did y'see that? One good turn deserves another.

I imagine they were glad to get their pal back, but they don't seem to like sand bein' chucked at 'em, wot?"

Sagax gathered up a double pawful of sand. "Then let's try out your theory and chuck some sand!"

Kroova loaded his paws with sand, grinning roguishly. "Aye, an' let's give em yore Salamandastron war cry just to show the blighters we mean business. One, two . . ."

"Eulaliiiaaaaaaa!"

The time-honoured battle cry of hares and badgers rang out as the three friends hurled sand at the grass above. Then, taking the slope at a run, they charged up the side, flinging sand and roaring aloud. "Eulaliaaaa! Give 'em blood'n'vinegar, buckoes! Eulaliiiaaaa!"

There was not a lizard to be seen when they gained the dunetop once more. Scarum chortled, "Hawhawhaw! Frightened of a bit o' sand, eh, who'd have blinkin' well believed it? Come out an' show yourselves, you lily-livered, sausage-skinned, pot-headed, slimy-bottomed cowards, come an' fight!"

Whether by invitation, or just angry inclination, there came a loud hissing noise. Suddenly the dunetops were teeming with not just hundreds, but literally thousands of the sand lizards. All looking rather angry. The three companions hurtled down from the dunes, sand spraying everywhere from beneath their pounding paws.

As they raced across the low hills away from the crater, Kroova shouted, "You and yore big fat mouth, why did ye have t'go an' challenge those reptiles, ain't you got no sense at all?"

The hare sped past his two friends onto the shore. "Steady on there, planktail, I didn't know they could understand me. I just got caught up in the heat of the moment, y'might say, blood roused by the jolly old war cry an' all that, wot wot!"

Suddenly Sagax could not help bursting out laughing. "Hahaha! I thought the only thing that'd ever raise your blood would be a double helping of apple pie. Hahaha!"

Now that they were in sight of the *Stopdog*, the humour of the situation hit Kroova and Scarum.

"Y'could be right there, old sport, hawhawhaw. I can get jolly warlike if anybeast tries to put a spoon in my soup!"

"Hohoho! Bet you'd scrap with twice that number o' lizards fer a steamin' bowl of skilly'n'duff. Haharr, harr, that'd be a sight t'see, mates!"

They made it to the boat in safety. Sagax was loosing the headrope from its driftwood stump when Scarum called out, "Look there, the flippin' lizards have stopped on the dunes. See, they're all standing there just watchin' us. Cheerio, you snot-nosed sand slopers, you string-tailed, pop-eyed, spotty-skinned, flirty-clawed sand swifflers!"

Kroova winked mischievously at Sagax and nodded toward the *Stopdog*. Leaping aboard, he yelled out fearfully, "Look out! The lizards are coming this way fast!"

The vessel sailed out from the shallows, with a panicked Scarum splashing madly after it. "Wait for me, you bounders! You wouldn't leave a chum behind to face those leaping lizards alone, would you? Rotters! Lend a paw or chuck me a flippin' rope, pull me aboard before they get their slimy claws on me. Cads!"

They hauled the hare aboard, joshing him unmercifully. "Oh deary me, you got wet paws, mind you don't catch a chill!"

"Hahaharr, wot about the sharks, mate? Didn't seem t'be botherin' ye as much as yore ole lizard pals!"

Evening shades lay gently over a calm sea. Sagax was making a pot of vegetable soup and warming barley scones against the firepot. Scarum hovered close to the food until the badger chased him away.

"I can't cook with you breathing down my neck. Go and help Kroova to open that bamboo thing. Be off with you!"

The sea otter was still struggling to release the stopper from the bamboo cylinder when Scarum, looking back over his shoulder at the supper cooking, tripped. He fell, cracking his head against the bamboo tube. It split in two pieces, lengthways.

"Ouch! Haha, I say, that solved your jolly old problem. Hello, what's that?"

Kroova unwrapped some greasy canvas from around the object that had been packed inside the cylinder. "A dagger, just like that'n you got in yore belt, matey. Lookit the carvin' on it. Well, ain't that odd? Same marks as on yore dagger an' the stern o' this vessel."

Sagax left off his cooking and hurried to join them. "I wonder what it's supposed to mean?"

It meant little to Scarum, who pushed past Sagax and sat watching the soup bubbling. "Huh, prob'ly means this soup'll be ruined if I don't tend to it. Good job that bamboo thingy wasn't as hard as my handsome head, wot!"

Kroova and Sagax ignored him. Mystified and puzzled, they both sat staring at the carving on the dagger handle.

12

Plugg Firetail had a reputation as the slyest, most blood-thirsty fox afloat. His ship, the *Seascab,* was the biggest Freebooting vessel in all the northern waters, crewed by the rakings and scrapings of vermin to whom savagery was second nature. Since dawn, Plugg had been watching the beacon burning on Riftgard Head. Seeing the signal fading from his stern cabin window, Plugg rose in high bad humour. Grabbing his long, skirted coat of plush green velvet, which had seen better days, he swung it around his shoulders and seized the huge double-bladed axe that was his favourite weapon. Sneaking purpose-fully up the companionway stairs to the aft deck, the sil-ver fox muttered darkly to himself. "The blisterin' barnacles on this ship's keel are more use t'me than this lardbrained crew!"

An enormous, fat wharf rat, with no ears to speak of, was fast asleep over the *Seascab*'s tiller. Plugg halted within a pace of the creature and spat on both paws. Hold-ing the axe sideways, he swung it hard, slamming the blade flat across the rat's substantial rump. Splat! It had the desired effect. Grubbage, the bosun, squealed in pain as he let go the tiller and danced in a little circle, rubbing frantically at his bottom.

"Yeeeeeowowow! Mercy, Cap'n, mercy!"

Plugg took over the tiller, bringing his vessel about until it was headed for the beacon. He kicked out at Grubbage. "I'll mercy ye, y'great wobble-bummed grubwalloper. Didn't ye see the beacon blazin' yonder?"

Tears poured from the rat's squinched-up eyes as, cocking his head to one side, he rubbed away at his smarting behind. "Wot's that ye say, Cap'n?"

Plugg roared aloud into his bosun's face, "Are ye blind as well as deaf, lardgut? I said, didn't ye see the beacon blazin' on Riftgard 'Ead?"

Grubbage pulled up both sides of his turban, revealing the severed stumps of both ears. "Wot's that ye say, Cap'n, somebeast eatin' an grazin' on a guard's 'ead?"

Plugg leaned over the tiller, clapping a paw across his eyes and sighing deeply. When he looked up again, his first mate, a thin, gap-toothed weasel called Slitfang, had arrived. He was pointing excitedly at the beacon.

"Haharr, lookit wot I jus' spotted, Cap'n, someplace afire!"

Grubbage looked toward where Slitfang was indicating. "D'ye think somebeast's 'avin' a feast? Roastin' fish prob'ly, eh, Cap'n?"

Plugg gestured to the two of them. "C'mere, stan' close together, right 'ere in front o' me."

They obeyed without question. Plugg banged their heads together hard, then smiled genially at them. "Take this tiller, Slitfang. Keep 'er dead on to that light, or I'll tie ye to a rock an' use yer for an anchor. Grubbage, rouse the crew an' tell 'em t'make full sail." The silver fox padded back off to his cabin.

Grubbage massaged the side of his head in bewilderment. "Grouse 'as flew with a cake full o' pail? Slitty, me old messmate, d'you think the Cap'n's gone soft in 'is 'ead?"

Slitfang was wiggling a paw in his ear, the one that had collided with Grubbage's head. "I wisht the Cap'n wouldn't do that, it makes a ringin' in me 'ead."

Grubbage nodded agreement with his mate. "Aye, I'd sooner be a-singin' in me bed too. Oh well, s'pose I'd better order the crew to make full sail. Huh, I got to do all the thinkin' on this ship, while the Cap'n strolls round talkin' rubbish!"

Soon all the motley vermin crew were on deck, hauling at the ropes to raise sails. Grubbage swung a knotted rope's end at any who were slacking.

"Come on, ye sons o'slopbarrels, put some backbone into it. Let's 'ear ye sing a Freebootin' shanty, an' sing out loud. I hates the way youse whisper yore songs, ruins a good tune!"

The *Seascab*'s crew roared out the ditty as they pulled on the ropes in unison:

> "When I was just a young 'un,
> I left me familee,
> Wid all that I could steal off 'em,
> I ran away to sea.
> An' me Cap'n cried 'ooray,
> That's the Freebootin' way!
>
> I took a course in wickedness,
> At plund'rin' I came first,
> In slyness an' at thievin',
> I was voted best o' worst.
> An' to anybeast I'll say,
> That's the Freebootin' way!
>
> I'll rob the eyes from out yore 'ead,
> If you ain't watchin' me,
> An' anythin' that ain't nailed down,
> I'll take with me for free.
> Who sez that crime don't pay?
> That's the Freebootin' way!
>
> When I rolls in to dinner,
> I smiles at all me mates,
> I robs 'em of their grog pots,
> An' vittles off their plates.

An' if'n they complain I say,
That's the Freebootin' way!

If early in the mornin',
I 'ears a bluebird sing,
I fixes 'im right smartish,
Wid a rock from out me sling.
An' me shipmates laugh 'n' say,
That's the Freebooters' way!"

Captain Riftun was still breathing hard from his run along the clifftops. Having made his report to the three Pure Ferrets in the throne room, he stood to attention, awaiting orders.

Agarnu shrugged. "Tell der Freebooters to anchor in de bay an' bring dem up 'ere. Ve must bargain mitt dem."

Kurda roughly jostled Bladd out of the way and stood in front of her father's throne. "No! I say tell dem to drop anchor outside de bay. Den dey must lower der rowin' boat. Only der Cap'n an' officers. I not havink de full crew o' scum inside here. Yarr!"

Agarnu did not like having his orders countermanded, but he saw the wisdom in Kurda's statement and nodded to Riftun. "Yarr, it be as she say. Bring de Cap'n an' a few odders. Keep dem under close guard."

Riftun went back to the headland, taking with him a company of well-armed Ratguards.

Plugg, however, flatly refused to trek overland to the stronghold. Filling his ship's longboat with almost a score of crewbeasts, the fox had them row him up the fjord to the jetty, leaving Riftun and the others to march back along the meagre shoreline.

Riftun watched the Freebooters disembark. Blocking the jetty with his guards, he confronted the silver fox.

"Leave yore weapons 'ere, you ain't allowed to walk in armed to a meetin' with the Royal Family."

Plugg drew his axe, smiling dangerously. "Stan' aside an' give way, soldier rat. Where a Freebooter goes, 'is weapons go too!"

Riftun held up a paw. His archers put shafts to string and stood with bows drawn. Now it was his turn to smile. "You'll carry out my orders or die!"

Plugg did not seem unduly upset. He gestured back over his shoulder to a weasel balancing a lethal-looking stiletto by its blade tip. "See Tazzin there? She kin throw a blade faster'n yore eye kin move. She can bring down a swallow on the wing. So if'n there's any dyin' t'be done, rat, you'll be the first t'go. D'yew reckon y'can get 'im through the eye, Tazzin?"

The weasel was a stone-cold killer. She replied coolly, "Yerrah, shore I can, Cap'n. Which eye d'ye fancy, left or right? I kin drop 'im afore they move."

Brandishing his axe, Plugg pushed roughly past Riftun, chuckling to the shamefaced rat Commander. "Don't never try 'n' stop a Freebooter. Yore only a landlubber, an' lucky to still be alive, I reckon!"

Shogg had lashed the tiller, leaving the small ship sailing on a straight course. He leaned over the side, surveying leagues of white-crested waves in every direction. Nowhere was there sight of land. Triss came up on deck from the cabin below, and she answered the otter's wordless glance. "Welfo still looks pretty ill."

Shogg squinted his eyes at the far horizon. "Stands t'reason, she took a bad knock from that slingstone. I ain't feelin' too grand either. There ain't a scrap o' food or a drop of fresh water aboard this craft. Are ye sure there isn't just a liddle bit o' somethin' stowed away, a flask of cordial or a mouldy old crust?"

The squirrelmaid stretched her paws wide. "Not a single thing. They were going to provision her that afternoon, but we stole the ship before they could. While you've been up here I've searched down below again. All I could find was a couple of parchment scrolls, nothing else."

Shogg tightened his belt another notch. "So, looks like we can starve t'death in freedom, mate. Let's go an' take a peek at those scrolls. Who knows, there might be an island somewhere not too far off."

As the ship had no cargo holds, the cabin was fairly large and roomy, but low ceilinged. Welfo lay on a bunk, her head wrapped in a damp cloth. The hogmaid was sleeping fitfully, tossing and turning. Triss did not like the look of her, seasick, hungry and injured. It was a worrying situation.

Shogg opened the two scrolls, shaking his head with disappointment. He rapped his paw on the first one, calling Triss away from her patient.

"Will ye come an' take a look at this lot of ole rubbish? Wot's all this gobbledygook supposed t'mean, eh?"

The squirrelmaid peered closely at the symbols neatly marked out in black ink, recognising only a few. "This little bit here at the top is the initials of the Royal House of Riftgard. A mouseslave who was a woodworker told me he'd carved it into different objects many times: R.H.O.R. See."

The otter traced the symbols with his paw.

$$\triangledown \vdash \mathbf{0} \triangledown$$

"Of course, that's even carved into the stern of this ship. But what does the other bit say, Triss?"

Gnawing on a pawnail, Triss studied the rest closely. "I can make out the odd letter here and there, but I'm sorry, mate, it doesn't mean anything to me."

She continued to stare at the symbols.

$$\mathsf{2}\vdash\triangle\triangledown\mathsf{R} \quad \mathbf{0}\mathsf{X} \quad \cup\square\triangledown\mathsf{A} \quad \mathsf{P}\triangle\triangledown\mathsf{O}\triangledown\mathsf{A}\mathbf{0}$$

"I can make out the R, H, and O a few times, but I can't make head or tail of the rest. Let's take a look at the other scroll. That may be more helpful."

Shogg grew quite excited as he viewed the other chart. "Haharr, 'tis a map! I know this bit, 'ere's the place we come from, Riftgard: There's the strong'old, the fjord, an' the sea beyond. Strike me rudder, Triss, this is one big sea we're sailin' on. I never knew there was that much water in one place!"

Triss traced the charted line, which had been marked out on the map. It came out of Riftgard fjord, straight into the sea, travelling due west, then taking a broad swinging curve southward. Farther down, land was indicated, but only one side of the coast. Then the route went south, taking a sharp dip east toward the land where it indicated what looked like a river running out across a beach. Triss sighed.

"Well, it all looks very nice, but how do we know where we are in relation to all this? We could be anywhere."

Shogg, however, did not share her bafflement. "See that compass drawn in the left corner there? The North Star's marked clear, right over the north point o' the compass design. 'Ere, wot's this? Is it a blot of ink or a tiny island, just off the route line where it starts to bend south? Look."

The squirrelmaid rubbed the dark speck with her paw. "Could be a blot, I suppose, or it may be an island."

Welfo moaned and rolled over. She was nearly falling from the bunk as Triss reached her and turned her back again. Wringing out the scrap of cloth, the squirrelmaid wetted it again in a shallow dish of seawater and bathed her friend's face with it. Still completely out of her senses, the hogmaid licked at the salty dampness.

Shogg pursed his lips grimly. "She's got to 'ave water soon, fresh water. We all need drinkin' water, or we'll perish afore too long. You tend to the pore creature, Triss. I'm goin' up on deck for a look about, see if'n I can fix our position."

It was fully night, with just a sliver of moon, like a silvery nail paring, surrounded by stars in a cloudless sky. Shogg sat at the tiller, his head thrown back, exploring the countless points of starlight that dotted the velvet dark skies in dizzying numbers. After a while, the otter's neck began to ache, but he had made his decision. Pointing up at one bright, still jewel of the night, he spoke aloud to himself.

"That'n's the North Star, it's got t'be!"

Setting the tiller on course, he trimmed the single sail and began heading away from the star.

Triss tended to Welfo until the hogmaid lay still. So that she would not roll out of the bunk again, the squirrelmaid lay down beside her. It was not long before Triss closed her weary eyes and fell into a slumber. In her dreams she saw the sea, ever restless, wave lapping upon wave, murmuring with that soothing noise that only the vast deeps can produce. Gradually she realised that a voice was calling her, softly at first.

"Triss . . . Trisscar, my daughter . . . I see you."

A squirrel and a mouse were floating towards her, their paws not touching the water, which flattened itself to make a path for them. Although she could not remember his face, Triss knew that the squirrel was her father. She called to him. "Father . . . Father!" He smiled at her and pointed to the mouse.

Triss felt tears spill down her face as she heard herself saying, "Trisscar, I am called Trisscar? I never knew . . ."

The image of her father began to fade as he spoke again. "Drufo would have told you . . . When the day came . . ."

He faded altogether, and Triss was left alone with the mouse. She sensed immediately that this was no ordinary mouse. He was clad in shining armour and held a wondrous sword, the like of which she had never seen. Not even among the best blades in Princess Kurda's armoury. The mouse had a kindly face, although Triss could see the light of a warrior shining in his eyes. He reached out with the sword and touched her right paw gently with its tip.

His voice was warm and friendly, but stirring somehow. "Trisscar, that is a name for a great swordmaid. Sleep, my little Trisscar. Sleep!"

Then the vision was gone and she descended into the comforting darkness of deep slumber.

It was bright day when she awoke. Welfo was still sleeping, but her breathing was shallow and laboured. Triss hauled herself stiffly from the bunk. Her mouth felt dry as a bone, her tongue swollen and awkward. Blundering up on deck, she stood dumbly, watching Shogg. He was sitting at the tiller, shredding the strands from a short length of rope. It was several moments before he realised she was there.

The otter blinked wearily. "Jus' seein' if I could put t'gether a fishin' line. Don't know wot I'm supposed to use for bait. How's Welfo t'day?"

The squirrelmaid sat down beside him, drawing her ragged gown about her in the slight morning breeze. "Hmm, what? Oh, Welfo, she's sleeping. What d'you think, Shogg, are we going to die out here on this great sea?"

The otter continued picking at rope strands. "Where would ye sooner die, missy, back at Riftgard as a slave-beast, or out 'ere on the deep with me at yore side?"

Triss managed a smile. She patted Shogg's paw. "I'd rather not die, if it's all the same to you, mate!"

The otter put aside the piece of rope. "Aye, I want to live, too, y'know. That's why I've set us a course by the North Star. We'll see if that dot on the map's a blot or an island."

Triss stared up at the bright morning sky. "But how can you do that? There's no stars about now."

Shogg explained. "I located the North Star last night, sailed through the dark with it t'guide us. Right up till 'twas startin' to dawn. Sun rises in the east, don't it? That's 'ow I fixed me position. With a bit of luck we'll find yore blot, missy, never fret."

Welfo appeared in the cabin doorway. She was shivering and could scarcely stand up. "I'm thirsty . . . so thirsty!"

Triss hurried to help her, murmuring to Shogg, "Find water, if only for poor Welfo's sake!"

She hurried the hedgehog maid back to her bunk and laid her down, talking soothingly to her. "There now, you have a little nap. We'll soon get you water. Let's take a look at that slingstone wound. Oh, it's looking much better today, I'll just bathe it with some seawater. There, that's nice and cool, isn't it?"

As Welfo's eyes were closing, she spoke to the squirrelmaid. "Is your name Trisscar?"

Triss was taken aback. "Yes, it is, who told you that?"

Welfo murmured as she sank into a daze, "You did, last night. 'Trisscar, I am called Trisscar.' You said it out loud."

The dream came back to Triss as she stroked her sleeping friend's brow. *Trisscar, that is a name for a great swordmaid!*

13

Redwall Abbey's twin bells pealed out to the new dawn. Down in the kitchens, Friar Gooch ceased ladling carrot and fennel sauce over a batch of mushroom pasties he was about to fold and crimp. Furrel, his faithful molemaid assistant, stirred a potful of hot honey ready for candying chestnuts. She allowed the ladle to rest, smiling fondly.

"Hurr, oi loikes ee bells, they'm wunnerful musick to start off'n a h'extra sunny mawnin'. Wot do ee say, zurr?"

Gooch nodded vigorously as he opened an oven door. "I say you're right, friend, especially as 'tis the first day o' summer our bells are ringin' out for!"

Furrel almost tripped on her long cook's apron as she trundled swiftly to the kitchen door and called out. "Ee zummer bee's yurr, joy an' 'arpiness to all!"

The Abbey bells began ringing out an extra peal, to welcome in the new season. Gurdle Sprink came bustling up from the cellar, puffing as he carried a small keg. Skipper, who was returning from his morning exercises, bumped into the fat Cellarhog and relieved him of his burden.

"Belay there, mate, let me carry that for ye. Oh, summer's 'ere, joy an' 'appiness to all!"

Gurdle shook the otter's paw, returning the traditional greeting for the new season. "Summer is 'ere, sir, aye, joy an' happiness to all, an' especially t'you, my big strong pal!"

Together they entered the kitchens, with the Abbot, clad in a fresh robe of clean linen, shuffling behind. Friar Gooch and Furrel met them, with much hugging, kissing, backslapping and paw shaking as they exchanged greetings for the jolly occasion.

"Summer is here, joy and happiness to all!"

The Father Abbot's eyes gleamed with anticipation. "And what, pray, is in that delightful-looking keg?"

Skipper placed it on the table. Gurdle took out his little screw tap and knocked it into the bung keg. Sister Vernal appeared with Malbun and Crikulus in tow. They carried a tray full of delicate rock-crystal beakers, tiny things, which tinkled as they touched.

Before Gurdle could answer the Abbot's question, old Crikulus chuckled. "Wild-cherry-an'-redcurrant cordial, made on the final day of last summer. Good beast, Gurdle, I knew you'd bring it up from the cellars today!"

The Cellarhog looked slightly nonplussed that anybeast should know what his surprise offering was to be. He grumbled. "Aye, brought it up 'ere, just like I do on the first day of every summer season."

Abbot Apodemus placed a paw carefully around Gurdle's spiky shoulders, smiling fondly. "What would Redwall do without you, my old friend? I'm sure this will be the nicest wild-cherry-and-redcurrant cordial ever tasted in our beloved Abbey!"

The Cellarhog blushed to his spiketips as he busied himself pouring the sparkling cerise-hued liquid into the glasses. "Kindly said, Father Abbot. Well, 'ere's long life an' good fortune to us all!"

Memm Flackery came hurtling in and relieved Gurdle of two glasses, which she quaffed instantly. "A jolly loud hoorah for summer, wot? Joy an' happiness to all you bounders, who never woke me t'say this was bein' served. I say, Gurdy old lad, this is absolutely toodle pip, well done, sah. Congrats!"

Foremole Urrm scuttled in and seized the last glass as Memm was about to reach for it. "Yurr gudd 'ealth, zurr an' marms, ee summer bee's yurr!"

Friar Gooch bowed to the Abbot. "Brekkist in the orchard I think, eh, Father?"

Apodemus beamed. "Why certainly, Friar, where else on such a day? I can't think of a more pleasant place!"

Memm Flackery interrupted. "Only after you've sat in Great Hall an' dealt with those dastardly Dibbuns who are on Abbot's Report, sah, wot!"

The Abbot's face fell. He disliked dealing out sentences, particularly to Dibbuns. Skipper saw this and provided an instant solution to the problem.

"Wot a mis'rable thing on the first day o' summer. Bring 'em up t'the orchard, pore liddle tykes. I was a Dibbun meself, y'know, we all were once."

The Harenurse cast a jaundiced eye upon the otter chief. "Perish the thought, you a Dibbun?" She shuddered.

Everybeast laughed at the indignant expression on Skipper's face. Seizing his otter friend's paw, the Abbot hurried him off to the orchard gladly.

"Thanks for getting me out of that task, you sensible ex-Dibbun. My my, but you have grown, haven't you?"

Beneath shady fruit trees, mottled by sunshine and shadow, Redwallers chattered merrily as they breakfasted at the long trestle tables and forms, which had been set up in the orchard by Log a Log and his Guosim shrews, who were enjoying a prolonged stay at Redwall.

Freshly scrubbed and wearing clean smocks, the Dibbuns were shepherded by Memm into their Abbot's presence. Adopting an attitude of mock severity, Apodemus sat back, looking over the top of his spectacles at the two lines of apprehensive infants. He shook his head several times.

"What in the name of fur'n'whiskers am I to do with you, eh? Dearie me, what have you got to say for yourselves?"

Turfee the mousebabe stared hard at the ground. "Rug-gum'n'Bikkle sez you gonna chop off us tails. It not fair! Roobil be a molebabe an' 'im gotta likkle tail, but I bee's a mousebabe wiv a long tail. Not fair, Farver Habbit."

Apodemus weighed this statement, scratching his whiskers. "Hmm, I take your point. What would you do with these villains, Skipper?"

Brandishing his javelin and scowling savagely, the big otter confronted the trembling miscreants. "Do with 'em, sir! Do with 'em! Why, I'd make the rogues dance twice round these tables singin' Honeybee Soup. That's wot I'd do, an' serve 'em right for their 'orrible crimes!"

The sentence was greeted with wild applause from the Dibbuns. Foremole Urrm took out a small moleedion and twiddled the opening bars of the jig, which was a great favourite with Abbeybabes. Ruggum and Bikkle deserted their seats and joined the little ones, prancing up and down.

Sister Vernal looked at them quizzically. "You two aren't on Abbot's Report. You don't have to do what Skipper asked!"

Grinning from ear to ear, Ruggum replied, "Hurr hurr, you'm troi an' stop uz, marm!"

Away the babes went, like a miniature whirlwind, jigging, hopping, leaping and singing wildly:

"Mix honey with honey an' honey in honey,
Get a big pot here an' pour it on thick,
Honey, fine honey, so golden an' sunny,
We'll stir it all up with a green willow stick.

Nod your head wag your tail,
Sup it from pan or pail,
Join up our paws an' go round in a loop,
Buzz like the bees do to flowers an' trees,
But fetch me a bowl of good Bumblebee Soup.

Oh bumblebee, don't stumble or tumble,
Come out of the flowers now, back to your hives,

Fly back to your home, sir, an' fill up each comb
  there,
For granma's an' granpa's an' babies an' wives.

Striped all with fluffy down,
Golden an' furry brown,
Bow to your partner an' yell a great whoop,
Now form a square, an' you may find it there,
A bowl of your favourite Bumblebee Soup!"

Right back to the first verse the little creatures went,
paws joined as they whizzed around the orchard at an
alarming rate.

Memm shook her head in despair. "Will you just look
at that villain Roobil! I've tried to teach him the flippin'
words a dozen or more times. But will he pay attention,
wot wot? Indeed he won't. Rumpitty tum, that's all he'll
sing, the little bounder. Listen to him. Rumpitty tum,
rumpitty tum, rumpitty bloomin' tum!"

Foremole Urrm nodded admiringly as Roobil vaulted
over his lap and shot off around the pear trees. "Burr hoo,
but ee doo 'ave a foine turn o' paw, marm. Thurr goes ee
mole choild arfter moi own 'eart, burr aye!"

Malbun Grimp agreed wholeheartedly with him. "Aye,
I don't think I'd be worrying about learnin' words if I
could dance half as good as Roobil!"

Crikulus, who was sitting on the other side of Malbun,
looked rather gloomy all of a sudden. He murmured to his
companions, "I don't expect it'll rain or storm tonight.
That's put the block on us goin' out to search for Brockhall."

Malbun pondered his words for a few moments before
replying. "You could be right there. But I don't intend lettin' the weather, or lack of it, get in our way. All we need
to do is to keep out of the way of those crows. Suppose I
was to ask Log a Log and one of those big otters from
Skipper's crew to come with us. Surely a Guosim Chieftain and that hefty young otter Churk could get us through
quietly, without upsetting those birds. Log a Log's an ex-

pert tracker, and Churk is well versed in woodland ways—I like her."

Crikulus nodded, keeping his eyes on the dancing Dibbuns. "Good idea, Malbun, but don't let anybeast save Log a Log and Churk know. No point in havin' them all worryin' about us. We'll slip off after supper, the four of us, eh?"

Malbun agreed. "Aye, after supper, but don't breathe a word. If the Abbot finds out, he'll forbid us to go."

It was right at that moment that the Abbot stood up and made an announcement. "My friends, Redwallers all. It is my wish that we celebrate the new season this evening with a feast!"

Everybeast applauded the good news wildly. A groan of despair came from Crikulus as he noticed that the two creatures cheering loudest were none other than Churk and Log a Log.

The ancient Gatekeeper sighed mournfully. "They'll never accompany us tonight, Malbun. We'll just have to put the whole thing off until another time."

Malbun's jaw set in a stubborn line. "Not me, my friend. I'm going. Who needs those two to guide us? Look at us, we're two well-seasoned creatures. Why shouldn't we do the job ourselves?"

Crikulus gnawed doubtfully at his whisker ends. "Out in the woodlands at night, on our own. Dearie me, I don't know, Malbun, I just don't know. . . ."

Malbun, however, was not ready to brook excuses or arguments. "Well, I'll go alone. I'm not a Dibbun who's afraid of the woodlands in the dark. Don't you worry, I can fend for myself!"

Crikulus clasped his old friend's paw. "No, no, I'll go with you. This is a joint effort, y'know."

The Abbot was watching the pair. He commented to Skipper, who was sitting next to him, "What d'you suppose those old fogeys are whispering about?"

The otter spread damson preserve thickly on a scone. "Wot, y'mean Malbun'n'Crikulus? I expect they're plannin' on singin' their song at the feast, Father. You know, that funny one where they both dress up."

Apodemus turned his attention to a bowl of oatmeal. "Yes, that'll be it. I like that song, it's good fun!"

Throughout the day the buzz of excitement continued. Skipper and an assortment of moles and shrews went to lend a paw in the kitchens. Log a Log and some of the others vanished into the cellars with Gurdle Sprink. Memm Flackery and Sister Vernal took the Dibbuns off to gather flowers and lay the tables. Foremole Urrm recruited Malbun and Crikulus to help him serve buffet lunch and afternoon snacks on the steps outside the gatehouse. Redwall Abbey became a hive of activity in preparation for the coming feast. Everybeast was busy and cheerful.

Memm and the Sister were hugely pleased at the way the Dibbuns behaved themselves. The Abbeybabes' conduct was exemplary; not one objection was heard at bath time. They even stood uncomplaining whilst getting dried and dressed.

The Harenurse kept praising them as she combed and brushed each one. "Oh I say, J.G.D., you chaps, A and B the C of D. Wot!"

Sister Vernal gave Memm an odd glance. "What are all those letters you're spouting, marm?"

The Harenurse explained. "J.G.D. means Jolly Good Dibbuns, an' A and B the C of D? Thought you'd know that 'un, Vernal. It means above and beyond the call of duty. Good, eh?"

Lining the Dibbuns up and inspecting them, Sister Vernal nodded approvingly before dismissing the little creatures. "Very good, right. G and P and T.T.S.C. . . . O.E.!"

Bikkle sniffed and wrinkled her nose at the Sister. "Wot dat all mean, Sissa?"

Vernal waved a cautionary paw under Bikkle's nose. "It means, go and play and try to stay clean. . . . Or else!"

* * *

Crikulus and Malbun sat down on the wallstairs during a lull in their duties. Malbun murmured to her friend in low, frustrated tones, "Did y'hear that, everybeast's saying that you and I are going to do our dress-up monologue at the feast. Huh, that's the last thing we'll want to be doing this evening!"

The ancient gatekeeper shrugged. "Nothing for it, we'll just have t'do it, I suppose."

Malbun's eyes lit up as an idea occurred to her. "Right! After the feasting is done, we'll volunteer to go first with our performance. When we've finished, we'll pretend that we feel tired and excuse ourselves. Nobeast will suspect us of leaving the Abbey then, eh?"

Crikulus still felt slightly unhappy about the venture. "Hmm, I suppose you're right."

From its commencement at early twilight, the feast was a complete success. Brilliantly decorated and lantern-lit tables groaned under the weight of superb food. Still warm from the ovens, fresh-baked breads with crusts ranging from gold to deep brown vied with vegetable salads, fruit junkets, cheeses, pasties, tarts, cakes and turnovers, plus a huge cauldron of the moles' favourite, deeper'n'ever turnip'n'tater'n'beetroot pie. There were hot herbal teas, cordials of all types and a barrel of Special October Ale on tap for the elders. Back and forth the delicious fare went from paw to paw amid banter, laughter and animated conversation.

Extra lamps and lanterns were lit as darkness fell and the entertainment commenced. Malbun and Crikulus performed their monologue, which was actually a duologue. It was a great favourite with all Redwallers, especially the Dibbuns, who had armed themselves with slapsticks for the finale. Malbun was dressed as a searat, with padded stomach and bottom, large floppy hat, brass earrings, a patch on one eye and a wobbly sword made from soft tree bark. Old Crikulus had garbed himself as a grandmother mouse. He wore a billowy frock, a lacy shawl and a fussy, beribboned bonnet. They strode toward one another, as if

meeting on a woodland path. Malbun eyed Crikulus
fiercely and declaimed aloud in a rough voice:

"Here be I a searat fierce, an' this to all I say,
I'm evil, villainous, bad an' tough,
Let nobeast stand in me way!
I've got two paws like iron claws,
Granite teeth an' steely jaws,
I chopped me ole grandma up fer stew,
An' I'll do the same fer you!"

Both elders and Dibbuns hissed and booed him heartily.
Crikulus rendered the grandmother's part in a quaky squeak.

"I'm a little grannie mouse, frisky as a flea,
An' I say what ho, this is my motto,
No bullies dare mess with me!
'Cos though I'm old, I'm feisty an' bold,
I've got twenty-two grandmice too,
I can spank the tail off any of 'em,
An' I'll do the same for you!"

Applause and cheers rose from the onlookers, with many
Dibbuns calling out. "Spank the naughty rat, grannie!"
Malbun rolled her eye and waved the floppy sword.

"Hoho, liddle grannie mouse, scurry off to yore
 'ouse,
Whilst I'm still in a good mood,
I eats a grannie fer brekkist each morn,
'Cos grannies are my fav'rite food!
I'll chop off yore tail an' whiskers,
I'll whack off yore nose an' each ear,
Then you'll be the lunch on which I munch,
Wot think ye of that, me old dear?"

The booing and hissing of the audience rose to fever
pitch. Crikulus winked broadly at the Dibbuns to make
them ready, then he began haranguing Malbun.

"Hah, just try an' eat me, an' you'll soon see
Us grannies are tough ole things.
I'll climb in your mouth an' pull your teeth out,
Then use your tonsils for swings!
But why should I bother to dirty my paws,
On a sloppy great bully like you?
Here come all my grandmice, ahoy there,
Show this searat a thing or two!"

This was the part the Dibbuns enjoyed most. Grabbing
their slapsticks, they bounded out and began chasing Malbun, spanking away at her rear, which was heavily cush-
ioned. Whooping and roaring, Malbun the searat fled the
scene.

Crikulus whipped off his grannie bonnet and did a
flourishing curtsy as the Redwallers applauded heartily.
Skipper and his two otters chased after the Dibbuns, pre-
venting them from spanking the villain further. Malbun
came back and took her bow to loud cheers.

The Abbot wiped tears of laughter from his cheeks and
congratulated them. "Thank you, my friends, heeheehee. I
don't know how many times I've seen your performance,
but it gets funnier every season. Heeheehee, splendidly
done!"

Malbun grinned ruefully, rubbing at her rear. "Dearie
me, those Dibbuns can really whack. I'll have to get extra
cushions in the future. Whew, I'm tired. How about you,
Grannie Crikulus?"

The ancient Gatekeeper mopped at his face with the
bonnet. "Ain't as young as I once was, friend. I think
we'll take an early night in my gatehouse. You take the
big armchair, I'll take the bed. Goodnight to you, Father
Abbot, goodnight all. Thank ye for a wonderful evening."

With the good wishes of everybeast ringing in their
ears, the two old friends left the orchard and the continuing revelry of a happy Summer's Day Feast.

Shortly thereafter, Malbun and Crikulus, cloaked and carrying a lantern apiece, left the Abbey and trudged off up

the path. On entering Mossflower Wood, they immediately became aware of one thing: the silence. Not a breeze stirred the still-warm air. The sound of night birdsong was completely absent.

Crikulus kept his voice to a subdued whisper as he remarked upon this to his companion. "Strange, isn't it? Not a breeze or a peep of anything about."

Malbun tried to make light of her friend's concern. "All the better for us, mate. I was dreading that any moment we'd hear the cawing of those rascally crows, but all seems nice and peaceful. That's a bit of luck, eh?"

Crikulus nodded wordlessly as they plowed on through the shrouded woodlands. He felt as if the atmosphere was not at all nice and peaceful. A misty haze had woven a milky carpet around the trees. It was almost waist high, formed by the day's heat turning the earthdamp into vapour. The ancient shrew decided that everything seemed rather sinister.

Malbun trod on a twig. Its sharp cracking sound made Crikulus twitch nervously. "What was that?"

Malbun tried to tread more carefully to reassure him. "Only a twig I stepped on. There's nothing t'be afraid of."

Following the path they had travelled along previously with the Brockhall search party, they pressed onward into the woodlands, their lanterns held high, twinkling in the night like two fireflies. Now Malbun began to feel uneasy. She could not say for certain the cause of it, but a sense of foreboding hung over her. Crikulus was right—it was too quiet. Normally the woodland was alive with nocturnal sounds: owls, nightingales, insects, a healthy breeze rustling the tree canopy.

Just to reassure herself, the Healer Recorder spoke to Crikulus. "We are on the right path, aren't we?"

The old shrew turned, his lantern light illuminating Malbun's face. She looked as scared as he himself felt. "Aye, this is the path sure enough. Look, there's where we stopped to have lunch and the crows attacked us."

Malbun found herself wishing that she could hear the caw of a crow, anything to break the oppressive silence.

Fear and fatigue were beginning to overcome both creatures. Crikulus pushed through the undergrowth to the tiny clearing and leaned his back against a tree.

"Let's stop awhile for a breather here. My footpaws have gone all sort of wobbly an' shaky."

Malbun hung her lantern on a branch. Not wanting to sit down in the mist, she stood alongside Crikulus. "Well, where do you think Brockhall is? I know we're somewhere in the area."

The shrew shrugged at her whispered enquiry. "Could be anywhere in a wide circle from here. I haven't a clue. I wish those Dibbuns could've remembered the way."

Slits of moonlight penetrated the trees, slivers of pale silver against the gloomy night. They stood wordless, each wishing they were back in the comfort of Redwall's gatehouse. Though it was not cold, their dew-laden cloaks felt clammy clinging against them. Malbun removed hers first, with Crikulus following suit. A sound came from the grass nearby. Crikulus whipped his head round in its direction.

"What was that?"

It was not an actual noise, more of a slight wet swish. The ancient shrew thought he saw some ferns tremble in a moonlit shaft. Then another sound was heard, from the opposite direction of the first one. Malbun held up her lantern, paws atremble as she peered into the blackness. Her voice took on a strained, panicky edge.

"Th-there's another sound, like somethin' moving through the grass towards us!"

Then they smelt the odour, musty and bittersweet. It grew stronger. The grass swished in both directions, then it swished behind them, getting closer. Crikulus's voice was tight with terror. He swallowed hard.

"That sound . . . th-the smell . . . We're being hunted by somebeast we c-c-can't see!"

Malbun felt every hair on her body standing up. The sounds and the vile, powerful smell were almost upon them. Her voice was little more than a petrified squeak. "There's m-more than one of th-th-them. Yaaaaaaah!"

Dropping lanterns and cloaks from nerveless paws, the two ran headlong into the pitch-black woodlands, away from whatever was seeking them as prey. Blundering, bumbling, tripping, stumbling. Crashing through ferns and nettlebeds, stubbing footpaws on roots, they raced. Mists swirled about them, their habits ripping and tearing on tree branches that seemed to be grabbing at them as they passed. They plunged onward, heedless of any direction save that in which the unknown peril lurked. They splashed through a small stream and raced through a bog, so fast that they hardly sank enough to impede their wild charge.

Crikulus grabbed the cord girdle on his friend's habit as they fled across a clearing and into a pine grove. Overcome by fright, Malbun turned her head to see what was holding on to her. Still running, she slammed side-on into the trunk of a thick fir. There was a sudden stab of pain as a broken branch stub pierced her cheek. Then she fell down senseless. The ancient shrew collapsed by her side, his hoarse rasping breathsounds mingling with those of his companion. He scrabbled around in the dark with the clean scent of pine needles banishing the musty odour from his nostrils. His paw struck Malbun's face. He felt the broken branch splinter sticking from it and the sticky wetness, which he knew to be blood, upon his paw. "Malbun, are you all right? You're not hurt, are you? Speak to me! Say something, Malbun, oh please, say something!"

There was no sound from her. Crikulus tried hard to get a grip of himself, moving along until he had his friend's head resting in his lap. They were not being followed; he sensed that they were out of danger. But they were lost. Malbun was breathing heavily, still lying senseless. The wood had gone deep into her cheek. He set his teeth round the broken fir twig and tugged it free. Spitting it out, he tried to compose his nerves by speaking aloud.

"There's no real harm done, mate, though a bit further up and you might have lost an eye!"

The thought of such an injury, combined with the memory of swishing grass and musty odours, suddenly sent the old shrew into a violent paroxysm of shivering and shuddering. His teeth clattered like castanets and his entire body shook uncontrollably. He sat there alone in the night, trembling and nursing Malbun's head in his lap, weeping.

"Didn't want to come. Good thing I did. Couldn't leave you on your own, old friend. Hope somebeast finds the main gate unlocked. I only jammed it shut with that stupid bonnet. Oh, say something, Malbun, say something. Don't leave me alone here like this!"

14

Moonlight danced on the waves. It was a clear night and the breeze was running fair. Kroova and Scarum lay sleeping under the bowspace. Sagax sat at the tiller, taking his turn as steersbeast. The shoreline was still in sight as the *Stopdog* steadily plowed her course north. All the young badger had to do was to tweak the rigging lines and check the vessel from veering landwards. He was also tweaking his conscience, trying not to think too hard about his mother and father back home at Salamandastron. Sagax had an idea that his parents had secretly allowed him to leave and go roaming; it was customary with young male badgers. Yet somehow he had a feeling that he and Scarum had forced the issue through their rebellious behaviour. He decided that when they did eventually return home, he would become the model of good behaviour and obedience. Sagax chuckled to himself. But for now he would enjoy being a runaway!

Sitting there musing, he became aware of a flickering light coming across the waves toward the *Stopdog*. He sat, calmly watching until it appeared as a small boat with a tiny sail and two occupants. Hastily he roused Scarum and Kroova.

"Wakey, wakey, you two sleeping beauties, we've got company coming. Better arm ourselves in case they're unfriendly."

Kroova took the cutlass. Scarum tossed a dagger to Sagax, clenching the other one between his teeth.

Trying hard to look fierce, he scowled. "Haharr, buckoes! Woe to anybeast who crosses the path o' Scarum the jolly wild tailslitter, wot!"

The boat pulled alongside the *Stopdog*. It was crewed by a sleek grey seal and an old female sea otter. She sat calmly and cast an eye over the three, smiling at the sight of Scarum, who was trying to keep the dagger in his mouth whilst scowling around it.

"Barnacles'n'binnacles! Will ye look at that puddenheaded young rabbit. What'n the name o' flukes'n'fishes are ye tryin' to do, chop yore own tongue out?"

Sagax could see that they were friendly. He extended a paw to help the sea otterwife aboard the *Stopdog*. "It wouldn't be such a bad thing if he did chop his tongue off, marm, it'd give us all a bit of peace. I'm Sagax."

The sea otterwife seized his paw in a grip that belied her many seasons and leapt sprightly aboard. "My name's Raura Shellrudd, pleased t'meet ye. That there seal is Slippo, me ole shipmate. Ahoy there, seadog, wot d'they call you?"

Kroova winced as she shook his paw mightily. "They calls me Kroova, marm, an' that longeared scoffbag, well, y'can call 'im anything, as long as ye don't call 'im late fer supper."

Scarum spat out the dagger, spluttering, "Now see here, you two wavewallopers. One, I'm not a bloomin' rabbit, an' two, my name is Bescarum Lepuswold Whippscut, but you may call me Scarum. Tut tut, dear lady, no need for apologies, wot!"

Raura shook his paw until Scarum flinched visibly. "Wasn't goin' to apologise, matey. Kroova, I'm surprised at you. Yore no landlubber—can't ye see a risin' spring tide approachin'? Yore ship'll get pounded t'splinters on the shore rocks if'n ye stays on this course, eh, Slippo?"

Raising a shiny webbed paw, the grey seal called out, "Hoom, kahonk woopa buhonk!"

Scarum blinked at the seal. "I say, what's all that flippin' great honkin' row supposed t'mean?"

Raura took a ropeline from Slippo and secured the prow of her boat to the stern of the *Stopdog*.

"That ain't no honkin' row. Slippo's just agreein' with me. Shift yoreself, Sagax, I'll take that tiller. Ye can come to our den an' shelter from the 'igh tide. I take it ye ain't backward in coming forward if I was to offer youse a bite or two o' supper, eh?"

Scarum bowed gallantly to the sea otterwife. "Beauty combined with brains, m'dear, a rare combination in these watery parts, wot. Supper! The word hangs on the bally night air like a lingerin' melody!"

Raura winked at Kroova, nodding toward Scarum. "I bet that'n could eat the four legs off'n a table if'n there was no vittles on it."

Kroova sat next to Raura and trimmed the sails. "You never spoke a truer word, marm!"

High tide began rising as they beat their way up the coast. Seaspray shot in on the port side of the *Stopdog*. Raura took her visitors skilfully through a shoal of rock-strewn reefs. Slippo watched the friends' faces, horrified as they sped through the perilous stone maze. The sleek seal clapped his flippers and laughed.

"Ahuunk ahuunk ahuunkaaah!"

Raura's den was situated up a channel between some small cliffs. The passage twisted and doubled back upon itself so many times that it took all the force out of the sloshing water.

Slippo slid expertly onto a thickly seaweed-fringed ledge. He moored both vessels loosely, allowing them to ride up and down on the swell. Raura explained.

"Lashin's o' seaweed 'ere, our liddle ships can bump against the rock forever. They won't come t'no 'arm. Away, boat's crew, shift yoreselves, messmates, step lively now!"

* * *

Sagax would never have guessed there was a cave at the
rear of the ledge until Slippo drew aside a curtain of long
trailing kelp. The friends hurried inside and stood staring
wordlessly. It was a natural cave in the solid rock, with a
crack in the roof serving as a chimney vent. A fire, complete with stone-slabbed hearth and a rock oven, burned
low but warm. Raura fed the flames with driftwood and
sea coal as she chattered away.

"Sit ye down there, you three. Slippo, where's yore
manners? Serve 'em a drink an' fetch me some bowls!"

The seal rolled his huge liquid eyes. "Kumhoo kohay!"
They sat on a shelf of rock padded with sailcloth cushions
stuffed full of dried sea moss. Slippo presented them with
beakers fashioned from nautilus shells.

Scarum sipped warily. "Hmm, this tastes like a bit of
all right, wot!"

Kroova smiled broadly. "Crabapple an' sweet
woodruff tonic. I ain't tasted this since I was nought but a
shrimp!"

Raura looked secretly pleased as she pulled a deep
basin from the oven. Fragrant smells wafted round the
cave. "Makes it to me own recipe. Nought like crabapple
an' sweet woodruff t'put a gleam in yore eye an' a wag to
yore rudder. Wait'll ye taste my seastew an' laverbread!"

Scarum swigged away at his tonic drink heartily.
"Yours truly is willin' to try anythin', marm. But 'laverbread'? What the deuce is that when it's at home, wot?"

Kroova accepted a wedge of the dark green loaf.
"Laverbread's made out of a special kind o' seaweed. It's
a delicacy in coastal parts."

Sagax liked the laverbread. It was savoury tasting, a bit
salty, but not unlike spring cabbage made into a loaf. The
seastew was rare good eating, comprised of many types of
shrimp and shellfish, thickened with cornflour and full of
mushroom, potato, leek and carrot.

Kroova sampled it from his deep scallop-shell bowl.
"Beg pardon, marm, but 'ave ye got any hotroot pepper?"

Raura produced two small wooden boxes and a tiny
spoon. "This 'un's yore normal 'otroot, but this other 'un,

hah, this is from my ole granpop's store. 'E used t'make a livin' fightin' pirates. This pepper came from a corsair galley wot sailed from the far isles o'er the big ocean. I calls it Red Firebrand Pepper, ten times stronger'n 'otroot!"

Kroova sprinkled both peppers liberally on his seastew. He tried it, put the bowl down and bent double, making loud gasping noises. Grabbing his tonic, he quaffed a deep swig and straightened up. Tears poured from his reddened eyes and great beads of sweat stood out on his nosetip. He recovered himself and grinned from ear to ear. "Phwooooh! Now that's wot I calls prime good pepper!"

Scarum accepted another bowl of the stew, ignoring the boxes of pepper. He remarked cuttingly to Slippo, "These confounded seadogs, got no respect for their blinkin' stomachs, wot wot?"

Slippo raised his head from his bowl. "Wharuumph buloooh!"

The hare nodded drily. "Couldn't agree with y'more, old lad!"

Waves could be heard from afar, booming against the rocks, with a strong wind driving them. Inside, the cave was snug and secure. Raura served the friends some of her special crusty plum slice and a small beaker of old elderberry cordial. They sat enjoying the flickering fireglow whilst Kroova told them of their journey, where they had come from and the destination they were bound for, Redwall Abbey.

Raura took down a little harp and passed it to Slippo. "Redwall Abbey, eh, I've 'eard tell of it, but I never got that far inland. 'Tis said to be a wondrous place fer sure. But you young 'uns must be tired—lie down an' sleep now. Slippo, play us somethin', maybe I'll sing. I ain't sung fer a while. I've fergotten most o' me songs, but I can recall this one, 'tis a nice ole ballad."

Stretching out gratefully on the covered ledges, the travelers closed their eyes and listened to the otterwife's song.

" 'Tis a far cry from home for a poor lonely thing,
O'er the deeps and wild waters of seas,
Where you can't hear your dear mother's voice
    softly sing
Like a breeze gently stirring the trees.

Come home, little one, wander back here someday,
I'll watch for you, each evening and morn,
Through all the long season 'til I'm old and grey
As the frost on the hedges at dawn.

There's a lantern that shines in my window at night,
I have long kept it burning for you,
It glows through the dark, like a clear guiding light,
And I know someday you'll see it, too.

So hasten back, little one, or I will soon be gone,
No more to see your dear face,
But I know that I'll feel your tears fall one by one,
On the flowers o'er my resting place."

Raura and Slippo crept quietly out to check up on the
vessels. Sagax and Scarum wept brokenheartedly, moved
by the old otterwife's sentimental song. Then Kroova
could not resist joining them. Tears welled up in his eyes
and spilled out over his cheeks, wetting the cushions.

"I never knew me mum, but I'll bet she was jus' like
the one in Raura's song, a dear grey-'aired old thing.
Waaaah!"

Scarum rubbed at his eyes with both paws.
"Boohoohoo! My old ma will be standin' at the cottage
door with a jolly brave smile on her face, hidin' the blinkin'
tears, I know she will. Boohoohoo!"

Sagax sat up, sniffing and wiping at his eyes. "Waaha-
haaa! But you don't live in a dear old cottage, you live in
a whacking great mountain, just like me. Waahaaah!"

The hare used his long ears to mop at his eyes. "Jolly
nice thought, though, ain't it. Boohoohoo!"

Raura and Slippo sat outside until the otterwife was
sure her young guests had cried themselves to sleep. She

listened awhile, then nodded. "There, y'see, Slippo, me ole mate, that'll teach 'em a lesson!"

The grey seal threw back his head and honked mournfully. "Kuhoo umhoon kahooka, mowwwwwwwwww!"

Raura sniffed in agreement with Slippo. "Aye, that's the young 'uns of these seasons for ye. Runnin' off from 'ome widout a second thought for their parents. Now me, I never 'ad young 'uns, but if'n I 'ad, well, I wager they wouldn't go skippin' off an' leavin' me, eh?"

Slippo smiled from ear to ear. "Kuurhaaam oooh kohonkahhh!"

The sea otterwife smiled back at her friend. "Yore right, mate, I would bring 'em back an' skelp the tails offen em. Come on, let's go in an' get some shuteye."

Breakfast next morning was an uncomfortable affair, with the three travellers avoiding their host's accusing gaze. Raura commented drily, "I've filled up yore bags with vittles for the trip."

Scarum kept his eyes fixed on the meal. "Terribly decent of ye, marm, a thousand thanks from us."

She busied herself raking ashes from the fire. "No need t'thank me, I'd do as much fer anybeast. Weather's cleared up out there, 'tis a prime day. There's plenty o' vittles to get ye back 'ome, if'n youse was thinkin' to sail that way. The goin' is easier, too, if'n ye travel south."

Kroova rose, dusting crumbs from his paws. "If 'tis all the same with you, marm, we was figurin' on goin' to find Redwall Abbey, 'cos that's where we're bound."

Raura passed her little harp to Slippo, smiling at them in a fond, motherly way. "There's no great rush t'get to Redwall, as I sees it. Why don't ye stop until lunch? I'll make us a nice apple an' whortleberry pudden an' sing ye a few old songs. I've remembered a few my ma used t'sing. There's one called 'A Mother's 'Eart Is Made o' Gold,' aye, an' another ditty called 'I'd Give the World fer a Slice o' Mamma's Nutbread.' Then there's the one about a mother's tear bein' like a pearl o' grief . . ."

Sagax grabbed the foodpacks. All three travelers were

closely jammed as they fought to get through the cave doorway. "No, thankee, marm, you've done quite enough for us!"

"Aye, we'll miss the tide if we don't go now, we wouldn't dream of imposing on your hospitality any further, marm!"

"Sorry we've got to jolly well go, marm, er, toodle pip an' all that, wot. Bye bye now, got to tear ourselves away!"

Piling hastily into the *Stopdog,* they sailed off down the narrow rocky passage, fending off the stony walls with their oars. Only when the bright morning and the open sea lay before them did they chance to look back. Raura was standing on top of the rocks, singing at the top of her voice as Slippo twanged the harp for her.

> "Though she is wrinkled, grey and old,
> A mother's heart is made of gold,
> And her smile is like a quiet sunny day,
> So hearken to my lonely song,
> Don't stay away from home too long,
> There's nothing crueller than a runaway."

A tear was springing to Kroova's eye as he put on all sail and passed around chunks of laverbread. "Stuff this in yore ears, shipmates, afore we ends up blubberin' an' puttin' about to sail 'ome!"

By early noon the *Stopdog* was well out at sea, with the coastline a mere smudge of dark strip on the horizon. Sagax and Scarum were sitting atop the bow seat, their happy, carefree mood now restored.

"Haha, imagine us wailing like babes just because we're taking a short holiday from Salamandastron!"

"Rather! Did you see old Kroova? He was cryin' buckets, an' the silly great seadog hasn't even got a home t'go to, wot. Look at him, sittin' there fast asleep at the tiller, snorin' like a toad with a toothache. Hawhawhaw!"

Scarum rolled a pellet of laverbread and flicked it at

the sea otter. It pinged him neatly on the nose. Kroova wakened with a start and blinked at them.

"Ho, very funny, mateys, pingin' me nose an' wettin' me footpaws, aye. Very funny, I must say!"

Scarum flicked another pellet and missed. "Bit of an unjust accusation there, old lad. I pinged your nose, but neither of us wet your flippin' footpaws, wot!"

Kroova diverted his gaze to the water slopping round in the bottom of the ketch. Dismay crept across his features. "Must've banged 'er prow a bit 'ard on those rocks when we came down the channel from Raura's cave."

Scarum grinned mischievously as he rolled another pellet. "Y'don't say, me old scout. Nothin' too serious, is it, wot?"

Kroova turned the tiller, sending the vessel shoreward. "Serious? You two shift yoreselves an' git bailin'. It means we've sprung a leak an' we're sinkin'!"

BOOK TWO

Of Serpents
and Paradoxes

15

Plugg Firetail sat studying the chart in his cabin aboard the *Seascab,* while Grubbage poured him a beaker of seaweed grog. "Put that over 'ere, where it won't spill all over this chart. 'Tis the only one we've got wot shows the route."

Tazzin, the knife-throwing weasel, was hovering close by. She relieved Grubbage of the beaker and set it down carefully before she spoke. "Cap'n, beggin' yer pardon, but when do we do away wid the Princess an' that fatbellied Prince?"

Plugg gave her a smack that set her sprawling. "Y'ain't been lissenin', Tazzin, yore like the rest o' the numbskulls I've got fer a crew. Now 'earken t'me, an' you, Grubbage, you, too, Slitfang. Clean the mud outta yore ears an' pay attention. Right, 'ere's the plan. We don't kill nobeast until this ship's 'omeward bound fer Riftgard. Agarnu promised me booty twice the value of anythin' wot's brought back from this Mossflower place."

Slitfang poured himself a beaker of Plugg's best grog. "Oh did 'e now, an' wot are we supposed t'be bringin' back?"

Plugg sneered. "Ole King Sarengo, or 'is bones if'n he's dead, an' a golden crown an' a pawring. But I ain't as green as I'm grass lookin'—there's got t'be more to it than that, mates! So let's not git too 'asty. We goes along wid everythin', make 'em think they're in charge, even that bossy Cap'n Riftun. Now, when we're comin' back from Mossflower, we gets rid of 'im an' that score o' Ratguards 'e brought with 'im, accidental-like."

Tazzin sniggered and licked at her knifeblade.

"Heeheehee, I likes the sound o' that, Cap'n darlin'. Could I be the one who makes Riftun 'ave an accident?"

Plugg nodded. "Aye, when the time comes, but not afore then. When we reaches Riftgard, we delivers Kurda an' Bladd back to their daddy, old Agarnu. Of course, Agarnu gives us our reward then, twice the booty we brought back. Now, 'ere's the nice part. We slays Kurda, Bladd an' Agarnu, all three of 'em. We takes the reward an' wotever they brought back, be it crowns or pawrings or a good haul o' treasure. Simple! We ends up wid the kingdom o' Riftgard, a lot o' booty, a throne fer me to sit on, an' all those liddle slaves to build us a big fleet o' ships. You lot can all be cap'ns!"

Slitfang grinned in admiration as he poured another drink. "Yore a Freebooter born, Cap'n, the slyest beast as ever walked a deck. I drink to ye!"

Plugg pointed his dagger toward the weasel. "Aye, an' you'll be the sorriest beast ever walked a deck, if'n you keeps 'elpin' yoreself to my grog. Now, that's the plan. 'Ave youse all got it in yore thick 'eads?"

Grubbage looked indignant. "Why 'ave we gotta take to our sickbeds, Cap'n?"

Plugg came from behind his table. Wordlessly he faced the deaf rat to the cabin door, pressing on the back of his head until he bent over. Taking a pace back, the Captain swung his seabooted footpaw and delivered a powerful kick to his bosun's bottom. Grubbage shot forward, whooping. At that moment the cabin door opened and he careered out.

Princess Kurda acted as if nothing odd had happened,

as she strode in, sabre in paw, to face Plugg. "Vy you can't make dis ship go faster? You be t'ree days out an' ve don't seem to be goink much far."

The silver fox regarded her sourly. "That's 'cos the ship'll only go as fast as the winds carry 'er, dearie. Or ain't ye ever been t'sea afore?"

Kurda did not like Plugg. She pointed the sabre at him. "I must catchen up mit der slaves who steal my boat. You vill make dis ship go faster. Dis is my vish an' my order!"

The Freebooter captain, ignoring the sabrepoint, grinned. "Ho right, ye 'igh royalness, I kin see yore used ter givin' orders. But I'm only an ordinary ship's cap'n, ye see. Why don't ye go up on deck? Go on, missy. Wave yore sword round an' give orders t'the wind an' waves. Yore a princess. The sea'n'weather'll 'ave to listen to you, ain't that right, mates? Haharrharrharr!"

Laughter froze on the crew's lips as Kurda, with a murderous glint turning her eyes from pink to ruby, levelled the sabre blade a hairsbreadth from Plugg's eye and hissed, "You are insolent, fox. Dis could make you lose de head, yarr?"

The Freebooter continued grinning, as he reached beneath the table and brought his big double-edged battleaxe into view. "That there's a pretty liddle sword ye've got, darlin'. We've all seen ye flourishin' it round, real fancy-like. Now, git it outta me face afore I show ye wot a Freebooter cap'n can do with a proper weapon!"

The grin had gone from the fox's face, and his eyes were narrowed, icy slits, matching Kurda's stare.

Bladd blundered into the cabin, breaking the tension as he complained aloud, "De bed in my cabin, it is too hard! I vant a nice soft von!"

Plugg's grin returned. He brushed past Kurda, knocking her sabre aside, and threw a paw around Bladd's shoulders.

"Ahoy there, Slitfang, git a nice soft mattress for me shipmate, the Prince 'ere. Wot are ye thinkin' of, eh? Lettin' a royal ferret like 'im sleep on an 'ard bed?"

Slitfang was chuckling as he bowed mockingly to

Bladd. "Ho dearie me, wot a shame. You come wid old Slitty, yer royal princeness. We'll soon get ye a decent bunk!"

Kurda sheathed her sabre and stormed out of the cabin, followed by Slitfang and Bladd, who were chatting away like lifelong companions.

"You make sure it be nice an' soft, diss bedbunk, yarr?"

"Why, bless yore 'eart, matey, you'll think yore floatin' on a cloud o' feathers!"

"Diss iz good, you are der fine fellow. I am likin' you, Slitty. You vill be mine shipmatey, yarr!"

As the cabin door closed behind them, Plugg turned to Tazzin. "When the time comes, you steer clear o' Princess Kurda. She's mine, d'ye 'ear? All mine!"

With neither food nor water, the days at sea began to take their toll. Welfo had slipped into a deep sleep. She lay limp and unmoving on the bunk. Triss lay alongside the hogmaid, gaunt-faced and hollow-eyed, drifting in and out of listless slumber. Shogg sat draped across the tiller on the open deck, licking at cracked lips with a swollen tongue. He shaded a paw across his eyes, staring up at the beaming sun, which seemed to mock him out of a clear blue sky.

The otter croaked despairingly, "Rain, why don't ye! Rain, jus' a liddle shower!"

He fell asleep, his bowed head against the tiller, holding the vessel on course as his strength ebbed low.

Alone, like a leaf on an eternal breeze-ruffled pond, the little craft bobbed along aimlessly. With all hope gone, the three friends lay, overcome by weariness and starvation.

Triss was past caring. It might have been hours, days, or a full season that she languished in the cabin, alternately shivering and sweating. Then one day there was a soft radiance; the voice of that strange mouse warrior visited her clouded mind. She saw him advancing through a mist, carrying his splendid sword, calling to her. "Trisscar, Swordmaid, come with me, have no fear." He reached out to her. Triss held forth her paw to him.

Bump! The ship struck something, knocking her out of the bunk onto the cabin deck. Her eyelids fluttered. She was barely aware of a large, rough, prickly face filling her vision.

"This 'un's in better shape than yon pore liddle 'ogmaid. Lend a paw 'ere, Urtica. Don't fret ye, missy, thou'rt safe."

Triss felt strong paws lifting her, then she passed out.

Unaware that it was the following dawn, Shogg opened his eyes slowly and looked about him. He was no longer at sea on the ship! The ground was still and firm. He tried to sit up, but a gentle paw pushed him back.

"Lie thee still, riverdog, thou art with friends. Thou lookest hungered. Fear not, we will be breaking fast soon now."

The otter stared up into the face of an enormous but kindly-looking hogwife. He tried to talk, but his tongue was so swollen that only a husky noise came forth. Dipping a gourd ladle into a pail, the hogwife supported his head and fed him some water. It was the coolest, sweetest thing Shogg had ever tasted. She checked him from gulping it greedily.

"Nay, drink slow, 'tis not good taken fast. My name is Downyrose. My husband, Bistort, and our son Urtica found thy craft whilst we were gathering kelp. What is thy name?"

The otter's voice sounded strange to him as he spoke. "Name's Shogg, marm. Where are me mates, Triss an' Welfo?"

Downyrose allowed Shogg to sit up, leaning his back against a rock wall. "They be safe, worry not. Here, sip now, I must be about my chores."

Shogg took the gourd ladle and did as she instructed. Whilst drinking, he took stock of his surroundings.

He was seated on a ledge at the edge of a cave, overlooking a steep, terraced valley. It was like some huge inverted bowl, with high rocks surrounding the entire area. Other caves were dotted about the slopes. Families of hedgehogs could be seen, either breakfasting or tending the fertile green steppes. All manner of vegetables and fruit were flourishing in the soft, cool climate. A small waterfall threaded its way down the far slope, cascading over the rocky outcrops to end in a beautiful little forest situated on the valley bottom. One of the biggest hedgehogs Shogg had ever seen came ambling up to him. His facial quills were silvery, and he wore a rustic brown farmer's smock.

Sitting down next to the otter, the big fellow proffered his paw. "A good morn to ye, sir. I be called Bistort, Patriarch of Peace Island. 'Tis a fair an' pleasant spot."

Shogg shook paws with Bistort. "Aye, mate, it is that. How long have ye lived 'ere?"

Bistort moved his great head back and forth solemnly. "My clan an' kin have been here since the days of my parents. They sailed here seeking peace and contentment away from all strife, slavery and war. I was the firstborn here, and have never been away from this isle."

The young otter nodded admiringly. "Can't say I blame ye, Bistort. Do otherbeasts ever come to yore island?"

The big hedgehog winked. "Nay, never. Thou art the first. Look ye at this rock. Strange, is it not?"

Shogg inspected the rocks around him. They were a bluish-green colour. "Nice rocks, but what've they got t'do with it?"

Bistort spread his paws to the valley beneath. "Outside of all this, our island is practically invisible, a mere smooth-sided lump of stone sticking up out of the sea. Freebooters, corsairs and pirates have all sailed right by us. They see neither beach nor anchorage, so they think this nought but a big piece of stone, if they chance to sight it at all. 'Twas once a fire mountain, though no more. The soil is fertile, and we have only one hidden cove—thy ship lies moored there."

Shogg chuckled. "A secret island, eh. I want to thank ye for savin' our lives—we'd 'ave perished out there at sea. Me 'n' Triss—that's the squirrelmaid—we was worried about pore Welfo. She looked sure t'die soon. She ain't dead, is she?"

The hedgehog Patriarch nodded back toward the cave. "Thy friend lives. She is in there now, with our healer. But it will be some long time ere she is well again, methinks."

An apple came spinning through the air at Bistort. He ducked neatly and spiked it on his head quills. Another young hedgehog showed up. He was a jolly-looking creature, winking at Shogg as he called to Bistort, "See thee, old hog, my apples are ready before thine this season. Try that one for taste!"

Bistort unspiked the apple from his head and munched on it. "Mmm, good an' firm with sap aplenty. Shogg, this cheeky beast is my son Urtica—he helped to rescue thee."

The otter rose and shook Urtica's paw. "Thankee, mate. 'Ere's my paw an' 'ere's my 'eart. I owe ye my life, an' my friends' lives too!"

Urtica kept one paw behind his back as he shook paws. "Welcome to Peace Island, Shogg. Thou art recovering well."

Bistort craned his head to see what his son was hiding. "Art thou keeping something from thy father?"

The young hedgehog scrunched his spines together, a sign of obvious embarrassment among his species. He produced a posy of brightly hued flowers, freshly gathered.

"'Tis nought but some flowers for Welfo, the hogmaid we rescued. When she wakens 'twill be a welcome to her." He hurried past them into the cave, his spines bunched tight.

The big Patriarch took another bite of his apple. "My son seems greatly taken with thy friend. I have never seen him so attentive to another creature. Still, she is a pretty young maid. Would thou like to visit her, Shogg?"

The otter patted Bistort's paw and winked knowingly. "Oh, I'll see 'er later, mate. Let Urtica keep 'er company awhile. We'll visit Welfo after brekkist."

Triss emerged from the cave when Downyrose called their new acquaintances to eat. Shogg was pleased to see her up and about, even though she still looked a bit shaky.

"Ahoy there, shipmate, yore lookin' pawfresh an' perky!"

Triss sat beside Shogg as Downyrose and several other bustling hedgehogs served them a breakfast of fresh fruit, new baked bread and cool pale cider. "You don't look too bad yourself, young seadog. My, this looks good! I'm famished. They have a wonderful old healer here—she's treating Welfo with all kinds of herbs. I think she'll be able to sit up soon. She was awake when I left her."

Shogg sunk his teeth into a farl of the crusty bread. "Sink me rudder, that's good news. Mmm, this bread's great. It's full o' hazelnuts an' almonds. Tastes wunner-ful!"

They did the delicious breakfast full justice. Downy-rose insisted on heaping their plates several times. "Lack-aday, such skinny young things!"

Bistort chuckled as he watched them tucking in. "Not for long, my dearie, not with the way thou'rt feeding 'em!"

After breakfast they went into the cave for a visit with Welfo. Her eyes were open, and she was propped up on cushions, being fed fresh vegetable broth by Turna, the old healer. Welfo took the food without even glancing at the spoon as it was brought to her mouth; her eyes were fixed on Urtica. The young hedgehog sat staring silently back at her, the flowers still clutched in his paw. The visitors stood in silence for what seemed an age, as both Welfo and Urtica seemed unaware of their presence.

Shogg interrupted, asking and answering his own questions. "Ahoy there, Welfo, me ole mate, 'ow are ye?" "Oh, Shogg, I'm fine, I'm much better, thank you!" "Ho that's nice, now you git yoreself well, missie, an' eat lots o' good vittles." "Oh, I will. Thank you for coming to see me!" "Aye, an' thank ye for chattin' t'me, mate. Nice talkin' t'ye!"

He nudged Triss and Bistort, indicating the outside. "We might as well be talkin' t'the wall. Let's go."

Turna followed them as they left the cave. "I'll join

thee. The little maid will recover, but poor Urtica looks stricken—he'll never be the same again!"

They left the pair still gazing into one another's eyes.

Bistort took Shogg and Triss up a long, winding path with many steps cut into it. Morning was well advanced when they reached the crater rim. Smooth and sheer, the bluey-green rockface plunged to the sea far, far below. It was a dizzying prospect. Triss sat with her footpaws dangling over the edge.

"I feel as if my head is touching the clouds!"

Bistort hitched his smock and sat down beside her. "See the crack in the wall o'er yonder?"

Shogg was first to spot the fissure running from top to bottom, though he had to peer hard to find it. "Hah! I sees it, though it's very 'ard to find."

Bistort pointed it out for Triss to see. "'Tis there where thy ship is secretly moored. Nobeast will ever see it from the sea. Thou art safe here, friends."

He took them along the rim and down again by another path. Cutting off the path momentarily, the big hedgehog showed them a cave, screened by bushes. He pulled the foliage aside and bade them enter. The interior was stacked with sturdy home-made weaponry. Shogg inspected the array, which consisted mainly of bows, arrows, slings, pikes and lances. All were tipped with razor-sharp shards of the natural bluegreen stone of the island.

The Patriarch indicated them with a wave of his paw. "There are no swords here, as long blades cannot be made without metal. Most of our knives are made from stone. No weapons are allowed in our valley, but we made these, lest we ever had to defend ourselves from enemies. They have never been used, for we follow the ways of peace here."

Triss commented respectfully, "That's because no vermin ever found their way to Peace Island. Fate forbid that they ever will. We came from a land that was conquered by evil ones. Our lives were nothing but war and slavery."

Bistort placed a gentle paw on her shoulder. "I was

about to ask thee to stay here with us. But I see in thine eyes that this cannot be so."

The squirrelmaid touched one of the lances. "No sir, not while there are still slaves in Riftgard!"

Bistort turned his gaze on Shogg. "Are ye of like mind?"

The otter picked up a bag of sling pebbles, three pointed and sharp, every one knapped from the island rocks. "We made promises to our mates that we'd return someday an' free them. We're not beasts to break our vows."

The hedgehog Patriarch gave a long sigh and nodded. "So be it. Ye must do what ye are bound to. Thy ship will be stocked with some of these weapons when it sails. We will provision it with rations also. But 'twill not be for a while yet—thou are not ready to face the seas again so soon. Come, forget thy woes whilst ye are with us."

Hedgehogs throughout the valley ceased work on their crops for the remainder of that day. Everybeast gathered on a grassy plateau to feast and sport. Food was cooked in shallow trenches on fire-heated rocks. Broad, shiny, dark green leaves were wrapped around the various fruits and vegetables, causing aromatic steam to rise. Welfo, borne down to the plateau in a form of palanquin, was carried by eight stout beasts, with Urtica walking alongside holding her paw. Though most of the hedgehogs were great strong beasts, they did not indulge in spike tussling or wrestling—there were no displays of fighting skills. The competition was mainly prizes for the best grown fruits and vegetables, and each hedgehog stood beside carefully arranged tableaus of their own produce.

Triss and Shogg found themselves acting as judges, in company with Bistort. They were followed by a group of hogbabes, who had never seen creatures different from themselves.

Hogmothers chased after the little ones, chiding them. "Grinfee, if ye pull yon squirrelmaid's tail again, I'll tell thy father, be warned!" "Come off the otterbeast's tail, 'tis not for thee to ride upon, come off I say!"

Triss and Shogg took the babes' curiosity in good part. The food was superb, harvested only that morning. Shogg swore he had never tasted bread so fine, and so many types, too. Cider was the main drink, but that also had a lot of different varieties: cider with damson, plum'n'apple cider, dandelion burdock cidermix, to name but a few. Then two empty barrels were rolled out and used as drums, a hogwife played a rustic melody on a reed flute and a stout farmer sang out in a fine tenor voice:

> "My valley is green, the soil is good,
> An' I grows what I please,
> All in the spring when birds do sing,
> My wife grows flowers like these.
> Pepperwort, trefoil, celandine,
> Daffodil, woodruff, dandelion,
> Paleflax, pansy an' speedwell,
> Sweet violet an' bluebell.
> She's helped by all the busy bees,
> An' I grows what I please!
>
> My valley is green, the soil is good,
> With lots of shady trees,
> So when the work is done each day,
> 'Neath them we take our ease.
> Hazel, willow, birch an' all,
> Oak an' beech an' elm so tall,
> Chestnut, elder, aspen, too,
> Make shade for me an' you.
> There's laurel, lime, an' rowan trees,
> 'Neath which to take our ease!
>
> My valley is green, the soil is good,
> Our table for to fill,
> I plant my fruit an' veg'tables,
> With pride an' right goodwill.
> Lettuce, turnips, carrots, beans,
> Leeks an' scallions, winter greens,
> Damsons, plums, an' apples red,
> An' pears grow overhead.

When we sits down, we eats our fill,
With pride an' right goodwill!"

Having been slaves at Riftgard since they could remember, Shogg and Triss had never experienced anything
like the feast on Peace Island. It was the happiest, most
joyous of days. In the evening they sat round a fire with
their new friends, watching the sky above the rim fade
from powder blue to rich crimson gold. Hogbabes draped
both their heads and necks with garlands of buttercups
and daisy chains, while elders plied them with even more
good food and drink.

Triss poked at the flames with a stick, watching bright
sparks rise like dancing jewels to the gathering twilight
shades. She felt a deep pang of regret for the passing of it
all. "Imagine if each day were like this, Shogg. Anybeast
would be foolish to think of leaving this wonderful isle."

The otter noticed her eyes glinting damp in the firelight. "Aye, matey, but fools such as we know wot must be
done. We can't live our time out 'ere, knowin' that others
are still kept in wicked slavery, can we?"

Triss sniffed and looked aside. "No, we'll be on our
way in a few days, though I think there's one who won't
be sailing with us."

She was looking at Welfo, who was still wordlessly
staring into Urtica's eyes. Both seemed unaware of everything around them, completely entranced with each other.

Shogg chuckled quietly. "I see wot y'mean, Triss, it'd
be a shame to part those two. Pore Welfo was never very
strong, she's a gentle creature. Leave 'er with young Urtica. She's found 'appiness 'ere on Peace Island."

Triss patted her friend's paw, smiling through moist
eyes. There was no need for words.

16

Morning sunlight filtered through Redwall's orchard trees, adding warmth and brightness to the merry chaos of breakfast. Foremole Urrm was ladling out a porridge of oats, chestnut and honey, a special favourite with Dibbuns. He was having difficulty keeping up with the demand. Noisy Abbeybabes banged wooden spoons on the tabletops, roaring for second helpings.

"I wanna more porrige, I finish mine all up!"

"Me on'y gorra likkle bowl, gimme more, more!"

"H'over yurr, zurr, quick, afore oi starven away!"

Foremole glared at Ruggum with mock fierceness. "You'm already 'aved three porshings, villyun!"

Memm Flackery grabbed the bowl that Turfee mousebabe had decided to use as a helmet. "Don't do that, you infant cad. Just look at y'self, you've got more porridge on your face than you've put in y'mouth, wot! Sit still while I wipe it off. Sister Vernal, grab that blinkin' miscreant, will you? Quick, before he escapes under the table, catch him!"

Abbot Apodemus covered both ears, shouting over the din to Gurdle Sprink, who was sitting alongside him. "I

know they're excited about taking summer meals out-
doors, but this is too much, old friend. Let's go and find a
bit of peace with Malbun and Crikulus in the gatehouse,
eh!"

Gurdle was about to help the Abbot up when suddenly
he halted. "Father, 'ere come our Skipper, an' Ovus, too.
Wonder wot that ole owl wants? He ain't visited us in seasons."

They hurried to meet Skipper and the big tawny owl
waddling at his side. Apodemus beckoned them away
from the orchard. The four creatures walked back slowly
towards the gatehouse, with Skipper explaining the reason for the owl's visit.

"I noticed the gates weren't locked early this mornin',
so I took a peek. They was jammed t'gether with that
bonnet old Crikulus was wearin' at the feast last night—
the lockin' bar wasn't in place. So I goes t'the gate'ouse
an' it was empty. Crikulus was gone, Malbun too!"

The Abbot halted. "Malbun and Crikulus gone!
Where?"

Ovus the tawny owl blinked his huge jet-black eyes.
"Can't say where they were going, but I can show you exactly where your friends are now. Er, breakfast looked
quite nice, a tad rowdy, but quite nice. Don't suppose
there's any left—haven't had much since yesterday."

Curbing his impatience, Apodemus nodded graciously.
"I'm sure we can find you breakfast, friend, but will you
please tell me immediately where Crikulus and Malbun
are?"

Ovus nestled his chin into his puffy breast feathers.
"Thank you, Father Abbot. Now, your two Redwallers, let
me tell you their location. I'd left my home south of here
and gone to visit some family, in the north, you know.
Can't say why they chose there to settle—cold, hostile
country, I've always thought. Never really liked the north,
y'know."

Gurdle whispered to the Abbot, "Beats round the bush
a bit, don't he? You think he'd get on with it!"

Ovus swivelled his head in the Cellarhog's direction.

"I heard that, y'know. I didn't come here to be insulted. Huh, I think I'd be better off keeping myself to myself!"

Apodemus nudged Gurdle sharply, warning him to be silent with a severe glance. "I must apologise for my friend. His back is playing him up a bit, touch of rheumatism. He didn't mean to be rude."

The tawny owl gazed down at his own enormous talons. "Hmm, the rheumatiz gets us all once the young seasons are gone. Take me, now, my talons give me dreadful twinges, especially in the winter. You wouldn't think owls would have that complaint, would you? Well, we do, let me tell you!"

Apodemus gave a polite cough. Ovus blinked several times, then got on with his account.

"Hmm, let me see now, ah yes. I was on my way back south from visiting family in the north, night flying, of course. It must've been three, no, I tell a lie, two hours before dawn. I heard weeping and sobbing, southeast of here, just beyond a patch of bogland in Mossflower Woods. Recognised the pair right away, your old Gatekeeper shrew and that woodmouse who does a bit of healing. Malbun, is it?"

Gurdle was about to speak when Ovus held up a wing. "I know what you're going to ask. Let me continue. I saw it was the old shrew who was crying. The woodmouse was unconscious, not badly injured, merely knocked out by something or other. So I had a brief chat—I can be brief, y'know—with the shrew. Told him to stay put and not to move. Said I'd fly to Redwall and get help. Well, here I am!"

Apodemus heaved a sigh of relief. "Many, many thanks, Ovus, many thanks! I take it you will be so kind as to lead us to them?"

The owl spread his wings as if to take off, then thought better of it and folded them again. "Of course I'll lead you to them. I can put my talon on the exact spot where they are right now. Straight after I've had breakfast. Oh, one other thing—don't expect me to gobble my food down. I suffer from indigestion, too, y'know!"

Skipper looked at the Abbot resignedly. "We'd best git our mate Ovus some brekkist, Father."

Crikulus tapped his paw upon a treetrunk impatiently and judged the sun's traverse. "Where in the name o' seasons are they? It'll soon be midmorn. D'you think the owl has really gone back to Redwall?"

Malbun sat with her back against the tree, holding a compress of herbs against her injured cheek. "No reason why he shouldn't. Ovus knows he's sure of a meal there. I never knew the owl who could resist a bite or two at our Abbey. Relax, they'll come for us, I'm sure."

Neither of the pair had discussed the fear and horror that had caused them to flee on the previous night. Nor did they feel that they wanted even to mention it—the dreadful odour, the rippling grass, the horrific feeling. It seemed like a bad dream in the broad, sunny light of day, so they avoided speaking of such things.

Crikulus rubbed his lean stomach. "Breakfast at the Abbey, I could use that right now!"

Malbun pressed her paw gently to the bump that had developed on the side of her head, smiling ruefully. "I'm absolutely useless without my first beaker of hot mint and comfrey tea in the mornings. I'd love to have one right now, with a drop of feverfew to reduce this headache."

The ancient shrew paced up and down, guessing who would come searching for them. "It'll be Skipper for sure, with them two big young otters. I'll wager Log a Log an' his Guosim shrews come, too. Malbun, d'you think I'd best take a walk and see if I can spot them coming? I won't be long."

Malbun held up a paw for silence and craned forward, listening intently to a distant sound. "No need for you to go anywhere, Crikulus, I think I hear them coming. Listen, can you hear it, too?"

The old shrew could not, even though he waggled a paw in his ears to clear them. "No, I can't hear a thing yet."

Malbun relaxed and leaned back against the tree.

"Let's hope they've brought some food with 'em, eh."

Crikulus rubbed his paws in anticipation. "I'll give them a shout, that'll jolly 'em along a bit. Let them know our position, too."

Cupping both paws around his mouth, he yelled aloud, "We're over here, over heeeere! Come on, you lazy lot, over heeeeeere! Bring us some foooooooooood!"

He sat down next to Malbun. As they waited, Crikulus would give out with the odd shout, "Over heeeeeere!" He persisted in doing this until Malbun stopped him.

"Great fur'n'feathers, d'you have to bawl your face off like that? My head is really beginning to bang!"

Crikulus stopped then, but he became a bit sulky. "Only trying to help. Letting them know where we are."

"Aye, so ye were. Thank ye fer the 'elp, old feller!"

Three rough-looking stoats strolled out of the trees. Malbun eyed them suspiciously. "Who are you?"

Their leader, a lanky specimen with yellowed broken stumps of teeth, drew a curved sword from his tattered robe. Grinning nastily, he pointed the blade at them.

"Never mind who we are, mousey. Who are you, an' who's yer noisy liddle pal? Wot are ye doin' in our woods, eh?"

Swallowing hastily, Crikulus tried not to look scared. "You'll pardon me saying so, but Mossflower Woods do not belong to anybeast. They are free to all creatures."

One of the stoats, a fatbellied beast with a marked stoop, leaned on his spear, cackling. "Heeheehee, ye'll pardon me sayin', ain't that nice. Heehee, 'ow about that, Wicky. Are yer gonna pardon 'im, or slit 'is throat? I'll do the job if ye like. Heeheehee!" He advanced on Crikulus with his spear held ready.

Malbun stood up and called out indignantly, "Don't you dare! We are creatures of Redwall Abbey!"

The third stoat, an undersized vermin with a big single brass earring, whipped out a hatchet, leering nastily. "So wot's that to us, eh? Yew shut yer mouth, or I'll part yore ears. Where's yore vittles an' valuables, quick!"

Crikulus bravely placed himself in front of his friend.

"We don't carry valuables an' we haven't any food. Now leave us alone, I warn you. Some other Redwallers will be here any moment, three big otters an' a band of Guosim shrews."

The one called Wicky shaded a paw across his eyes and leapt about, waving his sword. "Otters, shrews, I don't see any otters or shrews, d'you, mates? May'aps they're 'idin' close by."

The spear carrier thought it was all very funny. "Hee-heehee, Redwallers comin', otters'n'shrews. Who d'ye think yer foolin', granpa? That's the oldest trick in the book. Tell us where yore vittles'n'vallibles are an' we'll let ye go. But no fibbin'—fibs make us angry."

Wicky unwound a long, thin line of greased cord from under his cloak. He made a running noose and lassoed both Crikulus and Malbun with an expert cast. In a trice they were both bound to the tree that they had their backs to.

Crikulus whispered urgently to Malbun, "Where in the name of seasons have Skipper an' Log a Log got to? What's keeping them?"

Wicky cuffed the old shrew's ear. "Shut yer gob, I'll tell ye when to talk! Now, I'm goin' to ask ye once more. Where's the valuables an' vittles?"

The wound in Malbun's cheek and the ache in her head was doing little to improve her temper. She snapped sharply, "And I'm telling you once more, vermin, so dig the mud out your ears. There aren't any. Is that plain enough?"

The stoat swung his sword, chipping a chunk of bark from the tree a fraction above Malbun's head. He snarled, "Me next strike'll be lower, about where yer ears are!"

His companion with the hatchet waved him out of the way. "Yore not 'avin all the fun, Wicky, gimme a go. Right, old shrew, you tell us. Cummon, where's the stuff 'idden?"

Crikulus kept his voice reasonable, eyeing the hatchet. "We have nothing but the robes we are wearing, nothing."

"Well, let's see 'ow yer 'op round with only one foot-paw!"

The stoat flung his hatchet. Crikulus pulled his foot-paw aside just in time. The hatchet buried itself in the ground, a hair's breadth from the old shrew's paw.

A rough growl came from the spear carrier as he hefted his weapon. "Aarrh, I'm sick o' playin' around. I'll slay one of 'em, the other'll talk soon enough then!"

Looking directly at Malbun, he leaned back for a throw.

Skipper came hurtling out of the bushes and grabbed the spearbutt, pulling the stoat flat on his back as Log a Log and the others dashed in, surrounding the three vermin. Log a Log snatched the sword from Wicky and cut the captives loose. Skipper snapped the spear as though it were a twig. Roughly he hauled the floored stoat upright and shoved him toward the other two. Huddling miserably together, the three vermin stood dull-eyed, expecting no mercy.

Log a Log turned to Malbun and Crikulus, inspecting them. "Are you all right, friends? Did these three harm you?"

Malbun held the herbal compress close against her cheek. "We're all right, thank you. They were just about to start on us when you arrived. Please don't slay them, they're only three thickheaded, ignorant vermin!"

Log a Log looked enquiringly to Skipper, who shrugged. "Mossflower'd be better off without such evil scum. But if'n that's yore wish, marm, then so be it. Ahoy there, vermin, ye've got this good mouse t'thank for sparin' yore worthless lives. Speak up now, thank 'er!"

Hope gleamed in the stoats' eyes as they cried out together, "Thank ye, marm, thank ye kindly!"

Skipper picked up the stoat's hatchet and hefted it. "Tie their footpaws t'gether, Churk."

The burly young ottermaid took the severed rope and lashed the stoats' footpaws together, as though they were competing in a three-legged race, the middle one's footpaws bound to the left and right of his companions.

Skipper spoke. "I'm goin' to count to ten. I wouldn't be 'ere after the count if I was you. Take warnin', vermin, next time you're seen in Mossflower country yore dead-beasts, all of ye! One, two . . ."

Hobbling and stumbling, they fled off into the wood-lands. There was no need for Skipper to count further.

Log a Log gave a snort of derision, shaking his head at Malbun. "Yore too soft-'earted, marm. They'll live to slay other pore honest beasts. Oh well, come on, you two, let's get ye back to the Abbey. I suppose yore hungry, eh?"

Crikulus rubbed his stomach. "Hungry's not the word, friend—try famished. What happened to the owl? I didn't see him arrive with you."

"That's because you didn't take the trouble to look up here!"

Ovus was perched in a tree directly opposite. He swooped down to the ground and clacked his awesome beak at them. "I'm not exactly famished, but I could man-age lunch. Or if we're too late, a spot of afternoon tea would be nice."

The party moved off, with Crikulus striking up a friendship with the talkative tawny owl. "Toasted teacakes with a smear of honey on 'em, now that's my choice, with a good beaker of dandelion burdock cordial. Be my guest, sir, we'll take it in my gatehouse. Would you like to join us, Malbun? Maybe we'll have some of that soft white cheese with the celery bits in and a mushroom pasty or two, with lots of onion gravy, of course."

Squinching her eyes, the Healer Recorder shook her head gingerly. "No, thanks. A bit of quiet and a lie down'll do me."

17

Late-afternoon sunlight poured in through the Infirmary window at Redwall Abbey. Malbun lay on her bed, fiddling with the edge of the tasselled counterpane. Sleep was eluding her. There was a gentle tap on the door, and Abbot Apodemus entered, carrying a tray. Skipper and Log a Log came in with him. The Abbot checked to see if Malbun was awake.

"Ah, having trouble taking a nap, eh, Mal? I thought you'd like a teacake and a nice beaker of mint and comfrey tea."

Malbun sat up. "Indeed I would. Thank you, my friend."

As Malbun ate and drank, the Abbot began talking to her of the previous night's events.

"I take it, then, that you and Crikulus left the Abbey late last night during the feast. Still searching for Brockhall, probably. Well, Malbun, what did you find?"

The Healer Recorder shrugged dismissively. "Oh, nothing."

Log a Log and Skipper exchanged suspicious glances. The Guosim Chieftain kept his voice deceptively casual.

"Ye don't mind me askin', marm, but 'ow come we found you an' Crikulus miles from anywhere?"

Malbun suddenly became interested in the teacake crumbs on her plate. She hesitated. "Er, we got lost. Took the wrong path in the, er, dark."

Skipper dropped his question in casually. "Wot were the two of ye runnin' away from, marm?"

Malbun looked surprised. "Running? What makes you think we were running? There was nothing chasing us, we never ran."

Seeing she had finished her snack, the Abbot removed the tray. "Our Guosim trackers said that your trail looked as if you were dashing through the woodlands in a panic."

Detesting the lies she was telling to her friends, Malbun carried on unhappily. "When creatures are lost in darkened woodlands, they crash and stumble about a bit, through bushes, across streams. . . . I assure you, we weren't running or being chased."

Apodemus held his friend's paw, staring into her eyes. "Are you sure there's nothing more you want to tell us?"

Malbun pulled her paw free and lay back, closing her eyes. "I can't tell you anything more. I'm tired and injured, I need to have a sleep. Please leave me alone."

Apodemus signalled to Skipper and Log a Log that they should leave. He patted Malbun's footpaw. "Of course you need to rest. Forgive us for intruding."

As Skipper opened the door, Malbun called out, "Thank you for rescuing us from those vermin. Don't know what we'd have done if you hadn't arrived in time."

Log a Log bowed gallantly. "Think nought of it, marm. You take a nice liddle rest now."

The door closed. Malbun opened her eyes and rubbed her aching head miserably, still fighting to rid her mind of the sickly-sweet odour of death and grass rustling in the night.

Halfway down the stairs, the Abbot turned to his companions. He looked mystified. "Well, what d'you make of

that? Malbun was telling lies, I'm certain of it. That's not
at all like her."

Skipper sat down on the worn sandstone steps. "I'm
glad you said that instead o' me, Father Abbot. It grieves
me t'think of any Redwaller bein' a liar. Especially that
nice ole mouse!"

Log a Log scratched his whiskers thoughtfully. "She
must've had a reason. Hmm, I wonder wot ole Crikulus
would say if'n we asked 'im?"

Apodemus folded both paws up his wide sleeves.
"Now, that's a thought! Leave this to me, friends. Let me
go and have a word with our Gatekeeper, on my own."

With an appetite that belied his long seasons and frail appearance, Crikulus ravenously tucked into everything
within paw range. He stuffed himself with toasted teacakes, slices of heavy fruitcake, cucumber sandwiches, a
cheese-and-celery pasty, and a large tankard of October
Ale, after which he retired to his beloved gatehouse and
slumped in the big armchair with his footpaws resting on
a dusty old hassock. Almost immediately he fell into a
deep slumber.

Apodemus lifted the latch carefully and crept in, closing the door quietly behind him. Seating himself on the
wide chair arm, the Father Abbot whispered into the ancient shrew's ear, "Ah well, we're safe back in your gatehouse now, old fellow."

Crikulus moved his lips. "Mmm, mmm, aye, safe . . .
safe . . . Redwall . . . mmm . . . Who's that?"

He stirred, and the Abbot stroked his paw, relaxing
him. "Ssshhh, 'tis only Malbun. My my, we were lucky
out there in those woodlands, my friend, very lucky."

Crikulus nodded in his sleep, smiling at the recollec-
tion. "Aye, near chopped my footpaw off with that
hatchet. Vermin scum! Good job Skipper arrived. Log a
Log, too. Redwallers, true friends, y'know. Those stoats
were goin' to kill us. Haha . . . Bet they're still runnin' . . .
mmm."

Apodemus leaned closer, whispering urgently, "We

were running, too, last night, through the woodlands, me and you, running. What was it that was after us?"

Crikulus thrust a paw out in front of him, his face screwed up. Shaking his head from side to side, he gave a hoarse, high-pitched whimper. "Eeehh! They're in the grass, coming toward us! Malbun, oh, that smell, it's everywhere! Can't you hear the grass moving? . . . Run!"

"I say, either of you two chaps spotted that scallywag Ruggum? Oops, sorry, were you takin' a nap?" Memm Flackery stood framed in the open door, sunlight streaming into the gatehouse around her.

Crikulus's eyes popped open. He sat up, blinking. "Eh? what's th . . . Oh, it's you, Memm. Father Abbot, what're ye doin' sitting on my chair? What's happening?"

Swiftly the Abbot slid from the chair arm, making a pretence of searching around the gatehouse. "Oh, nothing, sorry we disturbed you. We were searching for little Ruggum, weren't we, Memm?"

The Harenurse stared stupidly at the furiously winking Abbot. "Got somethin' in your eye? Here, let me take a squint." She rolled an apron corner and licked it.

Apodemus was quickly at her side, muttering, "Play along with me!"

Memm did not have a clue what was going on. "Play along, sah? Righto, what d'you want to play? Hunt the acorn, toss the pebbles? Bit silly playin' flippin' games instead of lookin' for that confounded Ruggum, wot?"

Crikulus regarded them both curiously. He was not in the best of humour at having his nap broken. "What, pray, are you two gabbling on at, eh? Can't I have a bit o' peace after all I've been through? Clear off!"

Memm sauntered out of the gatehouse huffily. "Hmph, wish we could all sleep the bloomin' day away, instead of gettin' our bally jobs done. Fine state the jolly old Abbey'd be in then. Wot wot wot?"

Crikulus was settling back down. As the Abbot was leaving, he tried one more time to fathom the mystery.

"I'll leave you to get on with your nap, old fellow. But

just a moment ago, as I came in the gatehouse, you were talking in your sleep. You seemed quite upset."

Crikulus opened one eye. "Did I? What was I saying?"

The Abbot spoke hesitantly, as if trying to remember, "Something about a smell being everywhere and the grass moving. You seemed very unhappy about it all, because you were telling some other beast to run, shouting it aloud. Almost as if something was chasing you both."

Crikulus was wide awake now, and on the alert. Apodemus noted the look of horror on his face as he answered, "It was nothing . . . only a dream . . . leave me alone, Father!"

Apodemus bowed. "As you wish." He left the gatehouse.

Log a Log and Skipper were on the ramparts at the northeast corner, staring into the silent fastness of Mossflower Woods, when the Abbot joined them and told them what Crikulus had said.

The Guosim Chieftain felt the fur on his nape prickling. "At first I thought they might've been attacked by the crows, but this is different. I don't like it, Father Abbot. Wot d'you say, Skip? A smell bein' everywhere an' grass movin'?"

Grasping his javelin, the big otter shook his head. "Crows don't attack at night, leastways I never 'eard of 'em doin' so. Mebbe 'twas those three stoats trailin' Malbun an' Crikulus. They smelt pretty strong, but no worse'n any other vermin that ain't washed in two seasons. Hmm, 'tis a puzzler, right enough. May'ap you'n me might go an' take a look tomorrow, eh, Log? In the meantime, Father Abbot, you'd best forbid anybeast leavin' the Abbey to go wanderin' round Mossflower."

Apodemus patted the otter's well-muscled back. "At least until this matter is cleared up. Thank you for your advice, my good friend."

The three stoats had gnawed through the ropes that bound their footpaws together. They sat in the thick woodlands, far from the spot where they had met up with the Red-wallers. Vanquished and humiliated, their mood was far from happy.

Wicky, the self-appointed leader of the trio, flung the rope scraps viciously into the bushes. He curled his lip scornfully at the other two. "Hah, youse two was a lot of 'elp. That shrew 'ad me down, took me by surprise, 'e did. Kligger, why didn't yew grab yore 'atchet an' chop 'im? An yew, Burgogg, fancy lettin' a h'otter bust yer spear in arf like that. Idjits!"

Kligger bared his uneven teeth at Wicky, snarling, "Will ye lissen to 'im? 'E jus' stood there an let the lid-dle shrew take the sword outta 'is paws. I was too far away from me 'atchet, I 'ad four shrews' rapiers at me throat. Huh, I didn't notice yew goin' for 'em wid yore sword!"

Burgogg picked rope strands from his teeth with a filthy claw. "Didyer see the size of that h'otter? I didn't stan' a chance. That spear belonged to me old granpa. The shaft was strong as an oak, but 'e busted it like a twig!"

Wicky kicked out at him. "Next time you lets a h'otter break your spear, I'll bust you like a twig!"

Burgogg spat at him, but missed. "Huh, yew an' who else, scringenose? Jus' try an' put a paw near me!"

Wicky stood up and cast about for a stick. "Scringe-nose, is it? Right, I'll show yew, barrelbum, toadbelly, plinkypaws!"

Burgogg looked hugely offended. "Ooh, didyer 'ear that, 'e called me plinkypaws. I'll fetch a coggy lump on yore 'ead, soon as I finds a good rock!"

Kligger rose in disgust. "Why don't youse two give yer gobs a rest. We won't git our bellies filled by callin' each other daft names. I ain't 'ad vittles fer two days now. Let's search around fer roots an' things to eat."

Burgogg clapped a paw to his nose. "Phwaw, wot's that stink?"

Wicky caught a waft of the foul odour and blanched.

"Pew! Yew'd better find a stream an' gerra bath, yew greasy-eared wibble!"

Burgogg looked quizzically at Wicky. "Wot's a wibble?"

Wicky spotted something hanging from a tree behind Burgogg and pushed past him, remarking scathingly, "I dunno, but if there was a wibble, I bet it'd smell jus' like yew. An' you ain't gettin' one o' these!"

He gathered up the two cloaks and two lanterns that had belonged to Malbun and Crikulus.

Burgogg's face fell. "Give us one o' those cloaks. I ain't got a warm cloak."

Wicky poked out his tongue like a naughty vermin babe. "Ho no, yew ain't gittin' nothin'. I'll give one o' these cloaks an' a lanting to Kligger, that'll teach yer t'call me a scringenose. Hoi, Klig, 'ere's some booty fer ye!"

The odour grew more powerful as he looked around, calling, "Kligger, mate, where are yer, 'ave yew found some vittles? I'll trade ye, vittles fer a lovely cloak an' a lanting!"

Kligger had found a door, partly open, in the trunk of a great spreading oak. Though the smell was overpowering, he could not resist opening the door fully to see what lay inside.

Wicky and Burgogg heard his scream cut the quiet woodland air like a knife. "Aaaaarrrreeeeegh!" They dashed toward the sound and saw Kligger as he was dragged into the tunnel beneath the oak. They also saw the thing that had him.

No sound issued from their fear-clamped mouths. Eyes bulging with terror, both stoats stood petrified for a moment. Then the overpowering stench of the thing hit both stoats like a solid wall moving forward. They took to their paws and fled, running twice as fast as Malbun and Crikulus had run.

A short while thereafter, the sounds of Wicky and Burgogg had receded into the distance as they tore through the woodlands running due north. Around the area of the spreading oak, all was silent in the sunlit summer noon. Two cloaks and two lanterns lay forgotten on the ground amid the musty, bittersweet odour.

18

At first the water coming in through the *Stopdog*'s prow
was no more than a healthy trickle. But the flow increased
as she sat lower in the sea. Kroova, Scarum and Sagax
bailed until they were weary. Then they saw the wind had
changed and was blowing away from the shore, which
was still a good distance off. Little time was left for tacking, so they furled the sails. Kroova took the bowrope
around his shoulders and dived into the waves, towing the
Stopdog toward land as his two shipmates, backsore and
paw weary, continued bailing.

Scarum's voice was shaky. "I say, hope we make it to
dry land, wot. Not too good at the old swimmin' lark, y'-
know. The jolly old parents raised a hare, not a flippin'
fish, wot!"

Sagax watched Kroova regretfully. "There's the only
proper swimmer amongst us, mate. Oh, I can manage
what they call a doggie paddle, but I'd hate to have to
swim any distance. Land still looks pretty far off. What in
the name of fur'n'feathers are you doing, eating at a time
like this?"

Despite his woeful demeanour, Scarum was packing

down food as though he were facing a famine. "Mmff, grrmmfff! Eatin' me fill before all this scoff gets ruined by bally seawater, old lad. Grrrmmmffchomp! No use leavin' it for the fishes—waste not want not, y'know. Scrmmff!"

Sagax sent a chunk of laverbread spinning from the hare's paw. "If you can't swim and you stuff yourself, you'll go right to the bottom with that weight of food in your stomach. Now, leave that food alone and bail!"

Scarum stared guiltily at his midriff. "You're right, of course, never thought of that. Oh, what a confounded, absolutely rotten predicament: not bein' able to swim on an empty tummy or drownin' on a full one. Oh, rats'n'fiddlesticks an' beastly bad luck, wot!"

Kroova could really feel the drag now—they actually were sinking. But the worthy sea otter laboured on until he heard Sagax calling, "Kroova, we're nearly under, we'd best abandon ship!"

Judging the distance and trusting to his knowledge, Kroova shouted back to his distressed friends, "Just a bit more. Sling the water out, keep 'er head up. I ain't goin' to lose me dear old *Stopdog* just 'cos of a leak. Get t'- work, mates, I'll tell ye when to jump for it!"

Water was pouring in as fast as Sagax and Scarum were bailing it out. From a distance the scene would have looked like a badger and a hare standing on the surface of the sea, throwing water about. Sagax could see Scarum beginning to flag badly. The hare had started bailing like a madbeast, but the gruelling toll was wearing him down.

Then the waves splashed in over the rails, swamping the ketch completely as the *Stopdog* sank.

"Away, crew! Abandon ship, me 'earties!"

At the sound of Kroova's call they both leaped into the sea. Scarum let out an almighty spluttering yell. Floundering wildly, he grabbed at Sagax. The young badger was about to shout for Kroova to come and help them when his footpaws touched bottom.

The sea otter floated on his back, still holding the rope

and laughing at them. Sucking up a mouthful of seawater, he squirted it at his bewildered friends. "Haharrharr! We made it, mateys, we made it!"

Sagax and Scarum were standing with the water at chest height in the shallow seas offshore. Forgetting his former panic, Scarum waded toward Kroova, berating him.

"You! Y'great barnacle-ruddered, slipskinned, splay-pawed bounder! Allowin' a chap t'think he was drownin'. Not very funny, I'd say, wot. No sah, not the least bit droll!"

Sagax splashed water in the hare's face and chuckled. "He saved us, didn't he? What more d'you want? Ahoy, mate, why did you wait so long before you told us to abandon ship? You had me a bit worried there!"

Kroova explained the reason for his strange behaviour. "See those rocks stickin' up out of the sea yonder? Well, I tell ye, I was worried too, until I spotted 'em. Then I knew: This is a great big reef! Look be'ind you, see where the water goes from light to dark blue? That's the edge. I figgered if'n we could sail 'er out o' the deep an' onto this ledge, we could not only wade ashore, but I could save ole *Stopdog* by runnin' 'er onto the reef. If the tide takes a good long ebb around 'ere, there's a chance we can tow 'er ashore an' beach 'er for repairs. Come on, mateys, 'tis only a brisk wade to dry land!"

Making the headrope fast to a small rock poking out of the water, Kroova ensured that their boat would not be swept away. Side by side, they waded wearily forward. The beach looked to be sandy, though strewn with outcrops of rock. The water was now about waist height.

Scarum's mood had changed, and he was feeling happy. "One thing about bein' a jolly old shipwrecked seabeast, it works up a good appetite, wot. Right chaps, when we get ashore I'm in charge of the foragin' party. Though I warn you, I'm a pretty stern commandin' type, so you'd best find loads of scoff, or you'll have me to deal with!"

Sagax glanced back over his shoulder. The *Stopdog*'s masts could be seen sticking up at a tilt out of the waves. Suddenly a sinister triangular fin appeared, passing the sunken craft, heading their way.

"Shark! Quick, charge for the shore, shark!"

However, charging through waist-deep seas would be slow and difficult. Kroova slapped their backs.

"Get ahead, mates, move yoreselves! It's comin' after us!" Turning away from them, the sea otter plunged into the waves and swam straight for the big fish.

Without looking back, Sagax and Scarum plunged ahead, the going getting better as the water ran shallower. With tiny ripplets splashing round their paws, the pair made it onto the firm wet sands.

Scarum sat down, badly frightened and shaking. Sagax threw himself next to him, panting heavily as he stared around. "Where's Kroo . . . Oh, great blood'n'vinegar, look out there!"

Kroova was at waist depth, with the shark circling him. The sea otter had hold of something. He tugged it this way and that, sometimes tugging it sharply, which seemed to send the great seabeast in another direction. Seawater, pounded creamy white by the struggle, leaped high about Kroova and the shark.

Scarum gnawed at his whiskers in anguish at the dangerous spectacle. "Oh my fat aunt, it's followin' him in!"

Then Sagax saw what Kroova had hold of. "No, he's towing it! That's a rope—it's stuck to the shark somehow. He's playing it as if he were fishing!"

They both jumped up, yelling and bawling.

"Don't let it get you, mate, stay clear!"

"Watch the blighter, old lad, he's got better teeth than me!"

Rolling and thrashing, the shark showed its huge pale underbelly. They saw its wicked round eye and rows of curved, razorlike teeth. It made a dive at Kroova. The sea otter leaped the opposite way and hauled the rope hard, forcing his adversary to flounder off in another direction. All the time the two were getting closer to the shore.

Now the shark's body was sticking up out of the water. It would not give up, though it was beginning to roll and flop slightly. Suddenly Kroova whipped the rope deftly round a nub of rock and raced to the safety of dry land.

The two friends helped him ashore, where he sat blowing and heaving awhile before turning to Scarum with a comical grin on his tough face.

"That there shark's an ole pal o' yores, messmate. See the rope 'angin' out its mouth? That's the one you caught it on. The villain's still got yore 'ook stuck in its mouth!"

Scarum stared in amazement at the fish, which, now that it could stretch the rope by pulling against it, was biting through the fibres.

"Good grief, so it is." The hare began shouting at the shark. "Hi there, old lad! Remember me, the chap you took for a boat ride? Hoho, missed me again, didn't you? Silly great blighter, that'll teach you t'mess with fearless seafarers. Go on, be off with you, fishface!"

At that moment the rope snapped and the shark wallowed awkwardly out to deep water again, still towing a small tail of rope from its mouth.

Scarum flung several pebbles after it. "Call back anytime if y'want more of the same, wot!"

"Arrh, weel now, sorr, ye must be awful brave beasts!"

They turned to see a little hogmaid standing watching them. She had her headspikes tipped with flowers and wore a clean tunic of green woven linen with a flowery patterned pinafore over it.

Scarum put on a courageous, carefree face. "All part of the job, pretty miss. We're shark hunters really, chase the old sea monsters hither an' thither, wot. Not a bally shark in the seas won't turn tail an' run at the mention of us. So then, me spiked beauty, where d'you live?"

Completely friendly, the little hogmaid took Scarum's paw. "If yore honour'll come wid me, I'll be showin' ye."

The hare nodded at his companions to follow. Making an elegant leg at the little hogmaid, he allowed her to lead him off to some dunelands backing the shore.

"It'll be a pleasure, m'gel. I'll go with anybeast who looks as plump an' jolly well fed as you. Your family got plenty of grub, have they? Hawhaw, lead on, little charmer!"

A hogwife appeared on the dunetops, waving a ladle as she called to the little hogmaid, "Is that yourself, Fridilo Migooch? An' wot've ye been told about wand'rin' off alone? 'Tis a ladle I should be takin' to yer tailspikes. Ah shure an' where in the name o' fleas did ye find those three raggity ould tramps?"

Scarum murmured to Kroova, "Raggedy ould tramps, I say! Bit much, isn't it, wot wot?"

The sea otter winked at him. "Leave this t'me, mate." He bounded up the dune and smiled disarmingly at the hogwife.

"Pleasant day to ye, marm. We're pore shipwrecked creatures who found yore liddle 'un lost, so we was just bringin' 'er back 'ome to ye."

The hogwife waved her ladle at Fridilo. "That'n lost? Arrh, 'way with ye, she's no more lost than a dumplin' in a soup pot. So now, 'tis yoreself an' those other two a-fetchin' the babe home. At least yore not pirates. Ye look fair famished, all of ye. I'm thinkin' ye'd best come t'the tenty an' take an' ould gobfull."

Scarum was beside her in a bound, holding the little one in his paws, grinning bravely as he was prickled by her. "My dear lady, I take it that you mean we're invited to dinner. May I express the hope that it tastes as good as you look, beautiful creature, wot!"

A half-smile appeared on the hogwife's homely features. "Away with ye, y'great silver-tongued ould hooligan, I'm not yer dear lady. I'm Mammee Migooch, so I am!"

The "tentys," as Mammee called them, were great sand-coloured tents of hessian weave, almost invisible among the dunes. They were the home of the roving Migooch tribe, nomad hogs who wandered the coastline. There were roughly a hundred of them, all shapes and sizes, cheerful creatures who lived from day to day without any thought for the morrow. The travellers stood to one side as Fridilo related the shark incident with lots of comical dancing and rapid baby talk. When she was done, a fat old male, wearing a tattered straw hat and a soup-stained smock, shook Kroova's paw heartily.

"Arrh, an' 'tis yoreself the great shark wrestler? I raise me hat t'ye, sorr, I do indeed. Cumarnee Migooch is proud t'be shakin' the paw that shook a shark!"

Scarum strode forward, flexing his ears. "Actually, old chap, 'twas me who wrestled the blighter, doncha know. When the jolly old shark was worn out, I sent Kroova in to deal him a whack or two. Scarum Sharkslayer at y'service, sah!"

Cumarnee raised his bushy eyebrows. "Weel now, aren't ye the bold feller? We'll take a trip down t'the shore later an' let ye show us how you wrestle wid d'great sharks. How'll that suit ye?"

The garrulous hare had his answer ready. "Er, I'm restin' at the moment. Besides, y'won't see a fin for miles around. Sharks know I'm here, y'see. Oh yes, mention Scarum Sharkslayer an' they paddle off pretty fast. Can't blame the poor cads really, can you, wot!"

A pretty hogmaid of about sixteen seasons gazed adoringly at Scarum. "Faith, sorr, ye must've had some turrible times wid the ould sharks. I'd be afeared just to see one!"

Sagax and Kroova were having trouble stifling their laughter. The hare glared at them and whispered, "Titter not, chaps, got to impress the locals. They don't give tramps very big portions, y'know. But I'll bet they feed heroes like bloomin' kings."

He turned to the hogmaid. "No need t'be feared of sharks, m'dear, not whilst I'm around. Just before we go in to dinner, let me tell you the story of how I fought the great giant monster hog-eatin' shark. Hah, that was a day I'll never forget, eh, wot!"

The Migooch tribe loved nothing better than a good

story. They sat down on the sand and listened to Scarum's horrendous, and totally untrue, account. He strutted about with his chest puffed out, shutting one eye and glaring ferociously at his audience.

"This happened down the coast, south from Salamandastron, about, er, two summers ago. Were any of you chaps there at the time?"

An oldster raised his paw. "Meself was there, sorr!"

Scarum twitched his whiskers. "Er, no, 'twas three summers back, now I come t'think of it. Paws up, anybeast who was there three summers back?"

No paws were raised, so the hare continued with his lies. "Ah yes, chaps'n'chapesses, 'twas a bright sunny day an' I was walkin' along the shore, when all of a bally sudden two small hedgehogs, dear little types, came chargin' out of the sea, cryin' an' wailin' in pitiful voices. 'Ho, Scarum Sharkslayer,' they cried, 'save our granma!'"

A hogmaid tugged at Scarum's footpaw. "Pray, sorr, what was their names?"

He stared down at the hogmaid. "Don't know, m'dear, I'd never met 'em before. Now sit quietly an' listen."

But she would not. "Arrh, weel how did they know your name if ye didn't know theirs, 'cos you'd never met 'em afore?"

Scarum fixed her with an icy smile. "Because, my inquisitive beauty, everybeast down that way knows the name of Scarum Sharkslayer, wot!"

The oldster raised his paw. "But I was never knowin' your name afore today, sorr, an' I been down thataways many times."

Shaking with mirth, Sagax and Kroova held their sides as Scarum began losing patience with his audience. He bellowed at the oldster, "Well, y'must be flippin' well deaf if you've been down south of Salamandastron an' never bloomin' well heard of Scarum Sharkslayer. Now shut your snout an' listen!"

He was about to continue when another paw was

raised. "Beggin' yer pardon, sorr, but what was that shark's name?"

"How should I flippin' well know?" Scarum roared. "The blighter didn't have a name, it was . . . it was the blinkin' great, bloomin' giant, confounded monster, wotjermacallit, hog-eatin' shark. At least that's what all the hedgehogs called it. Satisfied, eh, wot?"

A hogwife shook her head wonderingly. "Ah now, isn't that the grand ould name for such a beast!"

The hog sitting next to her ventured his opinion. "D'ye think so? Well, I'm a hedgehog, so I am, an' I never knew a shark with a name like that. What was it called again, yer honour, I might be rememberin' if'n ye tell me?"

The hare danced up and down, waving his paws. "The thing wotsabloomin' name shark-eatin' monster hog!"

The little hogmaid tugged his footpaw again. "Ah now, that's not what ye said the first time, sorr."

The rest of the audience began discussing it among themselves, ignoring the storyteller.

"Shure the maid's right, he said a different name!"

"Away with ye, how'd you know, you was half asleep!"

"What, a monster shark-eatin' hog? I'm thinkin' that Scarum feller's been out in the sun too long!"

"Ah now, you leave him alone, doesn't he tell a fine ould tale. You go on, sorr, we're lissenin' to ye!"

"You lissenin', hah, 'twas you doin' all the interruptin'!"

"I take that from nobeast, stand up an' say it t'me face if'n ye dare!"

The storytelling became an argument, which broke out into a fight. Scarum gave up and sat down with his head in his paws. Sagax and Kroova were helpless with laughter as Cumarnee led them off.

"Come an' get some vittles. I forgot to tell your friend that the Migooch tribe is turrible at arguin' an' fightin', so they are!"

They were treated to huge bowls of vegetable soup, hot brown bread and some delicious mixed berry cordial, followed by an apple and pear turnover. Whilst they dined, the tent shook and bellied as the conflict raged outside. Cumarnee and Mammee carried on eating as though nothing was happening.

Cries from the combatants echoed round the dunes as Cumarnee and his wife passed the pie and poured cordial.

"Take that, y'ould pincushion!"

"Yowch! Wait'll I get me paws on ye!"

"I say there, chaps, steady on. Oof!"

"Owp! Kick me, would ye, well try this fer size!"

"Yerrrk! Ye great lump, you bit me nose, take that!"

"Steady on, chaps, now stop all this fightin'. Ooch!"

Scarum staggered into the tent, one eye half-closed and rapidly changing colour, his nose looking puffy and swollen. Cumarnee moved over and made a place for him to sit.

The hedgehog chuckled. "So now, me bold beast, how did the story end?"

Scarum touched his swollen nose and winced.

"The shark ate me, I think. Jolly ungrateful lot, your tribe. I say, that turnover looks rather good!"

Kroova licked his lips and grinned happily. "It certainly was, me old messmate. I'm just eatin' the last slice."

The hare's ears drooped in dejection as he gazed longingly toward the pot. "An' the soup?"

Mammee picked up her ladle. "'Tis all gone nearly, but I'll scrape ye up a drop from it. Here, take this ould crust of bread, sorr, 'tis the last bit. Have ye any cordial left fer the great Sharkslayer?"

Little Fridilo shook the empty flagon. "None at all, Mammee, but there's a beaker of fresh water over here. Drink that, sorr, 'twill do ye good."

As Sagax and Kroova discussed the possibility of the Migooch tribe helping with the repairs to their ship, Scarum could be heard muttering complaints to himself.

"Rotten lot, hoggin' all the scoff while a chap's out

there defendin' his reputation an' tryin' to restore order. Huh, I'd sooner face a score of sharks any day. Savage cads, bad-mannered bounders, hope a bloomin' great shark comes along an' eats them all, wot!"

19

In the misty dawn of the following day, they went out to the ledge, accompanied by all the able-bodied hogs of the Migooch tribe. It was the time of day when the tide was at its lowest ebb. The ketch *Stopdog* lay heeled over, almost high and dry.

Kroova stood on the tideline, explaining what was to be done. "We've got to get 'er back 'ere for fixin'. I know she ain't a big craft, but 'twill be 'eavy goin'."

Cumarnee spat on his paws and rubbed them together. "Ah, now don't ye fret. Us Migooches are well up t'the job!"

He was right. The tribe were expert salvagers, having spent their lives living off the flotsam and jetsam thrown up by the seas on all types of coastlines.

Carrying huge coils of rope and pushing a cartload of rounded wood logs, they padded out over the wet sand. When they reached the ketch, Cumarnee began shouting orders to his tribe. Sagax was surprised at the energy and obedience of the normally disorganised beasts.

"Hear me now, buckoes," Cumarnee yelled. "Make fast those lines t'the bowsprit, for'ard peak an' amidships. I'll draw ye a grand ould line in the sand with me stick, lay the logs straight on it. That's the way, yer doin' a lovverly job. Right now, shoulder those ropes an' I'll mark the pullin' time for ye with an ould shanty!"

Cumarnee perched in the lopsided bows of the *Stopdog,* singing the hauling shanty, the pullers joining him on the appropriate lines as the ketch rolled forward on the logs.

> "Ahoy, me lads, when I was young,
> Many's the lively song I sung.
> Way haul away! Way haul away!
> Me paw was strong, me back was, too,
> I'd pull a ship from under you.
> Way haul away! Way haul away!
> An' though 'tis not me way t'boast,
> I've towed a ship off many a coast.
> Way haul away! Way haul away!
> We'll pull 'er to the sandy shores,
> So bend yer back, dig in yer paws.
> Way haul away! Way haul away!
> For when I was a babe so young,
> Me mother o'er me cradle sung.
> Way haul away! Way haul away!"

Kroova and Sagax were out in front, ropes looped about their shoulders, hauling heartily with the hedgehogs. The badger nudged the sea otter.

"Scarum's on the midship side with a rope, can you hear him?"

Kroova smiled as he listened to the hare's nautical bellows.

> "When I get our ship to the shore,
> I'll need some scoff an' then lots more.
> You can haul away! I'll just eat all day!
> Soup'n'salad, pudden an' pie,
> Just load me plate up, don't ask why.
> Bloomin' rotten hogs! Scoff-pinchin' dogs!"

Mammee and some others were waiting the other side
of the tideline with a couple of pails full of nettle-and-
dandelion beer. No sooner was the *Stopdog* dragged onto
the warm dry sand than the toilers cast aside their ropes
and gratefully gulped down great beakers to quench their
thirst. However, their rest was short-lived. Cumarnee soon
had them up on their paws again, bustling about as he sent
his orders left, right and centre.

" 'Tis a good fire I'll be needin'! Light one right here!
Build me an ould sandhill, a long one, about the height of
the *Stopdog*'s decks. Here now, start pilin' up the sand
alongside the ship. Mammee, did ye bring along the pitch
an' resin with ye? Bring it here t'me. Fridilo, me likkle
darlin', fetch me that ould bushy rope. Aye, that's it!"

Sagax and Kroova helped to build the long sandhill
and wedge the *Stopdog* hard up against it. Another sandhill was built on the vessel's other side, so that she stood
straight and upright. They sat, taking a rest, sipping
beakers of nettle-and-dandelion beer, watching the pitch
and resin bubbling together in a cauldron over the fire.

Kroova's eyes searched among the workers. "I don't
see Scarum around, ain't seen 'im in a while. Any ideas
where that flopeared layabout's got to, mate?"

Sagax refilled his beaker. "Anywhere there's food,
that's where you'll find him, I suppose. That pitch and
resin looks about ready."

The crew went back to work, plugging up the gaps between the planking staves of the *Stopdog*'s bows. Old
rope was hammered into the cracks with mallets and flat-
bladed chisels, after which the molten pitch and resin
were poured liberally over the whole job. By early
evening the ketch was completely shipshape and water-
tight once more.

Sagax congratulated Cumarnee and the Migooch tribe.
"Thank you, friends, thank you for your hard work and
fine skills. I don't know how we'd have managed without
your help. Alas, my friends and I have nothing to offer
you in return but our gratitude."

Cumarnee swiped playfully at them with his straw hat.

"Arrh, away with ye, we did it 'cos yer grand beasts an' we've takin' a likin' to ye. A Migooch doesn't look for any reward from friends, at all at all!"

All the Migooches shook their heads and echoed the words. "At all at all, ah no, not at all!"

Mammee waved her ladle at them. "Faith, an' will ye be after standin' there all day, tellin' each other wot fine creatures ye are, or will I go back to the tenty to cook dinner an' eat it meself?"

The sudden mention of food to hungry workers sent them all trudging smartly back to the tents.

Sagax covered his eyes and groaned at the sight that greeted him on entering the tent. "Oh no!"

Snoring blissfully, Scarum lay amid a debris of half-eaten pies, breadcrusts, salad scraps, empty flagons and the remains of what had once been a large fruitcake. The hare's stomach resembled an inflated balloon. His whiskers, ears and nose were liberally sprinkled with crumbs.

Some of the Migooch hogs regarded him with awe.

"Muther Nature, will ye look at him!"

"Ah shure, he must be a grand ould scoffer!"

"The bold feller must have t'keep up his strength after wrasslin' an' slayin' all those sharks!"

Kroova and Sagax had never felt so embarrassed in their lives. Shamefaced, the otter averted his eyes from Mammee. "Marm, what can we say, after all yore 'ospitality, for a friend of ours t'do this!"

The good hogwife patted his paw comfortingly. "Ah now, don't be fussin' yerself, 'twas not yore fault a hare has the appetite of a wolfpack. Wot d'ye say we do about it, Cumarnee?"

The Chieftain of the Migooches had the answer instantly. "Do? Is it me advice yer after askin'? Well, I'll tell ye! We goes to yer sister's tenty for dinner—she's gotten more vittles than ye could shake a stick at. Arrh now, Mr. Sagax, an yerself, Mr. Kroova, if'n ye'll permit me, 'tis meself will decide a penance for the bold Scarum. Now don't be worryin', I won't go too hard on the ould beast. He can't help bein' a hare, after all."

Sagax bowed respectfully to Cumarnee's wish. "You can do what you like with the villain, sir. No penance could be too severe for a creature who abuses a friend's good nature. We leave him in your capable paws."

Mammee's sister Roobee was a jolly fat sort, and the equal of her kinhog at cooking. They sat down to a spread of cabbage'n'turnip pasties, carrot'n'mushroom bake topped with cheese, wild beetroot soup, and Roobee's special baked fruitloaf, with elderberry and plum cordial, or pennycress and comfrey tea for those who liked it. Roobee's husband, Birty, thought Scarum's gluttony was hilarious and kept remarking upon it.

"Heeheehee, curl me spikes, that Scarum Shark-slayer's a real boyo. He's got a belly on him like an ould stuffed duck. I wager his ma danced a jig the day he left home!"

Roobee noticed Sagax and Kroova's silence at Scarum's gluttonous acts. She nudged her husband none too gently. "Arrh, will ye shove some vittles in yer ould gob an' give it somethin' useful t'do, Birty. Eat up an' hold yer peace!"

That night they all slept in Roobee's tent, leaving the disgraced Scarum to himself.

Dawn came misty, with a light drizzle that would give way to brighter weather in the course of the day. Scarum slowly sat up, clutching his stomach, alone in the deserted tent.

"Ooooh, me poor old tum. I say, you chaps, just leave me here to die, would you? Tell my ma that the last words her sufferin' son spoke were 'no breakfast this mornin' for me!' "

He groped around in the grey half-light and groaned. "Cor, sufferin' icecakes! What sort of a bally good mornin' is this, wot? A faithful pal lyin' here with his head bangin' an' his tummy bustin', and not a flamin' beast around to comfort him. Rotters, I s'pose they're all out fixin' that blinkin' boat, thoughtless lot o' bounders!"

Staggering out of the tent, he spotted a firelight shining

through the walls of Roobee's dwelling. "Hah, now that's more the ticket, wot. A jolly good fire to sit by whilst some good-natured hogwife fetches a chap a drop or two of herbal tea to bring him round. Splendid!"

Entering the tent, Scarum got quite the reverse of what he had been expecting. It was a makeshift court, with Migooch hogs sitting solemn-faced and silent. Cumarnee seemed to be presiding, with Sagax and Kroova standing stiffly either side of him. Scarum gave them a feeble smile, but received only stern glares.

"Er, haha, I say, wot. Bit gloomy this mornin', ain't it?"

The tribe leader's voice lanced into his aching head. "Be it known to all the hogs of Migooch that this creature stands accused of idleness, slacking, laziness, vittle robbery and damage to pies, cakes, salads and other sundry eatables. What has the accused to say in his defence?"

Clutching his stomach, Scarum stammered and waffled. "Er, wot, er, steady on, chaps, can't blame a young hare for havin' a measly snack, especially a shipwrecked type."

Cumarnee stamped his footpaw down hard. "Silence!" He approached the hare, pointing accusingly at him.

"Babes had to go hungry to their beds because of you! Hogwives were left weeping over their spoiled supplies because of you! Workers who had laboured hard all day, repairing your vessel, were left starving because of you! I want a show of paws. Do we find this hare guilty?"

Every paw in the tent shot up, and there was a loud shout. "Guilty!"

Pleadingly, Scarum looked toward his two cold-eyed friends. "Sagax, Kroova, my faithful old messmates, can't you put in a jolly good word or two for a chum, wot wot?"

The young badger shook his head. "Sorry, it's not up to us. The Migooch tribe's laws have been broken; you must answer to them. The only advice I can give is, stand up straight like a Salamandastron hare and take the medicine Cumarnee dishes out to you."

Scarum tried to straighten up, but his aching stomach

kept him half bent. His ears drooped limply. He looked mournfully at Cumarnee and spoke in a hoarse whisper. "Sentence me t'be slain, sah, it'll put me out of my misery. Tell me dear old ma an' pa that it was my stomach which caused all the trouble, not me!"

Cumarnee shook his head resolutely. "Death? Hoho, me fine buckoe, that'd be too easy. Your punishment'll be to serve the Migooches as a slave for ten seasons, no, better make that twenty!"

Several hogs nodded. "Aye, twenty, that's about right for the turrible ould glutton, twenty good long seasons!"

Scarum's face was the picture of shock and misery. "Twenty blinkin' seasons, that's a bit jolly much, wot? I'll be on a perishin' walkin' stick, old'n'grey by the time twenty confounded seasons have passed. O mercy!"

However, the stern, righteous faces of the Migooch tribe dashed any of the hare's hopes for leniency.

The *Stopdog* bobbed at anchor, repaired and provisioned, straining at her bowline as high tide swelled, like a dog eager to be unleashed. Followed by all of the Migooch hogs, Sagax and Kroova waded out to the ketch. The pair climbed aboard and made ready to sail.

Cumarnee and Mammee exchanged paw shakes with them. "May the wind be at yer back an' the sun not in yer eyes!"

"Thankee, marm, an' our thanks for loadin' us up with yore fine vittles. We'll think of ye when we're eatin' 'em!"

Sagax saw Scarum standing dejectedly nearby, ears drooping, tears dropping from his cheeks to mingle with the salt water. Cumarnee shook the young badger's paw, passing him a secret wink.

"Weel now, me buckoe, I'm hopin' ye find Redwall. Good fortune attend ye on yer voyage!"

Sagax made sure Scarum was not watching as he returned the Migooch Chieftain's wink. "My thanks to you, sir. I'm just sorry that our visit was ruined by that hare's unforgivable behaviour. I trust you'll make him serve every day of his sentence and work him hard!"

Cumarnee stroked his headspikes pensively. "Ah now, I was meanin' to mention that to ye. Twenty seasons is a long time t'be feedin' some ould gluttonfaced rabbit. Would ye not think of takin' him back to do his penance aboard the *Stopdog,* afore he eats us out o' spikes'n'home?"

Sagax shook his head firmly. "No sir, a glutton's a glutton no matter where he is, on land or sea. He'll never repent."

Scarum knelt. With the water lapping his chin and his paws clasped beseechingly, he moaned aloud to his two friends, "I'll change me ways, I'll be good! Only take me aboard! I'll do all the work, scoff'll scarcely pass my lips, you'll see! Don't leave me here for twenty seasons with these spiky savages, oh, er, I mean dear little hoggybeasts. Sagax, Kroova, dear old jolly old faithful old pals, I'll do any bally thing for you, just take me aboard!"

Sagax looked doubtfully at Kroova. "What d'you think?"

The sea otter tapped his rudder up and down. "Hmm, ain't much of a catch, is he?"

As he was talking, Kroova was untying the bowrope from its rock mooring. "But I wouldn't feel right, inflictin' Scarum on our good 'edgehog friends for twenty seasons. Oh well, I s'pose we'll 'ave to put up with 'im. Come on, you lopeared excuse for a messmate, git aboard!"

With a bound, Scarum landed on the *Stopdog*'s deck, playing his new role as beast of all work. "Now, sit back an' put y'paws up, you chaps, leave this t'me. I'll see to the wotsits an' unfurl the hoojimacallits an' till the turner—I mean turn the tiller, wot wot wot!"

With a twinkle in his eye, Cumarnee called out as he and his hogs waved goodbye, "Now, go easy on those pore sharks, an' don't slay too many!"

Evening sun reddened over a placid sea as the three travelers continued their course northward. By this time Scarum had taken on a change of mood.

"Huh, are you two blighters goin' t'sit there forever

with your paws up? Lazy bounders, a chap needs help
around here. What d'ye think I am, a one-hare crew?
Sagax, why don't you take the tiller, an' Kroova can manage those ropes an' sails. I'll make the supper. Ah, supper,
what a jolly nice thought. All's I've had to eat was a snack
last night. Flamin' famine-faced hogs, wot? That Mammee gave me a whack on the paw with a ladle when I
mentioned brekkers this mornin', flippin' spiky old
tyrant!"

Sagax reached out with a powerful paw and grabbed
Scarum by the scruff of the neck. He had him half overboard in a trice. "One more word and I'll make you swim
back to serve your twenty seasons with those spiky old
tyrants!"

Kroova smiled wryly, shaking his head. "Ole Scarum
don't change much, does 'e?"

Sagax was also smiling as he whispered in Kroova's
ear. "I wouldn't want him to, would you? This would be a
dull, boring trip with a well-behaved hare for company."

20

Kurda pointed with her sabre at the rock sticking up in the distance, framed purple by the setting sun. "Vot is dat island called?"

Plugg Firetail had already seen it; he did not even turn to look at Peace Island. "That ain't no island, 'tis nought but a big rock stickin' up out o' the main. A big lump o' stone, that's all."

The ferret Princess kept her sword pointed at the object. "You vill sail over dere. I vant to see it, yarr!"

Slitfang was on duty as steersbeast. Plugg gave him a look. "Keep 'er steady on course, I'm the Cap'n o' the *Seascab*." He turned his attention back to Kurda.

"Yore daddy didn't say nothin' about stoppin' ter look at rocks. My job is t'get ye to Mossflower country an' catch those runaways if'n we spots 'em. Now, why don't yer let me gerron wid me job. Go an' lissen t'the crew entertainin' themselves on the fo'c'sle 'ead. Run along now, there's a good liddle missy!"

The Pure Ferret's eyes blazed scarlet in the setting sunrays. "Von day I cut out your insolent tongue, Freebooter."

179

Seething with rage, she strode off to the forecastle of
the big ship.

Plugg grinned at Slitfang. "That proud liddle beauty
frightens me t'death. Hawhawhaw!"

Prince Bladd was seated amidst the crew. Tazzin and
Grubbage had their paws around his shoulders, teaching
him an old Freebooter ditty:

"Ho 'tis nice t'be a villain, wot all honest creatures
    fears,
An' terrorise the beasts for miles around.
Their scringin' wails fer mercy is music to me ears,
Aye us bad 'uns loves to 'ear that mournful sound!"

A weasel twiddled the last two words on a one-string
fiddle as the Freebooter crew echoed them soulfully:
"Mawhawhawhawnful soooound!"

A searat with a ribbon-braided beard took the next verse.

"Lissen, mate, I'm tellin' you, we're a dirty desper-
    ate crew,
Each wid a cloud o' flies around 'is 'ead.
Filthy Fox an' Fatty Ferret an' old Stinky Weasel,
    too,
We're enough to fill an 'onest soul with dread!
Wihhihith derrrread!"

He threw his paw affectionately around another searat.

"Lookit my old matey 'ere, we all calls 'im Ripper
    Rat,
Wid no tail, one eye, an' 'arf a greasy ear,
Burnt down 'is granpa's 'ouse, now wot do ye think
    o' that,
Just because 'is granny called 'im 'er sweet dear!
Sweeeheet deeeeear!"

Ripper smiled bashfully. Pointing at another crewbeast, he sang:

"Now you take this bully 'ere, Scummy Stoat's 'is
    given name,
'E's never 'ad a bath, 'e's proud ter say,
'Til one day far out at sea, 'e fell in the watery main,
An' the fishes all jumped out an' ran away!
Rahaaan awaaaaay!"

Grubbage wiped away a tear and blew his snout on
Prince Bladd's embroidered sleeve. "Ain't it luvverly?
That's me favourite ditty. Though I can't 'elp sheddin' a
tear at the verse where old Scummy fell overboard, it
breaks me 'eart, mate, every time!"

Kurda did not like what she saw. The Riftgard soldier
rats were mingling with Plugg's crew in a free and easy
manner. She called their captain to her. "Riftun, get de
guards down der maindeck. You vill tell dem to stay avay
from de Freebooters. Make dem see to their uniforms an'
keep de spears sharp an' polished!"

Keeping his expression blank, Riftun saluted with his
spear. "I'll see to it right away, yore 'ighness!"

Watching from the stern deck, Plugg nodded approvingly. "Now, there's a maid after me own 'eart. It ain't
good manners t'make shipmates o' those Riftgard rats, especially when we're gonna slay 'em later on. Not nice,
Slitfang, I don't 'old wid false'ood."

The steersbeast chuckled. "Yore a real gentlefox, Cap'n!"

The vast dark bulk of the *Seascab* plowed on into the
night.

Next day was well advanced when Triss and Shogg took
their leave of Peace Island. Bistort waited patiently by as
they made their farewells to newfound friends.

Welfo stood paw in paw with Urtica, tears shining in
her eyes. "Say you'll come back one day, please!"

Triss was lost for words, but Shogg replied, "We'd be
lyin' if we did, you know that, mate. But no matter where
we goes, you'll be in our thoughts, you'n'Urtica. So both
of ye, 'ave a good'n'appy life, an' remember us fondly,
that's the best thing for all. Goodbye, friends!"

Bistort caught the otter's glance and nodded. "Come now, else 'twill be dark ere you reach your ship." He strode off swiftly, and they followed him without a backward look.

A long meandering fault in the rock ran from the crater rim down to their vessel, which lay hidden in a secret cove. There were pegs, a long rope and some rough steps at intervals. Bistort left them on the rim.

"Thy craft lies ready. I wish to thank thee for bringing Welfo to our island. She will be a wife to my son and a daughter to Downyrose and myself. Mayhap the seas will carry ye back this way one day, who knows? Speak no more now, but go. Let good fortune attend thee and may thy desires be fulfilled, the earth needs good creatures like thee."

No sooner had they cast off than the small craft was swept out into a swiftly running sea, even without the aid of a sail. Triss took the tiller as Shogg unfurled the sail and trimmed up the ropes. The sea made little noise. There were no crests of white foam on the grey-green waves, which moved with an alarming speed and smoothness. When Triss looked back, Peace Island was far away and rapidly diminishing below the horizon.

There was little time for talk or reflection as they hurtled along with the massive oily swells. Shogg relieved the squirrelmaid at the tiller, allowing her to prepare some food for them both. Triss glanced anxiously at the towering green walls of water as the ketch scudded from valley to peak of each one. There was hardly any wind, yet the current was running faster.

She enquired cautiously of her friend, "Are we still on course, Shogg?"

Staring dead ahead and clenching the tiller tight, the otter replied, "Can't say, matey, we've even lost sight o' the island to use as a point. I reckon we'll do well just to stay alive in waters like these. Better reef in our sail, Triss, afore a wind springs up. It might come from the wrong direction, an' these waves'd swamp us."

* * *

There was no sign of the high seas abating as darkness fell. It was going to be a long and sleepless night. Taking a crust of bread and a flagon of water, Triss stationed herself in the bows, keeping a lookout for anything at all that lay ahead. She found herself gazing over desolate watery wastes every time they rose on the waveswell.

Shogg manoeuvred the tiller, hoping against hope that Triss might sight land. Dark cloud masses, muddy purple and smoky cream, began obscuring the stars as they boiled up over the horizon ahead. There was no hint of a breeze. Then suddenly an earth-shattering boom crashed overhead and lightning ripped the heavens into fleeting brightness.

Shogg roared at Triss, "Get back 'ere with me, there's a big storm brewin'!"

The wind came then, howling out of nowhere. It soaked Triss, whipping water over the bows as she retreated to the stern and grabbed the tiller with Shogg.

Squinting their eyes against the blinding rain, they huddled together, awed by the mighty forces of nature. Every moment Shogg expected one of the mountainous waves to crash down on the tiny craft, but miraculously it stayed afloat, still whipping onward over the storm-rent deeps.

Triss dashed water from her eyes, pointing ahead. "What's that?"

Shogg saw it also. "A light, it's a light!"

Seaspray washed into the squirrelmaid's mouth as she shouted to make herself heard. "Is it land, Shogg?"

Prince Bladd lay in his bunk, a blanket wrapped about his head as he wailed in terror, "Der shtorm, it vill sink de boat! Help me!"

At that same moment, Kurda staggered across the deck, holding on to Captain Riftun's spearhaft as he went ahead of her. They barged into Plugg's cabin, where the fox was swilling grog with Tazzin and Grubbage. He looked up.

"Aharr, 'tis the lovely Princess 'erself. Wot can ole Cap'n Plugg do for ye on such a pleasant night, me dearie?"

Kurda was shaken by the sudden storm, but she would not let the Freebooter see her fear. "Is der ship in danger? Vill de shtorm sink us?"

Plugg, grog slopping down his chin, grinned crookedly. "Nah, it wouldn't dare sink a ship carryin' a prince an' a princess, specially one who's as good wid a sword as you!"

Riftun banged his spear angrily on the table. "Watch yore mouth, Plugg. Is there a safe cabin aboard, one where Princess Kurda can ride out the storm?"

Plugg gestured upward with his grog beaker. "Aye, there's one above this on the stern peak, comfy liddle berth. I usually sleep there meself, but 'er 'igh royalness can 'ave it fer the night. Best cabin on the ole *Seascab,* still as a rock an' safe as 'ouses!"

Kurda rapped out imperiously. "It vill do for der night. Captain Riftun, you vill take me dere!"

A mixture of wind, rain and seaspray whooshed into the cabin as Riftun opened the door. He was slammed back against the bulkhead, Kurda with him.

Plugg roared at them, "Gerrout an' shut that door!"

The pair departed, with the rat captain struggling to close the door behind them. In the silence that followed, the silver fox hooted with laughter.

"Aharrharrharr! Still as a rock an' safe as 'ouses? Hawhawhaw! She'll spend the night goin' up an' down like a toad in a bucket. I'll teach the snotnosed liddle whelp t'stand there givin' Plugg Firetail orders. Hawhawhaw!"

Grubbage, as usual, had not heard his captain properly. But he joined in the laughter, pretending he had. "Heeheehee! A frog an' a fly take borders. I like that 'un, Cap'n. Heeheehee!"

Out on deck, Kurda and Riftun negotiated the small set of stairs to the stern peak, their heads bowed against the storm's onslaught. Immediately after they gained the top deck, Kurda knew that Plugg was playing one of his wicked jests on her. The *Seascab* was rolling wildly, plunging up and down like a madbeast in its death throes. The Princess was flung against the stern rail, where she clung grimly for dear life. Riftun slithered and skated about on the seaslick deck, then dug his spear point in the timbers and hauled himself to her side. Thunder rumbled out of the distance and banged overhead in a loud explosion. A sheet of lightning followed. Kurda was bent over the rail, facing the sea. In the brief illumination from the lightning flash, she screeched, "There dey are, there dey aaaaaare!"

Not half a boatlength away and slightly astern of the *Seascab* was the small stolen vessel, with Shogg and Triss, soaked to the skin, clinging to the tiller. The small, light craft was rapidly overhauling the huge Freebooter ship. Kurda saw the pair look up, their faces showing clearly in the lights from Plugg's rear cabin window. She seized Riftun's paw.

"Get one of dem mitt your spear, de streamdog. I vant de other von alive. T'row, kill der streamdog!"

Shogg and Triss were horror-stricken. The light they had been sailing for was a huge Freebooter ship, with their archenemies, Kurda and Riftun, aboard. Frozen with shock, they sat staring up at the mad-eyed Princess urging her captain to slay Shogg. Riftun raised his spear, grinning cruelly down at them. It was a throw he could hardly miss. He brought the weapon back over his shoulder for a stronger cast. *Bang! Craaaaaack!* A bolt of lightning struck the iron spearblade.

Hurling the tiller to port, Shogg sent the little craft skipping nimbly by, narrowly missing the *Seascab*'s stern. Kurda did not know what had happened for a moment, as she had been watching Shogg, waiting for the spear to strike him. Turning, she saw the rat Captain lying rigid on the deck, every hair on his body standing up like a needle. His paw was welded to the smoking and shattered spear, rain sizzling as it spattered on the momentarily red-hot iron blade. Riftun was dead as a doornail.

The beautifully built little ship, which Agarnu had commissioned for his royal offspring, flashed by and was swallowed up into the gale-torn night.

Plugg shielded his grog from the wetness that blew in as the cabin door slammed open again. "Was you born in a field? Shut that clatterin' door!"

Looking anything but regal, the saturated Pure Ferret left Grubbage to struggle with the door as she staggered into the cabin, flailing her paws like a windmill.

"Mine ship, I haff seen mine ship, mitt two slaves in it, sailing by . . . out dere!"

The Freebooter fox took a gulp of grog and belched. "Well, ain't that a turnip fer the ship's log. Where's ole pastyface Riftun, swimmin' after it?"

Kurda ignored the fox's heavy-pawed sarcasm. "Riftun is slayed by der lightnink, he vos stricken! Mine ship is getting avay, you vill catch her!"

Plugg shrugged noncommittally. "I never took to that Riftun, 'e was a snootynosed rat. Don't worry about yore pretty liddle ship. If'n she's still afloat by mornin', we'll run 'er down all right. Just one other thing, missy, if'n ye ain't got double the value o' that ship, well, 'tis mine. Yore pa said I gets double the value of any booty we bring back. So if I sails back inter Riftgard with 'er in tow, ye can kiss yore ship goodbye. She'll be sailin' under Plugg's colours!"

Kurda did not have her sabre to paw. She stood in front of the Freebooter, shaking with murderous rage. "If I had not left my sabre in der cabin, you vould be a deadbeast now, seascum!"

Plugg winked at Slitfang and smiled sweetly. "Ain't she the one, mate. Pity ye didn't bring yore sword out on deck—the lightnin' would've struck you, me pretty one. That might've brightened yore night up, aharrharr!"

The Princess stamped her paw as she poured forth venom. "You stupid mudbrained slug, von day I vill haff your head on a spike, den ve see how you laugh, yarr! I vill tell mein father how I vas treated by you. De only double revard he vill give is to haff you chopped in two halves!"

Plugg tossed his empty grog flagon aside and got another. "Tch tch, naughty naughty! A bargain's a bargain when anybeast makes it wid Plugg Firetail, missie, ye'll soon find that out. Well now, ye can stand stampin' yer liddle paw there as much as ye like. There ain't a thing t'be done 'til this storm blows over an' we got daylight enough t'see wot we're chasin'. So you toddle off now, to that there snug liddle cabin I let you 'ave fer the night."

Kurda curled her lip and scowled at him. "I go back to mine own cabin, but first I vill choose a Ratguard to attend me. I do not trust you, yarr!"

Plugg turned to his messmates, speaking with mock sincerity. "D'you lot 'ear that? She don't trust dear old Plugg! That's 'ow you never got t'be a princess, Grubbage, by puttin' yore trust in me."

Grubbage nodded sagely. "Aye, a rusty flea, Cap'n, that's me. Shall I show the Princess back to 'er cabin?"

Kurda pushed Grubbage roughly aside. "I find my own vay!" She strode regally from the cabin, with the raucous laughter of Plugg and his cronies ringing in her ears.

21

Sometime just before dawn the storm abated. Thunder echoed dully, far off across pale, slate-streaked skies. Rain slacked to a drizzling curtain in wan daylight. The sea was still running high. Shogg and Triss were sleeping, sitting draped over the tiller, worn out and exhausted after their tempestuous ordeal. The otter slid forward bit by bit, until his nose bumped against the tiller arm. He sat up straight, blinking through salt-crusted eyes, immediately aware of the sound of waves pounding across reefs and breaking on the shore.

"Triss, wake up, mate! 'Tis land, straight ahead. Land!"

The squirrelmaid woke, shivering, damp and cold. She stared at the approaching coastline, rocks and shingle broken by patches of sandy shore. It did not appear very welcoming, but it was a marvellous sight to a pair of escaped slaves.

"Where are we, Shogg?"

Her friend applied his attention to the tiller. "I ain't got a clue, but we'll be in big trouble if we runs afoul o' those reefs, matey. Let's try to slide in easy-like."

Recalling the previous night, Triss scanned the horizon. "Where's the big ship gone, d'you see it anywhere?"

Shogg smiled grimly. "T'the bottom o' the sea, I 'ope. I don't see it about, but there ain't any sense in takin' chances. We won't put up the sail in case it gives us away—a sail can be seen from a good distance off. You see if'n there's any dry vittles left, an' water, too. I'd give me rudder for a mouthful of fresh water right now. Attend to that an' keep yore eyes peeled. I'll try an' get us to shore safely."

Viewing the strange new land, Shogg felt a thrill of anticipation as the shore loomed closer. He used all his skills to tack between the perilous rocks, some poking up out of the sea, others lying beneath the surface. Centering his attention at a sprawling stone outcrop on the tideline, Shogg sent the vessel toward it.

Triss found some apples that were undamaged. She uncorked a flagon of drinking water and tipped it to her mouth, washing out the heavy salt taste of the sea. It was sweet and refreshing. She passed it to Shogg, who wedged it against the tiller.

"I'll take a drop when I gets us past this tricky bit, mate. There! 'Tis a straight run to land now. Let's drink to our escape, Triss, we made it!"

As the keel scraped upon sand, Shogg leaped over into the shallows and hauled on the headrope. Triss was about to join him when she spotted the double sails bellying out on the horizon.

"It's the big ship! Look!"

The otter acted promptly as he sighted the *Seascab*. "Quick, let's pull 'er in behind these rocks. I 'ope they ain't caught sight of us!"

Between them they managed to push and shove the vessel to the lee side of the outcrop. Shogg began stripping the sail from the mast and rolling it up, whilst Triss salvaged what food she could from their spoiled stores.

Empty grog flagons rolled about on Plugg's cabin floor as the ship swayed gently. He sat with his head on the table, snoring in his chair.

"Laaaaaand hoooooooo!"

A moment later the silver fox was stumbling out on deck. "Land ye say, where away?"

Tazzin, who was on duty as steersbeast, pointed. "Straight on as she lies, Cap'n, dead ahead!"

Kurda came bounding up from amidships. "De land, mine new captain see it first, yarr. He say somet'ink move, over by der rocks. See!"

Plugg was too preoccupied with their position to pay the Princess much heed. He scanned the coast up and down.

Kurda slapped her sabre blade against the rail. "Vot you lookin' for, vy you don't listen to me?"

Plugg spoke as he continued inspecting the shoreline. "There should be a river runnin' out across the beach. That's where the chart says we make our landfall. I'm lissenin' to yer, missy. Now who saw wot, eh?"

Kurda beckoned a tall, grave-faced Ratguard to her side. "Diss von, he is Vorto, mine new captain. Tell him!"

Vorto saluted with his spear before reporting to Plugg. "I saw it, a liddle boat, runnin' fer those rocks, showin' no sail. May'ap 'tis moored behind the rocks, Cap'n."

Plugg turned, bringing his face close to the new officer and squinting into his eyes. "Vorto, eh, you got a fair ole pair o' peepers on ye. Oh well, I'll 'ave to take 'er in an' scout the coast 'til I finds a landmark. Tazzin, you steer 'er landwards, but stop before those big reefs. I'll be in me cabin, a-studyin' the chart. Shout out when yore droppin' anchor."

Kurda blocked Plugg's way, gesturing with her sabre. "You t'row down de anchor by de reefs, how ve get ashore?"

The Freebooter pushed past her, heading for his cabin. "Yore free to wade or swim, but if'n you stops playin' wid that toy sword, I'll let ye ride in the ship's boat wid me. Slitty, make ready the jollyboat fer when we anchors."

From their cover in the rocks, Shogg and Triss watched the *Seascab* heading in a direct line for the outcrop. The otter shouldered the rolled-up sail. "Cut an' run, Triss, 'tis all that's left to us. We ain't stoppin' round 'ere fer Kurda to practise 'er sabre on us."

The squirrelmaid hefted a stone-tipped spear, part of the simple weaponry Bistort had left aboard for them. "I wish I could stay and pay her back for murdering poor old Drufo. I'd give her the same chance she gave him. None!"

Shogg weighed the bag of slingstones and the sling he had armed himself with. "Aye, but there's prob'ly a full crew o' Freebooters an' a pack o' Ratguards with 'er. We wouldn't stand a chance, Triss. Right, we'd best move. Let's go east an' a touch north, keepin' those rocks atween us an' them so they don't see us. Kurda will try to track us, ye can rely on it."

They set off at a brisk jog toward some dunes.

Kurda did not wait for Vorto to assist her. She leaped from the jollyboat and splashed off through the shallows toward the rocks. Plugg had brought Prince Bladd along with him but, when the Freebooter captain jumped overboard into the shallows, the fat young princeling kept his seat in the jollyboat's centre.

"I get mine paws vetted if I jump in dere, I not like vet paws!"

Plugg shook his head in despair. "Slitty, you 'n' Ripper give Prince slobberchops a lift ashore, an' don't get 'is paws wet, 'e don't like it!"

Vorto waited until all the Ratguards had waded ashore. Lining them up, he marched off to find the Princess.

Kurda was standing on the lee side of the rocks, leaning against the stolen boat, studying the pawprints that ran off toward the dunes. Vorto arrived with the Ratguards and saluted smartly.

The Princess smiled. "Yarr, mine good Vorto, you vere right. Here is der ship, and der tracks, see!"

Plugg came swaggering up with a few of his crew. He inspected the vessel, stroking its sides and patting the stern in admiration. The Freebooter liked what he saw.

"Haharr, she's an 'andsome liddle beauty. The slaves

who built this'n knowed wot they was doin'. Now then, yer 'igh royalness, I wouldn't be stannin' gapin' at those pawtracks all day, if'n I was you. This drizzle will soon wash 'em out."

Kurda gave him a supercilious stare and drew her sabre. "Tchah! You know about der sea, but I know all about der land. Vere is Riggan?"

At Vorto's command, a rat stepped forward. She was of wiry build, older than the rest, with a long nose and slitted eyes. Kurda's sabre pointed to the fugitive tracks.

"You can find dese creatures, yarr?"

Riggan crouched and sniffed the prints. She rubbed a few grains of sand in one paw and licked them lightly. "Find 'em? Yer 'ighness, Riggan can find 'em as easy as findin' vittles on a plate fer dinner!"

The Pure Ferret smirked at the Freebooter Captain. "Nobeast has ever escaped Riggan. She is mine father's special slavecatcher. Dis rat can track a butterfly over de solid rocks. A drop of der drizzle vill not stop her!"

Plugg's voice oozed sarcasm as he answered. "Ye don't say? Now, ain't that nice. Right ho, me beauty, you take yore rats off an' play yore liddle 'unting game. As fer me, well, I'm only a simple ole Freebooter. I'll 'ave me crew cast about fer landmarks so we kin find this Moss-flower place, while I stops 'ere an' polishes me new liddle boat up. May'aps ye'll bring me 'er sail back when you catches up wid those slavebeasts. Now, be careful ye don't rip it, I'm partickler about me property, eh, Slitty?"

Slitfang grinned. "Aye, very partickler, Cap'n!"

But Kurda was not listening. She had set off with her Ratguards, slightly behind Riggan, who was travelling at a fast, easy lope over the wet sands.

Shogg and Triss headed east over the dunes, making for an outcrop of trees in the distance. The squirrelmaid got slightly ahead of her otter friend. She stopped and waited for him to catch up.

He hitched the bundle of sailcloth higher on his back. "Runnin' takes some gettin' used to, matey, after all that sittin' on me rudder in a boat fer long days. Let's keep on goin', me paws are beginnin' to feel better now."

The land was mostly scrub grass, with patches of broom and thistle. They ran steadily, side by side, with Shogg occasionally glancing back over his shoulder.

"We don't know if they're on our trail or not. This drizzle should blur our tracks, Triss. I 'ope it keeps up."

The squirrelmaid indicated the trees ahead. "When we get to those, I'll shin up one and scan the land."

Riggan did not stop or even pause to check the pawprints. She knew she was on the right trail.

Kurda clipped a thistle bloom with her blade edge. "Vorto, ven ve find dem you do nothink, surround dem and leave der rest to me. I vill show dem how I deal mitt runavay slave thieves, long and slow I show dem, yarr!"

Vorto could tell by the look in Kurda's red eyes that she meant every word of it.

On reaching the tree fringe, Triss dropped her foodpack and went up the trunk of a sessile oak with all the skill of a born climber. Vaulting and swinging, she passed the middle branches and was soon up in the topmost boughs. Shogg craned his neck back and looked up to where she perched on a high limb.

"Wot's the word, mate, any signs o' the vermin?"

His worst fears were confirmed as Triss called down, "Aye, I can make out Kurda with about a score of Ratguards coming this way fast. It looks like Riggan slavecatcher is leading them—no wonder they got onto us so quick!"

Shogg bit his lip with worry. Every slave at Riftgard knew the name and reputation of Agarnu's relentless tracker. None had ever escaped Riggan.

"'Tis bad news for us, mate. The only thing we can do is t'keep runnin' until they're so far from their ship that they gets tired o' chasin' us an' turns back, maybe."

As Triss began climbing down the oak, she suddenly noticed another squirrel climbing alongside of her. He was a jolly-looking, fat beast, his shoulders crossed with webbing that was stuffed tight with hard green pinecones. She nodded to him; he nodded back and struck up a conversation.

"So you're going to run for it. Well, good luck to you, good luck, that's what I always say."

Triss noticed that there were many more fat squirrels, all climbing down from neighbouring trees. She arrived back on the ground accompanied by roughly fifty of the creatures.

Shogg bowed politely.

"Good day to ye, friends!"

The one who had spoken to Triss was obviously their leader. He shook rainwater from his huge bushy tail. "Good, what's good about it? Nothing good about sitting up in a tree getting drenched, that's what I always say!"

Now that she knew the squirrels meant them no harm, Triss felt a lot more at ease with them. She spoke to the leader. "I'm sorry for trespassing in your wood, but we'll be gone right away. Sorry we can't stop to talk."

Tossing up a pinecone and catching it without even looking at it, the squirrel remarked, "No hurry. I'm Whurp, Chieftain of the Coneslingers. You don't have to run if you prefer walking, that's what I always say."

He tossed the pinecone high, shook paws with them both, and caught the cone before it fell. Triss was impressed.

"I'm Triss, and my friend's called Shogg. We really do have to go, Whurp. There's not much use walking with those Ratguards hard on our paws. We need to run."

Whurp tossed his pinecone, batted it with his tail and caught it one-pawed as it bounced off the sessile oak. "Oh, don't fuss yourself about a few rats, Triss, we can snarl them up here for a good while. You and Shogg follow my daughter Burnby, she'll lead you through the woods and out the other side. We'll see to the rats for you. Rats are bad creatures, that's what I always say."

Shogg noticed the thong wound about Whurp's paw. "I see ye carry slings. What d'ye throw from them, cones?"

Whurp tossed the cone he was toying with to Shogg. "Aye, cones just like that one, good and hard, quite sharp, too. They wouldn't kill a beast, we're not in the business of slaying any creature. Only use them in defence of our territory, that's what I always say."

Shogg took out his pouch of slingstones from Peace Island. "These are some stones I was given to use by a friend, far across the seas from here."

Whurp took the pouch and opened it, pouring forth into his paw the bluey-green, sharp-edged stones. His eyes lit up. "From far across the seas you say, Shogg. Wonderful, beautiful treasures like these, and you waste them by throwing them away with your sling? Never throw away precious things, that's what I always say!"

He passed the pouch back carefully, but Shogg refused it. "Keep 'em, mate, as a gift from us. Look, we've really got t'go now. Nice meetin' ye, Whurp."

As Burnby led them off through the trees, Whurp called out, "Goodbye, friends, and good fortune go with you. I can't thank you enough for these stones. The Coneslingers will treasure them forever. A treasure of great worth is a treasure worth treasuring, that's what I always say!"

Burnby took Triss's paw, giving her a quiet smile. "I could tell you other things that my dad always says, but I'd need ten seasons to do it."

Triss squeezed her paw. "Thank you for your help, but can your dad really stop the Ratguards?"

Burnby plucked a grass stalk and chewed on it. "Ask yourself, Triss. Did you see us when you entered our forest? Did you even know all of us were watching you? Coneslingers are invisible when they want to be—we can defend our wood against any number. Shogg, follow behind me. Watch that willow branch, don't touch it!"

When the otter saw the thin cord holding a whippy branch strained in an arc, he understood. "Haharr, a trap, eh, that'd soon stop anybeast who didn't see it. A good idea, Burnby."

She nodded. "That's why you must follow directly in

my trail. These woods are full of such traps, pits, cata-
pults, nooses. But those rats won't be bothered by them."

Shogg looked puzzled. "Why's that, mate?"

Burnby chuckled. "Because my dad won't even let
them get this far. Never let the foebeast enter your
home—"

Triss interrupted. "That's what he always says!"

Their laughter echoed through the trees as they strolled
in leisurely fashion through the Coneslingers' wood.

Riggan halted at the tree fringe. Kurda came hurrying up
with Vorto and the Ratguards.

"Dey go in dere, yarr?"

The slavetracker inspected the ground, then peered up
into the trees, sniffing the air suspiciously. "Aye, yore
'ighness, they've gone inter these woods, but there's sum-
mat I don't like about this place. I ain't put me paw on it
yet, but I'll find out."

She took a pace into the trees . . . and found out. Three
iron-hard green pinecones hit Riggan, one on the head,
another on the paw, and a third in the throat. She toppled
over, senseless.

Immediately the Ratguards threw themselves flat.
Vorto placed himself in front of Kurda, shielding her.
"Somebeast up in the trees is attackin' us, marm!"

Kurda signalled as she backed off. "Archers, shoot arrows at dem, slay der beasts!"

Four Ratguards set shafts to their bows. The first one
fired off at a shape high in the trees.

Kurda popped her head up from where she was
crouching. "Gutt, dat teach dem!"

Half an arrow, the pointed part, nicked her paw, and
she yelped. "Yowch! Vot happen?"

The archer gasped in amazement at what he had seen.
"Marm, somebeast up there in that tree, 'e caught me ar-
rer an' snapped it in arf, 'e's throwin' it back!" He ducked
as the feathered half bounced off his ear.

Vorto whispered orders to four Ratguards. "Crawl out
an' git Riggan back 'ere. We need 'er."

The four began to crawl forward, but were peppered so hard with green cones that they were forced to shuffle backward, their shoulders, backs and behinds smarting furiously. His paws numbed by two more flying cones, Vorto dashed off to a small rise in the ground where Kurda was crouching.

"Yore 'ighness, I think we'd better retreat!"

The flat of Kurda's blade whacked him in the midriff. "Retreat? Vot you t'ink I am? De Princess of Riftgard does not run from sillybeasts who t'row pinecones. Ve stay here and teach dem lesson for insolence!"

She poked her head up and screeched angrily, "You hear dat, ve teach you der le . . . Unkhh!"

A particularly fine specimen of the fir tree whacked solidly down between the Pure Ferret's ears, stunning her. This was followed by a matter-of-fact voice calling out, "Sorry, could you repeat that? I don't understand what 'Unkhh' is supposed to mean. State your intentions clearly, that's what I always say!"

Burnby led Triss and Shogg out at the far side of the trees that marked the Coneslingers' domain. She gestured eloquently at the open lands.

"There, my friends, you may go whichever way you please. I must return now and lend a paw to pin your foes down for a while. I'm rather looking forward to it. Bye bye!" She sprang up into the trees and was instantly gone.

The two friends waved, not knowing whether Burnby could see them.

"Goodbye, and thank you for your help!" Triss called. "Well, what do you make of that? What an easy escape! Burnby couldn't wait to get back to a bit of cone slinging. You'd never think it to look at her—such a quiet, pretty maid, so reserved and well-mannered, but so warlike!"

Shogg fluttered his eyes. "Aye, a bit like meself: quiet, well-mannered, pretty. Ouch! Mind that speartip, mate!"

Triss chuckled. "Come on, you rogue, which way now?"

The drizzle had stopped, and sunlight was peeping out

from between the clouds. Shogg shaded his eyes, gazing around.

"See that dip over there? I'm bettin' there's a stream runnin' through it. So 'ere's wot I think we should do. We'll get our paws wet, follow the stream west. They're bound to get away sooner or later. Riggan'll pick up our tracks, ye can rely on that. But she'll only trail us as far as the stream, then she 'as a choice."

As they made their way to the dip, Triss echoed Shogg's words. "A choice. How do you mean?"

The otter gave a sly wink and explained. "Riggan's choice is simple, mate. Which way did we go after enterin' the water, west or east? Now ask yoreself, which way d'you suppose two runaways would go? East an' inland, or west an' back t'the sea, where there's a Freebooter ship loaded with vermin who'd slay ye as soon as look at ye, eh?"

The otter's canny scheme dawned on Triss. "Of course! She'll head east, that's the sensible choice. You mightn't be pretty and reserved, but you've got a shrewd head on your shoulders, mate. Come on."

Shogg's guess proved right. There was a thin stream winding through the dip, and it was quite shallow. They proceeded carefully, trying hard not to leave any telltale traces that the slavecatcher could follow. Both fugitives hoped fervently that Whurp and his tribe of Coneslingers would keep Kurda and her Ratguards pinned down for a long while: the longer the better, for the survival of Triss and Shogg depended upon it.

22

Memm Flackery and Sister Vernal sat on two chairs close to the Abbey doors in Great Hall. A trolley served as their table. On it was toasted bread, a jar of comb honey, the first of that summer's strawberries, and a steaming pot of dandelion tea.

The Harenurse yawned. "Rotten old storm, hope we don't get another this season. There was one time last night when I thought the bloomin' roof was comin' in, the way that blinkin' thunder sounded!" She munched listlessly on her thick, honeyed toast.

Sister Vernal stopped herself from nodding off and blinked owlishly. "Up on our paws all night, with crying Dibbuns and others who wouldn't come down from the windows because they wanted to watch the lightning. Dearie me, I'm exhausted."

"Boom boom! Bangybangybang! Boobooboooom!"

A herd of shrieking little ones dashed past, followed by Ruggum, Roobil and Turfee mousebabe, who were chasing them, pretending to be stormdogs. Memm and Vernal covered their ears.

"Boombangeeboom! I'm a t'under comin' to getcha! Boom!"

Little Dibbun maids squealed, running in circles with their aprons thrown up over their faces. "Yeeeek, it's a storm!"

Turfee waved two long cornstalks. He was the lightning. "Tish! Flash! Tish! Tish! I burn you tails off. Tish!"

Memm collared him as he dashed past for the third time. Sitting the mousebabe on her lap, she popped a strawberry into his mouth. "Be still, y'little bounder. Chew on that an' keep quiet, wot!"

Immediately she was surrounded by Dibbuns, clamouring aloud,

"Wanna strawbee! Gimme strawbees, Memm!"

"Bo urr, oi'm gurtly 'ungered for strawbees, marm!"

"You nebber sayed pleeze. Can I hab a strawbee, pleeze!"

Memm and Vernal emptied the bowl as they dished strawberries to the open-mouthed infants. Vernal threw up her paws wearily. "Go and play now, they're all gone!"

Ruggum folded his paws defiantly and faced up to her. "Urr miz, uz be a goin' to ee h'orchard an' picken more!"

Memm fixed him with her severest Harenurse stare. "Oh, no you don't, young sah, you're not to go outside, any of you. It's drizzlin' heavy out there. Go an' play!"

Ruggum held his ground, returning her stare with what he thought was his fierce moleface. "Ho, do ee say so, marm, well let oi tell ee. Grizzle doant bee's a botheren us'n's, we'm gurt tuff h'aminals, burr aye!"

Memm moved her chair so that its back was against the door. She wagged a warning paw under Ruggum's snout. "Well, tough or not, you ain't gettin' by me, master Ruggum, so you can go off into the corner an' bally well grizzle about that. Now, that's my final word on the subject. Wot!"

"Ahem, permission to get by, marm, if'n ye please!"

Memm looked up to see Skipper and Log a Log standing there. The otter Chieftain and the Guosim leader were heavily armed. Skipper carried a sling and stone pouch, a newly tipped javelin and the sword of Martin across his back. Log a Log carried a sling and pouch alongside his shrew rapier, with a small bow and quiver of arrows in addition.

Ruggum snatched up one of Turfee's cornstalks. "Oi bee's a cummen too, zurrs!"

Log a Log whipped out his rapier and pointed at the stairs leading down to Cavern Hole. He yelled urgently, "A big rat with a bag of strawberries just ran down there. We can't 'ave that, can we? Get 'im!"

Whooping and roaring, the Dibbuns tore off in pursuit of the imaginary villain. Memm moved her chair and opened the door to allow them outside.

"I say, old lad, that was pretty crafty, wot. Don't suppose you'd like to stay indoors an' entertain a flippin' herd of wild infants. Vernal an' I could get a bit o' shuteye."

Skipper touched his rudder politely. "Sorry, marm, we got other business to attend."

Vernal watched the two warriors heading for the main gates. "Business to attend, hmm, wonder where they're off to?"

Skipper and Log a Log made rapid progress into Moss-flower, unburdened by cloaks and wearing only short tunics. They conversed little, each keeping well-trained ears and eyes on their surroundings as they pressed on through the trees. There were no unusual sounds, just the steady drip of rainwater from leaf, bush and fern. Skipper nodded at an old aspen tree on the edge of a small clearing. It had been broken in half, pale sappy wood showing white against its green background. Log a Log noted it, pointing briefly at the sky and making a quick moonlike circle with one paw. Both knew that the tree had been brought down by lightning in the previous night's storm.

Reaching the point where they had been attacked by the crows, they halted. Now they spoke, keeping their voices very low and standing close together. "No crows t'day, Skip, must've moved on to better shelter."

"Aye, mate, I don't smell nothin' odd, like the Abbot said Crikulus was talkin' about in 'is sleep. Let's listen."

The otter and the shrew stood still, only their eyes moving as they honed in their keen senses to the woodlands. However, neither could feel anything amiss.

Log a Log spoke. "Best split up, Skip. You go this way, I'll go yonder. Give a cuckoo call if ye find anythin'."

They went their separate ways like two silent smoke wraiths.

Skipper was casting about close to a massive old oak when he came across some familiar objects: the cloaks and lanterns belonging to Malbun and Crikulus. The big otter did not disturb them. Bending low, he sniffed his find, wrinkling his nose in distaste.

"Cuck-oo! Cuck-oo!"

Treading carefully, he moved off in the direction of Log a Log's call. Pointing to broken nettles and ferns, the shrew Chieftain nodded northward.

"Two beasts, runnin' hard. Storm never made these tracks!"

Skipper inspected some blurred dents in the ground. "Rain's ruined these prints, but I'd guess they was made sometime yesterday, by the water that's collected in 'em. Let's foller an' see who's makin' the pawprints."

Broken shrubbery, disturbed loam, scratched earth and torn-off leaves were simple to see. No storm could have left such a clear, narrow pattern.

Now that the drizzle had stopped, sunrays cast a mottle of light and shade over the still waters of a peaceful stream, drifting through the woodlands. Pale blue smoke twined lazily upward from a small fire on the bank. The remains of four ruddfish lay amid some half-eaten pears in the smouldering ashes. The two stoats, Burgogg and Wicky, sprawled on the bank, footpaws dabbling in the shallows as they picked their teeth with the ruddfish bones. Burgogg smiled contentedly and belched.

Wicky flicked a fishbone at him. "Beggin' yore pardon!"

Burgogg shot him a quizzical glance. "Why, what've yer done?"

Wicky shook his head at the other's ignorance. "That's wot yer supposed t'say after doin' that. 'Aven't yew got no manners at all?"

Burgogg belched again. "No, enny'ow, who needs manners? I never begged nobeast's pardon in me life. Let 'em go an' pardon theirselves!" He giggled. "I think we should stay 'ere ferever. Those daft fishes 'ave been swimmin' right up to us since we been on this spot. Plenty o' pears, too. Old Kligger liked a pear, y'know, very partial to pears 'e was. Yowch!"

Wicky swished a willow withe back for another stroke. "Wot've I told yer, eh? Shut yer gob about Kligger, d'yew 'ear me, shuttit! One more word about Kligg—"

Skipper's sling was around Wicky's neck like a strangling noose. Log a Log bounded lightly down onto the bank and put the tip of his rapier against Burgogg's nose. The helpless stoat wailed miserably.

"We wasn't trackin' nobeast! We was goin' to break camp an' keep goin' north, wasn't we, Wicky?"

Trying to ease the sling around his neck, Wicky gasped, "Burgogg's right, we wasn't doin' 'arm to anybeast, sir. You ain't got no reason ter slay us!"

Skipper loosened the noose a touch and growled, "Two things can save yore lives, vermin. One, where's yore mate gone to? There was three of ye. An' two, wot were ye runnin' from? Speak, or die!"

He tightened the sling again. Wicky yelled in a hoarse voice, "Awright, awright, I'll tell yer if'n yew let me breathe!"

Skipper slacked the sling off. "Now talk. . . . Fast!"

Wicky massaged his neck and began talking, his voice a low whisper. His eyes darted from side to side, as if watching for some terrible thing to come bounding out of the woodlands at him.

"It was after yew let us go yesterday. We staggered

along fast as we could wid our paws bound t'gether. When we couldn't run no more, we found a quiet liddle spot to sit an' bite through the ropes wid our teeth. Ole Kligger went off, foragin' fer vittles, an' I found a couple o' cloaks an' some lantings. I tell ye, though, there was an awful smell round that glade, a frightenin' smell. It was like . . . like death an' rottin' things, but sickly sweet. . . ." Wicky hugged himself and shuddered.

Skipper prodded him. "Go on, vermin, spit it out!"

Burgogg blurted out as if he could not control himself. "Wicky wuz goin' ter give Kligger a cloak an' a lanting. Then we 'eard the pore beast screamin'. I've 'eard lots o' creatures scream afore, but none like that, sir. None! So we dashed round ter see wot trouble our mate was in. It was worse'n a nightmare, I tell ye! There was this big fat ole oak tree, see, wid a liddle door in it, an' the door was open, an', an' . . . ugghh, it was 'orrible!" Hugging himself, he closed his eyes and mouth tightly. It was obvious that he would not talk further.

Log a Log gave Skipper a quick wink. Leaning across, he unwound the sling from Wicky's throat and patted him sympathetically. "Come on now, me old mate. We want to let you two go, but ye must tell us first. What did you see inside that tree door? Wot 'appened to yore pore ship-mate?"

Wicky sat wide-eyed, staring straight ahead, as if he could see the sight clearly in front of him. "It was a three-'eaded dragon, hissin' an' makin' noises like it was fightin' wid itself. The middle 'ead 'ad ahold of Kligger, an' the two 'eads either side was tuggin' an' rippin' at 'im! That smell, the screams, I'll 'ear them fer the rest o' me days, sir!"

Wicky broke down, sobbing and weeping. Skipper grabbed the stoat and shook him like a rag, roaring at him, "A dragon, are ye mad? Wot did it look like?"

The stoat managed to gasp out between clattering teeth, "It wuz all coils'n'scales, with three 'eads, sir. But the middle 'ead was the worst. Bigger'n the other two, with four eyes, two black an' two green. It 'ad big golden 'orns on its 'ead. I take me oath it did!"

Burgogg wailed out in panic, "Wicky's right, sir, that's just 'ow it looked. Oh please let us go, sir, don't ask us t'go back there an' take ye to the spot!"

Skipper stood up, winding the sling around his paw. "Ye've no need to. Come on, Log, I know where the place is!"

Log a Log kicked the two stoats upright. "Put that fire out an' run for yore lives!"

Wicky and Burgogg kicked earth over the smouldering fire.

"Thankee, sir, we're goin', thankee kindly!"

"Aye, we don't wanna see Mossflower agin, ever. Thankee!"

Noon was running to long shadows as Skipper and Log a Log approached the glade where the cloaks and lanterns lay. Both drew their swords and crept silently forward. Suddenly the sunlit afternoon woodlands had become a place laden with menace.

Log a Log's nose twitched, and the shrew blenched. "Good grief, d'ye smell that?"

Skipper did. Then he heard the grass rustling, slowly at first, then speeding up and becoming faster as it got closer to them.

Log a Log grabbed his friend's paw and dashed off, away from the hidden terror, all his instincts telling him not to stop, but to run. Throwing caution to the winds, he shouted at Skipper, "Quick, mate, or we're deadbeasts! Run for it!"

The otter ran then, but as he did he chanced a swift backward glance and saw what was hunting them. The sight lent wings to his flight. Seizing Log a Log, he bounded forward, pulling the shrew along so fast that at times his footpaws lost contact with the ground.

Long after the danger had passed and the hunter had quit pursuing them, they were still running, out onto the path and down toward the ancient Abbey reflecting the first evening light from its warm-hued sandstone bulk. Toward Redwall, home and safety to all who dwelt therein.

23

That night, after the Dibbuns had gone up to their beds, all able-bodied Redwallers gathered in Cavern Hole to hear Skipper speak. Grave-faced, the big otter faced his audience. He pointed a paw dramatically.

"Out there in Mossflower Woods is a great danger. Ye can believe me 'cos I saw it for meself this very day. I know we smiled a bit when liddle Ruggum said that 'e saw a monster serpent an' a white ghost, but I believes 'e was tellin' the truth, after wot I saw with me own two eyes."

As he paused, Memm called out, "Then tell us, what did you jolly well see?"

Urged on by Log a Log's nod, Skipper told them. "Three of the biggest adders I ever 'opes t'see, but all twisted together like one beast. The biggest was the middle one, an' I knows this is 'ard to believe, but it was wearin' a great golden crown with two big black jetstones set in the front. At first glance it looked like it had four eyes. Never seen anythin' like it in me life, an' 'ope I never do again, mates. 'Twas somethin' you wouldn't expect t'see, even in a bad dream!"

In the stunned silence that followed Skipper's words, Malbun held up the heavy gold pawring, with its two jet-stones glimmering in the lantern lights.

"Did the crown on the serpent's head look anything like this?"

The otter nodded. "Aye, save that the crown was many times bigger, an' the stones were, too. But it matches the crown, shore enough, marm."

The Abbot shook his head in awe. "It sounds very scary!"

Log a Log was glad that their incredulous story was getting home. He glanced around at the Redwallers' fearful faces. "Oh, 'tis scary all right. We know that it ate one o' those stoats who attacked Malbun an' ole Crikulus. The other two told me'n'Skipper that the vermin's screams was like nothin' they'd ever 'eard. I never ran from anybeast in me life, an' neither 'as Skipper, ye all know that. But this thing, the smell, the speed it came after us! Make no mistake, 'tis a great an' terrifyin' evil!"

Seeing that the Abbot wanted to take the floor, Log a Log and Skipper stood to one side. Apodemus raised a warning paw. "Now you have all heard, so I am going to issue the strictest orders. Nobeast is to leave the Abbey!"

He stared pointedly at Malbun and Crikulus before continuing. "Skipper will organise a wallguard. You must all take your turn at watching from the battlements. But more important, keep a sharp eye on the grounds inside. I do not want to hear that Dibbuns have been trying to get out by the wallgates, or any other possible exit. Memm, will you and Sister Vernal take a headcount of the Abbey-babes twice daily?"

The Harenurse saluted. "Yes sah, double roll call, got it!"

After the meeting dispersed, Abbot Apodemus took a stroll around the orchard, in company with Log a Log, Skipper, Crikulus and Malbun. The otter Chieftain felt it was his duty to voice an opinion.

"Father Abbot, you gave good counsel back there. We'll all be safe, long as we stays inside an' keeps watch.

But there is danger out there, sir, an' we won't make it go away by 'idin' from it. Somethin' needs t'be done."

Apodemus spread his paws expressively. "Aye, but what?"

They stood in the evening scent of blossom and fruit, listening to a blackbird's melodious warble, pondering the question. Log a Log was first to break the silence.

"Is the old tawny owl still around?"

Crikulus pulled a wry face. "Aye, he's taken to the beam below my gatehouse ceiling. Ovus isn't much trouble, except that you can't leave food lying about when he's near."

Log a Log agreed. "Worse'n a hare, some owls. Could you tell Ovus we want t'see him? I think an owl's wisdom might 'elp."

Looking a bit grumpy, the tawny owl waddled into the orchard behind Crikulus. He blinked several times and swivelled his head at them.

"I missed supper, y'know. Not good for the digestion, missing supper. Well, what is it?"

Log a Log gallantly offered a paw for the owl to rest his wing upon. "Come on, mate, we'll find ye somethin' in the kitchens. But tell me first, d'you know anythin' about gettin' rid of adders?"

The owl's black eyes widened. "Hmph! You don't get rid of adders. What you do is stay away from them, make your home in another place. Leave adders alone, don't mess with them!"

It was not a solution that pleased the Abbot. "But suppose you cannot, or don't want to, move away. What happens then, pray tell?"

Ovus waited as Skipper opened the Abbey door for him. "If you stay put, then the adders will find you, sooner or later. Those reptiles are totally evil. They're great hunters, too, and can range far and wide. I say move, that's the best and safest way of staying alive."

Skipper snorted. "'Tis out o' the question, mate. Is there no other way?"

Ovus paused on the top step of the kitchen. "Hmmm, strawberry and redcurrant turnover, can't mistake that gorgeous smell. Hope there's plenty left."

Skipper blocked the owl's path. "I asked ye if there was any other way!"

Abruptly the tawny owl snapped, "Bluddbeak, I suppose!"

Ovus would speak no more until he had despatched a large turnover. The Abbot's gesture signalled them all to be patient until the owl had finished eating. He picked a few crumbs from his talons and sighed.

"Ahhh, that's much better. Ahem, now about Bluddbeak. I'm surprised you haven't heard of him. Big old red kite, lives nor'west in the mountains, a goodly way off. Suppose that's why you don't know him. Anyhow, if anybeast can take care of adders, then Bluddbeak is the bird."

Malbun found another turnover that had been left cooling on a stone slate. She pushed it in front of Ovus. "Could you find Bluddbeak and bring him to Redwall?"

Again they had to wait whilst the owl ate his turnover. Then Ovus began making his demands for the task.

Skipper took the first watch on the walltops with Churk, the hefty young female otter. He told her of what had taken place in the kitchens. Churk leaned on a battlement, watching the night-cowled woodlands, shaking her head in disbelief.

"A day afore he can make the trip, ye say? Cheeky old featherbag. I'd 'ave sent that owl packin' tonight, Skip!"

Skipper rested his chin on the wallstones. "Ovus ain't hurryin' fer nobeast. Says 'e's got to feed 'imself up fer such a long flight. Huh, an' the load o' vittles 'e wants t'take with 'im. A fruitcake, two mushroom-an'-carrot pasties, a bag o' candied chestnuts, a whoppin' slab o' cheese, an' a big flask of greensap milk mixed with clear honey, if ye please!"

Churk could not resist a chuckle at the owl's gluttony. "Carryin' that lot, I think Ovus'll 'ave to walk all the way!"

Skipper shrugged. "I think the Abbot's far too soft wid that bird, but 'e agreed with everythin'."

Zassaliss was the biggest and oldest of the three adders. His brother Harssacss and his sister Sesstra were bound forever to him, not just by family blood, but also by the mace and chain of King Sarengo. Long seasons ago, when all three were young, the Pure Ferret Ruler and his crew of Ratguards had invaded the vipers' home. The attack had been brief but terrible. Their mother, the great snake Berrussca, had met Sarengo head-on, knocking the iron mace and chain from his paws and engaging him in a struggle to the death. The mace was a fearsome weapon, with a metal bar handle, an iron chain flail, and a spiked iron ball.

Berrussca's three children were hardly half grown. Huddling together in the cavern beneath the oak, they hissed venomously and struck out at the Ratguards surrounding them. Flailing through the melee, the discarded mace and chain wrapped itself about their writhing tails. Screams of stricken rats rent the gloomy air of Brockhall as the three young snakes struck again and again. Only six rats and Sarengo's fat, terrified son Agarnu managed to scramble out with their lives.

King Sarengo fought like a madbeast. Weaponless and trapped in the giant coils of Berrussca, the Pure Ferret sunk his teeth into the adder's spine, just below the skull. He hung on, hoping for rescue by his son and the Ratguards, but it never came. Sarengo died of wounds from the viper's poison fangs. Berrussca died, too, her spine broken by Sarengo's clenched teeth.

When it was all over, the three young vipers, Zassaliss, Harssacss and Sesstra, lay exhausted, the cruel weight of Sarengo's mace and chain embedded in their tails. The more they struggled, the worse it bit into their bodies. It was many days before they could move. Exerting his greater strength and authority over the other two, Zassaliss forced them to coordinate their movements until all three moved as one.

The brood of Berrussca learned to grow, to hunt and survive together, and Zassaliss took Sarengo's crown for himself. Now fully matured adders, they were the terror of every creature unfortunate enough to behold them. They were cold, swift, poisonous and deadly. Killers three, with none to oppose their ever-widening territory.

The dreadful trio slithered together through the night-dark woodlands, their tongues flickering as they used them to quest the air for prey. Separated, they might have been totally silent, but joined in unison the adders could not prevent the swish of grass caused by their dragging tails and the mace handle constantly trailing behind them. However, their combined speed and ferocity proved a deadly combination.

An old crow soon found this out to its cost. The bird, who had injured its wing and could not follow its kin, stood dozing on a low-dipping hawthorn branch. The crow heard the rustling grass far too late. Sesstra tugged the slender tree limb, toppling the ancient bird down into the gaping mouths of her two brothers. She joined them speedily, eager not to miss her share of the quarry.

Rigid with terror, the crow stared up at three pairs of eyes peering down at it.

"Sssssleep, do not sssssquawk or ssssscreech!"

"Ssssssleep in ssssssilence and darknessssss!"

"Do not dissssssturb otherssssss, we need to hunt more thissssss night!"

Dawn's first pale light washed gently in over a calm sea. A
lone gull's plaintive call echoed to the opening day. Scarum
sat at the tiller taking dogwatch, the shortest duty, as darkness gave way to light. The incorrigible young hare eyed
his two companions, sleeping in the bows with the ship's
rations between them. In the hope of waking Sagax and
Kroova to make breakfast, as he was not allowed to touch
the food, Scarum began composing a ditty and singing it
aloud:

> "O the life of a handsome young hare is sad,
> Jolly sad, believe you me,
> With two rotten measly grubswipin' mates,
> He sails the bloomin' sea.
> He's considered rude if he begs for food,
> Tut tut, that's far too bad.
> He's bossed by an otter who's nought but a rotter,
> An' a badger well known as a cad!
>
> Sing hey fol dee dee, sail hither an' there,
> Spare a tear for a famished young hare.

213

If this hare should die, would his comrades cry?
Wot wot, fat chance I'd say,
They'd cook skilly'n'duff, laugh hearty an' rough,
Scoff pudden an' chortle all day.
As for that pitiful, starved-to-death chap,
Why, they'd toss him over the side,
Where a rotten great shark, just for a lark,
Would be waitin' with mouth open wide!

Sing hey fol dee doh, through storm an' bad fogs,
Just look at 'em snorin' like hogs.

So all you jolly young handsome hares,
Pay heed to my sad tale.
Beware those blinkin' bounders who want
To take you for a sail.
They'll snigger an' whoop, as your poor ears droop,
An' make flamin' insultin' remarks,
Just bid 'em farewell, an' hop into the sea.
You're far better off with the sharks!

Sing hey fol dee doh, I've still got my pride,
So ignore me 'cos I've just died!"

Kroova opened one eye and nudged Sagax. "I 'ope ole
Scarum means that. At least we'll get a bit o' peace!"

Sagax replied with both eyes still closed, "No such
luck, mate, he's too hungry to die. Oh well, we'd better
get up and see about breakfast. Anything to report,
Scarum? Disasters at sea, ships in the night?"

The mention of breakfast had cheered the hare up con-
siderably. "What, er, oh, not a confounded thing, just the
bally usual. Water, water an' more flippin' water, wot! I
say, I'll bet that jolly good sleep you've had is makin' you
feel a bit peckish. What d'you say I make brekkers, eh,
wot?"

"Put one paw near that grub an' I'll chop it off!"

Scarum stuck out his tongue at Kroova. "No y'won't,
'cos then I wouldn't be able to steer!"

Sagax was about to start preparing the breakfast when

Kroova's sharp eyes caught a dark mass on the eastern horizon. The otter yelled out in fine nautical fashion, "Land ho! Take 'er bow east, matey!"

Scarum managed to turn his eyes from the food. "Wot, er, righto, me old messmate, me salty seadog, er, er, bow east it is, shipmate!"

The otter sighed wearily as he retrieved the tiller from the jaunty hare. "Yore 'eadin' out t'sea, bow east is the other way. Go an' do somethin' else, I'll take 'er in."

This did not diminish Scarum's happy mood a whit. "Do somethin' else, right ho, Cap'n. Shall I bail out the bilges or scuttle the masthead, wot? I say, perhaps I'll lend a paw an' help me old messymate Sagax with brekkers!"

The badger stowed the rations back under the bow seat. "Breakfast will have to wait until we make land, so forget your stomach and help me to look out for reefs."

Scarum's long ears wilted. He sat in the bows staring down into the clear blue water, muttering, "Forget about breakfast, the very idea! First shark that comes along can have me. Huh, providin' sharks like scoffin' thin, sickly-lookin' chaps!"

As they drew closer to the coast, Sagax could feel excitement beginning to bubble up within. "I can see a stream running out across the shore, coming right through those woodlands and out of the hills. Do you think we've reached Mossflower country, Kroova?"

The otter grinned triumphantly. "I certainly do, mate!"

Scarum set the craft rocking to and fro as he leaped up and down on the bows in a victory jig.

"Well hey ho and a nonny no, good old us, wot? We finally made it, chaps, the land of scoff'n'honey. Hoorah!"

Sagax grabbed the leaping hare by his tailscut. "Keep bouncing about like that and you'll capsize us. I'll watch the water. If you want to use some energy up, go and furl the sails. Take them down completely and roll 'em up. We'll need them to make a shelter."

Scarum's attempts at sail-furling were pathetic. He tugged the sternsail down on his head, enveloping him-

self. Sagax and Kroova exchanged winks as they watched
the mass of sailcloth wriggling about. They joshed him:

"That's the stuff, mate, fold it nice'n'neat now."

"You can tell Scarum's a trained seabeast. Wish I could
furl a sail like that—you'd think he was born to it!"

The parcel of canvas sprouted lumps as Scarum tried
madly to extricate himself from his prison. "Yaaagh,
gemme out, you fiends, it's dark in here. Come on, you
dreadful rotters, help a chap out. Don't you dare make
breakfast until I get m'self free of this lot. Gurrrr!"

Midmorning saw the ketch *Stopdog* glide smoothly into
the stream's outflow. Kroova dismantled the bow seat, and
together he and Sagax began paddling the craft upstream,
across the shore.

Scarum had finally managed to extricate himself from
the clutches of the sail. He folded it carefully, muttering
darkly against life's injustices. "Might've bally well
smothered in there, huh, a lot those two would care. Almost half blinkin' well through the day and food hasn't
passed my perishin' lips. Next time I go t'sea it'll be with
a fat duck an' a jolly frog, wot!"

The *Stopdog*'s keel ground to a halt on the sandy
streambed.

Kroova shipped his makeshift oar. "That's as far as
she'll go until the evenin' tide washes up this way an'
deepens these shallows. Away, boat's crew mates, all
ashore that's goin' ashore!"

Sagax was first overboard. He took a deep drink from
the streamwater—it was fresh, though slightly sunwarmed. He drove a stake into the sand and moored the
ketch to stop her being washed seaward.

Kroova gathered driftwood from the tideline and set
about lighting a fire with flint and tinder. Soon they had a
camp pitched on the dry sands, with an awning of sailcloth and a concoction of supplies bubbling merrily away
over the fire.

Sagax sat under the shade of the awning, facing land-
ward. The warm umber sands gave way to high hills

topped with grass and backed by thick woodland. It was a pretty sight on a bright summer's morn.

They had relented and allowed Scarum the position of cook. He was throwing ingredients willy-nilly into the pot and gurgling happily. "Just wait'll you chaps taste this. Ooch! It's a bit hot right now, but delicious all the same, wot. Even though one says it oneself, absoflippinlutely delicious!"

Headed by Slitfang, a score of Freebooter vermin wandered the coastline, looking out for the landmarks that Captain Plugg had described to them. Tazzin panted as she climbed a steep sandhill.

"Is this the one Cap'n Plugg said ter look out for?"

Slitfang shrugged. "Could be. We won't know 'til we gets to the top an' takes the lay o' the land."

The stoat Scummy gritted sand between his few teeth. "Wouldn't ye think old Plugg'd come an look fer hisself? Bet 'e's playin' wid 'is new likkle boat, 'im an' that fat white sissy Prince."

The weasel Stinky grabbed at a tussock of grass. It came out by the roots and he tumbled backward. Wiping sand from his eyes, he flung the grass away savagely. "Yore right there, bucko, I don't see the sense in traipsin' up an' down the beaches. 'Tis a flamin' vinegar trip if'n yew ask me!"

Slitfang turned to face the complainants. "Well, I didn't ask yer, Stinky. Vinegar trip, eh? That's wot ye call carryin' out Cap'n's orders, eh? I ain't askin' ye now, I'm tellin' youse two. Shut yore gobs an' stop talkin' mutiny, or I'll report ye to the Cap'n when we gets back. Now I've warned yer, one more word—"

Tazzin had reached the hilltop. She called out to Slitfang, "Ahoy, Slitty, come an' take a dekko at this!"

The weasel turned his back on the two crewbeasts and scrabbled his way to the top.

Below them the shores stretched south, broken only by the broad stream that flowed across from the woodlands. This was what they had been looking for, exactly as Plugg

had described it. However, it was not the stream that
caught most of the Freebooters' attention.

A smile of villainous delight crossed Slitfang's ugly
face. "Well, scrape me barnacles, will ye look at that. I
swear, 'tis the old ketch wot King Sarengo used to tow
abaft of 'is big ship. I remembers it from when I was
young. Haharr, an' there's a camp alongside it, all nice 'n'
cosy like!"

By this time the others had climbed up and joined him.
The rat Ripper licked the edge of a sharp sickle he carried.

"Couldn't be crewed by more'n 'arf a dozen, an'
there's twenny of us. Wot do yer say, Slitty?"

Slitfang spat on his paws and rubbed them gleefully. "I
say we takes a walk down there, nice'n'quiet, so as not ter
frighten 'em off. That fire's burnt low, bet they're 'avin a
peaceful noontime nap under that there lean-to. Now lissen, youse lot, I don't want no killin'. We'll take 'em as
prisoners back to the Cap'n. I gotta feelin' Plugg'd want
to 'ave a word with 'em. Foller me, an' no noise."

Tazzin tossed her blade skilfully and caught it. "Right
y'are, Slit, let's pay 'em a visit!"

Beneath the awning, Scarum was snoring gently. Something tickled his nose; he brushed it away. It tickled again,
and he hit out at it. His paw struck something hard. Opening his eyes, the hare found himself staring into Slitfang's
grinning face.

The weasel was dangling a dagger over his nose. He
winked at Scarum. "Wakey wakey, rabbit, you got visitors."

The Salamandastron hare came awake fighting. His
long back legs shot out into the weasel's stomach as
Scarum shouted, "Eulaliaaa! We're being attacked,
mates!"

His companions leaped up, Sagax flooring a rat with a
hefty blow. Kroova caught a ferret's footpaws and sent
him flat. Then the Freebooters swamped them. Fighting
like madbeasts, the three companions tried to battle with
overwhelming odds. Scarum seized their makeshift pad-

dle and broke free. He batted the campfire with it, sending showers of hot embers at his foes. Sagax exerted his mighty strength. Grabbing the rat Ripper, he whirled him bodily over his head.

Slitfang roared out, "Surrender, or this 'un's a dead-beast!" Slitfang had stunned Kroova from behind with his cutlass hilt. Both he and Tazzin crouched over the otter, their blades at his throat.

Fear for their friend's life caused Sagax to drop Ripper. Scarum ceased scattering fire. Immediately they were set upon by vermin and bound with ship's ropes.

Slitfang spat out a tooth he had lost in the melee. He looped a rope around the half-conscious otter, nodding with satisfaction. "That's better. No sense in slayin' youse . . . yet!"

Four vermin had Sagax lying bound upon the sand. He tried to struggle upright, but was kicked back again. "What's the meaning of this attack? What do you want with us?"

Slitfang held his cutlass point to the young badger's chest. "Oh, nothin', stripedog, just a bit of information, but that'll wait 'til ye meet Cap'n Plugg Firetail."

Scarum was lying facedown, the ropes biting cruelly into his paws. Lifting his head, he blinked sand out of his eyes. "I should've booted your belly through your backbone, you scumfaced villain. If I wasn't jolly well trussed up, I'd give you such a blinkin'—"

"Yah shuddup, rabbit!" The stoat named Scummy ground his paw on the back of Scarum's head, pushing his face into the sand.

Tazzin felt heat on her back. She turned. "The ship's burnin'!"

Blazing embers from the scattered fire had stuck to the pitch and resin coating of the bows. With such inflammable materials, the *Stopdog* immediately burst into a sheet of flame. Everybeast leaped back from the blaze. Slitfang tried running forward to see if he could fight the fire, but a breeze caught the conflagration. He, too, was forced to leap back from the blistering heat. Then the awning caught light from a salvo of pitch- and resin-soaked splinters. Dragging their captives, the Freebooters abandoned the site, beating at their smouldering clothing as more sparks leaped out from the burning vessel.

Slitfang kicked out viciously at the young hare. "Yew caused that, rabbit! It was yore fault, whackin' fire all over the place like that!"

Scarum bit at the weasel's paw, but missed. "Rabbit y'self, you great smelly bully!" He looked over at Kroova apologetically. "Sorry about your ship, old chap."

Half dazed, the otter managed a lopsided grin. "Better'n lettin' the *Stopdog* fall into the paws o' vermin, eh."

Slitfang waved his cutlass at Ripper and Stinky. "Youse two get back to the *Seascab*. Tell the Cap'n wot 'appened, an' tell 'im we've found the stream wot crosses the shore. We'll wait 'ere for 'im. Go on, git goin'!"

Reluctantly the pair moved off, muttering under their breath.

"Huh, while 'e waits there, all nice an' easy-like."

"Aye, picks the good jobs fer 'imself, don't 'e?"

Before they had made it to the hill, which they had earlier descended, Tazzin caught up with the pair. She smiled slyly and twirled her knife expertly.

"Slitty sez I'm t'go with ye. Oh, an' 'e said somethin' else, too. Gave me orders to cut off yore 'eads if'n ye start talkin' mutiny or not movin' fast enough."

Slitfang watched them scrabbling back up the hill with Tazzin and her knife close behind. He turned to his captives. "Yew three just lay there quiet an' try not to annoy me. Ye wouldn't like to see me annoyed. We'll all wait 'til Cap'n Plugg comes sailin' up in the ole *Seascab* an' see wot 'e's got to say about all this. Haharr, shouldn't imagine that snooty Princess Kurda'll be too 'appy when she sees 'er old grandad's ketch burnt to a cinder!"

Scarum whispered to Kroova, "Who in the name of my auntie's pinny is Princess Kurda?"

Slitfang cuffed Scarum across the ears. "I tole ye t'be quiet, rabbit."

Scarum could not resist having a last word. "Actually, I'm a hare, old chap."

Slitfang raised his cutlass threateningly. "Yew ain't an 'er, yore a him, but one more peep out o' ye an' you'll be twins, 'cos I'll make two of ye!"

Sagax gave his friend a glare, warning him to be silent.

Evening fell with the three prisoners still lying bound upon the sand, listening to the vermin's coarse banter about their eventual fate at the tender mercy of the one they called Plugg Firetail. Sagax closed his eyes. It did not make for cheerful listening.

25

The stream that Shogg and Triss were following took a
curve into thick woodland. Both kept to the water, sometimes waist deep, other times paddling through the bank
shallows. It was not easy going, trying not to leave signs
that could be tracked. In the late noon they took a rest, sitting on a mossy ledge overgrown by hanging willows.
The otter peered back up their trail.

"Luck's with us so far, mate. I can't see nor 'ear any
sign of 'em, thanks to those Coneslinger squirrels."

Triss stretched out on the velvety moss, tired and hungry. "Maybe fortune is favouring us for the moment, but
we'd be fooling ourselves by thinking Riggan won't pick
up our trail sooner or later. Kurda won't rest until she's
got us back in her clutches—you know that."

Shogg slid back into the water. "Aye, yore right.
Though if we can make it to the shore an' get our ship
back somehow, we'll show em a clean pair o' paws. A big
clumsy Freebooter vessel like theirs wouldn't keep up
with us if'n we sailed close to the shallows an' reefs.
They'd find it 'ard to follow."

* * *

Evening began falling over the tree-shaded stream as they plowed their way onward. Triss was wading alongside her friend when she began feeling a touch uneasy. Leaning across, she whispered in his ear, "I don't like it hereabouts, but I don't know why."

Keeping his gaze straight ahead, the otter replied, "I don't like it either, Trissy. I think somebeast's watchin' us. Keep movin', maybe we're just passin' through their territory an' they'll let us go by. Don't look around, keep goin'."

Triss peered downstream and saw shadowy figures flitting about on the banks. "Don't have to look around, Shogg, they're up ahead."

But the otter had already chanced a backward peep. "Then 'tis woe to us, mate, 'cos they're be'ind us, too!"

The squirrelmaid felt her paws tremble. "As if we haven't got enough trouble. What d'you think is the best thing to do? I'm too tired to think straight."

Shogg halted, placing his back against Triss so that he was facing upstream. "We got nothin' to lose, matey, so let's brag it out. You any good at the braggin'?"

Triss faced downstream, glad of her friend's back to lean on. "It's worth a try, I suppose. You go first."

Clenching both paws, Shogg shook them above his head and roared aloud to the unknown watchers, "Come an' face a champion streamwalloper! Don't skulk around like maggots in a rotten log! I've cracked skulls, sailed stormy seas an' leaped o'er mountains! I ain't got a foe in the world, know why? 'Cos they're all dead!"

Gruffing her voice, Triss yelled out her challenge. "I was born in the thunder, I'm a warrior, the child of warriors! Stand in my way an' I'll tramp right over ye!"

There was a splash in the water as something dived from the bank. A moment later a large water vole's head popped up, almost directly between the two friends. He shook his fur, bushing out his big hairy face, and smiled, addressing them in a slow rustic voice.

"Oi do berleeve we means you wayfarers no 'arm. Oi be named Arvicola. Me'n my voles allus been friendly wi' streamdogs an' treemouses. Hush ye now, though oi do berleev oi did enjoy lissenin' to such good braggers as you be."

Triss heaved a sigh of relief and held out her paw. "I'm Triss and he's Shogg. We're runaway slaves trying to reach the shore. Some very bad rats and an evil white ferret are probably on our trail. That's why we stuck to the stream, to save leaving tracks."

Other water voles popped up all around the fugitives, each one as big and bushy as Arvicola, who was nodding his head sagely as he digested the squirrelmaid's information. He plucked a reed and began nibbling on it.

"Dearie me an' lackaday, you creatures be in trouble greatly, no doubtin' o' that. We got families an' babes nestin' in these 'ere banks, can't 'ave otherbeasts a-botherin' 'em. Do ye follow us now, we'll be takin' ye down to the shores. Oi be thinkin' 'tis the best solution. Come you now, voles, let's be helpin' these two."

Surrounded by water voles, Triss and Shogg continued their journey, with Arvicola pointing the way ahead. "Our stream splits an' joins another up yonder, oi do berleev that will be a-takin' you to the shorelands."

Kurda was relieved when darkness fell. She beckoned Vorto to her side. "Vot you t'ink ve do now, Captain?"

Vorto answered, knowing he would be saving the Princess's face by suggesting the obvious. "They could keep us pinned 'ere forever, yer 'ighness. Best thing is to back out an' slip away. Then we can circle the trees an' let Riggan find the slaves' trail. Unless, o' course, they're still 'idin' in there."

A pinecone whizzed out of the darkened tree fringe, pinging off Kurda's sabre blade. She began wriggling backward.

"Nah, slaves not 'ide in dere no more. Ve do like you say, yarr!"

Shuffling backwards on their bellies, the Ratguards retreated, still pelted by stray pinecones. When they were out of range, Kurda ordered Riggan to scout the area for signs.

Less than an hour later, the slavecatcher returned to make her report. "They left these trees, a bit round the other side, Princess. I found a stream close by. Runners always try to lose yer by takin' to a stream."

Kurda touched Riggan's paw with her bladepoint. "You are de best. Ve vill go catch dem, yarr?"

The tracker led them off, giving the trees a wide berth. "We'll lay 'em by the paws, never yew fear, marm!"

Vorto held the guards back whilst Riggan inspected the streambank. Kurda watched her closely.

The tracker's keen eyes missed nothing. She smiled to herself. "Aye, just like I figgered, they went downstream, west."

Kurda pointed her sabre. "You sure dey not go upstream? I t'ink dey go dat vay, east!"

Riggan waded a short way downstream and returned with a broken reed. She held it up for Kurda to see. "Yore a princess, marm, I'm a slavecatcher. This came from down yonder. It'd be natural for anybeast t'think they'd gone inland, but I knows me slaves. They always try an' fool ye by goin' the opposite way. 'Tis west, sure enough!"

Kurda and Riggan led off downstream. Vorto and the rest followed, marvelling at the tracker's skills as she confirmed the route by noticing bent reeds, disturbed pebbles and bruised leaves hanging down from streambank trees.

Plugg Firetail had misjudged his landfall by anchoring too far north of Mossflower. Immediately after Tazzin and the runners arrived with news of Slitfang's discovery, the silver fox had the *Seascab* under way, rousing the rest of his crew from their night's sleep. With the recovered craft in tow, he sailed south down the coast.

Grubbage spotted the smoke and flame from the *Stopdog* shortly before dawn. He roused Prince Bladd, who was sleeping out, snuggled in rope coils on the afterdeck.

"Ahoy, mate, go'n' tell the Cap'n we'll be droppin' anchor soon. Move yerself, Princeness, Cap'n don't like t'be kept waitin'!"

Bladd, who had got used to being bullied by Freeboot-ers, staggered upright, scratching his midriff. "I go, but den I take another shleep in mine nice soft bed."

Grubbage, whose hearing had not improved, waggled a grubby paw in his ear and nodded. "I allus said you 'ad a nice soft 'ead. 'Op along now, mate!"

Slitfang ran down to the sea and waded in, shouting up to Plugg, who was standing in the bows. "This is the place, Cap'n, I found it. An' I got three prisoners for ye, too!"

Two of the crew lowered Plugg down on a rope. On reaching Slitfang, he boxed the weasel's ears soundly.

"Three prisoners, eh? Then why aren't ye back there guardin' 'em? An' why did yer let that ketch git burned down?" Stumping up to the burned-out campsite, he glared at Sagax, Kroova and Scarum distastefully.

"A streamdog, a stripedog, an' a rabbit, wot good are they t'me? Why didn't ye destroy them an' save the ketch, instead o' savin' them an' lettin' the craft get ru-ined?"

The crew got out of Plugg's way. It was obvious he was in a bad mood. Grubbage came up the beach, fol-lowed by Prince Bladd and the rest of the *Seascab*'s crew. A sudden thought struck Grubbage.

"Cap'n, 'ow's the Princess an' those Ratguards goin' to find us again, now that ye've moved the *Seascab* down the coast?"

Plugg sighed. "I forgot about that lot."

Bladd giggled. "I hope dey are losed forever, 'specially mine sister. I not vant to see her again, dat's for sure!"

Scarum had been listening with interest to the conver-sation. The talkative hare could not resist taking part. "I say, old chap, that's a bit heartless, wot, not wantin' to see your sister again. I bet she misses you terribly!"

Plugg waggled his axe threateningly under the hare's nose. "Who asked you, rabbit? 'Ere, Tazzin, gut these three an' toss 'em in the sea fer fishfood!"

Tazzin twirled her knife, smiling eagerly. "Aye aye, Cap'n!"

Sagax decided it was time for him to speak up. "Only a fool would do that. D'you know who we are?"

The young badger tried to look as regal as he could, which was not easy, lying dumped and bound on the sand. "I am the son of a great mountain Lord. The hare, Bescarum, is from a very wealthy family. Our otter friend is the son of an emperor of sea otters. If you slay us, think of the ransom you'd miss out on."

Scarum interrupted. "He's right, y'know, old lad. Our families would prob'ly swap a jolly great shipload of treasure t'get us back. No sense in slayin' us, wot wot?"

Plugg sat down on the sand beside Scarum. "Haharr, 'tis long seasons since I 'eld anybeast to ransom. Righty ho, rabbit, we'll let you'n yore mates live, but you'd better 'ope yore rich pappas an' mammas stump up plenty, or ye'll be fed to the sharks, one at a time. D'ye unnerstand?"

Scarum shook his head in mock admiration of the Freebooter. "I say, sir, you're a born genius, what jolly clever thinkin'. I'd shake your paw heartily if I weren't tied up at the moment!"

Slitfang placed a paw on his hip and swaggered about, trying to imitate Scarum's speech. "Ho I say, wot wot, jolly ole rabbit! Don't 'e talk pretty?"

Plugg fetched Slitfang a whack that sent him sprawling. "That's 'cos 'e's a gentlebeast, not like you, slabnose. That there rabbit's 'ad a h'eddication, more'n wot we've ever 'ad. My old uncle was a gentlebeast wid a h'eddication. I liked 'im. My old uncle could sing wunnderful h'eddicated ditties, too!"

Plugg whirled on Scarum, shoving his double-headed axe under the hare's chin. "Kin yew sing h'eddicated ditties?"

Scarum gulped. "Educated ditties, sah, I was brought up on 'em, could sing ditties before I could talk!"

Plugg aimed a cheerful kick at the floored Slitfang. "See, I told yer, that 'un come from the quality. Go on, then, h'eddicated rabbit, sing us a ditty."

Scarum bobbed his ears politely. "These ropes are pretty tight."

The silver fox raised his axe meaningly. "Never mind tellin' us the name o' the ditty, just sing it!"

Scarum pulled a wry face at Sagax and Kroova, then launched into his song.

"O 'tis marvellous what an education does for a
    chap,
His eyes light up when he puts on the old thinkin'
    cap,
His brain begins to whirr an' click,
Ideas pour in fast an' thick,
'Cos that's what an education's for!

If it takes one mole to dig a hole,
Ten seasons and a bit,
How many moles could dig that hole,
If they were fat an' fit?
Then if two squirrels helped them,
As deep as they could reach,
If those two squirrels made a pair,
The answer is a peach!

That's what an education does for a chap,
It leaves the blinkin' duffers in a bit of a flap,
For learnin' facts you may depend,
One spouts out answers without end,
So hearken now an' I'll astound you more!

If two sparrows had six arrows,
And set out to shoot a duck,
Just how long would it take them,
Before they had some luck?

The answer's jolly simple,
As clever types will know,
To bag that duck they had no luck,
Because they had no bow!

'Cos that's what an education does for a chap,
When learnin' dawns upon him like a big thunder-
    clap,

As they hear his knowledge flow,
The clods will cheer and shout what ho,
Now that's what an education's for!

If I had two an' you had two,
And she had two as well,
If they had two, just like we two,
The truth to you I'll tell,
If one knew far too little,
Those facts would be too few,
But if one had education,
One would find the answers, too!"

The Freebooter crew, who had gathered around to listen, sat slack-jawed with wonderment at Scarum's rapid delivery of the song, for he had sung it at an alarming rate, without a single stumble.

Kroova could not help smiling. "Well done, matey, I'd clap ye if'n me paws was free!"

The hare sniffed. "Think nothin' of it, old lad. Huh, you'd wait a long time expectin' applause from these vermin oafs!"

Plugg swiftly cuffed a few ears and kicked some tails. "Come on, ye dimwits, if'n ye ain't got a h'eddication, the least ye can do is to show the rabbit you've got some manners!" He strode among his crew, making sure they all cheered.

Sagax moved closer to Kroova and murmured quietly, "Good old Scarum. While he's keeping them amused, they're not talking about slaying us, eh, mate?"

Kroova looked at the cheering vermin, knowing that their mood could change in the blink of an eye, depending on their captain's good or bad humour.

"Aye, mate, but it'll only last as long as ole Scarum can keep 'em entertained."

Sagax watched his friend. Scarum was launching into a funny story about a rhubarb pie fight between two frogs. The young badger shook his striped head.

"I know he's the world's worst glutton and we've had to yell at him from time to time, but we'd be in a bad way right now if we didn't have him along. To think that our very lives are depending on Scarum keeping a crew of vermin amused."

Kroova had to raise his voice to make himself heard above the guffawing crew of the *Seascab*. "Yore right, mate, I'll never shout at 'im again for robbin' vittles. If'n we gets out o' this lot, ole Scarum can stuff 'is face to 'is 'eart's content!"

Sagax shot the sea otter a warning glance. "Not too loud, mate. Keep your voice down—he might hear us!"

26

After wading through the small stream they had been following, Triss felt as though the one it flowed into was almost a river—broad, deep and fairly swift-running. Almost up to her neck, she clung to Shogg's paw, which supported her stoutly. Arvicola went ahead with them, his watervole tribe bringing up the rear, no strangers to overhanging foliage and a night-darkened waterway.

Triss peered anxiously into the gloom ahead. "Are we anywhere near the shore yet?"

Arvicola answered in his slow, rustic drawl. "If'n you do berleev that yon vermin are sure to track ye, then I do think it be time to divert 'em, missy."

Shogg shook his head doubtfully. "There's one among 'em, Riggan the slavecatcher, she's clever, matey. Ye'd 'ave trouble bluffin' 'er from a trail."

Arvicola pulled a reed and chewed reflectively on it. "Mayhap she's smart, but I berleev you'll find us not t'be fools. This be our territory, we knows it like no other beast. Hop out of this water now an' I'll tell ye my plan."

They pulled themselves up onto the bank, Arvicola and

his tribe following suit. The watervole Chieftain issued orders in an unhurried manner.

"All of ye now, circle an' mill. You two as well, friends."

Obediently they joined the watervoles, milling about in circles, stamping the ground hard until Arvicola called a halt. He inspected the ground, satisfied with the result.

"I do berleev it be nicely flattened an' well marked now. Look you, friends, see where my paw be a-pointin'."

Triss nodded. "Over the water to the far bank."

The watervole's homely face broke into a brief smile. "Well said, missy. Now, yonder there is an overgrown ledge, I do berleev 'twill fit ye both snug. You jump in the water an' make your way across to it, an' we'll bide 'ere till you be goodly hidden. Hasten now, waste not the time."

Shogg took Triss by the paw and the two leaped into the broad stream. He guided her across and felt around in the dark until he had located the ledge beneath lots of hanging grass and fern. They ducked under the water and surfaced beneath it. Taking care not to touch the screen of vegetation, Triss peered through. She could barely make out Arvicola standing on the far bank.

Shogg called across to him, "'Tis a good 'idin' place, mate. Wot now?"

Arvicola chuckled. "Stay put there, friends. My voles will mill around a bit more, then go south through the woods. We'll be leavin' a fine ole messy trail for your vermin foes to follow. Whatever ye do, stay there silent. Wait until they leave the waterway to follow us. When they be well clear, ye can both carry on through the water. 'Tis not a great distance to the shores and the sea. Fare ye well now, I do berleev we'll be off!"

Milling and stamping away, Arvicola and his watervoles crashed off through the woodlands.

After a while, the silence and darkness began making Shogg feel edgy. He murmured uneasily, "I don't like it, Triss, sooner be on the move than stuck 'ere stannin' still. What if Riggan spots us?"

The young squirrelmaid clasped her friend's paw. "This is the best chance we've got, believe me. I trust Arvicola. He looks like a woodland bumpkin, but that watervole has got a crafty old head on his shoulders!"

Shogg was forced to agree. "Aye, I know 'e wants to take Kurda an' the vermin away from both 'is own camp an' us as well. Looks like we'll just 'ave to bide 'ere an' 'ope we don't get spotted."

It was easier for Shogg than it was for Triss, standing neck deep in their watery hideout. For what seemed an interminable age, the broadstream flowed silently by. The young squirrelmaid bit down on a pawful of reeds to stop her teeth chattering as Shogg murmured, "At least it ain't as bad as bein' in a cage at Riftgard's fjord—now that was real cold. Hush, somebeast's a-comin'!"

Kurda waded alongside Riggan. The slavecatcher had deployed half of the Ratguard behind them and the other half walking either side of the banks. The Pure Ferret Princess was still not convinced they were on the right course, complaining regularly to Riggan.

"You sure dey vent dis vay? Dere are no signs."

Peering ahead, the slavecatcher growled confidently, "Don't ye fret, marm. We're 'ard on the trail, I knows it!"

Vorto, who was up on the bank, called out excitedly, "Up 'ere, tracks all over the place!"

Riggan hopped out onto the bank. "Back off, I want those prints clear! Keep the others away from 'em an' keep yore voice down. No need to shout all over the woodlands."

Kurda halted in midstream, with the rest of her Ratguards catching up to her. She was directly opposite the hidden ledge—Triss could see her clearly through a slight gap in the reeds. Both she and Shogg remained completely still. At one point, when Kurda turned to maintain her balance, Triss looked directly into the wicked pink eyes of the Princess, convinced that Kurda was staring straight back at her. Mercifully, the Princess turned around to face Riggan.

"You see der tracks, yarr, tell me!"

Riggan was down on all fours, inspecting the area. "Ho, I sees 'em shore enough, marm. They mostly belongs to a crowd o' voles, but I kin make out the otter an' squirrel marks, very faintly. They've cut off south through the trees, not so long back, either."

Kurda allowed Vorto to assist her up onto the bank with his spearhaft. The rat Captain saluted smartly.

"No need t'move slowly now, 'ighness, this trail's easy to follow. They prob'ly figgered we went upstream an' east."

Kurda released the spear pole. "Gutt, den vot you vaiting for, Vorto? Go and capture dem. Riggan and I vill follow."

Riggan protested. "But, marm, I should be up front, trackin'."

Kurda fixed the slavecatcher with a haughty glare. "I give de orders. You track too slow. Der trail is clear, yarr, let dem get hot onto it. Go, Vorto, hurry. Ve vill be behind you, making sure der slaves haven't cut off to left or right. Riggan vill know if dey have."

When the woodlands were still and quiet once more, Shogg poked out his head and sighed. "Phwaaaw! Good ole Arvicola! That liddle dodge worked well."

Triss climbed up onto the bank, flexing her cold limbs. "Come on up here, mate, we'll travel much faster to the shore on good dry land!"

Plugg Firetail was immensely proud of his new boat and wanted to show it off. He winked roguishly at the three prisoners sitting bound paw and limb on the sands. "D'ye see the big ship? That's me ole *Seascab*. But I'm cap'n o' two ships now. Wot d'ye think o' that likkle beauty lyin' moored astern of the big 'un?"

Kroova knew they had to keep the Freebooter happy. "She's a beauty, no doubt o' that, Cap'n, pretty as a picture. I never seen one nicer!"

Plugg stood and thumped his swelling chest. "Aharr, an' she's all mine, though she ain't got a sail fer the moment. Some runaway slaves made off with it."

Scarum played along, shaking his head sadly. "Tch tch, can't trust anybeast these days. So then, sah, what's the name o' that handsome craft, wot?"

"I ain't thought of a name yet. Wot would you call 'er?"

Sagax could not help admiring Scarum's crafty reply. "Hmm, difficult to say, sah, not havin' seen the vessel close up, bein' aboard her an' so on. If you were to untie us, an' I promise we won't run away, perhaps we could go and look the craft over and decide on a well-educated name."

Plugg closed one eye, letting the other rove over them. "Untie ye? I ain't no fool, that's why I'm a cap'n. But I'll tell ye wot I'll do. I'll get me crew to carry the three of ye down an' put ye aboard o' me new ship. I'll sit with ye an' we'll 'ave an eddicated talk about namin' 'er!"

As they were carried down the shore by the *Seascab*'s crew, Sagax managed to whisper to Scarum, "Nice try. Pity it never worked, but don't give up."

Plugg had them propped up in the bows. He ordered extra ropes and had them lashed securely to the seat. The silver fox sat astern, leaning on the tiller of the beautiful slave-built ship. He peered over the side, where his crew stood, waist-deep, waiting patiently.

"Belay there, wot d'you thick-'eaded lot want, eh?"

The rat Ripper looked rather hurt at this remark. "We wants to 'ear wot the eddicated rabbit is goin' to name yer pretty ship, Cap'n."

Plugg adjusted his tattered coat hem haughtily. "That's private. Youse git back ashore, go on. Huh, I'm a cap'n an' I got eddicated things to discuss wid these gentlebeasts. Slitty, yore in charge, take 'em back to the fire, will ye? Oh, an' keep an eye out fer Kurda an' those rats of 'ers. If'n we're still 'ere come dawn, then, Grubbage, you bring us some brekkist."

As the crew waded sullenly to the beach, Grubbage muttered, "Wot's all that about rubbish gettin' kissed? Huh, they'll prob'ly sit out there the rest o' the night, an' I'll 'ave t'bring 'em some brekkist!"

Plugg rubbed a paw fondly along the tiller and smiled happily at his three prisoners. "See, I told ye. Pretty as a painted cockleshell, ain't she? C'mon now, which of ye is eddicated about ship names?"

Sagax and Scarum hesitated, so Kroova volunteered. "I think that might be me, Cap'n."

Plugg produced a flask of grog from his voluminous coat. He took a long swig, belched and pointed at Scarum. "That there riverdog don't talk as nice as you."

The young hare hastened to assure him. "Beg pardon, sah, but Kroova is a boat-namin' expert!"

The silver fox took another long pull at his flask. "An expert, y'say? Go on then, riverdog, do yer stuff!"

Still following the broad stream, Shogg and Triss emerged from the woodlands onto a plateau of dunes. Below them the stream coursed along a canyon it had carved from running for countless ages through the dunes. It flowed outward across the shore to unite with the sea. Immediately both threw themselves flat on the coarse grass, viewing the scene before them. A whole crew of vermin were lazing around the embers of a burnt vessel. Beyond that the big Freebooter ship bobbed at anchor, like a huge dark bird of ill omen. Behind it their little boat swayed on the start of an outgoing ebb tide.

Shogg scratched his rudder thoughtfully. "Look, mate, there's our boat! Wot's it doin' down this far? When we left, it was further north up the coast."

Triss shrugged. "Lucky for us we found it. We must have gone in a sort of half-circle. The captain of the big ship moved it south down the coast. So here we all are."

The otter patted the rolled-up sail, which was still tied across his back. "Then let's git down there an' steal our vessel back. We can cut round those vermin dozin' about the fire."

Triss narrowed her eyes as she peered at the small craft. "It won't be so easy as that, mate. I think there's a few of them aboard our ship, about four of 'em, I reckon. We don't have a weapon between us—you gave away your slingstones to the Coneslingers. As for my spear, I've no idea where it is. I must have lost it along the way. So, what now?"

The light of determination shone in the otter's eyes. "We ain't waitin' about 'ere for Kurda an' 'er slavecatcher to find us. I've still got my sling, but there's no stones about. So there's only one thing for it. This is the plan, Triss: We sneak down there an' pinch some weapons off'n those vermin. Then we swim round the big ship an' surprise whatever beasts are in our boat. If we're quiet an' fast enough, we can slip 'er line an' sail off after we toss 'em overboard. So, matey, are ye with me?"

Triss gripped her friend's strong paw. "Sneak down there, steal weapons, sneak round the big ship and steal our craft back. That's a lot of sneaking and stealing for one night, Shogg. I'm with you all the way, mate!"

Tazzin was sitting stooped by the glowing embers, her head bent, snoring gently. As Shogg inched up behind her, his paw encountered something in the sand: a broken oar pole. He grinned happily at Triss. The pole made a distinct thonk. Triss held her breath. Falling silently sideways, the knife-throwing weasel groaned faintly and lay still. Shogg relieved her of two stilettos from her belt. He passed one to Triss and indicated that the daggers, plus the oar pole, were sufficient. They backed off into the darkness outside the pool of light from the guttering fire.

Scarum had taken up the task of ship-naming, since Kroova's efforts had not satisfied Plugg. "Actually, I think *Gutslasher* isn't the right name at all, sah, far too sissyish for a villa . . . er, fine chap like y'self. What about *Rosebud Nosenipper*—how does that sound, wot? Yes, the *Rosebud Nosenipper*—pretty but fierce at the same time. Hmmm, but perhaps *Rottenrudder* does have a certain jolly old ring about it, quite a charming name, I think, wot?"

Sagax caught the hare's attention. "Ssshh, he's asleep!"

The empty grog flask slid from Plugg's loose grasp as his head lolled to one side, mouth open, snoring uproariously. Scarum stared disdainfully down his nose at the Freebooter. "I say, what a dreadful sight! Bet his parents were jolly glad when he upped anchor an' left home, wot?"

Kroova strained wearily at his tight bonds. "Oh, leave 'im be, mate. While Plugg's nappin' we don't 'ave t'keep on talkin' to save our lives. Let the scum snore."

The vessel rocked suddenly. Plugg began to awaken. "Whoozat mates, wha—!"

Shogg bounded swiftly over the stern, a dagger clutched in his teeth and an oar pole in his paw, which he swung. *Thonk!* Plugg collapsed in a senseless heap.

Triss heaved herself up over the prow, dagger at the ready. Shogg saw the three bound friends and hissed at her, "Don't strike, Triss, these beasts are prisoners!"

In a trice Shogg and Triss were slicing through the ropes that bound the trio of captives. The irrepressible Scarum almost whooped with delight. "I say, you chaps, spiffingly well done, wot wot. Allow me to introduce us, I'm—mmmmphhh!"

Triss had her paw across his mouth. She whispered urgently, "No time for all that now. We've got to cut and run, quick!"

Kurda was furious. She stood slashing with her sabre at the reeds of a vast water meadow. "Fools! Dey haff made fools of us!" There was no trace of any creature in sight. Her pink eyes glittering insanely, she turned on Vorto. "Vy did you not carry out mine orders? You should haff captured dem by now!"

Riggan waded about in the shallows of the water meadow, sniffing at bulrushes and inspecting weeds. She shook her head and sloshed back to dry ground. "Huh, we'll never see those voles agin, and the two runaway slaves, they wasn't wid 'em. I told yer you should've let me lead the way, marm. 'Twas all a false trail."

The slavecatcher took a step back as Kurda raised her

sabre. "Excuses, don't give me de excuses, vere did der slaves go?"

Riggan stepped even further back out of blade range. "As y'say, marm, they fooled us. They prob'ly never left the stream."

Kurda stared hard at Riggan. "You mean dey still back dere?"

The slavecatcher shook her head vigorously. "No, marm, they was followin' that broadstream t'the shore. Our best bet now is to 'ead west, that'll take us to the beaches. Then we can travel north 'til we picks up their trail again. They can't go far wid the sea at their backs."

Kurda leaped forward and slapped Riggan's paw hard with the flat of her blade. "Den do it, now! Vorto, get der guards moving on der double, follow Riggan. I vill get dose slaves, even if I have to follow dem to de crack of doom!"

27

Crikulus and the Abbot were in Great Hall, cleaning wax out of the candle sconces, when they heard the squeals of Dibbuns from outside. Before the two old friends could make a move, Skipper and Log a Log rushed by them, shouting as they headed for the Abbey door, "Leave this to us, stay inside, you two!"

Dibbuns fought to get past Skipper and Log a Log as they threw open the door. The little ones were shrieking, "Yeeeek! Big birdy, big birdy! Yeeeeeek!"

Bluddbeak, the great red kite, looked even bigger lying flat upon the lawn with both his enormous wings spread wide. Skipper took one look and commented to the Guosim Chieftain, "Yon must be Ovus's friend Bluddbeak, come to 'elp us."

Log a Log whispered as they approached the red kite, "Aye, though he looks as if he couldn't 'elp 'imself right now, the bird's exhausted, and he seems t'be very old. Look at 'is eyes, they're cloudy with age."

Squinting hard, the red kite clacked his lethal hooked beak. "Keerah! Stand still or die! Bluddbeak slay, be keeerful!"

Skipper held up his paws in a peace sign. "We're friends, matey. Ye've arrived at Redwall Abbey. You'll be Bluddbeak—we asked Ovus to fetch you 'ere. I don't see him, though—where's that owl got to?"

Cocking his head contemptuously on one side, Bluddbeak scoffed, "Kraah! Ovus is old, he will take long to get here!"

Sheathing his rapier, Log a Log bowed politely. "You look tired, sir, is there anythin' we can do for ye?"

Bluddbeak's head swivelled, as if just noticing him. "Karrah! I no tired, this bird just rest. You get me some greensap milk, mix with honey, that what Bluddbeak need right now, mouse."

Log a Log bristled. "I ain't no mouse, I'm a Guosim shrew. If'n y'could see me, ye'd know that right off!"

The red kite's milky eyes glared ferociously at him. "Kreegarr! I see you, nothing wrong with this bird's eyes. Still waiting for my milk an' honey. You very slow!"

All Redwall turned out to see the great red kite lying sprawled on their front lawn. The Abbot seated himself on the doorstep, next to Skipper. He listened to what the otter had to say.

"That rascal Ovus sent us an ancient red kite, Father. Bluddbeak's almost blind, deadbeat weary, an' real bad-tempered. We'd best keep 'im an' Log a Log apart—they put one another's backs up at first sight!"

Abbot Apodemus shook his head despairingly. "We were fools to listen to Ovus. That poor old kite should be back in his mountains, dozing on a warm rock."

"Gangway there, milk'n'honey comin' through!"

Skipper and the Abbot shifted, allowing Friar Gooch and Furrel to pass with the red kite's drink.

Bluddbeak guzzled away at a panful of the mixture, throwing back his head and swallowing noisily. Greensap milk and clear honey slopped down over his throat and chest plumage.

Memm kept the Dibbuns in check with a long window pole, nudging them back. "Steady in the junior ranks there, chaps, that blinkin' monster'll scoff you if y'get too flippin' close!"

Whooping excitedly, the Abbeybabes fled off to the orchard. Memm had created a new game for them: Ruggum, Turfee and Roobil became red kites, chasing the others and trying to scoff them. All good fun.

It was midnoon by the time Bluddbeak had sufficiently recovered himself. The onlookers got out of his way as he hopped awkwardly through the open door and into Great Hall.

Malbun met Gurdle Sprink coming out. "What's that bird up to in there?"

The Cellarhog shrugged. "Great silly thing, 'tis flyin' about an' bumpin' into everythin', see!"

Outside window casements rattled as the huge feathery form inside hit them several times.

Log a Log chuckled sourly. "Prob'ly tryin' to knock some sense into hisself."

Skipper gave a slight start as Ovus flapped out of nowhere to land beside him. The otter took him straight to task.

"Hah, so there ye are, matey. Wot in the name o' seasons made you send us that useless ole bag o' feathers, eh?"

The owl's eyes widened indignantly. "Have a care what you say about Bluddbeak, that kite saved my life more than once. He's the greatest hunter I've ever known, and a much faster flyer than I'll ever be! What have you done with him, where is he now?"

As if in answer, Bluddbeak staggered out into the sunlight. Blinking rapidly, he attempted to arrange his plumage, which was sticking out at all angles. He looked irritable. "Karrakarraka! Not like it in there, this bird bang head on roof, knock against stones. Arrekk! Dark in there, not good for kite! Ovus, friend, you here now. Yayhakkar! We go now an' hunt poisonteeth, slay adders. Come!"

Without another word, the two birds waddled off toward the gatehouse. Appearing very distressed, the Abbot called to Skipper and Log a Log.

"From your description of the thing out there in the woodlands, those two don't know what they're walking into. Hadn't we better stop them?"

The otter watched both birds flap their ungainly way over the outer walls. He turned to Log a Log. "Round up yore Guosim, an' I'll get my crew. We can't stop 'em goin', but at least we can stand by, in case of trouble."

As slowly as the two birds flew, it was difficult keeping up with them by paw. Skipper hurried the rearguard through the trees, whilst keeping sight of the winged pair drifting over the high foliage. Bluddbeak and Ovus finally descended, just short of the clearing where Skipper had found the cloaks and lanterns.

Stumbling from his perch in an elm, Ovus gazed sadly at his talons. "Rheumatiz, can't grip anything properly anymore."

Standing on the same branch where they had both landed, the red kite blinked at the space where the owl had been. "Karrh! What was that, what you say, where are ye?"

Ovus called up from the ground where he now stood. "Down here, friend, it's the rheumatiz."

Bluddbeak licked at the honey and milk stuck in his plumage. "Chakkarr! Wait till you get it in wingfeathers, like me!"

Skipper and his party emerged from the bushes. The red kite flapped his wings in surprise.

"Arreeka! Where you think you going?"

"To see ye don't get yoreselves in too much danger, mates."

Bluddbeak glared down imperiously, offended by the remark. "Krakkah! Not need your help, squirrel. You stay here, or I slay all. Bluddbeak has spoken, stay or die. Karrohakk!"

He launched himself off into the woodlands, followed by Ovus.

Log a Log flicked his rapier in their direction. "Who does that ole relic think 'e is? Come on, Skip, let's go an' see those two crusty birds get themselves eaten. Snake'unter, my footpaw! That kite couldn't tell if you was an otter or a squirrel!"

Skipper did not want his followers spread out—it was

far too dangerous. Keeping close together, they proceeded
cautiously toward the glade. The smell came then, strong
and almost overpowering. Hairs stood rigid on everybeast's neck.

Log a Log signalled them to halt, calling out in a
hoarse whisper, "Bluddbeak, Ovus, come back or that
thing'll get ye!"

There was a terrible sound of squawking, beating feathers and hissing. Raising his javelin, Skipper leaped forward. "We've got t'do somethin', come on!
Redwaaaaaalllll!"

They charged into a scene of what had obviously been
chaos. Branches were snapped, grass flattened, kite feathers strewn everywhere. Ovus was lying prone, with a
strange-looking, golden-furred mouse bending over him.
Of Bluddbeak and the monster there was no trace, save
for the vile sweetish odour enveloping the glade. The
golden mouse caught sight of them and suddenly bolted
off into the undergrowth. Log a Log and four shrews sped
after him.

Skipper hurried to the owl's side. Ovus could only half
open his great dark eyes as he spoke in a weak, fading
voice.

"Tried to save Bluddbeak . . . got bitten. . . . Where's
golden mouse . . . helped me . . . Skipper, that you?"

The otter placed a paw under the owl's head. "Aye, 'tis
me, mate. Lie still, yore bad hurt."

Ovus could not stop his eyes from fluttering rapidly.
"Funny . . . rheumatiz isn't hurting anymore . . . had to
try and save that old kite . . . saved my life several times,
y'know."

His eyes finally closed and his head lolled loosely from
Skipper's paw. The adder's poison had proved fatal. Skipper brushed a paw roughly across his eyes.

"Ole fools, brave, perilous ole fools, why did ye try
it?"

Log a Log and his four Guosim returned, dragging the
golden mouse along with them. He appeared to be in his

late seasons, painfully thin and completely terrified. He was pleading pitifully, "Don't 'urt ole Mokug, mates, I don't mean 'arm to nobeast!"

Skipper placed his paw firmly about Mokug's shoulders, signalling the shrews to release their hold on him. The otter Chieftain's voice was cheerful and comforting.

"We ain't goin' to hurt ye, ole matey. Mokug, eh? Where'd you spring from? Ain't seen you afore."

The golden mouse relaxed then, knowing he was safe. "You ain't Freebooters or Riftgarders, Mokug can tell."

Skipper gave him a reassuring little hug. "We're Redwallers, friendliest beasts y'could ever meet. So tell us, Mokug, wot're ye doin' around 'ere?"

Mokug's mood changed, his eyes darted to and fro, and he moved in close to Skipper, as if for protection. "Been 'ere since I was a young 'un, ever since Sarengo died. I was the King's personal slave, y'know, the only slave 'e fetched on that voyage. 'Course I was only a young 'un then."

Log a Log twirled a paw next to his head and murmured to Skipper, "Looks like ole Mokug's crazy as a fried frog."

Mokug peeped at the shrew from behind Skipper. He smiled. "Well, if'n Mokug's the only beast left alive from that voyage, he ain't so crazy, is 'e, mate?"

Skipper looked down at the pitiful creature. "Yore right there, ole feller, but where d'ye live?"

Mokug tapped the side of his nose secretively. "Where nobeast can find me, but 'tis an 'ard life. I likes you, streamdog. Come on, I'll show ye, 'tis a real golden hamster's den. Nobeast kin find it, 'cept me!"

The golden hamster led them to a bramble patch a short distance north of the glade, where he pointed to a tiny hole amid the thorny creepers.

"In there's where Mokug lives. All these long seasons gone, all on me own. Heehee, but I'm the only one left!"

Skipper looked at the tiny opening and shook his head. "Bit small for me, mate. I'd take the skin off'n meself tryin' t'get in there. You come with us, we'll find ye a decent 'ome at Redwall Abbey."

Mokug wiggled his snub nose. "Will Mokug like it there?"

Skipper winked at him. "Best berth anywheres, ye'll love it!"

The hamster scuttled into his hole, calling back, "Wait, wait, Mokug's got to collect 'is tackle."

While they waited, Skipper told Log a Log of what had happened to Ovus and Bluddbeak. Shaking his head regretfully, the Guosim Chieftain sighed. " 'Twas a foolish venture right from the start. Cold steel or beak an' talon are useless against that horror. Still, I'm sorry about Ovus, an' sorry, too, that I can't take back wot I said about that ole kite. 'E was a warrior born. Me'n my Guosim will bury Ovus where he fell, close to where 'is mate was slain. The owl'd like that."

It took Mokug some little time to pack up his belongings. At last he emerged backwards from the den, dragging a big sailcloth bundle with him. The big ottermaid Churk and her brother Rumbol kindly carried it between them. The party headed off back to Redwall, leaving behind them a lonely grave with a crudely inscribed wood marker:

"Ovus and Bluddbeak, friends and warriors."

Abbot Apodemus was desolated by the loss of the two brave birds. As evening fell, he stood on the west walltop and held his paws wide, calling aloud an old chant to the crimson fires of the setting sun:

"They are gone from the land,
We will see them no longer,
To a place where the fearless ones go.
In the valley of noonshades,
They will meet there to wander,
Where the tranquil green waters do flow.
But oh, their brave memory will rest with us all,
Through the flowers of summer so dear,
Through the winter's cold winds, after autumn
    leaves fall,

Lives a home in our hearts for them here.
Their brave lives were lost in the service of others,
They died so that we might live free,
O ye sad grieving friends, O ye fathers and mothers,
Spare a tear as the sun meets the sea!"

All along the other three walls, Abbeydwellers stood in silence, watching as Skipper moved to stand by the Abbot. As the otter Chieftain raised his javelin overhead, they honoured the dead with a mighty shout:

"Redwaaaaaaaalllll!"

28

Cavern Hall was lit with fresh candles, lanterns and torches. Everybeast took their place at tables ranged foursquare. Though the meal was held in celebration of Ovus' and Bluddbeak's lives, the Abbot had little stomach for food. He had seated Mokug between himself and Mal-bun, and they looked on in amazement as the hamster put away pasties, pies, salads, cakes and tarts, with the gusto of a regiment of hares.

Mokug chuckled through packed cheeks as he helped himself to October Ale, saying, "I ain't tasted a cooked vittle since I was a young 'un. Wunnerful stuff, ain't it, yore majesty!"

A faint smile crossed the Abbot's homely face. "I'm not a king, my friend. You may call me Abbot or Father, whichever you please. Tell me, though, you must have quite a story to relate. Perhaps you'd honour us later?"

The golden hamster nodded as he reached for more cheese. "Story, me? Hoho, I'll say I have. I'll tell it all to ye later, soon as I've taken enough o' these good vittles aboard. Wunnerful stuff, ain't it, yore Abbotship!"

It was a warm night, so lanterns were brought out into

the orchard. Memm and the two otters Churk and Rumbol took the Dibbuns down to the Abbey pond for a paddle before bedtime. Almost every other Redwaller gathered in the lantern lights beneath the orchard trees, to hear Mokug, the golden hamster, tell his story. Mokug arrived with a scroll he had dug out of his belongings. Taking a sip from a beaker of redcurrant cordial, he launched straight into his strange tale.

"I don't remember havin' a mother or father. All that I recall was bein' a very young slave at Riftgard, an awful place, up in the high north, beyond the great seas. A fierce white ferret called Sarengo was the King there. Huh, nobeast disobeyed ole Sarengo. But he liked my golden fur, so I became the King's personal slave. I was luckier than the rest o' the other pore beasts who were slaves at Riftgard. Sarengo's fat, lazy son, Agarnu, treated 'em cruel. He was a bad 'un!

"Well, one day, Sarengo goes on a plunderin' voyage aboard his big ship, the *Seafang*. It was crewed by lots o' Ratguards. I was taken along, too, an' so was Agarnu. He didn't like goin', but the King forced him to. Sarengo had a map with a plan to raid this Abbey, they say he slew some corsair vermin to get it. Yore Abbey wasn't marked on their map, but written there it said that it was up a river that ran onto the western shores, somewhere in Mossflower, a big red castle called Redwall, with many fine things, magic swords, valuable tapestries an' big bells."

Skipper smiled and shook his rudder at the Abbot. "Ole searat stories an' lies, they get more fantastic every season. Magic swords an' big bells. Huh!"

The Abbot nodded as he allowed Mokug to continue.

"But there was a place marked on that map, mates! A place said t'be full of badgers' treasure, an underground fortress called Brockhall. 'Twas said it had lain fergotten many long seasons an' Badger Lords had used it to 'ide their treasures away from vermin."

Malbun snorted. "Utter rubbish!"

The Abbot silenced her with a single look.

Mokug continued. "Well, seein' as it was marked clear

on the map, Sarengo decided to go for Brockhall first. 'Twas hard an' rough goin', I can tell ye, but we made it. Only trouble was, when we got there, the place was full o' poison snakes! Well, not really full. But a full-growed female adder an' three young 'uns ain't t'be sneezed at, as y'know. Old Sarengo wasn't King for nothin', though—he scouted the place out for days an' days, and guess wot he found? Brockhall had two entrances! Aye, a front an' a back one."

Crikulus interrupted. "How do you know, Mokug? What proof is there of two entrances, eh?"

The golden hamster winked knowingly at the ancient shrew. "Be patient an' I'll show ye. But on with me story. When they attacked the place, Sarengo went in the front way. He sent Agarnu an' some Ratguards in the back. Just like Agarnu, though, he arrived late. Sarengo was already caught by the big female adder, callin' for help. Agarnu, the coward, ran straight by his father an' out the front way. I was standin' in the open doorway an' I seen it all. Sarengo gave me his map showin' the secret entrance, told me to stay put outside an' guard it with me life!"

Leaning forward, the Abbot held up a paw. "Excuse my interruption, friend, but is the map on that scroll you have with you?"

Mokug waved the rolled-up parchment triumphantly. "This is it, yore Abbotness, kept it by me since that day. But wait'll I tell ye the rest. Sarengo was a champion battler. He died, but he took the big snake with him—they ended their lives locked t'gether! The three young snakes slew many a rat between 'em, and only six Ratguards got out alive. Well, eight if ye count Agarnu an' me. I've lived in Mossflower for 'ow many seasons I don't know. I always thought one day they'd come back from Riftgard to find the treasure, an' give ole Sarengo a king's burial. So I lived alone an' steered clear of everybeast. I didn't know who was friend or foe, see, an' I valued me freedom. But here I am now, with honest creatures an' goodly cooked vittles. I hope ye'll let me stay. I'm only an old golden 'amster, I won't be no trouble to anybeast in this wunnerful Abbey."

Abbot Apodemus patted Mokug's paw comfortingly. "Of course you can stay. I'm sure you'll be a valuable addition to our Abbey, my friend. So the white ghost and the giant serpent locked together! That explains Ruggum's story—he was telling the truth. And now, Mokug, let us take a look at this map you have kept faithfully."

The Abbot took the scroll and unrolled it. "I thought you said this was a map?"

The hamster tapped his paw on the scroll. "Well, 'tis a map of sorts. Sarengo wrote down the directions instead of makin' a sketch, but it tells everythin'."

Log a Log took a peek at the parchment. "Hah! It ain't even proper writin', just a load of ole squiggles, circles, dots an' loops. Nobeast could make 'ead nor tail o' that lot!"

Mokug nodded in agreement. "That's 'cos 'tis written in the royal script of Riftgard. Only Pure Ferrets of Sarengo's blood can read'n'write like that."

Crikulus groaned and threw his paws up. "You mean to tell us that you've held on to a written map since you were young, but you can't understand a confounded word of it?"

The golden hamster shrugged innocently. "I ain't no scholar, but I'll wager one day that some clever beast'll understand it."

Redwallers crowded round to look at the odd script. There was much scratching of tails, rudders and ears.

"Well, I'm sure I'm not that clever beast!"

"Burr, nay zurr, noither bee's oi!"

The Abbot rolled the parchment up carefully and put it to one side. "Oh dear, what a shame. Well now, have you anything else to tell us at all, think?"

The hamster looked the picture of dejection. "I told ye all I know, Abbotness, on me word I did."

Skipper placed a sympathetic paw about Mokug's shoulder. "Never mind, matey, you did yore best. Let's go inside, ye look tired. Sister Vernal, do you think we can find this good ole beast a bed of 'is own?"

Vernal took Mokug's paw. "I'm sure we can. There's a small room next to the Dibbuns' dormitory—it has a nice bed."

Great tears popped from the hamster's eyes. "D'ye mean a room of me own, with a real bed in it?"

The Abbot took his own kerchief and slipped it to Mokug. "I'll have the otters carry your belongings up. The room and the bed are yours from now on, friend."

Sister Vernal led Mokug inside to his new room. He kept the kerchief jammed to his eyes, stemming the tears. "I'll sweep it out every day an' make the bed up meself. I never 'ad me own quarters, ever. Thankee for yore kindness!"

Friar Gooch was bringing biscuits from his kitchens for the Dibbuns. He passed Vernal and Mokug at the main door. "Dearie me, wot's up with the old hamster? He's cryin' like a babe. Somethin' upset the pore beast?"

The Abbot took one end of the biscuit tray to assist the Friar on his way to the pond. "Mokug isn't upset, he's happy. Funny how we at Redwall take things for granted, isn't it, Friar? A bed and a room of your own: simple things. But if you were a slave who'd never had one, and if you'd lived in a hole in the ground for long seasons, it would be very different. Properly cooked food, lots of new friends, so that you're not alone anymore. Add to that a comfortable room and a clean bed. That's why the poor fellow's weeping—he's overcome by it all."

Crikulus sat on an upturned wheelbarrow in the orchard. Pulling a lantern closer, he stared hard at Mokug's parchment until his eyes began to water. He gnawed at his lip as he pored over the strange symbols.

Malbun ambled across to sit beside him. "Waiting for the solution to jump out at you?"

Putting aside the parchment, the ancient Gatekeeper rubbed his eyes wearily. "Hmph! One would be waiting a long time for anything recognisable to jump out o' that load of gobbledygook!"

Skipper peered over Malbun's shoulder at the puzzle. "Don't give up 'ope, mates. It means somethin'—it must do, if'n somebeast took the trouble to write it all down there."

Malbun yawned and stretched. "That's correct, Skip, but I'm too tired to concentrate on anything. Come on, Crikulus, time for bed. I'll walk you down to the gate-house."

Malbun's companion rose stiffly. "Ooh, my back. I'll take the bed tonight—your turn to sleep in the armchair."

Skipper gave them a lantern to light the way. "A good night to ye both. Don't ferget that scroll, take it with ye. I'll go an' lend a paw to round up the Dibbuns down at the pond."

Paddling and eating biscuits was all the Abbeybabes were interested in. No sooner were they pulled from the shallows by Churk and Rumbol than they would escape from Memm and dash straight back into the water. It was an endless task. The Harenurse rushed about, trying to be everywhere at once.

"Turfee, stand still on that bank, sah, don't move! I say, Churk, grab Roobil, he's back in again!"

"Me wanna nudder bikkit. Ruggum splashed mine, it all wetted!"

Ruggum grinned villainously, holding out a chubby paw. "Give et yurr, oi loikes ee soggy bikkits!"

Memm twitched her ears severely at the little mole. "Out! Out of that blinkin' pond this instant, sah. Out!"

"Don't get yoreself in a tizzy, marm. Leave this t'me!"

Memm smiled with relief as Skipper strode past her

into the water, a long shrimp net draped across his shoulders. "That's the ticket, Skip, fish the blighters out and we'll make soup of them!"

Churk and Rumbol took the net ends, while Skipper held the centre. They captured the little ones neatly in a single sweep. Keeping them confined within the net, the three otters and Memm herded the protesting mass of Dibbuns back into the Abbey and straight up to the dormitory.

But they would not go to sleep without a song. Mokug came out of his room and obliged. The Dibbuns were delighted. This was a song they had never heard, sung by a funny old golden mouse. Mokug had a reed flute, too, which he played quite well. Even Memm and the otters lay down on the little truckle beds to listen.

"O I caught a fish in the water,
I caught a crab an' his daughter,
I caught a flounder an' a sole,
An' I caught an ole tadpole.

They all criiiiiied,
'Mercy me, please let us free,
We'll swim back to our mothers.
My very kind sir, now please be fair,
An' go an' catch some others!'

Well, I saw a cod in the water,
Shoved in me net an' caught 'er,
I saw a clam, an' a fluke so fine,
So I caught 'em on me line.

They all criiiiiied,
'Mercy me, please let us free,
We'll swim back to our mothers.
My very kind sir, now please be fair,
An' go an' catch some others!'

Farewell they swam off singin',
'Til both me ears was ringin'

'Cos I fell in the sea so dark,
An' got caught by a shark.

Then I criiiiiied,
'Mercy me, please let me free,
I'll swim back to me mother.
My very kind sir, now please be fair,
An' go an' catch some other!' "

The Dibbuns learned the chorus and enjoyed it so much that they made Mokug sing it twice more. Obligingly, the golden hamster did this, and then sang a few more comic ditties. In the course of all the singing, Skipper closed his eyes and drifted off to sleep. He looked so peaceful lying on the little truckle bed, none of the others had the heart to wake him, so they left the big otter snoring gently in the Dibbuns' dormitory.

29

When pale dawn sunlight crept over the dormitory windowsills, Skipper sat up blinking. It took him a moment to recognise where he was. Then he remembered the dream. Silently he slipped off the bed. The Abbeybabes were still slumbering, some snoring, others whimpering and giggling in their sleep as they dreamt small dreams. Noiselessly the otter Chieftain padded out, closing the door gently behind him. Then he ran like the wind, down the stairs, taking two at a time and charged across Great Hall.

Furrel, the assistant cook, was coming in from the orchard, carrying a trug of fresh strawberries with morning dew still glistening on them. As Skipper dashed out the door, the molemaid bobbed him a swift curtsey.

"Gudd mawnin', zurr, be ee not a stoppen furr brekkist?"

However, breakfast was the last thing on Skipper's mind.

Malbun Grimp was wakened by the knocking on the gatehouse door. She pulled herself out of the armchair, grumbling, "All right, I'm coming, leave the door on its hinges, will you!"

Framed by a flood of sunlight and dust motes, Skipper bounded in. Crikulus scrambled from his bed, tousle-headed. "Great seasons, are we being attacked by a vermin army?"

The otter raised his rudder politely to them both. "G'mornin', marm, mornin', sir. I 'ad a dream last night!"

Scratching his head frowsily, Crikulus yawned. "That must've been very nice for ye, but not uncommon. I had a dream, too, an' so did Malbun, I'll wager."

Skipper sat down on the bed. The urgent tone of his voice caught their attention. "Aye, but not like this 'un, mates. My dream was of Martin the Warrior—he spoke to me. Get that pawring we found in Mossflower, an' the scroll, too!" The wood mouse and the shrew were now wide awake and listening.

The scroll was still on the table. Malbun produced the heavy gold pawring from a wall cupboard. She struggled to keep the excitement from her voice. "Here they are. Now take your time, don't hurry, try to think clearly. What was your dream about?"

The otter slowed himself visibly as he explained, "Martin came into my mind when I lay sleepin'. He was holdin' the scroll an' wearin' that pawring. Then 'e pointed at the pawring an' said, 'The leaf is three times five, you must remember. Tell Malbun an' Crikulus that the leaf is three times five.' Then Martin was gone. I dreamed no more, but I remembered wot 'e said, word for word!"

Malbun bowed her head slightly. "Thank you, Skipper, you did well. Crikulus, my friend, it seems that we've been given our first clue by none other than Martin the Warrior. So you open up the parchment and I'll study this pawring. Let's make a start."

Skipper hovered anxiously over them. "Anythin' I can do to 'elp you two goodbeasts, anythin' at all?"

Crikulus smiled hopefully at him. "Er, breakfast?"

The big otter bounded off, chuckling. "Right y'are, brekkist for three comin' up, mates!"

Malbun placed the pawring in a shaft of sunlight, its two jetstones glowing darkly on either side of the four symbols.

"Hmm, Skipper said that Martin pointed at the pawring. Now let me see, the leaf is three times five." She studied it briefly, then pointed at the next-to-last symbol. "This is leaf-shaped. It even has a mark like a leaf vein running through its centre. Yes, this is the leaf."

Crikulus showed her the parchment. "That shape shows up all over here, and the other two shapes as well, because obviously both end symbols are the same. But here's your leaf: twice on the top line, three times on the second line, once on the third line, three times on the fourth line, and once on the bottom line of those two rows that are set apart. Ten times in all, what d'you make of that?"

Malbun shook her head. "Ten times, that's only two times five. We're looking for three times five. Count them again."

Crikulus did as he was bade, but his first count proved right. "That leaf only appears ten times, I'm positive!"

Mokug was up and about early on his first morning. He went downstairs to explore his beautiful new home, strolling hither and thither with a radiant smile on his face and whistling softly between his teeth.

Friar Gooch popped his head around the kitchen door. "A good morn to ye, friend. Come in, we're just getting the breakfast ready. I'm Gooch, the Friar of Redwall."

A few moles were pulling hot scones from the ovens. Furrel was busy ladling a blob of meadowcream onto each scone and topping it off with a strawberry. She wrinkled her nose in a jolly manner at Mokug. "Do ee loike to try wunn, zurr?"

The hamster eagerly accepted her offer. "Thankee, pretty miss, I'd like that fine!"

The molemaid giggled. "You'm keep callen oi pretty an' oi'll let ee 'ave 'em all, zurr!"

Skipper trundled a trolley out of the steamy mist from a line of bubbling pans, nodding affably to Mokug. "Top o' the morn to ye, mate. Load yore brekkist on this trolley an' we'll take it to the gatehouse. Crikulus an' Malbun are lookin' at yore scroll down there. If'n ye eat with all the Redwallers, those Dibbuns'll mob ye. They always do that to newcomers an' guests."

Malbun and Crikulus made Mokug welcome. Over breakfast they told him of Skipper's dream and their efforts to interpret the symbols. Malbun took the pawring from her apron pocket and showed it to Mokug. "Ever seen anything like this before?"

Fear and hate suffused the hamster's face. "That's the pawring of King Sarengo. I've seen it many a time, aye, an' felt it too. Ole Sarengo often lashed out at me when 'e was wearin' it. See that scar over me left eye? Those black stones did that. Sarengo just laughed when 'e saw me lyin' on the floor with blood runnin' down me face. Oh, I've seen it before, mate, believe me!"

Malbun's voice softened. She felt sorry for the hamster. "What about these signs? I don't suppose you know what any of them mean, do you?"

Mokug did not even have to look at the symbols. "Oh, those, any slave at Riftgard could tell ye that, marm. It stands for Royal House of Riftgard. Ye see it stamped or carved on anythin' in the kingdom over there."

Skipper pushed a bowl across to Mokug. "Try some o' this, messmate, 'otroot'n'watershrimp soup. If'n it's good for otters, it should do you good, too. Put a sparkle in yore eye an' a spring to yore step!"

Whilst they were joking and laughing at the taste of food new to Mokug, Crikulus took the pawring and scroll,

along with his beaker of mint tea. The old Gatehouse
Keeper went outside to sit on the wallsteps in the morning
sun. He stared at the pawring and the parchment alternately, repeating to himself, "Royal House of Riftgard,
the leaf is three times five."

Churk the ottermaid wandered up with a scone and a
beaker of dandelion-and-burdock cordial. She sat beside
the old shrew. "Ah, a bit o' peace an' quiet at last. Ye
wouldn't believe the noise those Dibbuns are makin' in the
orchard."

Crikulus continued talking to himself, ignoring
Churk. "The leaf is three times five, Royal House of
Riftgard."

The burly ottermaid listened to the odd phrases. "Leaf
is three times five, wot's that supposed to mean, sir?"

Crikulus looked up, as if just noticing her. "Are ye any
good at puzzles and riddles, miss?"

Churk winked confidently at him. "You just try me.
Skipper says I'm too clever for me own rudder sometimes. I like tryin' to solve things."

Showing her the pawring and parchment, Crikulus explained. "You see these four symbols on the ring? Well,
they stand for Royal House of Riftgard. The sign shaped
like a leaf is the one I'm interested in. Now, the key is
hidden somewhere in all of the symbols on this parchment. The only clue to it are these words: The leaf is
three times five. So, miss, does that mean anything to
ye?"

Churk sat silent for a moment, concentrating hard on
the evidence presented to her. Crikulus was about to
speak when she held up a paw. He held his silence whilst
Churk continued scanning the objects. A slow smile began spreading across her face. Still studying the parchment, she spoke. "Can you get me some clean parchment
an' somethin' to write with, sir?"

As Crikulus bustled into the gatehouse, Malbun indicated a single strawberry cream scone. "We saved the last
one for you, my old pal. Where've you been, and where's
the pawring an' scroll got to?"

The ancient shrew rummaged a thin charcoal stick out of a drawer. "You can have the scone. Where's all the clean parchment gone, has somebeast hidden it all?"

Malbun slid a piece from under the armchair cushion. "It's right here where you put it the other day."

Crikulus snatched the section of birch bark parchment. "Young Churk is looking at the scroll an' ring, out on the wallsteps. I think she's onto somethin'!"

As they hurried from the gatehouse, Mokug grabbed the scone. "Waste not want not, especially strawberry cream scones!"

Churk took the writing materials and immediately began scribbling away. Skipper patted her back proudly. "Haharr, you just watch this young 'un solve yore puzzle!"

But the ottermaid was not about to allow them to.

"I'm not havin' you four breathin' down me neck. Now be off with ye, yore makin' me nervous an' I can't think properly. Go on, shoo, an' leave me alone!"

The four Redwallers strolled off toward the orchard. Skipper cast a backward glance at Churk working away. "That 'un's got some nerve, sendin' us off t'play like four naughty Dibbuns. Ah, but she's a brainy one, that niece o' mine."

Malbun remarked drily, "Don't know where she gets all those brains. Certainly not from her uncle."

Nimbly, she dodged a swing from Skipper's rudder. The otter Chieftain spoke out indignantly. "I taught Churk all she knows. Aye, there's nobeast like me at riddles. Lissen to this, mates:

"Y is a letter, yet why is a word.
Don't stalk among grass stalks, a stork's a bird.
I is a letter you see with your eye.
Can U mean you, or is it just I?
Ask me a riddle and I'll tell you Y.

Two's one and one, but there's to and too.
To understand too, I must tell you

There's a B and a bee which should really be
Like a letter C, you don't see in the sea.
I'll ask you a riddle and you tell me.

For what is four? Only two times two.
I can see you C, oh Y say U?
Is a hare with hair a him or a her,
Does it eat good fare, and have fur that is fair?
Two pears make one pair, that's your answer, sir!"

Mokug shook his head in amazement. "Can ye say that again?"

It was an old Redwall riddle, and Crikulus gave the answer that everybeast had learned at Abbey school.

"There's a pane in my window that never feels pain,
And he's at a loss to say it again.
So now is now, but as you know,
A know without K would still sound like no!"

Malbun smiled wistfully. "I remember old Brother Frumble teaching us that at Abbey school. Ah, happy days!"

Mokug sniffed ruefully. "Suppose that's why it puzzled me. I never went to Abbey school, there was no such thing as a school for slaves at Riftgard."

Skipper took the golden hamster's paw. "Never mind, mate, we'll teach ye bit by bit. Yore never too old t'learn."

"Yahaaaar!"

Crikulus almost fell over with fright at the sound. "Great seasons, what was that?"

Skipper was already running back to the wallsteps. "It's Churk—she always makes that noise when she's pleased!"

The ottermaid was beaming from ear to ear when the friends arrived at the wallsteps. "I've solved yore riddle! Come an' sit here while I show ye wot it's all about."

BOOK THREE

The Swordmaid

30

It was the Ratguard Captain Vorto who sighted the fire-glow further north up the shore. The embers formed a small island of red light in the waning night. He pointed it out with his spear. "Princess, look, there's fire burnin' up ahead!"

Not to be outdone, Riggan was pointing also. "There's a ship beyond the tide line yonder, looks like Cap'n Plugg's *Seascab*."

Kurda looked from the fire to the ship, quickening her pace. "Yarr, dat Plugg moved der ship down, she vas anchored further up north, de odder side of dat big hill. I soon find out vot he is playink at!"

Pawsore and weary, the Ratguards were forced to break into a run in order to keep up with her. She checked her pace without warning, scowling as Vorto ran into her back. Kurda's glance was fixed on the stern end of the *Seascab*. Suddenly she was pointing with her sabre and dancing about in agitation at what she could see.

"Mine boat, it is sailin' avay, dey be stealing it back again, dose slaves!"

Riggan watched the sail go up as the small, elegant

craft heeled away from the larger vessel. "See, marm, I told ye I'd lead yer to 'em sooner or later."

The sabre hilt smacked into the slavecatcher's chin, sending her sprawling. Kurda kicked and berated Riggan. "Idiot! You haff not led me to dem, dey are escaping!"

She dashed off up the beach, yelling hoarsely, "Plugg, stop dem, de slaves are makin' off mitt der boat!"

Kurda came storming into the Freebooters' camp, tripping over the unconscious Tazzin. Slitfang and the others, roused from sleeping around the fire, staggered forward, yawning and scratching.

Ripper the searat, no respecter of royalty, snarled irately, "Yew ain't in command 'ere, we takes orders from Cap'n Plugg!"

A whack from Vorto's spearhaft sent him sprawling. The Ratguard captain yelled at the sleepy Freebooter crew, "Then ye'd best get the sand out o' yore brains an' let Plugg know that a vessel's bein' stolen by slaves!"

The *Seascab*'s crew began milling about, bumping into one another.

"Where's the Cap'n? Find Cap'n Plugg, somebeast!"

"Look, they're makin' off wid 'is new sailin' boat!"

Grubbage stared about in bafflement. "Wot's all this got t'do wid a blue trailin' coat?"

Kurda seized the deaf steersbeast by the scruff of his neck. "You come vit me, lunkhead. Vorto, get everybeast aboard de big ship, ve vill catch dem ourselves!"

Triss watched from the stern as the small vessel was swept westward on the outgoing tide. "I can see Kurda—she's driving them all aboard the Freebooter ship. We'd best put on a turn of speed, they'll be coming after us as soon as she gets under way!"

Shogg and Kroova were sharing the tiller between them, whilst Sagax and Scarum took up the slack in the ropes until the mast creaked and the sail billowed tautly on the breeze. Shogg peered grimly at the grey breaking dawn.

"We're goin' to sail out west, then turn an' take 'er back into shore among the reefs. Wot d'ye say, Kroova?"

The sea otter watched as the *Seascab*'s sails began un-furling to catch the wind. "I think yore right, mate, that big ship'd soon run us down in open water. Tack an' weave through the rocks an' shallows. But we've got to draw 'er away from the shore first. All the vermin are aboard 'er—they can't be left on the beach, where they can wade in an' cut us off!"

"Oof! You keep der boat still, I bang mine head!"

Prince Bladd crawled out from under the stern seat, where he had been sleeping. The Pure Ferret gazed up at them. "You not Ratguards or Freebooters, vere you come from?"

He attempted to rise, but Triss kicked him flat. "Well, well, look who it is. We're asking the questions now. How did you get here? Speak!"

Bladd tried to scuttle back beneath the seat as Triss drew her dagger, but Shogg cuffed his ear sharply. "Lay still, an' answer the question!"

Bladd glanced at the unconscious form of Plugg and began to whimper. "Dose Freebooters, dey alvays teasin' me. I come here for der bit of peace und quiet, sleep under der seat. I am der Royal Prince, who are you?"

Triss tapped Bladd's nose with her blade. "You don't remember us, do you? Well, and why should you? We were only two miserable slaves, imprisoned at Riftgard just for the pleasure of your family. You hardly knew we were alive, save for the times you kicked us out of your way, or had some guard beat us for not bowing to you!"

Recognition dawned on Bladd's stricken features. "You der slaves who steal diss boat from Riftgard. Please, it vas mine sister who put you in der cage, not me, no no!"

Scarum called to them from his perch on the bows, "I say, you chaps, don't like to butt in on your jolly old re-union, wot. But I rather think those villains are hard on our trail. If we don't shift ourselves, they'll be dropping in for tea shortly, wot."

Shogg grinned wolfishly. "Mayhap we'd be better lightenin' our load by sendin' these two fer a swim."

Kroova took a backward glance at the progress the
Seascab was making. The big ship was gaining bit by bit.

"Not right now, mate. If'n I ain't mistaken, there'll be
archers an' slingers firin' at us from 'er bows, soon as they
get in range. Tie those two up an' sit 'em both back 'ere."

Scarum wiggled his ears. "Super wheeze, old lad. Right,
you two unsavoury types, prepare to defend our vessel!"

Kurda braced herself in the bows of the *Seascab,* holding
tight to the bowsprit riggings. "Vorto, bring up de archers,
diss ship be close enough soon. Den I slow dem up a bit.
Yarr!"

Tazzin climbed up alongside Kurda, rubbing at a lump
the oarpole had raised. "Look, they're up to somethin'!"

Hurrying to their positions, Ratguard archers set shafts
to their bowstrings. The *Seascab* hove closer to the small
craft. Riggan's sharp eyes identified the two figures sitting
upright and bound on the vessel's stern seat.

"Marm, 'old yer fire, that's Prince Bladd an' Cap'n
Plugg!"

An evil smile lit up Kurda's pink eyes. "Yarr, so 'tis.
Who needs dem—I don't."

The business edge of Plugg's battle-axe prodded
Kurda's spine. Slitfang's voice ground out menacingly, "I
don't care about yore fat stoopid brother, but Plugg Firetail's our Cap'n. One arrow from yore guards an' I'll
make two of ye with this axe, believe me, yer royalness!"

Kurda never turned around, her body trembling with
rage. "Scum, you vill die for diss!"

Slitfang prodded a bit harder. "Aye, but not right now I
won't, missie. I'm givin' the orders, 'cos I'm Cap'n when
ole Plugg ain't aboard the *Seascab.* Tell 'em to stow those
weapons."

Kroova whispered urgently to Shogg, "We better do
somethin' fast, mate, afore they ram us! That ship's too
big, an' she's comin' up too fast."

Shogg sniffed the air and dabbled a paw over the side.
"Yore right. Give it a moment!"

A stream of curses came from the wakened Plugg. "Blister yore blubberin' guts, streamdog. The tide's startin' to turn, ye connivin' plank-tailed pup!"

Shogg laughed. "Thankee for backin' up my judgement, Cap'n. Yore right, the tide is turnin'. Good'n'heavy, too. Right, mates, 'ang on tight, 'ere we go. Kroova, take the tiller. Send 'er round with all ye've got. Haharr, haul on those port lines, Sagax, 'tis our turn to slow them up a bit now!"

Spinning almost on her own keel length, the little craft did a nimble half-circle turn, running a semicircle round the big, ungainly *Seascab.*

Slitfang roared back to Grubbage, "Take 'er round, they've turned tail on us. Take 'er round!"

Tazzin's shout cut across the command shrilly. "Slitty, git ropes out! That streamdog's just pushed the Cap'n an' Prince Bladd overboard. They're in the sea!"

Shogg had cut Plugg and Bladd's bonds before he kicked them off the stern into the waves. Both beasts were floundering, waving wildly as the *Seascab*'s bow waves washed over them.

"Bring 'er about! Glubbleubble! Throw me a line, ye swabs!"

"Gallugallug! Help, I'm drownink, I cannot svim!"

Slitfang kept the battle-axe pressed against Kurda's spine. "Cap'n's in the water, bring 'er about quick! Ripper, Scummy, get those lines to midships. Yew 'ang on, Cap'n, we'll get ye out o' there!"

Kroova sent the vessel skimming and skipping over wave-crests, sailing dead east on the powerful sweep of a heavy running floodtide. Triss bared her teeth as she watched Bladd and Plugg being hauled aboard the *Seascab.* "I would've liked to have tied a stone to that white ferret's paws!"

Shogg winked at the squirrelmaid. "No ye wouldn't, Triss, yore made o' better stuff than that. When the right day arrives, we'll take our revenge face-to-face an' sword-to-sword."

Triss's paw trembled as she patted her friend's back.
"You're right, Shogg. I just felt so angry at letting him go
that I had to say something. Right now we're relying on
you and Kroova to lead them a dance around the reefs and
shallows, where they can't follow us."

Shogg sat down next to Kroova and placed his paw on
the tiller. They looked ahead at the pounding surf breaking on the shore.

Shogg spoke. "Due east, dead ahead, eh, mate?"

Kroova nodded. "Dead ahead it is, mate, let's do it together!"

Sagax was bending his back, straining against the
humming sailropes, when he straightened up, alarmed.
"Dead ahead will take us crashing straight onto the shore.
You'll run us aground!"

Triss blinked against the sun rising in splendour to the
east. "Oh, no it won't. I know what you rascals are up to.
Tell him, go on."

Both the otter's paws were clasped on the tiller, as
Kroova told Sagax what was on their minds. "There's one
place that big ship don't 'ave a chance o' follerin' us,
mate. Straight up the stream across the shore!"

Scarum's ears stood straight up in alarm. "I say,
steady on chaps, bit risky, ain't it? What about the jolly
old *Stopdog*? I know she's burned out, but the blinkin'
wreckage is still lyin' in that stream. I mean, won't that
stop us, wot?"

Shogg kept his eyes on the coastline ahead. "Not at the
rate we'll be goin', mate. I 'ad it in me mind to do this
afore we ever boarded this craft to rescue ye. It'll take all
of me an' Kroova's skills, but we'll run on that floodtide
like a pike after a waterfly. We'll either crash through that
wreckage or sink. Either way, 'tis the best course to leave
Plugg's ship be'ind!"

Scarum looked around for something to nibble on, but
could find nothing in the way of food to comfort him.
"Good grief, is that really the plan, Kroova?"

The otter nodded. "Once we're past that wreckage,
we'll row an' sail into the woodlands, through the stream

current. It'll be tough goin', so git yoreself ready for action."

The young hare's ears drooped mournfully. "Huh, should've told old Pluggface to pack us a lunch. I'll face any jolly thing on a full stomach, y'know."

Triss could not help chuckling as she asked Sagax, "How could anybeast think of food at a time like this? Is Scarum always hungry?"

The badger answered the question with another question. "Does night follow day?"

Kurda was still perched on the *Seascab*'s bows, watching the smaller craft's progress. She turned anxiously to Plugg, who was standing nearby, draped in a blanket and swigging hot grog.

"Dey go straight 'head, sailink for der stream, you t'ink?"

She recoiled as the silver fox belched a fraction from her nose. He did not seem unduly worried. "Aye, that's their liddle game. At first I though they'd sail in among the reefs, but they couldn't stay there forever. We'd be circlin', waitin' for 'em to come out. You mark my words, missie, if'n they plans on makin' a run up yonder stream, that'll do me just fine!"

Bladd pulled his blanket tighter about him. Taking a sip from a beaker of steaming grog, he coughed and spluttered. "How vill it do you just fine, Cap'n?"

Snatching the beaker, Plugg drained it at a gulp. "One o' two things, yer princeness: either they'll miss the channel an' run 'er aground, or else they'll smash the bottom out when they whacks into that burnt ole boat. Either way, we'll be in plenty o' time to lay paws on 'em. Though I 'opes they only runs my nice likkle craft aground. I don't like to see me property damaged, eh, yer 'igh royalness?"

Kurda sneered. "Long as ve capture dem, I don't care!"

Plugg pushed by Kurda and shouted out orders. "Lay south a point, Grubbage, take 'er in short o' that there stream an' drop anchor. Crew! Stand ready an' armed to jump ashore an' grab those imperdent beasts. I'll h'eddicate that rabbit in the ways of me battle-axe when I lays paws on 'im. We'll see 'ow pretty 'e talks then!"

With a strong breeze at their backs and the tide running high, the two otters held the tiller dead onto the stream mouth, which drew closer by the moment. Sagax dashed up to the bow point, shouting aloud into the bright blue morning, "Let's give her a good old Salamandastron Eulalia to send her in, mates!"

Triss turned to the hare. "I like the sound of that— what's a Salamandastron Eulalia?"

Scarum explained. "Somethin' to make the jolly old fur stand on end, marm, the battle cry of real warriors. Just yell it out loud and long. Right ho, chaps, altogether now."

They roared at the top of their lungs as the sleek vessel whipped head-on into the fresh water. "Eulaliiii-iaaaaaaaa!"

In the narrow mouth, wild following-wave swells drove them like an arrow up the channel.

Because of the time having been spent picking up Plugg and Bladd, the *Seascab* had lost ground, plus the fact that they had to haul in sail to stop them from running aground in the shallows. All this added up to slow the big ship's speed. Kurda was dancing with rage.

"Look, look, dey vent right into der stream, straight in!"

Plugg was donning another frock coat, even tattier-looking than the wet one he had cast off. He smirked confidently. "Don't fret yore pretty white 'ide, dearie, the wrecked boat'll stop 'em, won't it, Slitty?"

Slitfang nodded dutifully. "Aye, Cap'n." What he did not say was that the Freebooters had hauled quite a bit of it, still burning, to feed their fire the previous night.

Ripper raised a paw, but dropped it at a glare from Slitfang, who muttered, "Shut yore gob or 'e'll skin us both!"

As the *Seascab* sailed in closer to land, Plugg went aft to question Grubbage, shouting down the deaf rat's ear, "'Ow far up the stream d'ye reckon that wreck is?"

Grubbage winced. "Ye don't need t'shout so loud, Cap'n. They're about right at that spot now."

"I'd say they've gone clear past it!"

Plugg looked sharply at Riggan the slavecatcher, who had just made the remark. "An' how d'ye figger that out?"

Riggan pointed overboard at the broken and burned struts of timber floating in the shallows. She observed drily, "I watched that float out o' the stream mouth—that means they've broke through an' passed the place. The fire prob'ly burned right through the ketch an' broke 'er up afore they arrived."

A few of the crew standing about nodded guiltily. "Aye, yore right there, matey, she burned right through!"

Plugg kicked out at them and cuffed a few ears. "Then why didn't ye say, why didn't anybeast tell me, eh? Get over the side an' catch 'em, the useless lot o' ye!"

Several Freebooters promptly leaped overboard, but the water closed in over their heads. Grubbage watched them. "Water ain't shallow enough yet, Cap'n. We needs t'be closer in t'shore."

Kurda came running to berate the Captain. "Iz too deep 'ere. Ve need to be closer in!"

Leaning over the rail, Plugg buried his face in both paws. "You 'eard 'er, Grubbage, take the ship in closer to shore."

Grubbage manoeuvred the tiller, muttering darkly, "I ain't throwin' my clothes ashore fer nobeast. I'll just take 'er in closer to the beach!"

Poling and paddling energetically, the friends took their vessel into the high, sandy canyon walls of the dunes. Scarum paused to swat at a curious fly.

"Shove off, you bounder, go an' eat somebeast who's fatter."

Triss could see the *Seascab* drifting to a halt, side-on, far down at the tideline. "Scarum, don't stop to argue with insects. Keep poling!"

Sagax could see overhanging tree foliage further ahead. "We'll be in the woodlands soon—keep going, mates. Kroova, have they left the ship yet? Are they ashore?"

The otter took a quick glance. "One or two of 'em. Wait, they're lowerin' the ship's boat!"

Plugg sat in the jollyboat facing Kurda and Bladd as it splashed gently into the water. "Slitfang, git yoreself in 'ere, you'll be rowin'. Tazzin, Grubbage, Ripper, yore at the oars, too. Come on, move!"

"An' vot about mine captain and Ratguards?"

Plugg leaned back in the most comfortable seat. "Oh, them, they can run both sides o' the bank wid the rest o' my crew. If'n yew wants ter give up yore seat to another beast, you'll 'ave t'get out an' walk too. I ain't takin' on any more passengers. Wot d'you say, Bladd, me ole mate, eh?"

The fat Prince snorted indignantly. "I not gettink out der boat for others, let dem valk!"

The silver fox toyed with his battle-axe, teasing Kurda. "Yew travel in style, me beauty, wid yore beloved brother an' yore dear old uncle Plugg. Don't fret now, we'll punish those naughty slaves an' get my nice likkle boat back."

Kurda smiled back at the Freebooter. "An' ven 'tis all over, you deliver me back to mine father?"

The Freebooter winked broadly at her. "Why, bless yore 'eart, pretty one, of course I will!"

Kurda's eyes went cold. "Gutt, den I vill see him hang you in chains over his gates."

31

Sunshine and shadow dappled through the trees onto the stream's surface. It was far more calm running in the woodlands. Shogg took down the sail and furled it. The others kept rowing and poling, with Scarum expounding his list of complaints.

"I say, my bloomin' paws are jolly well sore, must be worn down to the flippin' bones by now. Blisters on top of my blisters, that's what I've got!"

Sagax poled stoically onward. "Should have blisters on your tongue, the way you're yammering on there. Give it a rest."

However, Scarum was not to be deterred so easily. "A rest? Jolly good idea, if y'ask me. A rest and a whacking great feed. We're going to have to stop soon and eat, y'know. It's not fair, a chap starvin' to death, all because a few mangy vermin are chasing us. Can't one of you bright sparks think of somethin' to slow 'em up or put 'em off a bit, wot?"

Sagax snorted. "We could always chuck you overboard like we did those other two. That'd slow them up."

Kroova stumbled as his pole hit a root.

Shogg peered through the crystal-clear water. "Look! See that root running across the bottom of the streambed? There's lots of 'em from the trees on the bank. Just the sort o' thing we need, mates."

Picking up the broken oarshaft that he had used as a weapon earlier, Shogg felt the broken end; it tapered down to a blunt point. The broken oar was almost as tall as he was. "Kroova, I think we need two otters for this job, matey."

They huddled together at the stern of the boat, whispering. Shogg had his knife out, whittling the broken end of the oar to a point until it began to resemble a sharp wooden stake. Kroova leaned over, peering steadily down into the stream.

"There, that's the place. Come on, we got work t'do. Sagax, keep 'er goin' upstream, don't stop. We'll join ye later, won't be long."

With scarcely a ripple, both otters slid overboard into the stream. Scarum glanced astern. "D'you think they've spotted a good fat fish? I'm famished—the jolly old tum's making an awful noise, wot?"

The hungry hare was a constant source of amusement to Triss, who smiled as Sagax berated him: "Listen, twiddly ears, stop moaning about your stomach and get this vessel moving. We're deadbeasts if those vermin catch up with us. You don't hear Triss and me complaining all the time. Now, get on with it!"

Scarum poled away resentfully, chunnering to himself, "Huh, you don't complain, 'cos you're not a hare. We're noble beasts, with bloomin' noble appetites, too. Blinkin' badgers an' squirrels can live on a pawful of nothin', but not this mother's child. I need a good six square meals a day, at least!"

Triss whispered in his ear sympathetically, "I know they don't understand you, but don't fret. Keep working and I'll personally see that you get a good big feed as soon as we get time to rest."

As Sagax watched Scarum poling diligently away, he spoke out of the side of his mouth to the squirrelmaid.

"Look, he's stopped complaining. I could never get him to work like that. What did you say to him, Triss?"

"Oh, I just told him I'd get him something to eat as soon as we get the chance."

The badger shook his great striped head. "You might be sorry you said that."

The deck shook as Kroova and Shogg leaped aboard. Scarum noticed immediately that they had returned empty-pawed.

"Flamin' bounders, I thought you were bringin' back that big fat fish as a surprise for me!"

Shogg patted the hare's back. "Sorry, mate, we left the surprise back there for those vermin to find."

Plugg Firetail had the ship's jollyboat speeding like an arrow upstream. His method was simple: The moment his four rowers showed signs of tiring, he sent them ashore to run along the banksides and chose four fresh vermin to replace them.

Princess Kurda sat stonefaced as the Freebooter harangued four of her own Ratguards scornfully. "Row, ye lily-livered swabs—come on, bend yore backs an' pull those oars. Youse rats've had an easy life, yore all fat'n'lazy. I'll show ye 'ow a Freebooter works. Row, ye slab-sided, bottle-nosed bangtails, yer not bowin' an' scrapin' to a princess now, yore rowin' a boat!"

Bladd giggled. He liked the Captain's colourful curses. "Yarr, you row like de Capting say, bottle-nosed svabs! Yowch! Capting, Kurda pinch me vit 'er sharp claws."

The Princess glared hatefully at her fat brother. "Shut your slobberin' face, stupid, or I t'row you overboard!"

Plugg shook a paw at her, his voice dripping sarcasm. "Now, now, beauty, ye shouldn't be usin' language like that to yore dear brother. Come on, kiss 'im an' make up."

Bladd recoiled in disgust. "Yekk, she not kissin' me!"

The silver fox rounded on the four rats at the oars.

"Who told you idle scum t'stop rowin', eh? Now put some energy into it, afore I chop off yore tails an' make ye eat 'em. Row, ye pickle-pawed oafs!"

Oars dipped swift and deep as the jollyboat sped from the dune canyons into the sheltering shade of woodlands. Plugg reached up and snapped off a long green willow branch. "First one I spot idlin' gets a taste o' this!"

Vorto called across the bank to Riggan, who was trotting along the other edge, "Are we still on their trail?"

Plugg interrupted before the slavecatcher could answer. "No, matey, they've took to the sky an' they're flyin' south like the birds. Idjit! This is the only way they can go in a boat. Huh, an' I thought my crew was stupid!" He lashed out at the rowers with his willow withe. "We should be plunderin' an' loadin' up wid loot, instead o' chasin' a few lousy slaves. . . . Aaaaaargh!"

Without warning, the rowers had sent the jollyboat speeding straight onto the sharpened wooden stake that Shogg and Kroova had lodged tight between two roots on the streambed. It protruded upward at an angle, facing downstream, the point lurking fractionally below the surface. As the boat hit the stake, it smashed through the side of the prow like a huge spearpoint. Water came gushing in. Plugg's agonised scream was not without reason—the stake had gotten him in the lower back, just short of his haunches.

Pandemonium reigned. Kurda seized two of the Ratguards who had been rowing, screeching at them as the boat rapidly filled up, "Get me to de shore, quick!"

The two of them bore her to the bank, with the other two carrying Prince Bladd, who was wailing in terror, "Don't let me drop, I cannot svim!"

The crew of the *Seascab* hurled themselves into the stream. Cutlasses and hatchets crashed into the sinking boat timbers as they hacked wildly, striving to free their captain. Plugg had passed out with the pain, and Grubbage held the silver fox's head above the waterline.

"Gerrim out, mates, 'urry, or the Cap'n will get drowned!"

Slitfang chopped away madly at the stake, which was holding Plugg in the boat. "Tazzin, lend a paw 'ere, bring yer dagger or we'll lose the Cap'n!"

They freed Plugg and carried him up to the bank. Scummy the stoat and Grubbage, who both had experience in treating wounds, attended the fox's limp, wet form, whilst the rest of the crew looked anxiously on. Without a captain, the Freebooters were like lost creatures.

Kurda watched them, a smile of pitiless cruelty on her face. "Dere is no need for de boat now, so I vill continue hunting der slaves mitt my Ratguards. Yarr, de fox does not have a lot to say now, does he? Tchah!"

She spun on her paw, only to find herself surrounded by Freebooters. Tazzin licked her dagger blade meaningly.

"Yew ain't goin' anywhere an' leavin' us wid a wounded cap'n. We all stays 'ere til Plugg's ready to move, see!"

Vorto came hurrying up, with his spear at the ready. "Back off, seascum, yew ain't orderin' our princess about!"

Slitfang sneaked up behind and felled Vorto with a hefty blow of his cutlass hilt. Placing a paw on the senseless rat, he leaned across and hissed in Kurda's face, "I'm cap'n while old Plugg's out of action, an' I says we stay. If'n ye wants to challenge my order, yer welcome to try. I'll fix it so you an' yore rats stays 'ere fer good, wid the insects to pick over yore bones. Well?"

Kurda dropped her eyes. There was no point in trying to argue with dangerous sea vermin. "Yarr, ve stay."

Midafternoon found the five friends taking a cutoff up a sidestream. Shogg rested his oarpole and listened to the stillness hanging upon the quiet sunny air.

"Wot d'ye think, Kroova, did our liddle plan work?"

The sea otter leaped from the boat to the nearby bank. "I think it prob'ly did, mate. Don't seem to be a sound of anybeast followin'. Can you 'ear anythin', Triss?"

Bounding ashore, the squirrelmaid shot up the trunk of

a tall elm. She was back down directly. "Not a move anywhere—I think we're safe for the moment. Right, let's get
some vittles organised, I'm hungry!"

Scarum was at her side in the wink of an eye. "Well,
thank me auntie's pinny for a handsome gel with a bit o'
sense, wot, excellent suggestion, marm. Capital!"

They split up and went foraging into the woodlands,
whilst Triss stayed behind to guard their boat.

Sagax was the first to return. He brought some wild
berries and a few early plums, which, while sweet, were
still quite hard. The two otters arrived next, followed by
Scarum, who assessed the fruits of their search. He was,
by turns, both critical and optimistic.

"Not bloomin' much, chaps, is it? A few measly
berries, some hard-as-rock plums, a load of roots, dearie
me! Still, I suppose we'll make somethin' of them once I
start cookin', wot?"

Triss shook her head. "Sorry, no fires to give off
smoke signals. Besides, what would you use for a cooking pot?"

Scarum's ears drooped. "I thought you were on my
side! What in the name of fiddlesticks d'you expect us to
do, scoff 'em raw an' drink streamwater? It's not jolly
well civilised."

Sagax pulled the boat into the land and moored it to a
tree. "Sshh! Listen, can you hear singing?"

The strains grew louder and clearer as they listened.
From round an upstream bend, four shrew logboats appeared. They were packed with shrew families, singing at
the tops of their voices to the accompaniment of drums
and tambourines. Stringed instruments blended with the
harmonious melody. The shrews did not appear to have a
single care in the world.

    "Summer, summer, what a lazy afternoon,
    Music, laughter, sun a-waitin' for the moon,
    Twilight, my light, stream is all a-slumber, too,
    Babes a-sleepin', willows weepin', skies so blue.

Nothin' like a good ole river,
On a sunny afternoon with you,
Sittin' in a dear ole logboat,
Plunkin' out a tune or two.

We'll sail off to a shady bower,
Kettle will be boilin' soon,
While we sport an' play, the livelong day,
An' sleep beneath a golden moon.

I'll find a place so filled with mem'ries,
Where the waters kiss the shores,
When yore ma an' pa ain't watchin',
You'll hold my paw in yours.

Then we'll have a good ole picnic,
With such nice things to eat,
While the babes all go a-paddlin',
Let's dance to the ole drum's beat.

Summer, summer, what a lazy afternoon,
Music, laughter, sun a-waitin' for the moon,
Twilight, my light, stream is all a-slumber too,
Babes a-sleepin', willows weepin', skies so
  blueooooooooooooh!"

Triss had never seen creatures so happy. There was no
question of their being foebeasts. She dashed into the
shallows, waving and calling to them, "Hello there, good
afternoon to you, friends!"

A fat shrew wife in flowered pinafore and bonnet
waved her parasol back at the squirrelmaid. "An' the same
to you, missy, that's a luvverly boat you got there. Want to
tag along an' join our picnic? There's plenty for everybeast, yore welcome!"

Scarum danced along the bankside, grinning like a
buffoon and blowing kisses outrageously. "Profusions of
thankfulness, gorgeous creature, we accept your wonderful offer gratefully, nay, jubilatorially!"

Shogg squinted one eye and scratched his rudder. "Ju-
bila . . . wotsit? I'd better warn 'em not to go downstream,

they'll run into those vermin. Ahoy, marm, comin'
aboard!"

He dived into the water, vanished momentarily, then
popped up on the logboat's deck. "Beggin' yore pardon,
marm, but we're bein' chased by a pack o' vermin. I
wouldn't go downstream if'n I was you."

A stout old shrew touched his snout respectfully.
"Thankee for tellin' us, sir. Looks like we'll 'ave to put
about an' go t'the water meadows. You follow us in yore
pretty boat. Nobeast'll find ye there, we'll make sure o'
that." He waved a paw back upstream. "Backpaddle,
we're goin' to the water meadows an' takin' these goodbeasts in tow. Backpaddle, Guosim!"

Poling along behind, they followed the logboats along
a series of cutoffs and backwaters. Scarum worked harder
than his four companions.

"Keep up, chaps, don't want t'get lost an' miss the picnic now, do we? Stop dawdlin' an' move yourselves,
wot!"

Scarum had a dreadful singing voice. However, that
did not stop him from breaking out into an off-key warble:

> "O I don't wish to be rude,
> But the very mention of food,
> Is the nicest word I've heard,
> Tumpty tumpty tum tum,
> Lalalah deedly dee,
> I've forgotten the next flamin' word . . ."

Shogg chuckled. "Keep singin' like that, mate, an'
they'll banish ye from the picnic for frightenin' the
babes."

Dragonflies hovered low over platelike water lilies, butterflies and gaily hued moths stood swaying on reed ends,
bees droned to and fro with a leisurely hum. The water
meadow was a haven of peace and tranquillity, fringed
with bulrushes and backed by willows, splurge laurel and

catkin-laden osiers. The Guosim shrews lashed their log-boats to the small vessel, forming an island in the shallows that was hidden by reeds and treeshade. Food hampers and picnic baskets were brought out, lots of them.

Scarum could scarcely restrain himself. "Oh corks, I say, these shrew chaps don't believe in stintin' themselves, do they, wot? Allow me to help you with that heavy grub container, marm. Hoho, your little ones look fine and chubby—I expect you feed 'em jolly well!"

He flinched as the hefty paw of Sagax drew him to one side. The young badger's eyes had a no-nonsense look about them. "Listen carefully to what I say, Scarum. If I catch you hogging food, or offending these good shrews, I'll personally deal with you. No excuses this time—put one paw wrong and you're on your own. Triss, Kroova, Shogg and myself will personally disown you, and our friendship will be ended. Now, did you hear me? Have I made myself clear?"

Scarum twisted neatly out of the badger's grasp. He appeared quite indignant. "Me, are you talkin' about me, old chap? Tut, pish an' fiddlesticks, how you can say such things is beyond belief. You mind your own manners, sah!"

He stalked regally off to join the feast. Triss murmured to Sagax, "Don't worry, I'll keep an eye on him."

The jollity, singing, dancing, drinking and feasting in the sunlit water meadow made Triss happy, but wistful. Mimsy, the kind shrew wife who had invited them, passed the squirrelmaid a leek-and-turnip pasty.

"Eat up, m'dearie, this ain't no day for mopin' about. What ails ye, little sad face? Have some raspberry fizz!"

Triss accepted her offer, forcing a smile. "Are your creatures always as happy as this, Mimsy?"

The shrew chuckled. "Only when we've got nothin' t'be sad about—we've got our ups an' downs, y'know. I can sense that you've not led a carefree an' happy life, Triss, but try an' be like us. When ye get the good times, don't stop to mope about the bad 'uns. Enjoy yoreself while ye can."

Scarum lifted his nose out of a high-piled plate to agree. "Well said, marm, that's my motto too, wot. Even though I was reared poorly, often beaten an' starved constantly. Crusts, roots an' springwater, that's what I was jolly well brought up on. Pale, thin little chap, that was me. Oof!"

Sagax, who had given the hare a playful buffet on the back, laughed heartily. "Plus being a terrible fibber, a great fat scoffbag, and the biggest bounder at Salamandastron. If your mum and dad could hear you talking like that! Pay no attention to the flopeared fraud, marm."

Mimsy stroked Scarum's paw. "Let him be. I like a beast who can tell a good fib—this hare is fun t'be with. Come on now, Scarum, I'm sure you can manage some damson crumble an' cream?"

From behind the backs of Triss and Mimsy, the incorrigible hare made a face at Sagax, as he allowed himself to be pampered. "Seasons bless you, marm, I've never tasted damson crumble an' cream in m'life. I've watched Sagax stuffin' it down many a time, though. He's the son of a mountain Lord, y'see, while I'm just a lowly peasant type. I say, that tart looks rather nice, wot!"

Mimsy carved off a large slice. "Oh, you poor beast, here, try some, an' have some more raspberry fizz."

Sagax looked on aghast as Mimsy and Triss plied Scarum with delicacies from every hamper. The gluttonous hare accepted everything coyly.

"Oh, I wonder if I'll be able to eat a portion that big? I'm only used to nibblin', y'know, but thank y'marm. I'll certainly try my best t'get through it, wot."

Kroova flicked an apple pip at the young badger. "You should see yore face, matey!"

32

Plugg Firetail awoke in the late evening and found himself lying by a fire, covered in an old blanket. Scummy and Grubbage hovered about, watching him anxiously.

"Take it easy, Cap'n, don't try to sit up, you been wounded."

Plugg lay still, listening to them relate what had taken place when the jollyboat was rammed by a stake. He put a paw to his lower back and grimaced. "It 'urts like the blazes, mates, but I'll be shipshape soon. No real damage done, eh?" He glared quizzically at the pair as they kept silent. "Wot? Tell yore cap'n, wot's up, am I bad 'urted?"

Scummy's paw scuffed the grass awkwardly as he explained. "That sharp cob o' wood, Cap'n, it stuck deep in yore, bot—er, 'indquarters. We managed t'get it out, me'n Grubbage. . . ."

Plugg was fast losing patience. He gritted at them. "Stop picklepawin' round an' tell me wot's wrong!"

They both moved out of paw range. Grubbage stammered, "You ain't got no tail, Cap'n, it sorta fell off."

The Freebooter's ugly face squinched up in horror. "Me tail? Fell off? Where is it?"

Scummy held up the severed tail. "I got it, Cap'n."

The fox covered his face and groaned in despair. Plugg's tail had been his proudest possession. He had been born silver-furred, unlike other foxes. However, his tail was a beautiful goldy-red–furred one. This had given rise to his second name, Firetail. Often as a young Free-booter Plugg would wash his tail each day, carefully shampooing it with soapwort and almond oil. On going into battle, he had always ordered a crewbeast to run be-hind, holding a lantern close to display the shine and sheen of that tail. But now the feared Freebooting Cap-tain, Plugg Firetail, had not even a stump of this former glory. Swiftly he snatched the tail from Scummy, looking about furtively.

"Who else knows I've lost me tail, eh?"

"Nobeast, Cap'n, we never told any of 'em!"

"Aye, on me oath, Cap'n, only us knows, an' you, too, o' course!"

Plugg's eyes danced shiftily as he pondered a solution. "Get sticky stuff."

Grubbage leaned forward, squinting. "Why d'ye want skilly'n'duff, Cap'n, are ye 'ungry?"

The fox swatted him with the tail. "You shurrup! Scummy, get me some sticky stuff, any kind, but make it good'n'sticky, 'asten now!"

He stuffed the tail under his blanket as Kurda ap-proached. She eyed him up and down in disappointment. "So, you don't be dead, yarr. Vot a pity, I vas hoping der shtake vould haff slayed you."

Plugg spat, but missed her. "So sorry not to please yer, but 'ere I am, fit'n'well, yore 'igh royalness."

Kurda shrugged. "Never mind, der vound might get poisoned and kill you, den I be very glad, yarr."

Plugg bared his crooked teeth at the Pure Ferret. "If'n it does, I'll come back an' haunt yew, missie!"

She stalked off, sniggering to herself.

Scummy returned with a beaker that contained a few lumps of pine resin. He placed it on the fire. "This should do the trick, Cap'n. I'll 'ave ye lookin' good as new in a

tick. Grubbage, you sit on the Cap'n an' 'old 'im still.
This is goin' to 'urt, Cap'n, 'old tight!"

"Yeeeeguuurrr! Blisterin' barnacles, that stuff burns.
Pour some in the wound, too, mate, that'll keep it clean. I
ain't about t'die, just ter please that snotty liddle madam.
Well, 'ow does it look, Grubbage? Tell the truth now!"

"Looks pretty as a summer morn covered wid roses,
Cap'n."

The Freebooter stood up, wincing. "Never mind no
summer morn wid roses, long as it looks like my tail, in
its proper place, too. Well, does it?"

Both crewbeasts nodded furiously. "Oh, it do, Cap'n, it
do!"

Before they could blink, Plugg had them both by their
noses. His claws sunk in ruthlessly. "Now lissen, buckoes,
one word of this gets out an' I'll be a laughin'stock. So,
you keeps yore gobs buttoned tight, or I'll skin ye both
alive an' make a cloak of yore 'ides. Do yew 'ear me? Say
'Aye aye, Cap'n' if'n ye do."

Tears flooding their eyes, both crewbeasts danced tip-
pawed on the spot as they obeyed the command.

"Hi hi hi, Capin, uth heerth yith. Yeeeeek!"

Plugg limped a few steps—the tail held firm. He
wheeled on Scummy and Grubbage. "From now on,
wherever I goes, you two follow right be'ind me. Everywhere! Keep yore eyes on me tail an' fix it if'n it slips,
afore anybeast can see. Aye aye, mates, look who's
sneakin' into camp, 'tis the slavecatcher."

Riggan padded noiselessly down the bank to where
Kurda and Vorto were sitting at their own fire, apart from
the Ratguards and crewbeasts. Plugg and his two followers trailed in her wake. Kurda stared haughtily at the three
Freebooters, but they did not move. Leaning on his battle-
axe, Plugg sneered back at her.

"We knew yore spy sneaked out o'camp. Well, go on,
Riggan, make yore report to liddle miss pinky eyes."

Kurda could see there was no fooling the fox. She nodded for Riggan to go ahead with what she had learned.
Firelight glinted off the tracker's keen eyes as she spoke.

"I picked up the slaves' trail, marm, further upstream. They stopped there awhile, then joined up wid some shrews. Nobeast spotted me—I kept 'idden. I tracked them up t'the far side o' that big water meadow, where we lost the voles. Fools! They was all singin' an' dancin' an' feastin'. So I got as close up to 'em as I could an' lissened. The stripedog said they was bound fer a place called Redwall Abbey, an' the leader of the shrews said 'e knowed where it was. Said 'e'd take 'em there. Tomorrow morn at dawn light they're settin' off. Four logboats an' yore vessel."

Plugg interrupted maliciously, "My boat ye mean, ratface. Haharr, Redwall Abbey, I've 'eard grand tales about that place. 'Tis a treasure 'ouse, ripe fer the pluckin'. We'd best break camp if'n we're goin' to follow 'em."

Kurda smiled thinly. "You injured, fox, not able to keep up mitt us, yarr."

The Freebooter winked roguishly. "Don't fret yore pretty 'ead about me, I'll be right up front with ye. An' if'n I finds the goin' a bit 'ard, well, I'll lean on yore fat brother's 'ead an' use 'im fer a crutch. Hahaharrr!"

Kurda ignored the insulting fox. Rising from her fire, she drew her sabre and pointed upriver. "Ve march now, to der Abbey of Redvall!"

Plugg set off at her side, but felt himself pulled back by Grubbage. He turned irately on the fat searat. "Will ye stop tuggin' at me, wot is it?"

Grubbage held the tail up. "This just fell off, Cap'n, must've been the heat from that fire," he whispered.

With a swift motion, Plugg grabbed the tail and punched Grubbage on the nose. "Why don't ye shout a bit louder an' let the 'ole woodlands know, bigmouth!"

Running stooped, Scummy panted as he fixed Plugg's tail back in place, with the fox marching forward boldly. Scummy muttered to Grubbage, "I 'ope this Redwall place ain't too far!"

Grubbage nodded agreement. "Aye, mebbe we shoulda used tar!"

* * *

The Abbot had finished his oft-interrupted breakfast in the orchard and was looking for means of escape from the boisterous horde of Dibbuns. Wherever he moved there seemed to be one or other of the Abbeybabes, clinging to his robe, wanting to know the answer to a thousand and one unreasonable questions.

Friar Gooch came to his rescue, fending off the little ones. As he shepherded the Abbot from the orchard, the squirrel cook pointed with his ladle at the midwest wall-steps and remarked, "Seems t'be a deal of disturbance over there, Father. Did ye hear young Churk whoopin'? Great seasons, I thought we were under some sort of attack!"

Nodding absentmindedly, the Abbot replied, "I was certainly under attack from those Dibbuns. D'you know why a gooseberry has its pips inside and a strawberry has pips on the outside?"

The good Friar looked nonplussed. "Never thought of it, really."

Shaking his head, the Father Abbot chuckled. "Neither did I, until molebabe Roobil asked me. Right, let's go and see what all the kerfuffle is about at the wallsteps. Nothing as difficult as Roobil's problem, I hope."

Skipper, Mokug, Crikulus and Malbun waved and cried out to them across the lawn, "Come and see, Churk has found the solution!"

Churk waited until Friar and Abbot were seated on the sunwarmed sandstone steps. Skipper puffed out his chest and waved his rudder proudly. "When ye come t'think of all the scholars within our walls, an' who was it solved the mystery o' the scroll an' pawring? Haharr, none other than me own pretty niece Churk. Let me tell ye, Father, an' you, Friar, this ottermaid 'as got an 'ead on 'er shoulders, ten, nay, twenny seasons beyond 'er age. Ain't that right, beauty? We'll find that entrance now, sure enough!"

Churk lowered her eyes politely. "Uncle Skip, will ye stop embarrassin' me in front o' these goodbeasts an' let me speak for meself?"

The otter Chieftain patted her paw. "Sorry, missy, you tell 'em all about yore discovery—me lips are sealed!"

Churk indicated the symbol on the pawring. "The leaf is five times three, that's the key to it all." She opened the scroll, pointing to the two bottom lines set apart from the rest. "I wondered why this bit was written separate, so I counted the number of symbols on the line: Twenty-six, and each one is different. Now, what's five times three, Father?"

An immediate answer came from the Abbot. "Fifteen, why?"

Churk smiled secretively. "Simple, really. Count along these signs, sir, an' stop at the fifteenth one."

Moving his paw along the parchment, the Abbot counted. "Twelve, thirteen, fourteen, fifteen. Why, it's the leaf!"

Churk asked her next question. "What's the fifteenth letter of the alphabet, Crikulus, sir?"

The shrew did a quick count on his paws. "Letter *O* is."

Churk spread her paws triumphantly. "Right! Don't ye see, those twenty-six signs at the bottom are an alphabet, from A to Z!"

Malbun seized the ottermaid and planted a resounding kiss on her cheek. "You, Churk, are a positive wonder!"

Crikulus gnawed on his straggly whisker ends. "Hmph! I stared at that scroll for long enough, but it didn't occur to me that it might be an alphabet. Well done, miss!"

Mokug began wriggling and rubbing his paws. "At last, I'll know wot it all means. Go on, Churk, put it all together an' read us the message!"

Friar Gooch straightened his apron decisively. "This calls for somethin' special. You bide here an' do your message solvin'. I'll nip off t'the kitchens an' make us a celebration mid-mornin' snack!"

Mokug and Skipper were at his side in a flash. "We'll come with ye, Friar!"

Churk looked up from her charcoal stick and birchbark writing materials. "Why don't ye all go. Leave Crikulus with me, we'll get more done with a bit o' peace'n'quiet."

Malbun leaped from the third wallstep and performed a small hopskip, quite out of character for one of her seasons and dignity. She led them off, striking up an old Abbey song:

> "When the sun sinks in the west,
> Sweet the nightingales do call,
> There's noplace I love best,
> Like the Abbey of Redwall . . . Redwall!
>
> When the moon does beam in splendour,
> See the dew upon the lawn,
> Mirror-bright twinkling starlight,
> Waiting for the golden dawn.
> No foebeast will I fear,
> Me and all my good friends here,
> Who live within our gates in peace,
> For we hold our freedom dear,
> And we've earned the right to sing,
> As long as our Abbey bells may ring . . . Redwall!
>
> So let others quake and weep
> As a stormy night will fall,
> While at ease our Dibbuns sleep,
> Safe within our Redwall . . . Redwall!"

It was actually closer to lunch than mid-morning when the party returned from the Abbey kitchens. Pushing a laden trolley, they sang the marching song once more as they returned across the lawn.

Skipper bounded up the steps confidently. "Ahoy there, charmin' niece, did ye solve it all?"

Crikulus answered, "Oh, we've translated the message right enough, but one puzzle always brings another in its wake."

Friar Gooch whipped the cover off the trolley. "Will this help t'feed your brains, then?"

Churk grinned from ear to ear. "Ooh, thank ye, I'm sure it will. Hazelnut wafers, candied chestnut cake, fruit salad with meadowcream, redcurrant cordial an' hot dandelion an' mint tea. I can feel my brain clickin' away at the sight of it. But come 'n' see wot we've done so far."

Between them, Churk and Crikulus had set it all out on the birchbark parchment, neat and clear:

A B C D E F G H I J K L M

N O P Q R S T U V W X Y Z

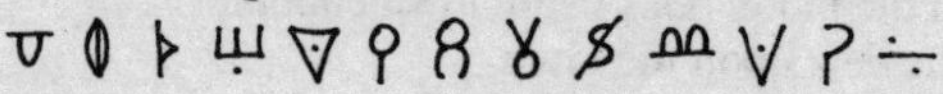

midday sun shines bright for you

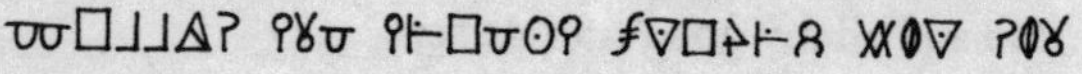

twixt leaning ash and poison gold

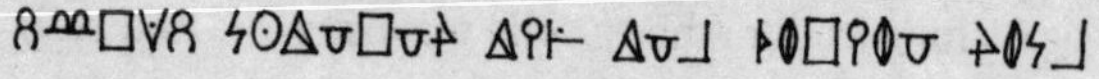

where the greenrock hidden lies

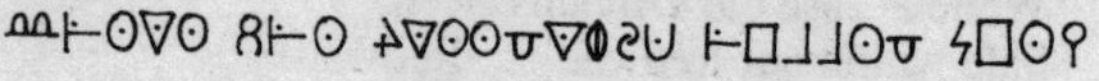

for keen eyes to behold

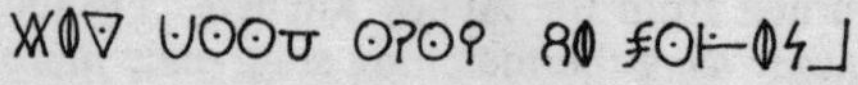

Churk and Crikulus took their friends' congratulations calmly, like true scholars. Ever practical, the ottermaid sat eating her lunch, but like all true scholars, her mind was still probing.

"What's it all supposed to mean? 'Tis a very strange rhyme."

Mokug helped himself to some candied chestnut cake. "That's the way to Brockhall, miss, the secret entrance. Ye could get in by that way without the serpents knowin'."

Malbun shuddered. "I wouldn't go inside that place for anything, knowin' those dreadful creatures could be lurking in wait for me. Ugh! All those poison fangs an' evil eyes!"

Crikulus agreed with her. "Nor me, I don't care what we can add to our archives by going down into Brockhall!"

Pouring himself some mint tea, the Abbot observed, "One thing is clear, friends. Nobeast will be going down there until the message in the poem is solved. Shall we get down to it? Let us look at the first line: 'Midday sun shines bright for you.' Can anybeast explain what that's supposed to mean?"

Skipper pursed his lips thoughtfully. "Sounds t'me like the midday sun is shinin' for wotever beast is searchin'. But midday sun shines on us all, not just the searcher. Huh, it beats me."

"But it's not beaten me." Malbun put aside the hazelnut wafer she was nibbling. "I think it means that the search must take place at midday. The line is telling us exactly what time to go searching—not dawn, or eventide, but midday."

Placing his paw on the second line, the Abbot agreed. "I believe you're right, friend. Tell me, then, what about this: 'Twixt leaning ash and poison gold'?"

Crikulus snorted. "Ash doesn't lean. To me the word *ash* means a heap of black and grey dust from a fire. Right?"

"Nay, sir, it prob'ly means some ole ash tree."

Churk turned to Mokug, who had made the remark. "That's good plain thinkin'. You lived a long time in the woodlands, mate, d'ye know of such a tree, a leanin' ash?"

The golden hamster shrugged. "I don't know the names o' trees, sorry, miss. Some of 'em got different-shaped leaves an' rough or smooth bark. Big 'uns an' liddle 'uns, they're all the same to Mokug, just trees."

Friar Gooch began loading empty platters onto his trolley. "Sure enough, 'tis all a riddle. I wouldn't even know where to begin findin' out what 'poison gold' means."

Churk volunteered a suggestion. "It looks like we're

stuck for answers. Why don't ye all go about yore business an' leave me to try an' sort it out."

Skipper had something to add. "Aye, that's good advice. I'll go an' get Log a Log an' some o' those Guosim shrews. We'll take young Rumbol, too. Mokug, yore comin' with us, mate. We'll take a walk north, up the path. Per'aps if'n we point out some trees an' tell ye their names, y'might recognise wot an ash tree looks like. We'll stick to the path, just in case those adders are prowlin' the woods."

33

A small flotilla wound its way upstream: the stolen craft and four shrew logboats. Mimsy and her husband Gulif, who were the unofficial leaders of the shrew party, sat in the prow of the little ship with Triss and Sagax. Scarum, who had become the model of politeness and decorum because of the amounts of food their hosts were feeding him, wandered up, munching on a honey and almond turnover.

"Jolly decent types, these chaps. I say, marm, I hope we aren't puttin' you out of your way by havin' you lead us to Redwall."

Mimsy peered ahead through the sunny green light created by overhanging trees. "Bless ye, no, we was plannin' on goin' to the Abbey in the next day or two. I've got a feelin' we should meet up with our Chieftain, Log a Log Groo. Him an' some Guosim were sailin' the streams not far from Redwall. They'd be sure to call in an' visit awhile."

Triss sat back, savouring the pleasant morning on the rippling water with tree foliage as a canopy. "This is nice. I could go along like this forever."

Gulif sat down beside her. "I knows the feelin', miss, but the ford that crosses the north path'll be a-comin' up soon. Won't be usin' the boats no more, then—we'll stow 'em away an' walk south down the path to Redwall."

The squirrelmaid trailed her paw in the cool streamwater. "Pity, I was really getting to enjoy the waterway."

Mimsy spoke up helpfully. "Well, p'raps we could tie up just before the ford an' take lunch there, whilst we wait for the backscouts to catch up."

Scarum interrupted. "Beg pardon, marm, but what are backscouts?"

Gulif pointed downstream. "I sent four of 'em to check on those vermin ye said were trailin' ye. It ain't good sense to leave things to chance. Mimsy's right, we'll moor up short o' the ford an' wait for 'em. Don't suppose they'll 'ave much to report, I took all the twists an' turns to shake any followers off'n our wake."

It was mid-afternoon by the time they moored the vessels beside a mossy bank. Kroova and Shogg hauled them into a small inlet and hid them beneath shrubbery and boughs.

Sagax watched the Guosim cooks prepare a meal. "Is there any way we can lend a paw, marm?"

Mimsy gave him a long, studious look. "Wot's up? Ain't our cookin' good enough for ye?"

Scarum drew the young badger to one side and lectured him. "My good chap, keep y'self to y'self, wot. We don't want to antagonise these good creatures. So mind your manners!"

Sagax pulled a meaningful face at Kroova. "Listen to the pot calling the kettle black!"

Triss amused the little shrews by singing them a song she had made up. They sat tapping their paws as they listened to the jolly air.

> "Bushes and treetops drifting by,
> Fish gliding 'neath our keel,
> Soft and gentle breezes sigh,

'Tis like a dream made real.
Whirl and gurgle, eddy and flow,
Past carp and dace and bream,
Dragonflies, mayflies, swooping low,
As we sail upon the stream.

Cuckoos call out from the trees,
Bees bumble busily by,
Telling of golden days like these,
When the sun smiles from the sky.
Some will pole and others row,
Let each one do their best,
Let the waters flow by slow,
Put up your paws and rest."

Blue smoke wafted through the trees. Kroova and
Shogg sat on the bankside, dabbling their paws in the
shallows. Sagax and Gulif checked that the boats were
well concealed. Scarum had wheedled his way into a new
position. Mimsy and the Guosim cooks had actually ap-
pointed him to serve the meal. Triss covered her mouth,
turning aside to stifle her merriment at the sight of him.
Scarum had bound a turban about his ears to stop them
from flopping into the food. Clad in a flowery apron, he
wielded a ladle officiously.

"Attention in the ranks, chaps, lunch is served. Line up
here in a jolly orderly manner. No nonsense now, I'm
your disher-upper, so watch your behaviour, wot!"

When Triss had been served with a delicious bowl of
something the shrews called Streambank Stew, she took
her beaker of cider and a small batch loaf of shrewbread.
She sat between Kroova and Shogg. All three giggled
helplessly as they watched Scarum chiding Sagax.

"Good grief, sah, look at those paws. 'Fraid I can't
serve you until you've washed 'em in the stream. Move
along, please, don't stand there glarin' at me like that.
Next!"

It was in the midst of all this that Gulif suddenly held
up his paws for silence.

"Hist! Sounds like our backtrackers returnin', but they're comin' this way runnin' like madbeasts. Break camp, Guosim, git the liddle 'uns ready to leave fast!"

The fire was quickly doused. Triss and her companions helped to round up the shrewbabes. There had originally been four backtrackers, but only two staggered into camp, one with a vicious spearwound in his paw. Sagax threw a cloth around the injury, binding it speedily as the shrew gasped.

"Git movin' sharpish, Gulif, there's a horde o' vermin on our track, armed t'the teeth an' out fer blood. They slew Cadro an' Elbun, but we got away. They're 'ard on our trail, mate, there ain't time to 'ang about!"

Gulif drew his rapier as he heard the vermin crashing through the undergrowth downstream. The tough little Guosim leader growled out orders. "Mimsy, Triss, get the old 'uns an' the babes goin', make for the ford an' head south down the path. Sagax, you two streamdogs an' the rest o' ye, we'll form a rearguard an' follow. Git goin' now, quick!"

Kurda, Vorto and Riggan raced ahead of the rest, while Freebooters and Ratguards thundered along both sides of the bank. Supported by Prince Bladd and Slitfang, Plugg Firetail stumped along not far behind.

"Haharr, we'll lay 'em by the tails this time, buckoes!"

Riggan put on a spurt, calling back to Kurda, "I think I caught sight of 'em, up ahead. There's smoke an' steam, though I don't see no boats!"

Kurda slashed at willow fronds with her sabre. "Never mind der boats, ve find dem later. Get der slaves!"

Vorto grinned triumphantly as they passed through the camp. "Some o' those ashes are still smolderin'—they broke camp in a hurry. We'll soon catch up with 'em!"

Mokug halted on the path, pointing out a tree. "Is that 'un an ash, Skip?"

Skipper shook his head patiently. "No, mate, that's a rowan. The leaves look the same, but the ash is stouter an' it don't 'ave red berries like the rowan tree. Log, old mate, will ye find an ash an' point it out to 'im?"

However, Log a Log's interest in trees had suddenly waned. Detaching himself from his score of Guosim, he cocked his head on one side, drawing his rapier. "Cut the cackle a moment, will ye, I can 'ear somethin'!"

The young otter Rumbol walked ahead a few paces. "Yore right, somebeast's a-comin' this way in an 'urry!"

Triss and the shrews appeared around a bend.

Log a Log dashed toward them. "Mimsy, wot's the rush, marm. Where's old Gulif?"

As he spoke, the rest of the party ran into view. Gulif sighted the Guosim Chieftain and roared out the shrew war cry:

"Logalogalogalogaloooooog!"

Sagax boomed out a warning as they neared the Red-wallers. "Vermin chasing us, a great load of 'em!"

Skipper had been staring strangely at Triss, but he recovered and took swift charge of the situation. "Git yore party down t'the Abbey, marm, tell the Abbot to hold the gate 'til we arrive. The rest of us, form up on the path 'ere, slings an' javelins. Look out, they're comin', I see the scum!"

The vermin were hard on the heels of their quarry as they rounded the bend, with Kurda waving her sabre and screeching, "Ve haff dem, kill, kill!"

She dropped swiftly back as an unexpected volley of slingstones hit her front ranks. Plugg passed her, brandishing his huge battle-axe. He laughed wildly.

"Haharr, me beauty, ye ain't in yore daddy's castle now. We'll show ye 'ow Freebooters gets the job done. Chaaaarge!"

Much to Skipper's surprise, Scarum picked up a fallen spear and saluted smartly. "Salamandastron trained hare, sah, ready for duty, stand aside if ye please. Javelin throwers to either side of this path! Pay attention in the ranks there! Shrews an' slingers, form up across the path in three ranks, look lively. That's the ticket, chaps. First slingin' rank, throw an' drop back two ranks. We'll give 'em blood'n'vinegar, me buckoes! Eulaliiiiiiaaaa! Second rank, throw an' drop back two ranks, make every stone count, steady the buffs an' hammer 'em!"

Amazingly, the tactic worked. Hail after hail of speedily hurled stones halted the vermin charge.

Plugg wrung his paws as a big pebble reverberated against the blade of his axe. "Press forward, ye spineless jellyfish, we outnumber 'em ten to one. Drop t'the sides o' the path an' circle 'em!"

Skipper and Log a Log had their swords and javelins on either side of the path. The Guosim Chieftain murmured to his shrews, "This ain't no fight t'the death—we only need to slow 'em down until we can get to Redwall. Don't let anybeast try to sneak by an' surround us, or we'll be cut off!"

Down the path the battle ensued, with Kurda and Plugg urging their creatures on. Both the Princess and the silver fox were enraged that their force could make no headway against the efficiently organised band. Vorto dashed recklessly forward, but was repulsed by Log a Log skilfully wielding his rapier. Nursing a slashed cheek, the Ratguard Captain bumped into Kurda.

"Princess, 'ow can they be retreatin' an' beatin' us at the same time? It ain't right!"

Kurda pushed by him and slew a shrew with a sabre thrust. "See, dey die, same as any odder beast. You turn back an' I slay you, too. Plugg, vere you goin'? Come back, coward!"

Leaning heavily on a cringing Prince Bladd, the Freebooter stumped off into the tree shelter, calling back to Kurda, "I ain't goin' up agin that . . . Look!"

They had fought almost up to the ramparts of Redwall Abbey. The battlements were thronged with young and old, flinging anything they could lay their paws upon. Abbot Apodemus stood out on the path, hurrying the remainder of the party inside.

"Straight in, friends, don't dawdle. You put up a brave fight there, come on in."

He stood calmly until the last one, Skipper, was safe

inside. Only then did Father Abbot deign to retreat. "Close the gates, Crikulus. Gooch, you and I will see to those extra bars. Get the gate locked safe and tight!"

Late evening faded to night over the vast acres of Moss-flower Wood. Somewhere in the undergrowth, not far from the Abbey, a mistle thrush stirred. The bird's head moved slowly, taking in the view all around. It skipped from cover and winged its way swiftly up into the clean night air, leaving behind it the terrifying odour of cloying evil.

Zassaliss the adder had taken his fill of a Ratguard carcass. Now Harssacss and Sesstra were dealing with the remains. Sarengo's crown slid back slightly on the giant adder's head as he watched the thrush slip off. Butting his brother and sister aside, Zassaliss leaned his lower jaw on the broken Ratguard spear, letting his forked tongue slither caressingly over it.

"Lotsss of new beastsss crosssing our pathsss!"

Sesstra lifted her head from the grisly meal. "Yesss, lotsss!"

The three bodies of the snakes wriggled pleasurably. Beyond where the mace of Sarengo remained buried in their flesh, the dead serpent tails lay still, bound together and exuding their rotten odor.

34

Forty creatures in all were guarding the battlements, ten
to each wall. Below, moles trundled trolleys of food
from the kitchens, out to where the Redwallers were
gathered on the lawn and gatehouse steps. Stories had
been related, introductions made and old friends re-
united. Memm Flackery had put all the Dibbuns up to
bed and found berths for the new arrivals. She shook
Scarum's paw.

"Heard good things about you, young buck, wot.
Served at Salamandastron m'self in the young seasons,
y'know. Hightor still Lord there, is he?"

Sagax took his nose out of an October Ale beaker.
"Aye, marm, I'm his son."

She refilled the beaker for him. "Hmm, stern old stick,
ain't he? I liked your mother, though. Lady Merola an' I
were good chums. Before you came along, of course."

Triss bore Skipper's penetrating stare for as long as she
could. Finally she felt she had to speak. "Excuse me, sir,
but do you know me from someplace?"

The big otter Chieftain nodded. Everything in his
dreams was filtering slowly back to him. "Aye, Triss, I

think we 'ave met afore. Come an' take a walk with me. Father Abbot, I'd like ye to come as well."

Registering only slight surprise, the Abbot rose from the steps and went with them.

Skipper took them both into Great Hall. Once inside, he spoke softly to the squirrelmaid. "Take a stroll around, Triss, see if'n ye recognise anythin'."

The Abbot was mystified. "What's this all about?"

Skipper placed a paw around the shoulders of the old mouse. "Hush now, Father, let's just watch the maid."

Triss stood rigid in front of the tapestry, gazing up at the likeness of Martin the Warrior. Moving in a dreamlike trance, she mounted the ladder that Skipper had placed there earlier. Her eyes were riveted on the sword that hung over the tapestry. She lifted it from its retaining pins and climbed back down. Not once did her eyes leave the fabled blade.

"Welcome to Redwall Abbey, Trisscar Swordmaid!" Skipper placed his paw on her. "Oh aye, I know ye, all right. Yore the stuff my dreams've been made of, though I didn't realise that 'til just now. Martin the Warrior showed you to me while I slept. It's all coming back to me."

The Abbot was astounded. "You dreamed of this squirrelmaid? Martin showed her to you? How can this be?"

Skipper squeezed Triss's paw gently. "Father, 'tis all a puzzle t'me as 'tis to you. But she was guided to Redwall by Martin—who are we to question 'im?"

The Abbot shrugged. "Who, indeed. You look as if you were born to hold that blade, miss; can you use it?"

Triss saw her own reflection in the bright steel as she spoke. "I am the daughter of Rocc Arrem. Nobeast in all the Northlands could cross swords with him. Though I was a slave, I was brought up around swords. But this blade, this is different. I know it like I know my own right paw."

Satisfied, the Abbot sized Triss up and down, smiling. "Then you must wear it. Redwall is fortunate to find one such as you in time of danger, Trisscar."

The squirrelmaid undid her waist belt and buckled it

across her back from left shoulder to right waist, then thrust the sword through, so it hung over her back. "If you please, Father Abbot, I prefer to be called Triss."

They watched her go back outside to join the others. The Abbot transferred his gaze to Martin on the tapestry. "Sir, I'll wager you used to wear the sword in the same manner. Thank you for sending her to us."

Since the vermin had entered the woodlands, Kurda seemed a touch more affable toward Plugg. Her archers had brought down a fine woodpigeon, and she beckoned him to join her at the fire.

"So, tell me, you haff conquered big stone places like diss?"

The Freebooter sat down gingerly, having first assured himself that his tail was still hanging intact. "The bigger they are, the richer they be, missy. If'n all the tales o' booty an' loot inside there are only 'arf true, ye can bet yore white 'ide old Plugg'll find a way to get at it. Aye, on me affydavit I will!"

Kurda stared into the flames. "If diss be true, you can haff der booty. I'll take dose slavebeasts, yarr."

Grubbage and Scummy lingered behind their captain, keeping an eye on the unfortunate tail. Plugg sniffed at the bird cooking on a spit over the fire.

"Is that bird fresh killed?"

Kurda gave it a turn with her sabre point. "Yarr, fresh diss very night. Vy you ask?"

The silver fox sniffed the air uneasily, then noticed his two crewbeasts lurking in the background. "Ahoy, Scummy, d'ye reckon yew could find a stream 'ere-abouts?"

The stoat touched his ear dutifully. "Aye, Cap'n, I could."

Plugg wrinkled his nose distastefully. "Then take Grubbage with ye, an' when yer come across the stream ye can chuck each other in an' scrub yoreselves 'til dawn. Rub some fresh mint on yoreselves, too."

The two vermin plodded obediently off, Grubbage

waggling a paw in his ear, or what was left of it. "Why've we got to put fresh mint on a shelf? Don't make sense."

When they had gone, Plugg continued sniffing. "Phew! That stink's still 'angin' about. Wot is it?"

Kurda was about to suggest that Plugg join his crew-beasts in the stream. But she thought better of it now that she really needed an ally. "Der shmell? I don't know, maybe all strange voodlands shtink like diss!"

The silver fox picked up a burning twig and blew on it. "No matter, we'll see if it smells any better inside that Abbey place, once we've burned their doors down. Haha-harr!"

Eight Redwallers, headed by Foremole Urrm, shouldered four stout poles running through the hooped iron handle of a massive cauldron. Urrm grunted.

"Yurr, altogether naow, give et ee gudd lift, wun, two, hupp!"

Filled almost to the brim with oatmeal boiled in honey, the great mass was lifted and carried, one step at a time, up the gatehouse stairs. Only Memm Flackery and some shrew wives, who were seeing to the Dibbuns, were not present. Just before dawn, Skipper had ordered everybeast up to the battlements to provide a show of force for the vermin's benefit.

Scarum strode the walltop jauntily. He threw an excellent salute to Skipper and Triss, who were both standing on the threshold directly over the gates. "Beeyootiful mornin', sah an' marm, no sign o' Plugg an' his perishers, no white ferrets or rats to blight the day. I'm about ready for a spot of brekkers, wot!"

Shading his eyes, Shogg peered up toward the north-west. "You spoke too soon, Scarum mate. 'Ere they come!"

Figures could be seen scurrying out of the woodlands. They crossed the path, negotiating the ditch on its far side. When a few score of them had made it, they began walking out west, across the flatlands, away from the Abbey.

Sagax watched the line of figures trudging through the

clinging remnants of groundmist. The badger scratched
his muzzle stripes. "Looks like they're going away."

Scarum merely shook his head. "Goin' away? 'Fraid
not, old lad, they're just movin' out of sling an' arrow
range."

Kroova saw them halt a good distance away, straight in
line with the Abbey gates. "Yore right. 'Ow did ye
know?"

Scarum winked confidentially. "Son of a colonel, sah,
attended Long Patrol School at Salamandastron, learned a
smidgeon there, y'know, wot wot!"

Sagax tugged his friend's tail playfully. "Hah, Long
Patrol School. We spent most of our time playing truant as
I remember. Go on, then, what did you learn?"

The young hare pointed to the vermin and scoffed,
"Pish tush an' fiddleydee, oldest trick in the book, that
one. Either they're tryin' to draw attention away from our
rear, or they're plannin' chargin' us head-on an' doin'
somethin' pretty awful to the front gates. See, told you.
See those flames, they're lightin' a blinkin' fire, the cads.
I'll wager you a salad to a sausage they're goin' to flamin'
well try an' burn their way in, wot!"

"Yurr, moi guddbeasts, makeways, us'n's bee's a-
cummin' oop thurr wi' brekkist!"

Scarum hopped nimbly to one side, all agog. "Oh,
splendid show, chaps, hot honeyed oatmeal. Let me give
you a lift with that, my good moletypes. Nothin' like a
spot o' the old honeyed oatmeal t'keep me handsome,
wot!"

Triss looked at the huge cauldron of steaming food. So
did Skipper, Shogg, Kroova and Sagax. They exchanged
grins.

Scarum had a ladlefull. He blew on it and tasted a little. "Huh, dunno what you chaps are laughin' at, this
stuff's jolly hot an' pretty heavy I can tell you."

Triss and Sagax were now conferring with Foremole
Urrm and his crew, leaning over the battlements and
pointing out toward the vermin and their fire on the flatlands. There was lots of whispering and nodding. Urrm

and his moles seemed to find the entire conversation hilarious.

Still trying to cope with his ladle of hot oatmeal, Scarum flapped his ears to cool it and muttered indignantly, "Nothin' funny about a chap tryin' to have brekkers, wot?"

Triss wiped the smile from her face. "Of course not, Scarum. Listen, why don't you take your oatmeal around to the east wall. Organise the sentries there. You said that the vermin may be trying to draw attention away from our rear. If there is anything going on over there, there's nobeast we'd like better than you to take command."

Any idea of being a commander appealed to the hare. Throwing Triss an elaborate salute, he swaggered off around the ramparts, leaving the steaming cauldron behind and bawling orders to the shrews on the east wall. "Attention there, you sloppy lot! Chins in, chests out, shoulders back! Steady in the ranks! First one who moves is on a fizzer! Officer comin' over, prepare to salute!"

Plugg Firetail stood with his back to the fire, enjoying its warmth in the misty dawn. The crew of the *Seascab* went about their tasks as they listened to him outlining his scheme. He was in high good humour.

"Haharr, who needs Princess Pinky-eyes an' 'er lackeys, eh? We'll show em 'ow Freebooters gets the job done. While they're skulkin' round in the woodlands, I'll 'ave us inside yon Abbey in time fer afternoon tea an' some liddle cakes!"

The crew roared with laughter. Their captain had never failed them when it came to plunder and the taking of booty.

Prince Bladd was with them. He giggled excitedly. "You be der sly old fox, Captain. Vot is der plan?"

Plugg threw a paw about the Pure Ferret, leaning on him like a crutch. "Listen now, mate, an' I'll tell ye. Those creatures on the wall will be watchin' this 'ere fire. That's wot I wants 'em to do, see. But they won't see old Slitfang and Grubbage and some others. They'll range out in two big 'alf-circles an' sneak up through the grass to the

Abbey gates. With them they'll be carryin' dry brush, some veggible oil an' ship's tar, an' a smoulderin' cob o' tow rope. I'll stay back 'ere by the fire with a few mateys. We'll distract those sillybeasts' attention. Then Slitty an' the rest'll build the brush up agin the gates, douse it wi' tar an' oil, blow on the smoulderin' tow 'til it flames, an' goodbye Abbey gates. Hahahaharr."

The fat Prince performed a little dance of delight. "Diss is gutt, yarr! Captain, I go vit dem, I make a gutt Freebooter. Let me carry der rope, I'll set fire to de gates. I like playink mitt fire."

Plugg tweaked the fat Prince's nose fondly. "Right y'are, matey, we'll make a Freebooter of ye!"

"Er, er, Cap'n, will ye move away from the fire, sir?"

Plugg growled distractedly at Grubbage, who was behind him. "Wot've you been told about interruptin' yore cap'n?"

Grubbage shrugged. "I dunno about a tin cup for flappin', but yore tail's just fell off with the heat!"

Plugg rasped out of the side of his mouth, "Scummy, stick it back on, quick! Now then, Grubbage me ole darlin', come round 'ere where I can see ye!"

The deaf steersrat knew what was coming. Plugg forced him to bend over by placing the flat of his battle-axe on Grubbage's neck, then winked at Bladd. "Let's see ye land 'im a good kick, me ole royal mate."

Bladd obliged willingly. Grubbage staggered a pace or two, then turned with a grin to his captain.

"Bless 'im, Cap'n, but 'e's got some kickin' t'do afore 'e's as good a booter as you!"

From the battlements, Churk's keen eyes watched the activity around the fire. Without taking her eyes from the scene, the ottermaid called out, "Is that oatmeal still 'ot, Triss?"

The squirrelmaid did not bother testing it. "Aye, there's still a bubble or two popping on it, and you can feel the heat from this iron cauldron a good pawlength away. Anything going on up there, Churk?"

"Looks like they're startin' to make their move."

Foremole popped up alongside Churk, squinting hard. "Burr, oi doant see nuthin' excep' sum vermints a-dancin' round ee flames, marm."

Triss came up to watch as Churk pointed them out. "They're fannin' out two ways an' circlin' in toward our gates. See, there they go now, layin' low an' crawlin' through the grass an' heather."

Triss followed the direction of Churk's paw. "Ah, I see them now. Hey, Shogg, Prince Bladd fatbelly is with them, though I don't see Kurda or any Ratguards."

Shogg was helping Skipper and Kroova place the carrying poles through the cauldron handle. "Let's take care o' this lot first, Trissy, then we'll worry about the others. You still keepin' watch down there, Father Abbot? Tell us when the time's right."

Abbot Apodemus was down behind the main gates with Malbun and Crikulus, peering through a gap by a lower hinge. "I see them now, friend, but they've still got a way to come. We'll let you know when they arrive."

Plugg and about six others were dancing a hornpipe around the fire, singing aloud:

> "Ho plunder, by thunder!
> Ain't nothin' nice as plunder.
> An' booty, me beauty,
> An' loads o' loot to boot!
>
> There's treasure, fine treasure!
> Ye can count it at yore leisure.
> All those not slayed an' thrown in graves,
> We'll trade 'em off as slaves!
>
> Freebooters, we're looters!
> Slingstone an' arrow shooters.
> They sigh now, an' cry now,
> O mercy, woe is me!

Wid cutlass, an' spears,
We'll carve off tails an' ears,
An' wid full sacks upon our backs,
We deals out blows an' whacks!"

The silver fox got so carried away at one point that he pulled off his tail and whirled it above his head.

Slitfang's ugly head showed over the ditchbank. He stared up at the seemingly empty walltop. "Come on, buckoes, over ye go!"

The Abbot saw Bladd scramble out onto the path, grinning wickedly as he blew on the smouldering rope end. Sagax looked down. Crikulus was standing on the lower wallsteps and waving wildly as he nodded his head. Skipper, Churk, Kroova and Shogg mounted the battlements as Foremole and his crew shouldered the poles, lifting the hot cauldron of honeyed oatmeal off the ground. Leaning over, Triss could see the Freebooters scurrying in pairs across the path, carrying dried brush, oil and tar. The four sturdy otters at her side leaned down and grabbed the poles, heaving the cauldron off the moles, then straightened up, lifting the cauldron above the walltops.

Crouching down close to the gate, the searat called Ripper splashed vegetable oil on the timbers. He started with shock as a cry rang out from behind a lower hinge.

"Yowch, there's oil in my eye!"

In the split second that followed, Skipper roared out loud and clear, "Brekkist comin' over, scum!"

The four otters twisted the poles to turn the mixture over the wall, but the poles snapped and the lot fell, cauldron and all. Crikulus leaped back as hot oatmeal flooded under the gate. "Malbun, are you all right, friend?"

The woodmouse was mopping her eye on an apron corner. "No damage, just some vegetable oil in my eye."

With his head ringing from the agonised screams outside the gates of his Abbey, the Father Abbot helped Malbun into the gatehouse and bathed her eye.

"A dreadful solution, Malbun. Listen to those wretched beasts."

Crikulus entered, wiping oatmeal from the hem of his robe. "Aye, Father, but the vermin could have saved themselves all that injury and agony by leaving Redwall in peace."

Slitfang rolled in the ditch bottom, where there was a lining of stale water and mud. The Freebooter weasel screwed his face up, whimpering from the pain of the scalding honeyed oatmeal that had flooded over his back. Ripper and a searat named Blear fell in on top of him, avoiding a lively salvo of slingstones from the walltop. Slitfang booted them aside and staggered from the ditch. Reeling from side to side, he headed in the direction of the fire on the flatlands.

35

Redwall Abbey's twin bells tolled out the close of day. It was a warm, quiet summer evening. The Abbot stood at the southwest corner of the high ramparts, discussing the day's events with his friends. Servers trundled trolleys along the walltops, dishing out meals to the sentries.

Scarum halted young Furrel the molemaid. "Marm, would you kindly push that trolley over here? Hmph! Goin' to make sure I get my grub this time, wot!"

The Abbot looked over the top of his glasses. "Dear me, you mean to say you've missed a meal?"

Helping himself to salad, a wedge of leek-and-potato pie, cheese, bread, an apple turnover and a beaker of cordial, the hungry hare sniffed in annoyance. "A measly ladle of oatmeal this mornin, that's all I've jolly well had. I was far too busy commandin' my troops most of the day, sah, dealin' with scurvy vermin an' whatnot. What really grieves a chap is how they disposed of the oatmeal. Whackin' good scoff it was, too, wot. Far too blinkin' good t'be fed to those scoundrels at the gate!"

Triss fetched him a bowl of rhubarb crumble. "No, no, Scarum, you've got it all wrong. We used the hot oatmeal to stop the vermin from burning the gates down. When Skipper and the otters tipped it over them, that oatmeal saved the day."

However, Scarum was not to be pacified. "Bloomin' waste of good tucker, if y'ask me. Now, if I'd been in command, 'twould have been different, marm, oh yes! Let me tell you how I dealt with those bounders at the east wall."

A joint groan arose from the listeners. Kroova scowled. "You've already told us ten times, mate, no need t'go on."

Scarum ignored him completely and launched into his heroic narrative once again. "Never wasted a crumb or a drop of scoff, officer trainin', y'see. Well, anyhow, I put an ear to the east wallgate, an' I heard that white ferret givin' her orders. Hello old chap, says I to m'self, what a bloomin' spot o' luck. So then . . ." He looked around and found he was talking to himself. They had all moved off to the centre of the west wall. "Ignorant bounders, you wouldn't know a hero if he fell on your confounded heads. Er, excuse me, pretty miss, don't go chargin' off with that trolley, I'm only on my first course, wot!"

Groans from the wounded and injured echoed around the vermin camp in Mossflower Wood. Kurda's pink eyes flashed contempt at the Freebooter Captain. "So, you showed dem how to do t'ings de Freebooter vay, yarr. It vas clever de way you stole de hot oatmeal from de Red-vallers. You got mine brother killed, too, is dat how to do t'ings de Freebooter vay?"

Plugg snarled back at the Pure Ferret, "You been bad luck ever since we took ye aboard, an' you ain't sheddin' no tears fer Bladd. Leaves the way clear for yew, don't it? Yore brother 'ad twice the guts you'll ever possess, 'twas just bad fortune an' a cast-iron stewpot got 'im slayed. Hah! I don't notice yore crew doin' any victory dances. I 'eard you was beaten by that big rabbit!"

A Ratguard was slumped nearby, nursing a broken footpaw. The silver fox grabbed the injured limb and dragged the rat forward screaming. "Tell us wot 'appened, matey, c'mon!" He loosed his grip, allowing the cringing beast to speak.

"Princess Kurda told some of us to try an' force a way in through the liddle east wallgate. While we was tryin' t'do it, the rabbit an' his pals dropped a big fishin' net over us an' snarled us up in it. We was trapped—they battered us wid slingstones an' anythin' they could drop on us. Banged big long poles on our 'eads, an' we couldn't get away. The rabbit was callin' us vermin cads an' rat bounders an' sayin' 'wot wot' all the time. We just 'ad to lie there an' take it, until they allowed us t'crawl away, still all knotted up in that big net!"

Plugg kicked the agonised rat away from him. Picking up his battle-axe, he pointed it at Kurda, his eyes slitted coldly. "You've got no room to curl yore lip at me, missie. I 'eard wot you was doin' while all that was goin' on. Skulkin' back in the trees, far away from it as ye could get, ye white-spined coward. At least I went back t'the ditch to 'elp me mates get away from the slingstones, ain't that right, Slitty?"

Slitfang could scarcely move his head because of the poultice of wet mud and dock leaves covering his back from tail to ears. "Aye, Cap'n, ye did that, you 'elped yore crew!"

There was a brief silence while both Ratguards and Freebooters watched their leaders. Plugg remained seated, but Kurda rose slowly, sabre in paw.

"Nobeast calls der Princess of de 'Ouse of Riftgard coward."

The silver fox came upright, gripping his axe haft. "Oh, is that so, me darlin'? Well, I just did—me, Plugg Firetail, an' I ain't pertickler who 'ears it. Yore a coward! A snooty-nosed, lily-livered, cringin', crawlin', gutless, spineless coward!"

Injured and wounded vermin scrambled to get out of the way. Danger hung on the air as Plugg and Kurda began circling each other, weapons raised. The parting of their ways had finally come, and one was bound to die.

Kurda locked eyes with Plugg as she returned his insults. "You are de scum of der sea, a common stupid foxbeast mitt not even a tail to your idiot name! You shtink, Plugg, de smell of you is all around us, even now! I t'ink dat smell gets stronger because you fear me, you are de coward!"

With a roar the Freebooter Captain charged. "Yoooo-haaaaarr!"

Kurda swung her sabre, but the Freebooter's huge battle-axe head struck it, turning the blade and sending the sword spinning from her grasp into the bushes. Carried on by his own momentum, Plugg rushed as she dodged aside. His battle-axe head thudded deep into a sycamore trunk. Kurda ran into the bushes after her sabre, as Plugg gave the axe a tug, but it was buried too deep, caught fast in the sappy wood. Growling with rage, the silver fox left it there and sped after Kurda with teeth and claws bared. Before the Princess could retrieve her blade, the Freebooter was on her.

Saplings swayed, leaves and grass flew in the air as they battled tooth and claw. Everybeast watched in fascination as shrieks, roars and growls rent the air. Plugg came stumbling backward out of the undergrowth, blood pouring from his wounds. He gave a mad laugh and charged back in, throwing himself at Kurda, who was lying flat on her back, recovering from the Freebooter's first sally. As the silver fox descended on her, she threw up all four paws rigidly. They struck Plugg, knocking the breath from him in a loud whoosh, and he went sailing over her, deeper into the bushes.

Scrabbling wildly, Kurda found her sabre. She wielded it and turned to face her adversary. The Freebooter jumped upright, ignoring his injuries. Everybeast present was witness to what happened next.

There was a loud hissing, and the bushes parted. Plugg half turned to see what was behind him. The three snakes hit him with terrifying force, sinking their fangs deep. The silver fox was wrenched screeching into the air, vanishing backwards into the woodland thickets with eye-blurring speed.

"Mates, 'elp meeeeeeeeeeeeeeeeeeeeee!"

His piteous last cries hung on the still air. Then there was total silence. Plugg Firetail, famous Freebooter Captain of the *Seascab,* was gone forever. The sabre dropped from Kurda's nerveless grasp. All around her, Ratguards and vermin crew stood or lay, open-mouthed in shock.

Grubbage's small whimper broke the stillness. "It's took our Cap'n."

A concerted wail arose from the *Seascab*'s crew.

Riggan picked up the fallen sabre and placed it back in Kurda's paw. "Blood, fur an' 'ellgates! Did y'see that thing, marm?"

Still staring into the woodlands, Kurda replied, "You can track it, Riggan?"

The slavecatcher gulped. "A blindbeast wid only a nose could trail that smell, but who'd want to track that thing?"

The sabre point was suddenly forcing Riggan's chin up. "Unless you vant to die here, you vill track it. Dat is mine command. De t'ing vas vearing de crown of Sarengo. Dat crown is mine by right!"

Morning arrived with pale skies and a light drizzle. The Abbot and Malbun followed the breakfast servers around the walltops, issuing blankets to the defenders. Scarum accepted his blanket and saluted.

"Drizzle shouldn't last long, sah, it'll break before noon."

Scanning the sky, the Abbot nodded. "You could be right, there. Enjoying a full breakfast this morning, I see?"

The young hare dipped his spoon into an outsized bowl of oatmeal. "I should jolly well say so, an' I ain't sharin' it with any vermin, sah. I say, those rotters don't seem to have shown up this mornin', wot?"

Malbun chuckled. "No, perhaps you scared them off altogether, after the brave show you put up yesterday."

Scarum made an elegant leg and allowed her a slight bow. "Only doin' my duty, marm, far too modest t'mention it. Though if they have turned tail, one would've thought the blighters'd let us know. It ain't much fun standin' atop of a bally wall for a couple o'days, wot?"

Patting Scarum's paw sympathetically, the Abbot replied, "You're right, of course. Mayhap you'd be better off inside the Abbey, looking after the Dibbuns. They get a bit restless after a few days indoors . . ."

Scarum shot to attention, his eyes roving theatrically over the woodlands, as if expecting immediate attack. "Wot, an' leave the little ones unprotected? Not I, sah. Never can tell, the flippin' bounders might be sneakin' up on us even as I speak. I'll hold my post, if y'don't mind. Faithful unto death an' true blue, that's me, sah!"

Triss was sitting within earshot of Scarum, taking breakfast with her friends. Sagax laughed. "Listen to him, the rogue, he could talk his way out of a beehive with that silver tongue of his!"

Kroova remarked drily, "Aye, after he'd eaten the honey."

The squirrelmaid chided them. "I think you two are being unfair to Scarum—he's very brave and dependable. I've grown to like him a lot since we met."

Shogg put aside his empty bowl. "Well, that's nice of ye, Trissy. Per'aps you'd like to go an' mind the Dibbuns. It'd save the Father Abbot havin' to ask Scarum again."

Triss murmured as she applied herself to the oatmeal, "There is such a thing as stretching friendship too far, y'-know."

Scarum had not heard the conversation, but he sniffed haughtily at the sound of their laughter. "Hmph, glad there's some chaps enjoyin' themselves, stuck up here on a drizzly mornin', wot!"

Over at the south walltop, Mokug and Crikulus took their blankets from the Abbot and made a small tent by draping them across the battlements. Mokug and Crikulus heard the laughter of Triss and the others. The golden hamster remarked to the Abbot, "Good t'see they're keepin' in 'appy spirits, Father. I likes to see that. Young Triss there, she told me she was a slave at Riftgard since she was a babe. Nice to know a pretty maid like 'er can come through it all an' still smile."

The Abbot watched Triss bantering and joking with her friends. "Yes, there's a lot more to that young squirrel than any of us realise. See how she carries the sword of Martin the Warrior, as though it were part of her. I think that our Triss will leave her mark upon Redwall Abbey, one way or another."

Crikulus paused over his bowl of oatmeal. "I'll second that, friend, that young 'un looks bound for greatness!"

36

Without Plugg to lead them, the Freebooter crew was hopeless. Huddling together at one end of the camp, they sat about, slack-jawed and dull-eyed. Kurda watched them as she discussed the next moves with Vorto and Riggan. The Princess had little else than contempt for the Freebooters, and she showed it openly.

"Tchah, look at dem, stupid bunch of mudbrains!"

Vorto was inclined to agree with her. "Aye, marm, they ain't foraged for food, nor lit a fire. Scum like that are no use to anybeast, eh, Riggan?"

The slavecatcher was not so quick to condemn the crewbeasts. Riggan was a thinker, with a wide knowledge of animal habits.

"Mebbe they do seem in a bit of a mess, but look at our own Ratguards. They ain't farin' much better, are they? We've all 'ad an 'orrible shock today. They're frightened, an' wid good reason, too."

Kurda respected Riggan's advice, though she tried never to show it. "So, den, tell me more."

Riggan explained, sure that Kurda would take her advice. "Well, first we needs to break camp an' find some-

wheres where that bad serpent smell ain't hangin' about.
Wot everybeast needs is a strong leader, like yoreself,
marm. Settle 'em down in a new camp, get a good fire
goin'—not two fires, but one good blaze for all. Post sentries, get foragers searchin' fer vittles. Crack 'em back
into shape."

Kurda was nodding as she listened. "Gutt, gutt, go on."

Riggan warmed to her scheme. "When everybeast's
lookin' better, you got to make it clear that yore chief,
marm. Don't take no backtalk or nonsense from Plugg's
ole crew. Y'see, I know yore bound to 'unt that monster
down an' git yore crown back. That's goin' to mean a lot o'
deaths. So why waste the lives of me 'n' Vorto an the Ratguards, when there's a full gang o' seascum fer ye to use?"

The Pure Ferret allowed Riggan one of her rare smiles.
"Yarr, ve might even spare der liddle deaf 'un, Grubbage,
to sail de *Seashcab* back to Riftgard for us, eh?"

The slavecatcher bowed her head briefly. "Yore idea is
a good 'un, marm. Right, Vorto?"

The Ratguard Captain agreed immediately. "Good
idea, marm!"

Kurda patted her sabre hilt. "All mine ideas are gutt!"

Nobeast objected to moving camp. Riggan chose a spot
closer to the path, a clearing in a fir grove with a clean
smell of pine. By nightfall things were beginning to look
up; a large fire burned in a freshly dug pit and the foragers
had brought in berries, roots and several fat woodpigeons.
The weasel Tazzin and a female ferret, aptly named Fatty,
were self-appointed cooks. They set about providing a
meal for everybeast. Riggan played her part well, jollying
both sides along.

"Ahoy, look at this, mates, the Ratguards just brought
in fresh water an' three nests full o' coots' eggs. Keep a
good big fire burnin' there, Freebooters, snakes don't like
fire. We'll keep it goin' an' sleep round it tonight. Wot's
that you got there, Scummy?"

The stoat had been laboriously scratching away at a
piece of slate with a shard of flint. He held it up proudly.

" 'Tis a poem I writ fer our good ole Cap'n an' pore Prince Bladd, just to remember 'em by."

Vorto could not help sneering at the stoat. "Hah, yew writin'? Rubbish. Freebooters can't write."

Riggan stamped on Vorto's paw and glared at him. "Leave Scummy alone, of course 'e can write. I'll wager 'tis a good poem. Come on Scummy, mate, read it out!"

The *Seascab*'s crew enjoyed the fact that one of their number had some learning. They encouraged him heartily.

"Aye, go on, Scumm, you show 'em, mate!"

The stoat stepped into the firelight and began reading his efforts, slowly at first, but gaining confidence as he rendered his eulogy to Plugg and Bladd.

"Cap'n Plugg 'ad an 'eart o' gold,
He was good at lootin' an' slayin'.
Plugg could lay out some whacks, wid his battle-
    axe,
An' laugh, just as if 'e was playin'.
Aye, but 'e was like a father to us,
Ain't a single beast 'ere can say
They didn't enjoy a kick from the Cap'n,
Once the *Seascab* got under way!
But I tell ye, mates, I cried salt tears,
When 'is tail fell off in me paw,
Robbed of 'is tail, by a foul sneaky trick,
Far from 'ome, on some foreign shore.
Whenever I thinks of dear ole Plugg,
The sight'll haunt me mind,
Of me an' Grubbage, fixin' that tail,
Wid sticky stuff, to his be'ind.
But our Cap'n is gone, an' everyone,
Must curse those 'orrible snakes,
An' live in 'opes, Plugg was tough as ole ropes,
An' killed 'em wid stummick aches!

But 'earken, mates, to the tale o' pore Bladd,
All fat'n'white, wid pink eyes,

Slayed by a cauldron of oatmeal,
Ain't that an orful surprise?
Whacked on 'is royal 'ead, by a big iron pot,
Bladd liked oatmeal as much as the next,
But not the full lot, served up pipin' 'ot,
I'll bet yer 'e felt rather vexed!
Aye, Cap'n an' Prince, we ain't seen 'em since,
Wot a sad gloomy story it makes.
One killed at lunchtime by brekkist,
An' the other et up by snakes!"

Scummy took his bow amid fervent applause from both sides. Many of the Freebooters wept openly, tears coursing down their ugly, bewhiskered faces. Under Vorto's watchful eye, the Ratguards bowed their heads, bodies shaking, as if racked by grief. However, they had difficulty controlling their laughter, as none of them had been particularly fond of the fat, spoiled Prince.

Kurda felt it was time to make her announcement. She stood by the fire, leaning on her sabre.

"Listen to vot I haff to say. No more do I go up against dat Abbey. Now ve must seek vengeance against der shnakes, der monsters vot slayed de good Captain Plugg! Hear me, tomorrow I hunt de serpints to der death, und you vill be at my side and make dem pay for our friend Plugg. Yarr?"

Slitfang emerged from behind the firelight and put the crew of the *Seascab*'s view bluntly. "We ain't goin'."

Vorto hurried forward, spear at the ready. "Silence! The Princess is the leader of this group now!"

Slitfang drew his cutlass and pointed it at Vorto. "Shut yore mouth an' keep outta this. Leaders, eh? I'm the leader of the *Seascab*'s crew when the Cap'n ain't 'ere, an' I say we ain't goin' on no snake 'unt, see!"

Kurda curled her lip scornfully at him. "So, you are de coward now, you don't care noddink about de Captain. Seascum, you are not fit to lead!"

Kurda was a bit taken aback when Slitfang laughed in her face. "Haharr, lissen to 'er, mates, she loved our Cap'n so much that she wants revenge fer 'im? Who do ye think yore foolin', pink eyes, I 'eard you an' Riggan talkin' together when Plugg got taken. Vengeance, me eye, you saw the crown on the snake's 'ead. Now ye know where the treasure lies, in the serpent's den! That's wot yore after, missy. Don't lissen to 'er, mates, she'll get the lot o' ye killed!"

Kurda was trying to hold her rising temper under control. "All right, all I vant is de crown, an' a pawring dat belongs to mine family. You can haff all der rest, shplit it like booty betveen you. It is mine command dat ve go, so obey!"

Slitfang was beginning to enjoy baiting the Princess. "Ho, we'll go all right, first thing tomorrer, straight back to our ship. We're Freebooters, not fools. I'll tell ye somethin' else, too: Don't try an' stand in our way. Right, crew?"

The *Seascab*'s company rose, cheering with him to a beast.

"Aye, we've 'ad enough, let's ship out!"

"Yore givin' the orders, Cap'n Slitty!"

"'Tis wot Plugg would've wanted!"

Kurda seemed to wilt under the weight of opinion against her. She lowered her sabre. Shrugging and smiling ruefully, she skirted the fire, her paw held out to Slitfang.

"So, you are a Freebooter who knows his own mind, yarr. Go if you must, no hard feelinks, eh, Slitty?"

The weasel chuckled. "Aye, an' good luck wid yore snake 'unt, Princess." Lowering his cutlass, he held forth his paw.

It was as if Kurda were back at Riftgard, chopping turnips in the armoury. Two lightning-swift strokes of the sabre, one across, one down. Tazzin reached for her dagger, but dropped her paw as a blade touched the back of her neck and Riggan whispered in her ear, "Just try it an' yore a deadbeast for sure!"

Kurda stepped over Slitfang's headless carcass, flicking his severed paw to one side. She nodded to Vorto. "Take diss out of mine sight!"

Later that night, Kurda lay down at the edge of the firelight to sleep. Riggan and Vorto spread their cloaks on either side of the Princess. She watched the flames
reflecting off the pile of weaponry taken from the
Seascab's crew by her Ratguards. These would only be
reissued at her command. The Pure Ferret sighed with satisfaction. "None of de Freebooters challenged me after I
make de example mit Slitfang, yarr."

Riggan half closed her eyes, ever watchful as she murmured, "None would even look yore way, marm, you was
quicker'n any snake wid that sabre!"

Triss stood on the northwest ramparts, sipping a beaker of
hot vegetable soup and watching a silver sickle moon
peeking out from behind a small, fluffy cloud. Seated with
his back against the battlements, Shogg yawned wearily
and stretched.

"Didn't come back, did they? I'm not complainin'.
'Tis good to 'ave a day's peace after wot we've been
through."

Scarum slid his empty beaker on the walkway and
picked up the otter's half-full one. Shogg nudged him
gently. "I saw that, mate. You go on an' finish it, though. It
might get yore ears out of their grumpy position."

The young hare's ears half rose, then fell back.
"Grumpy? Who said I'm blinkin' grumpy, wot? Stuck up
here for the flippin' rest o' me life with nothin' t'do. Huh,
I volunteered myself for duty in the kitchens, an' that
bloomin' Friar Gooch said he'd sooner have the vermin
helpin' out there instead o' me. The nerve!"

Log a Log watched a moth hovering round the glint
from his rapier blade. "Never mind, Scarum. I'll tell
young Furrel to pack ye an' extra-big lunch tomorrow."

Scarum nodded. "Friendly little molemaid, I like her.
Lunch, did you say lunch, old lad? Why would she be
packin' me a lunch, am I goin' anywhere?"

Skipper leaned over from his walltop perch and tickled
the hare's ear. "If'n the vermin don't show up afore mid-

morn, we're takin' a scoutin' party out t'see wot's goin' on in Mossflower woodlands. Are ye comin'?"

The hare tried to poach Sagax's soup beaker and got a rap over the paw for his audacity. "Count me in, old scout, anythin's better'n sittin' up here like a caterpillar waitin' to change into a bloomin' butterfly, wot wot wot!"

Sagax gave Scarum his beaker, but it was empty. He smiled at his friend's dejected expression.

"Oh, stop looking like a boiled bumblebee. I know you're bored, we're all bored, and it's a long time until dawn. Come on, Scarum, entertain us. Give us that monologue about your uncle Gurdilo—I like that one."

The hare sniffed. "It's Burdilo, not Gurdilo, an' all you've given me tonight is a flamin' empty soup beaker. Shan't!"

Triss picked up the beaker. "Oh, do it, please, I've never heard about your uncle Burdilo. I'll fill this beaker with soup again if you recite it for us. Promise."

Scarum rose stiffly. "You do know the way to a chap's heart, miss, or is it his stomach? Same thing. Oh, all right, here goes." The hare soon had them all chuckling with his comic poem.

"My uncle Burdilo was a chap that you'd like to know.
He'd paws like iron an' a back like oak,
All in all quite a handsome bloke!
They say he scoffed his own weight twice,
In the space of a bloomin' day,
An' licked ten times his weight in foes,
At least that's what they say, hey.
Beefer yoofer arfer deefer, eyefer elfer oh.
That's how he spelt his name, y'know. My uncle
    Burdilo!

His eyesight was so jolly good,
Do you know what they say?
He could spot a fly on an apple pie,
A score o' miles away . . . even on a foggy day!

So strong and tough a hare he was,
D'you know what he did one day?
He stood in a pail an' picked it up,
An' carried himself away, hey.
Beefer yoofer arfer deefer, eyefer elfer oh,
That's how he spelt his name, y'know. My uncle
   Burdilo!

He'd swim wide seas with skill an' ease,
And often for a joke,
He'd run so fast, as he sped past,
His footpaws puffed out smoke!
Y'know what they say, he raced one day,
Until his tail was burnin',
He ran, of course, with such great force,
He met himself returnin'.
Beefer yoofer arfer deefer, eyefer elfer oh,
That's how he spelt his name, y'know. My uncle
   Burdilo!"

During the laughter and applause that followed,
Scarum bowed and flourished both ears outrageously. He
flopped down beside Triss.

"Now, then, how's about that beaker o' soup, m'gel?"

She smiled sweetly at him. "Oh, that. No need for me
to go dashing off to the kitchens—here come Foremole
Urrm and Furrel with two big jugs of soup for refills."

The hare's face was the picture of outrage. "You knew
they were comin'. Hoodwinker, charlatan! I'll never trust
a pretty face again, wot, you see if I bally well don't,
huh!"

Sagax pushed him playfully. "Oh, stop grumbling, it
passed away a pleasant moment or two, didn't it?"

Scarum held out his beaker to be filled, muttering,
"Might have for you rotten lot, but it took quite a bit out
of me, wastin' my artistic an' poetic talents on a pack o'
soup-guzzlin' buffoons, wot. I say there, Furrel, you
charmin' young molemaid, keep pourin'. This blinkin'
beaker's only half full—keep goin', me pretty one!"

The molemaid wrinkled her snout. "Hurr hurr, you'm a gurt flatterer, zurr, h'oi can't resist ee!"

Kroova whispered to Sagax, "I'm glad somebeast can't!"

Scarum shot him an icy glance. "I heard that, y'know!"

37

As all the able-bodied Redwallers were guarding the walltops, there was nobeast to relieve them. Night's dark hours dragged by with painful slowness. The defenders paired off, one napping whilst the other kept watch. Beyond the walls, Mossflower Woods lay calm and peaceful, but to the sentries' eyes they looked different. Every shifting moonshadow or breeze-swayed bough represented the threat of a fresh vermin attack.

Triss watched the silent plain spread out in front of her. Many thoughts wandered in and out of her mind. The friends she had left on Riftgard's cold northern coasts, still trapped in a life of miserable slavery. Agarnu, the fat white King, stumping about on his false limb, while his tyrannical mind dreamed up new schemes that added to the harsh existence of the wretched captives who served his every whim. The vow she had made to poor old Drufo.

Triss touched the hilt of Martin's wondrous sword. Silently she renewed her vow to return and free the slaves. Martin the Warrior's spirit had guided her across the seas to Redwall. She would do what she had to and help her new friends to defend their Abbey against evil. But the day would come when she would set paw again on Rift-gard's shores to avenge Drufo's memory, and that of the father she had never known, Rocc Arrem.

Lying on a bed near the dormitory door, Memm Flackery stuck out a paw, stopping the Dibbun Bikkle from leaving the room. The Harenurse murmured. "Where d'you think you're off to, little miss?"

The squirrelbabe climbed up onto Memm's bed. "Br-effist, it bee's time for breffist, Bikkle, 'ear a larker!"

The bed creaked as Memm rose and carried Bikkle to an open window. Dawn's first lark twittered thinly, ascending into the pale light of a new day. Delicate rose hues stippled the horizon, dispersing the dark blue of night as soft gold sunrays threaded out between cream-puff clouds.

Ruggum trundled up beside Memm and Bikkle. "Yurr, ee larker bee's a-tellin' uz et's toime furr breffist."

Taking in the glorious scene before her, Memm absently patted the molebabe's head. "Hmm, the beauties of Mother Nature are never lost on you, Ruggum, wot!"

Nodding solemnly, the molebabe agreed. "Hurr, they'm surpintly b'ain't, marm!"

The morning wore on, with no sign of the vermin returning to attack Redwall. Skipper and Log a Log had shared their plans with the Abbot: a force was to be sent out into the woodlands. It was vital that they knew what had caused the Freebooters and Ratguards to break off the attack.

Triss was pleasantly surprised when they consulted her as to who should go and who would stay behind to protect the Abbey. Scarum was chosen to stay with the home-guard, as was Gurdle Sprink and all the shrews who had arrived with Mimsy and Gulif, most of whom had families. The rest would be Redwallers, those too young or old to travel, and possibly fight. Triss suggested that they leave at least one more capable warrior behind, to assist Scarum and Gurdle. They decided it would be one of the four otters. Shogg, Kroova, Churk and Rumbol drew lots, and it fell to the sea otter.

Kroova was slightly disappointed, but he made light of it. "Hah, it'll be easy enough defendin' the walltops, mates, but who's goin' to defend the kitchens against old Scarum?"

Foremole and his crew were out on the path, having just finished burying the slain vermin and cleaning the oatmeal from the gateway. He touched a heavy digging claw to his snout as the tracking party emerged from the Abbey.

"Hurr, gudd luck to ee, zurrs'n'marms, you'm be careful an' watch owt furr ee vermint villyuns."

The remaining Redwallers flocked to the west walltop as Skipper, Log a Log, Triss and Sagax led off their crew at high noon. Guosim shrews formed the main body, followed by the three otters, Mokug and a half-dozen Abbey dwellers. The Abbot stood on the walltop with Scarum and Kroova, waving and calling goodbyes. The hare bellowed down to the trackers, "Give 'em blood'n'vinegar, chaps, an' don't let that Sagax too near the blinkin' supplies. Badgers are born hogs, y'know. Hawhawhaw!"

Triss threw a salute to the Abbot. "Don't worry, Father, I'll bring Martin's sword back safe and sound."

Apodemus smiled fondly at her. "I'm sure you will, my child."

Shogg and Kroova had become close friends. The sea otter shouted down to Shogg, "I'll tell Friar Gooch t'make some shrimp'n'hotroot soup to share with ye on yore return, mate."

Shogg grinned from ear to ear. "Yore a good 'un, matey. I'll look forward to that. We'll scoff it t'gether."

Foremole and his crew were still out on the path. They watched until the last creature disappeared into the woodlands, then Scarum began exercising his authority from above.

"Attention now, all moletypes will come inside an' lock the gates, quick as y'like now, jump to it!" Scarum

saluted Kroova with a fine military flourish. "Got to keep
those wallahs on the move, y'know, wot!"

The otter, still staring at the small dust cloud the party
had left on the path, agreed absentmindedly. "Wot, oh
aye, right, mate, keep 'em on the move . . ."

Ripper the searat and Tazzin found themselves in the vanguard of the vermin as they marched through the quiet,
sunshafted woodlands. Without turning his eyes, Ripper
nodded backward. "I'll wager that Princess Kurda is well
pertected."

Tazzin took a quick peek. "Oh aye, yore right there.
She's right in the middle ranks, guarded by spears. Not up
front in the open like me 'n' you, mate. Still, there's 'er
tracker, Riggan, scoutin' up ahead of us. If anybeast gets
attacked by snakes, she'll be the first."

Ripper did not agree. "Not when we gets t'the snakes'
den, that's when we'll be given our weapons back an' told
to charge in the front door. Well, 'ere's one wot won't be
goin'. I ain't no fool. Let 'er guards do the chargin'."

Tazzin's gaze roved from side to side as she answered,
"You seen wot 'appened to Slitfang, didn't ye? Kurda
ain't a beast t'be crossed—I never seen a creature so fast
an' deadly wid a sabre. She'd 'ave slayed Plugg if'n the
snakes didn't get to 'im first. That ferret's a real swordbeast!"

Not only had Kurda ringed herself with Ratguards, but
she had split the unarmed Freebooters, keeping half in
front of the column and the other half behind. The
Princess was as frightened as any of them by the thought
of the three snakes, but her mind was working constantly
as she discussed plans with Vorto.

"Ven Riggan finds der serpents' den, you give de Freebooters der veapons back. I t'ink many of dem get killed
in de shnakes' lair. Who vill get mine crown back for
me?"

Vorto had been thinking up a new plan, which he outlined. "No real need for 'em t'go chargin' in, yore 'ighness. Suppose we was to stake one o' the Freebooters out

in front o' the den? We could be layin' in wait when the
serpents come out t'get the bait, then we could send
Plugg's crew in to finish the snakes off."

Kurda liked the idea. "Yarr, gutt! Den you an' mine
guards rush in an' take mine crown from der dead serpents. Und if de lair is empty, den you go in an' get der
pawring. Gutt!"

Vorto was not too happy about exploring the snakes'
den to find the royal pawring. But he said nothing, knowing that he could drive any surviving Freebooters in ahead
of him. It was a good plan; all that would be sacrificed
would be the crew of the *Seascab*.

Log a Log's scouts tracked the vermin trail to their previous night's camp. A Guosim shrew emerged from the undergrowth rather swiftly. "There's a slayed weasel in
there, with 'is paw an' 'ead lopped off. They must've been
quarrellin' among themselves."

With one mighty tug, Sagax released Plugg's battle-
axe from the trunk of the sycamore. He wielded it in
one paw. "I like the feel of this weapon. I think I'll
claim it."

Triss watched him heft the big axe. "I think you'd better have it, it suits you, Sagax. There's not many other
beasts could lift it, let alone use it!"

Log a Log stirred the dead fire ashes with his rapier,
listening to the report of one of his scouts.

"Still a smell of those adders yonder, faint, but track-
able. Looks like they're huntin' 'em, Chief."

Wiping his rapier clean, the Guosim Chieftain replied,
"Aye, an' we're trackin' them. So everybeast be double
careful, an' you scouts, watch yoreselves. Give a shout
if'n ye get into trouble, we won't be far behind."

Shogg threw some kindling on the dead fire and set
flint to tinder, blowing on the sparks. Log a Log saw what
he was doing and nodded approval.

"No sense in catchin' up to 'em too soon, eh, mate?"

Shogg dug bread and cheese from his pack. "I figger if
the vermin are huntin' these serpents, we'd be better off

lettin' 'em go ahead an' do it. No sense in runnin' into the middle of a vermin snakefight."

Log a Log winked broadly at Triss. "That's a smart matey ye got there, miss. Let's stop an' take a snack."

The squirrelmaid sat down with Shogg and Mokug, who was going over the map rhyme, which he had remembered by heart.

> "Midday sun shines bright for you,
> 'Twixt leaning ash and poison gold,
> Where the greenrock hidden lies,
> For keen eyes to behold."

All of the Abbey newcomers were familiar with the riddle. During the long watches on Redwall's ramparts they had been told of the story of the quest for Brockhall. Mokug sat repeating the lines under his breath, his brow furrowed with concentration. Triss passed him bread and cheese.

"Keep trying, mate, you'll get the answer sooner or later."

Packing food into his cheek pouches, the golden hamster chattered his teeth in frustration. "Well, I 'opes 'tis sooner, missy, I likes to 'elp me friends. These Redwallers 'ave been good to me! Skipper's showed me wot an ash tree looks like, but I don't know anythin' about poison gold an' greenrocks. Huh, nor does young Churk, an' she's cleverer than most of us put t'gether."

A glimmer of pride for his species shone in Shogg's eyes. "Aye, mate, us otters knows a lot more'n most beasts think!"

Mokug looked hopefully at him. "Could you solve it, Shogg?"

The otter shuffled his paws awkwardly. "Well, er, I dunno, I ain't had as much learnin' as Churk . . ."

Triss clasped his paw, encouraging her friend. "Give it a try, Shogg, go on. What do you think of it all?"

He stared hard into the fire, scratching his chin. "Hmm, it seems t'me that we're lookin' for an 'idden green rock, an' the clue to it is in the midday sun. But yore puzzle is in that second line. ' 'Twixt leanin' ash an' poison gold.' D'ye think I'm on the right track, Triss?"

The squirrelmaid ran mentally over the second line. "You could be. We've found out that leaning ash is probably an ash tree that leans in some way. Now, what about poison gold—could that be a tree as well?"

Mokug suddenly brightened up. "Aye, it might be a tree!"

Shogg became aware that other members of the party were listening to the conversation as they sat eating. So he attempted to enlist their help. "Ahoy, mates, any of ye knows about trees?"

Log a Log pointed out a serious-faced shrew. "Grifty, yore always spoutin' poems an' songs about the woodlands. Yore ole mum was a healer, wasn't she?"

The Guosim shrew Grifty prodded the fire with a stick. "Aye, best healer in all Mossflower, my mother was. She knew all the names o' plants, bushes, trees an' flowers. She needed to use all of 'em for 'er remedies."

"Well, wot can y'tell us about trees?"

Grifty was considering Log a Log's question as he poked at the fire. "Trees, hmm, now let me see. I can do ye a rhyme about trees. Would that be any help?"

Mokug chuckled. "We needs all the help we can git, mate. Do your rhyme for us, please."

It took Grifty a moment to recall the rhyme, then he looked up from the fire and began reciting:

"Most trees are old, long-standing friends,
With crowns of leaf and trunks of wood,
Their lives o'er countless seasons span,
And learn from them we should.
Great oak is king of woodlands,
It rules both copse and glade,
To give us acorns from its cups,
Midst wondrous spreading shade.
Bold chestnut, too, has nuts for you,
Some maples' sap is sweet,

Slim rowan, known as mountain ash,
Bears berries red to eat.
Dark baubles from the elder,
And juniper so fine,
Like fruits of good wild cherry,
Can all be turned to wine.
But other trees are not like these,
Take caution and beware,
Some are born to carry death,
Although they may look fair.
Bright berries of spurge laurel,
Laburnum's flowers of gold,
And blossoms from a guelder rose,
All beauteous to behold,
But poison in their nature,
I say to you, my friend,
Ignore this timely warning,
And your days will swiftly end!"

Shogg slapped his rudder sharply on the ground. "Ha-harr, there 'tis, plain as the crust on a pie! Laburnum flowers o' gold an' they're poison, too. ' 'Twixt leanin' ash an' poison gold.' We're lookin' for a laburnum crossed by an ash tree wot ain't growin' straight!"

Mokug tugged at Triss's robe. "Wot does a laburnum look like?"

Triss explained. "It's not a big tree, but quite slender, with smallish spearhead-shaped leaves and long chains of bright yellow flowers hanging from every branch. Laburnum's a deadly tree, though, not just the flowers, but the leaves, wood and bark and all."

She was interrupted by Log a Log calling to his scouts, "Take a look round the woods, mates, see if ye can bring back a laburnum branch to show ole Mokug."

Triss was surprised by the shrews' alacrity. They seemed to have been gone no time at all, when one came racing back. In his paw he clutched a laburnum branch, wrapped around one end with dock leaves to protect himself.

As soon as Mokug caught sight of it, he was beside himself with eagerness. "I've seen one of 'em before, a tree all covered wid those yellow flowers. I've seen one, I tell ye!"

Shogg was caught up in the excitement. "Where, mate, where?"

Mokug ceased jumping up and down. "Er, er, I couldn't put me paw on it right now, but I'll remember, never fear, mates. I know 'twas someplace east of where ye found me when that ole owl was slain. Aye, I'll know it when I sees it!"

Log a Log shook his head. "But that's away from the vermin tracks we're followin', well away."

There was a momentary silence, then Churk spoke up. "All the better for us, I say. If the vermin are trackin' the snakes to their den, they'll be goin' in by the front way. But if we can find the back entrance, we'll know where both the vermin an' the serpents are. Inside!"

Sagax left off whetting his axe blade and viewed the sky. "How far off would you say the two trees are, Mokug?"

The hamster scratched his ear. "Oh, a fair piece, I'd say, at least half a mornin's walk."

Log a Log thrust his rapier into the earth. "Right, then we camp 'ere tonight an' break camp at dawn. With any luck, that'll bring us to the place before midday sun shines bright for us!"

38

Redwall's rose-coloured sandstone walls still felt warm
from the summer day's heat. Blackbirds could be heard
warbling throatily in the evening's stillness. Father Abbot
had gone back to his Dibbun days; he was enjoying himself down at the Abbey pond with a group of Abbeybabes.
The old mouse cut a comical figure as, with his long habit
tucked up, he dashed into the shallows and joined in with
the fun of skipping stones, chortling happily, "Three, four,
five, look, my stone bounced six times!"

Ruggum glared at him suspiciously. "Yurr, oi only
counted foive bouncers, zurr, b'ain't that roight, Malbun,
marm?"

Malbun, who was sitting on the grassy bank with
Crikulus and Memm, agreed with the infant mole. "Aye,
Ruggum, five it was. You still hold the record for six
bounces. You counted wrong, Father Abbot!"

Abbot Apodemus pulled a face that had the Dibbuns
squeaking with laughter. "You just don't want me to win
the candied chestnut trifle, you old cheat—bet you're going to share it with Ruggum. You're both in this together!"

Crikulus looked sternly over his glasses. "Six bounces

gets the trifle, sir—yours was only five. I counted 'em me-self!"

The Abbot registered an expression of comic shock. "You're both on Ruggum's side now! Memm Flackery, tell them my stone bounced six times, please."

The Harenurse's ears twitched. "I certainly will not, sah! An Abbot of your age, cheatin'! What's Redwall comin' to?"

Friar Gooch solved the dispute by marching up with Furrel, his molemaid assistant, in tow. "My candied chest-nut trifle's been stolen!"

Wading out of the pond, the Abbot unhitched his wet habit. "Are you sure you're right, Gooch, stolen?"

Furrel assisted him up the bank. "Burr aye, zurr, ee troifle's bee'd stoled roight enuff. Oi see'd ee Friar putten et on ee gurt slate shelf, to let it be coolen."

Gooch cut in, fluttering his jaws wildly. "A moment later, there it was, gone!"

Paws akimbo, Memm stared accusingly at one or two likely Dibbun candidates. "Own up, you villains, who's sneaked back to the kitchens instead of playin' skimmin' stones, wot?"

Kroova's head broke the surface of the pond's centre, where he had been acting as lifeguard, and swam ashore. "None of these liddle 'uns been away from this pond, marm, I've kept a close check on 'em since we arrived 'ere. The question ye should be askin' is, where's Scarum?"

The Abbot gaped disbelievingly at Kroova. "Scarum? You don't mean he . . ."

The otter nodded decisively. "Aye, Scarum. As hares go, beggin' y'pardon, miz Memm, Scarum is the biggest glut-ton 'twixt 'ere an' the cracks o' doom. Come on, let's find 'im!"

The young hare in question was snoring in an upturned barrow at the orchard entrance. A candied chestnut was stuck to the fur between his ears, meadowcream liberally festooned his whiskers, and traces of redcurrant, black-berry, maple sponge and other trifle ingredients clung to his narrow chest and bulging stomach.

He grumbled dreamily as Kroova poked a paw into his midriff, "Gerroff, it's all mine, go an' get your own, rotter!"

Memm took the wheelbarrow and turned him out with a mighty heave. Scarum sat up, blinking.

"What 'n the name . . . I say there, chaps, have a care, wot. A gentle shake's all that's needed t'wake your jolly old military commander. Ho hum, what's up with you bounders, all standin' round with faces like flippin' fried frogs?"

Memm seized his ears and hauled him upright. "Candied chestnut trifle, sah, where is it?"

Scarum transformed into the picture of outraged innocence. "Candied chestnut trifle, marm, what're you wafflin' on about, wot wot? Never come across one in me life, no marm!"

He winced as Kroova ripped the sticky chestnut from between his ears and stuck it on the end of his nose. Quite deliberately, the sea otter wiped cream from Scarum's whiskers and smeared it along his top lip like a moustache. Kroova brought his face close until they were eye-to-eye.

"That candied chestnut trifle, you 'orrible great foodbag. Don't tell lies, yore only makin' it worse for yoreself!"

Scarum forced a weak smile. "Oh, that one! Well, why didn't you say, old lad? I, er, spotted it in the kitchen an' just took a small nibble, nothin' too drastic, wot."

The Abbot stared questioningly at him. "A small nibble?"

Scarum nodded emphatically. "Yes, sah, barely a smidgen. Don't know what happened to the rest of the confounded trifle. I expect those moles guzzled it. Small types, but incredibly greedy, those molechaps. I say, what d'you think you're doin'? Yowch! Owch! Lemme go, mercy!"

Memm and Kroova had him by an ear apiece. They hauled him off to the Abbey, with Malbun giving him the dressing-down of his life, accompanied by hard paw prods.

"That trifle was to be shared out among the Dibbuns as a treat, with the winner of the stone-skimming getting the first portion. Aren't you ashamed of yourself, depriving those poor babes of their special treat?"

Opening the Abbey door, the Abbot took charge. "Thank you, Memm and Kroova, you may release him now. Right, master Scarum, follow me!"

The door slammed behind them. There was an awed silence as the Dibbuns stood looking at one another on the doorstep. Ruggum spoke in a hoarse whisper. "Boo urr, oi wunners wot zurr h'Abbot bee's goin' t'do to Scarum?"

Mousebabe Turfee had some definite views on the subject. "Choppa off'n his tail an' baff de daylights out of him, an' make 'im go t'bed for fifty 'leven days. Ho yes!"

Memm picked the mousebabe up. "Is that all? Lettin' the cad off far too easy, if y'ask me, wot!"

Later that evening, Friar Gooch and Furrel made it up to the Dibbuns by creating another trifle and serving it out to them in the orchard. The Abbot came out to join them, gratefully accepting a bowl of the delicious trifle and a beaker of strawberry fizz. Crowding around him, the Dibbuns eagerly wanted to know what punishment had been meted out to the greedy hare. As each enquiry became more gruesome, the Abbot called for quiet.

"No, no, I never chopped off his tail or boiled him up in the soup—what a bloodthirsty notion!"

Crikulus could no longer restrain his curiosity. "Then how did you deal with the wretch, Father?"

Putting aside his bowl, the Abbot explained. "Well, the first thing I did was to put him on a diet for three days—only one portion of lettuce leaves and water per day. Then I locked him in the main Dibbuns' dormitory with pail, scrubber, broom and duster. Scarum must scrub the place from top to bottom, floor, walls, windows, everything. After that he must restuff all the mattresses, make up the beds with clean bed linen and wash all the old stuff. That should keep him amused!"

Opinions were divided, with Dibbuns still muttering darkly of tail chopping and soup boiling, whilst the elders nodded sagely.

Kroova smiled with satisfaction. "Three days with just one meal a day of lettuce an' water? You'll 'ear ole Scarum yowlin' a league away!"

Looking over the top of his glasses, the Abbot agreed. "I've no doubt we will. I've also stripped him of his command. Kroova, you'll be in charge of the wallguards. Every other beast can sleep out here in the orchard. 'Tis a fine warm night here, and out of yowling range, too."

The Dibbuns cheered gleefully. Sleeping out in the orchard was an adventure for them. Sister Vernal, Mimsy and Memm exchanged grim looks; their night's work was cut out for them, keeping the Abbeybabes together in one place.

Dawn was well up and a fresh summer's day was under way. A needlepoint of sunlight pierced the gloom of Brockhall. Zassaliss uncoiled, dealing the other two adders light blows with his blunt nose.

"Hissst! Sssomething goesss on outssssside, let usss ssseeee!"

Kurda had chosen the skinniest, most useless-looking Freebooter, an old searat called Whidge. The remainder of the *Seascab*'s crew were forced to watch, helpless and unarmed, as Vorto and three Ratguards laid paws on Whidge, dragging him shrieking to an open spot within view of the door in the oak tree. When Whidge saw the stake, driven deep into the ground, with a rope collar attached to it, he dug his footpaws in and wailed aloud to his comrades, "Don't let 'em do this t'me, mates, 'elp me, 'elp me!"

A blow to his jaw from Vorto's spearbutt knocked the old searat senseless. Ratguards menaced the Freebooters with their spearpoints as Kurda addressed them warningly.

"Dat von is old and useless. Anybeast tryink to rescue 'im vill take his place, yarr?"

Cowed and leaderless, they hung their heads in silence. Vorto swiftly bound Whidge's paws together and tightened the rope halter at the back of the searat's neck, where he could not reach it. Riggan signaled everybeast back to the cover of the undergrowth where Vorto placed two Ratguards with each group of Freebooters. They held the crewbeast's weapons, ready to distribute at a nod from their captain, while Kurda took to a high fernbed, where she crouched with Vorto and Riggan on either side of her. The Pure Ferret could see the door from her vantage point. She drew her sabre.

"Und now ve haff only to vait!"

From his spyhole behind the door, Zassaliss and the other two snakes had seen all that went on. Sesstra hissed softly, "They leave ussss food, they fear usssss!"

Her brother Harssacss flickered his tongue sensuously. "Brother Zassaliss, doessss not the ssssight of food make ussss ravenousssss?"

Zassaliss was bigger and more powerfully built than his brother and sister. He retreated down the tunnel, pulling them along with him. Sarengo's rusty mace chain clanked as he halted a safe distance away from the entrance.

"Can you not ssssee, it issss a trap. We will ssssstay here, ssssstill and ssssssilent. The day will be warm—at noon they will tire of waiting and ssssssleep. Then we will ssssstrike fasssst and ssssseize the bait! You two take him. I will watch over ussss and take care of any foolsss who try to attack usss!"

Triss left the main body of the column and went ahead to catch up with Mokug. The sprightly old hamster was scurrying along, with his eyes fixed on the woodlands ahead. He pointed. "Haharr, we're gettin' near there, missy, see. Laburnums, there's plenty of 'em in this neck o' the woods."

Triss saw the splotches of hanging yellow blooms amid the trees. "D'you know which is the right one?"

Mokug plowed onward. "I will when I sees it, I'm shore!"

Skipper caught up with them, looking doubtful. "We're a good way east o' the place where I found the capes an' lanterns—quite a ways, in fact. Ahoy, Mokug, are you sure it's round here someplace?"

The golden hamster halted. "'Tis our lucky day, mates—there's the leanin' ash, dead ahead!"

Some unknown force of nature had caused the ash tree to grow at a strange angle. A laburnum had caught the ash trunk in its fork as it sprouted. Being stronger, the ash had forced the laburnum to bend. Together they formed a rough diagonal cross with their trunks.

Skipper placed his chin in the cross joint. "All I can see is the sun in me eyes."

Churk shook her head at his efforts. "Then try comin' round the other side an' lookin' that way."

Skipper rubbed his eyes. "That's wot comes o' bein' born wid brains. 'Ere, Sagax, you give it a go, matey!"

The young badger took up his place on the other side of the tree. With his chin in the intersection, he gazed ahead. "I'm afraid I don't see anything except woodland, trees, bushes, ferns. No, sorry, can't see a thing!"

"That's probably 'cos it ain't midday yet." Shogg stared upward at the sky. "We'll just 'ave to wait."

Skipper winked broadly at Log a Log. "Wot would ye do without us otters, I ask ye?"

The Guosim Chieftain replied nonchalantly. "Share out yore vittles atween the rest of us, me ole mate!"

Sagax brightened up. "Vittles, that's a nice idea. Thank goodness we don't have Scarum along with us."

They dined on some of Friar Gooch's oatloaf, which had honey and nuts baked into it, together with apples and flasks of dandelion and burdock cordial.

Triss felt better than she had in a long time, surrounded by good friends, true honest beasts. A sudden wave of affection for Shogg swept over her. She watched him joking and chuckling with some Guosim shrews as they shared

their food. Good old faithful Shogg! He had been with her
from the start, through thick and thin. It would be pleasant
for them to live out their seasons at Redwall, with all its
happy atmosphere and trusty companions.

The squirrelmaid gazed at her reflection in the blade of
Martin the Warrior's great sword. She could see in her
own eyes that this could never be. Not whilst there was a
single creature living under the yoke of slavery, across the
seas in Riftgard. Drufo's voice was still burned into her
memory: "Get away from 'ere, Trissy. Get away! I ain't
goin' nowhere! This is as good a day to die as any. Remember me, remember yore father. You'll be back to free
the slaves one day, I know ye will. Now go, don't waste
the chance we gave ye!"

As Triss gazed at her reflection in the swordblade, the
noise of creatures talking, laughing and eating together
blended into a fuzzy background hum. The squirrelmaid's
eyes were fixed on the bright blade. However, it was not
her features staring back at her; it was Martin, the Warrior
of Redwall, whose strong, gentle voice echoed through
her mind:

> " 'Twixt leaning ash and poison gold,
> Trisscar Swordmaid, look, behold,
> What is sought by everyone.
> Now! Ere high noon light moves on."

Shogg poured out a drink for Triss, but as he held it out
to her, she rose dreamily and brushed by him. Log a Log
watched her go toward the two trees.

"She looks like she's sleepwalkin', mate. Hi, Trissy,
where are ye off to?"

Shogg silenced the shrew hurriedly. "Hush, mate, let
'er be!"

Triss's odd behaviour caused the entire camp to qui-
eten down. Churk whispered to Sagax, "Look, the sun's
dead centre, it must be exactly midday at this moment!"

Placing her chin in the treeforks, Triss narrowed her

eyes, peering straight ahead. Then it was as if the spell was broken, for she became her usual cheerful self.

Leaving her position, she strode resolutely forward. Passing Churk, she gave the ottermaid's ear a tweak and laughed aloud. "Haha, I caught a glimmer! Go and put your chin in that tree fork, mate. Don't look until I give you a shout."

Mystified, Churk carried out the request. Triss continued walking until she was almost obscured by trees and shrubbery. She halted at what appeared to be a hump in the ground. Picking up a rough, paw-sized pebble from the top of the hump, she began polishing it hard against her tunic. Having done this, she replaced the pebble and called out, "Churk, get your chin in the fork and take a look!"

A short moment went by. Then Churk could be heard yelling, "Yaharr! Great wallopin' rudders, mates, come an' take an eyeful o' this. Trissy, me pal, yore a wonder— how did ye know?"

Crowding round, the entire party struggled to get a glance.

"I see it, the light, it shines like white fire!"

Sagax and Shogg dashed through the woodland to Triss's side. She was leaning proudly on a massive bulge with bright green liverwort moss growing all over it. Small, tight and curling fronds completely obscured the stone. Triss pointed to the rough rock crystal pebble standing at its centre.

"I saw it glimmer in the midday sun. It was a bit dull and dirty, so I gave it a good polish to make it shine properly."

Sagax touched the bulge reverently. "So this big mound is the greenstone!"

Churk ran her paws through the moss covering the stone. "The rear entrance to Brockhall! But how did ye find it, Triss?"

The squirrelmaid shrugged, her vision of Martin unrecalled. "I don't know, really. Just a bright idea, I suppose."

Skipper gave a great belly laugh. "Hohoho! Bright idea, that's a good 'un. Lookin' at that crystal pebble, I'd say 'twas a shinin' idea, miss. Now, mates, anybeast got more bright ideas as to 'ow we move this big hump of rock?"

Churk and Triss were already on all fours, doing a tour of the rock's base. The squirrelmaid suddenly halted. Without looking up, she shot out a paw. "Sharp knife, please!"

A dozen daggers appeared like magic. She grabbed one, talking as she scraped busily away. "Moss isn't growing as thick here. Somebeast scraped it away a long time ago, but it takes a lot of seasons for liverwort as thick as this to grow properly again. What d'you make of this, matey?"

Churk was at her side, inspecting the symbols scratched into the bare limestone. She nodded knowingly. "'Tis that crazy ole alphabet again. Mokug, get me that key I made, it's in my pack. I'll soon tell ye wot this says!"

By the time they had cleaned off the stone sufficiently, Mokug found the translation and brought it to Churk. Using birchbark parchment and a charcoal stick, Shogg wrote the symbols as Churk called out the letters:

t u r n h a l f w a y a n d s l i d e s o u t h

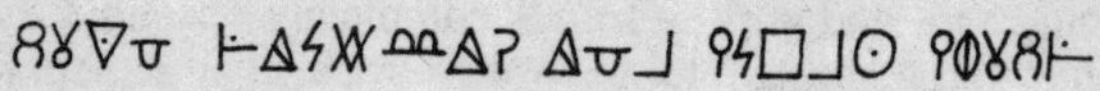

Sagax scratched his striped muzzle. "Turn halfway and slide south. Let's give it a try, Skip!"

Between them, both otter and badger possessed considerable strength. However, they could not budge the stone a bit, no matter how they threw their weight against it. Triss could not help smiling at their efforts.

"Stop pushing and shoving before you do yourselves an injury. It's pretty clear that nobeast has moved this stone for ages. Wouldn't it be better to clear the ground around the base first, get rid of all these weeds and rubbish?"

Skipper blew a sweat bead from his nose tip and grinned. "I was waitin' for me niece Churk t'suggest that, miss, but I'm willin' to accept yore solution!"

Log a Log swept his rapier blade along the ground. When he pulled away the moss where the rock met earth, he heard a scraping sound. "It's stone, a stone laid on a stone base. Let's get to it!"

It did not take long for the efforts of the entire party to clear a wide circle. The Guosim Chieftain was right. Their work revealed a wide flat stone base, with scratches in it that had been made every time the badgers of old had shifted the greenstone to open the rear exit.

Streamwater and soapwort were brought, and they washed the base off and rubbed soapwort plants onto the stonework. Skipper, Sagax and Shogg tried this time. At first the greenstone refused to budge, then Triss and Churk lent a paw. The ottermaid lent a suggestion, too.

"Try turnin' it left to right, instead o' right to left."

Skipper muttered to Shogg, "Y'know, I think she inherited a double portion o' brains!"

Shogg stifled a giggle. "Aye, but not from yore side o' the family, mate!"

The stone moved without too much difficulty. When it would turn no further, Churk gave it a healthy shove southward. It slid aside. Triss peered down a dusty flight of steps into the darkness below.

"Welcome to Brockhall, friends!"

39

Whidge had regained consciousness, finding himself bound to the stake in front of the serpents' lair. He moaned and whined piteously, until both Ratguards and Freebooters were tired of his whimpering.

Tazzin shook her head in disgust. "I wuz never too fond o' that ole misery. If'n 'e keeps that weepin' up, I'll finish 'im off meself!"

Kurda gave Riggan a sly wink before she answered Tazzin. "No, no, mine friend, ve need 'im alive or der serpents might lose de interest, den ve get no booty. Keep der rat quiet, but don't slay 'im."

Tazzin crept out from cover. Hurling herself on Whidge, she gagged the wretched searat with his own broad belt. "There, that'll keep ye quiet. You just lie there an' wiggle about a bit—I'll see ye get yore share o' the loot!"

Whidge lay wide-eyed, staring into his former shipmate's hard features. The only noise he could make was "Mmfff!"

Tazzin patted him reassuringly. "Aye, that's the stuff, but mind now, if'n ye get much noisier'n that . . . well."

She licked the blade of her knife, grinned wickedly at him and departed to hide behind a sycamore with Grubbage.

Kurda conferred with Riggan. "Get dem t'inking about loot und booty an' ve haff dose seascum on our side, yarr. You sure der serpents are in dere?"

Riggan watched the door in the oak trunk. "Oh, I'm shore, marm. Trackin' that 'ellish smell to yon oak was no trouble. Those snakes are in there, all right, I'd stake me life on it."

Kurda's pink eyes were as cold as ice as she tested her sabre edge. "You better hope you don't lose your stake."

The bright summer day drifted by with the pace of a leisurely snail, warm sun and humming insects combining to soften the menace that hovered over the still, green woodland. The stoat Scummy spread out on some moss behind an elm and closed his eyes. A nearby Ratguard prodded the Freebooter with his spearbutt.

"Hoi, yore s'posed to be watchin', not snoozin'."

Scummy opened one eye and glared balefully at the rat. "Mind yer own business, I'll do wot I like, see!"

The Ratguard was slightly taken aback. "Better not let Cap'n Vorto or Princess Kurda catch ye!"

Ripper the searat curled his lip at the speaker. "Wot are we supposed t'do, then, sit 'ere to attention all day? We've 'ad little sleep an' 'ardly a bite to eat. I'm gonna get some o' those whortleberries growin' over yonder. Yew stay awake an' keep guard—yore a Ratguard, ain't yer? We're Freebooters, we do wot we like!"

As time meandered slowly by, summer cast its warm spell over the glade. Anybeast out of Kurda and Vorto's sight took advantage of the torpor and dozed off, crewbeasts and soldiers alike. Even Kurda could not halt her eyelids from drooping.

Vorto tried to remain attentive, whispering to Riggan, who was still watching through half-closed eyes, "Those serpents would've showed theirselves by now if'n they was really in there. You sure you saw 'em go in?"

The tracker gave Vorto a pitying look. "I trailed 'em 'ere. I never saw the snakes enter, I got 'ere too late fer that. But they're in there, all right."

Whidge was lying quite still. Vorto did not realise that the old searat had been suffocated by his own belt. "Look at 'im. Don't seem t'be too bothered by it all, does 'e?"

Down inside the dusty gloom of Brockhall, Zassaliss slithered forward, pulling his brother and sister along with him. "Sssssssoft now, sssssssilent! Let usssss ssssssee what issss happening outsssssside."

As they passed the mummified remains of their mother and King Sarengo, locked together in death's eternal embrace, Sesstra hissed malevolently, "The time hasssss come to make them pay for thisssss!"

Leaving a rearguard of Guosim shrews aboveground, Triss led the woodlanders down the steps into Brockhall. It was gloomy and musty, with the awful odour hanging thick upon the still air. Sagax tried to keep his voice from echoing into the tunnel as he murmured to Skipper, "D'you think we should chance a light?"

The otter Chieftain mentally debated the point for a moment. "A light could get us seen. But I think we should 'ave one down 'ere, 'cos we need to see. Hmm, we'd be best off with a small 'un that don't flare up too bright."

Churk felt along the rough rock wall until she encountered a bend. "There's one here, will this do?"

It was a candle lamp, with a good thick candle stump in it. Log a Log set flint to tinder and lit it. "Aye, this'll do fine. The crystal glass is all dusty, but it'll give us enough light t'see wot we're doin'."

The lamp gave off a soft golden light upon an eerie scene. Brockhall, the once-legendary home of badgers and their woodland friends, was in a sad state of neglect. Cobwebs clung everywhere and tree roots hung like tentacles from wall and ceiling. The whole ancient place was deeply coated in dust, with sinister drag marks down the centre of each winding passage. There were side cham-

bers, some with the doors broken down, others screened
by curtains, which crumbled and disintegrated at a touch.
Sagax and Shogg entered one and looked around. It had
once been a comfortable bedchamber, but now the wonderfully carved furniture was woodworm-riddled and broken. Snakeskins, shed in previous seasons, caused
revulsion among the seekers as they burst and crinkled
underpaw.

Out in the corridor, Triss called in an echoing whisper,
"Stay together, don't anybeast stray off alone."

Mokug shuddered. "Good advice, missy, I'm all fer
that!"

Log a Log placed a paw against the hamster's mouth.
"An' don't speak lessen ye have to, t'ain't safe in 'ere!"

Scarum strode blithely up the path, munching on a hefty
apple-and-blackcurrant flan. Chuckling to himself, he cut
off into the woodlands. "Dozy old bunch, wot! Jolly im-
pudent, too, I'd say. Fancy thinkin' y'could demote a gar-
rison commander to a drudge of all work, cads! Chap of
my blinkin' skills, wot? Didn't take me a bloomin' tick to
escape that lot. Huh, starvin' for three days on lettuce
leaves an' water, fat chance! They'd find my young
wasted body dead after just two flamin' days o' that nonsense. Hey ho for the open air an' fiddle dee dee for those
old buffers. Join up with the chaps, that's the ticket! Comrades staunch an' true, with lots of rations an' so forth. Y'-
can't go paw-sloggin' without loads of fodder t'keep
fur'n'scut together, no sah!"

The incorrigible young hare strode jauntily along,
armed with a pillowcase full of food from Redwall's
kitchens and a window pole with a metal hook on one
end, his chosen weapon. With neither care nor conscience, he composed a marching song as he went on his
way:

> "I'm a one chap regiment,
> Don't y'dare stand in me way,
> No Abbey cell could suit me well,

> On such a jolly day.
> O trampitty tramp I'm marchin',
> Stand fast the Buffs, I sing.
> If I had a drum I'd go rumpetty tum,
> I'd biff it like anything.
> I'm a perilous hare y'know,
> Just like me dear old dad,
> A word's as good as a blow, hoho,
> Though some may think me mad . . ."

He paused and pulled a face. "Mad? No, no, not the right word at all—have t'change it. Let's see, mad, bad, glad, sad, old lad? Hmm, I'll have to think about that one."

In the midst of still-shimmering noontide, the trio of serpents struck. Everybeast was unprepared for the lightning move. One moment the glade was quiet and peaceful, save for an occasional muted snore. Then, in the blink of an eye, the whole scene changed. Zassaliss had spent the last hour inching the oak tree door open, fraction by fraction. Suddenly the adder saw that the way was clear. He hissed, "Sssssstrike!"

Together the trio of snakes boiled out of the entrance. Straight across the glade they rushed, with the mace chain clanking behind, right past the carcass of Whidge, whom they already knew to be dead. Crashing into the fern bed, they snatched a plump sleeping Ratguard, who shrieked as they seized him.

Kurda came awake immediately. Grabbing her sabre, she yelled urgently, "Stop der shnakes! Arm der crew! Don't let de serpents get back inside der den. Hurry!"

To their credit, the Ratguards roused themselves swiftly. Vorto kicked the pile of weapons, scattering them as he ran by, shouting, "You 'eard the Princess, git yore swords, cut 'em off afore they escape!"

But the adders were faster. Bunching their coils jointly, they slithered backwards like lightning, dragging the feebly kicking Ratguard into Brockhall with them. Vorto

paused momentarily, looking to Kurda for orders. Her
eyes shone madly at the sight of the coveted Crown of
Sarengo vanishing into the darkness.

"In! In! Get in after dem, kill de serpents! Get der
booty! De cowards run, dey are scared of us! In! In!"

Tazzin swung a dagger about her head, fired by the
mention of booty and the excitement of the chase. "Did ye
'ear that, mates? Booty! Chaaaaaarge!"

Both Ratguards and Freebooters piled into Brockhall,
roaring and yelling after Zassaliss, Harssacss and Sesstra.

Skipper had just led the party into the big main cavern beneath the oak tree roots. Log a Log held the lantern up as
the others stared in awe at the mighty structure. Then a
deafening cacophony of noise filled the chamber: clanking
chains, hissing, pounding paws and yelling vermin. Before
they had a chance to group themselves, it broke in upon
them like a dark tidal wave. The three snakes collided with
the Redwallers. Mokug turned to run, his head butting
Triss under her chin. She slipped and fell, the sword
kicked from her grasp by the milling paws of shrews.

Zassaliss spat the dying Ratguard from his mouth and,
pulling the other two adders up with him, reared over the
fallen squirrelmaid and struck. Shogg hurled himself between them, slashing wildly with his spearpoint. Zassaliss
pulled to one side, attacking the otter with his poisonous
fangs as the spear struck Sesstra straight down her open
mouth. There was a roar like thunder breaking over the
sea, as Sagax swung his battle-axe, leaping into the fray.
Zassaliss ducked his head, and the big axe slew his
brother Harssacss. Triss rolled over as the adder's chin hit
the floor. Her paws clasped about the sword hilt, she
sprang upright, driving the keen blade straight through the
throat of Zassaliss.

Then followed a scene of utter chaos as the Ratguards
and Freebooters came tumbling on them in the wake of
the snakes. Both sides were confused until Skipper took
out a Ratguard with his javelin and gave the battle cry:
"At 'em, mates! Redwaaaaaaalllllll!"

Triss gathered in the vanguard with Churk, Sagax, Skipper and Log a Log. Backed by Guosim and Redwallers, they rushed the vermin, catching them off guard. Warcries rang out, echoing and bouncing off the walls of Brockhall as they drove the vermin back up the corridor.

"Eulaliaaaaaa!   Redwaaaaaalll!   Logalogaloga- looooog!"

Spear cracked against javelin, sword clashed upon cutlass, rapier rasped against daggerblade. But above it all, two stood out: the young badger wielding the fearsome battle-axe, and the squirrelmaid armed with the sword of Martin the Warrior. They were like twin whirlwinds, slaying and roaring as they went. Triss was wreaking retribution for the death of her father and Drufo. Vermin fell before her like chaff beneath a scythe. Sagax's eyes shone red in the gloom—he was possessed of the dreaded Bloodwrath, inherent to great Badger Lords of Salamandastron. Neither injury nor foebeast could hurt him as his awesome weapon swung into the vermin ranks like a windmill.

Tripping and stumbling, the vermin broke and ran in defeat, the Redwallers swarming after them. Their cries echoed off down the gloomy passage as Kurda, Vorto and Riggan sneaked out of a side chamber. Leaping over the carnage of dead and mortally wounded creatures, Kurda grabbed the crown from the head of Zassaliss. She slashed cruelly at the dead snakes, growling frantically,

"Vere is der pawring, dat is mine birthright!"

Riggan jumped aside, narrowly missing the sweeping blade. "It ain't 'ere—ye can see that for yoreself, marm. Leave it, we got to get goin' afore those Redwallers come back!"

Kurda leaned on her sabre, breathing hard. "Yarr, you are right, but I must find mine pawring!"

Vorto, catching Riggan's glance, interrupted. "Yore 'ighness, we can come back 'ere when they've gone. Me 'n' Riggan'll find yore pawring for ye. Come on, Princess, there must be a way out the back, or 'ow did the Redwallers get in? Can ye get us out safe, Riggan?"

The slavecatcher nodded. "Just follow the trail backwards where they've disturbed the dust an' broke the cobwebs. C'mon!"

Taking their advice reluctantly, Kurda put up her sabre and followed them to the rear exit.

Triss and Sagax threw themselves on the grass to regain their breath. Vermin could be heard in the distance, pursued by Redwallers as they fled in ignominious retreat, scattering widespread.

Sagax picked up a fallen water flask. Taking a deep swig, he passed it to Triss. "Whew, I can't remember half of what went on in there. Don't think I want to, really."

Triss stared bleakly in front of her. "I can. I still remember the whip strokes I received from some of those Ratguards when I was a slave. I grew up with them!"

"Triss, Trissy mate, 'elp me!"

Dragging himself along on his stomach, Shogg emerged through the open door. Triss was at his side in an instant. "Shogg, what happened, where have you been, are you hurt?"

Without allowing him the time to answer, Triss poured water into the otter's mouth as Sagax held his head up. The otter drank a drop, the rest trickling from his lips as he gasped, "Snake . . . the big 'un . . . bit me neck . . . Triss, lissen. Kurda, still alive . . . Vorto an' the slavecatcher, too . . . She got the crown . . . Gone out the back . . . Get 'em, Triss!"

The squirrelmaid saw her friend's eyes beginning to mist over. She hugged him close, rocking to and fro, murmuring, "We'll get them, mate, together, when you're better. But first we've got to get you to the Abbey. Malbun and the Abbot will know what to do. You'll be all right, my Shogg."

Slowly the otter raised his paws until they held either side of the squirrelmaid's face. His voice sounded tired. "Too late fer that, me old matey. . . . Promise me, Triss, promise me ye'll go back to Riftgard an' free the slaves. That's wot we were always goin' t'do, wasn't it?"

Her tears spilled onto his paws as she looked into his
eyes. "Aye, right from that day we stole the boat and escaped. That's what we vowed and that's what I'll do, you
know that."

Shogg smiled. "That was a day to remember, eh, Triss?
The first slaves ever to escape from Riftgard." The otter's
eyes looked away from Triss, over her shoulder. "Welfo,
liddle maid, wot are ye doin' 'ere? Did ye come all the
way from Peace Island t'see me? 'Tis kind of ye, mate."

Shogg's eyes closed and his head lolled loosely to one
side. Sagax gently prised the otter's paws from Triss's
cheeks.

Triss stared in disbelief at the badger. "Shogg . . .
you're not . . ."

The young badger picked Shogg carefully up. He held
him like a babe, blinking back huge tears. "I'll let him rest
in the shade of that oak. When the others get back, we'll
take him to Redwall. Triss, I'm sorry."

The squirrelmaid just sat there and wept. Sagax came
back from his task and placed a paw about her shoulders.
"His heart has gone out across the seas to visit your friend
on that beautiful isle you told us of."

Triss wiped her eyes with the back of a paw. "I've
known Shogg ever since I can recall—we were slaves together. First I lost my father, then Drufo, and now Shogg,
the best friend I ever had, is gone. Stay away from me,
Sagax, I'm bad luck to know!"

The powerful badger heaved her upright and brought
his face close to hers. "I'm not leaving you anywhere,
Trisscar. When you return to Riftgard and free the slaves,
I'll be at your side. You can take my word as a warrior on
that!"

Mokug and Log a Log returned first. With them they had
an unhappy Grubbage. The hamster and the Guosim
Chieftain were desolated by the news of Shogg's death,
but Log a Log was not a beast to sit around grieving for
long. He took charge immediately.

"Mokug, tie our prisoner to a tree. Then stand by pore

young Shogg 'til our friends get back—together ye can take our mate 'ome to the Abbey. Come on, Triss me darlin', an' you, too, Sagax. We got business t'finish wid that white polecat an' 'er cronies. Weepin' won't git the job done. If'n our matey Shogg was alive, 'e'd be 'ard on the paws o' those scum right now. Wot d'ye say?"

With her eyes blazing hotly through the tears, Triss tightened her grip around Martin the Warrior's sword. "You're right, friend. What are we wasting time for?"

Sagax shouldered his formidable battle-axe. "I'm with you!"

Throwing caution to the winds, they lit a torch of pine and brushwood and marched boldly into Brockhall. Through the carnage of the battle they strode, ready for anything.

As Log a Log passed the trio of slain serpents, he commented harshly, "Yore killin' seasons are done. Mossflower's air will smell sweeter without ye!"

As Sagax mounted the steps to the greenstone exit, a shrew voice challenged him gruffly: "Who goes there? Show yoreself!"

The four Guosim guards they had left behind were in a sorry state. One lay dead, two were unconscious and the remaining shrew was wounded, though not badly. He pointed west into the woodlands.

"Three of 'em, Chief, the white 'un an' two rats. They pretended they was surrenderin' an' tricked us. Let me go with ye."

Log a Log applied a hasty bandage of dockleaves and grass to his clanbeast's injured side and made him comfortable. "You stay 'ere an' do wot ye can for yore mates. You'd only slow us down. Don't fret, we'll get 'em for ye!"

Riggan halted on the bank of a small, shady lake and sat down gratefully. "This'll do, we'll rest 'til nightfall. Then if'n you still want t'go back for that pawring, things should be quieter at that Brock'all place, marm. That's if'n ye want t'go, of course."

Kurda was polishing the crown with some dried moss. She breathed on it and rubbed busily, admiring the way the light caught the heavy gold circlet with its two large jetstones. The Pure Ferret paused and glared regally at her slavecatcher. "Dere is no question, I must return to dat place und find mine pawring. Vorto, go und get somet'ink for your queen to eat. I am hungry!"

Saluting with his spear, the Ratguard Captain obeyed. Riggan, the more forward of the two, commented drily, "So ye ain't a princess no more, marm—'tis Queen now, eh?"

Kurda drew her sabre. Sliding the crown over its blade, she held them both out to Riggan. "I am Queen by right und conquest. If you vant to be Queen, all you haff to do is lift der crown from dis sabre blade."

Riggan chuckled nervously, knowing what would happen the second she reached out to touch the crown. "Wot gave ye the idea I want t'be Queen, marm? My duty is to serve you an' yore father, Agarnu. Er, wot about 'im?"

Kurda's eyes narrowed, and she giggled like a naughty infant. "Dat von-legged fool? I giff him der same offer I make to you, mine friend. Yarr, I vill be Queen of all Riftgard!"

Vorto came stealing furtively back to the lake bank. Kurda gave him a questioning look. "Vere is der food I send you for?"

The Ratguard Captain placed a paw to his lips. "Not so loud, yore 'ighness, I just seen somethin'. D'yer remember that big rabbit at Redwall Abbey, the one who snared our guards in a net an' whacked 'em? I saw 'im by chance out in the woodlands, but 'e didn't see me, an' 'e's comin' this way!"

Kurda's face was the picture of smug self-satisfaction. "I remember dat von. Hide now, ve vill ambush 'im!"

40

Scarum was lost. Between stopping to eat, napping, and composing heroic ballads about himself, the young hare had wandered willy-nilly through Mossflower and missed all trace of his friends. But he was not unduly bothered; anything was better than skivvying at Redwall on a restricted diet. He rambled on, holding a lively conversation with himself.

"Lost? Oh come off it, old sport, a chap of my perfect qualities is never lost, wot! I'll wager anythin' that pretty soon I'll hear Sagax shoutin' it's time for lunch. Huh, that stripeheaded baritone pal o' mine has a voice like a bloomin' bushel o' bullfrogs, lets the whole world know when he's hungry. Not like me, of course, the tiniest whisper is all I jolly well give when it's time for the old nosebag. Not one to yell about scoff, never was!"

He caught sight of the pond with a loud whoop. "What ho! Fresh clean cool water, just the thing for a growin' hare. Hope there's some o' those flippin' tasty little watershrimp whizzin' about in there, wot wot?"

Scarum crouched in the shallows, making the most outrageous guzzling noises as he sucked up lakewater. He

belched and wiggled both footpaws. "Capital stuff, water!
Fills the old tum, drives away the drought, an' cools off
one's weary paws. Not as tasty as strawberry fizz, but it'll
do at a pinch, eh wot!"

Glancing down at the shaded surface, he saw the re-
flections of Kurda, Vorto and Riggan standing behind
him. Catching sight of a flashing sabre blade, Scarum
went into quick action. Grabbing his window pole, he
did a straightforward roll into the lake. Twisting about,
he came up almost waist deep, facing them with his
weapon at the ready.

"Bounders, what did your mothers tell you about
sneakin' up on a body, eh? Jolly bad form, if y'ask me!"

Kurda grinned out through clenched teeth. "Gedd 'im
out, Vorto!"

The Ratguard waded in, thrusting with his spear.
Scarum countered with his metal hooked window pole,
landing Vorto a thwack on one ear which set his head
ringing.

Kurda shoved Riggan forward. "Don't shtand dere!
'Elp Vorto!"

Scarum knew he was in trouble. The only advantage he
had was the water at his back. Vorto and Riggan moved
apart, getting on either side and outflanking their quarry.
The young hare swung his pole left and right, beating off
the menace of the spears, which were shorter than his
weapon. Kurda stood on the bank, waiting, knowing he
could not keep his defence up for any length of time.

After a while Scarum began to flag. The pole fell
lower until it was splashing the water at each stroke.
Posturing, with the sabre point held forward, Kurda entered the lake, wading forward toward her victim. The
hare thrust at her with his pole, leaving his sides momentarily unguarded. Riggan swung her spear powerfully, catching Scarum a hard blow to the back of his
head and knocking him senseless. Kurda retreated
swiftly from the lake, not liking having her footpaws
wet. "I hope you haff not slayed 'im. Pull der rabbit
ashore. He vill die bit by bit, yarr!"

* * *

Scarum's skull throbbed remorselessly. He opened his eyes to find the earth had turned upside down. Riggan was squatting nearby, chewing on a half-ripe pear. She winked at the young hare. "Yore goin' to wish I'd finished yer off in the lake!"

Craning his neck painfully upward, Scarum saw that he was bound by both footpaws, suspended from the limb of an alder tree. Riggan gave him a push, which set him swinging. "The rabbit's awake now, marm!"

Kurda had been honing her blade on a stone. She came over and stood in front of her prisoner. Scarum decided that he had better mind his manners. "Er, good day to you, madam."

The Pure Ferret clipped the top from a rush with an expert flick of the sabre. "I am not der madam, I am Queen Kurda of Riftgard. Nobeast in all der Nort'lands has mine skill mitt der sabre."

Scarum tried a warm smile. "Pleased t'meet you, I'm sure, skilful with the old sabre, wot. Need lots o' practice for that sort o' thing, I'll wager."

Kurda brought the point to rest against Scarum's nose. "Oh yarr, lots of practice, I alvays practice. Sometimes mitt turnips, but dat's no fun. I like to practice mitt mine sabre on livink beasts."

Scarum gulped. "Actually I come from a jolly long line of turnips—a dull bunch we are. Er, haha, you should see my old granny turnip, she's really goin' to seed this season!"

The sabre flicked sideways, shearing the whiskers from one side of Scarum's face. Kurda narrowed her eyes. "First de whiskers, den de ears, von at a time. Ve haff all day to play diss liddle game, yarr?"

Scarum could see by the way Riggan and Vorto turned their faces away that his time had come. He dropped all pretences and snarled at his tormentor, "Then do your worst, you milk-furred scum, I'll see you at Hellgates one day. Aye, and I won't be helpless then!"

Scarum raised his voice and yelled out the old Sala-

mandastron war cry, hoping to go out bravely. "Eualiiii-
iaaaa! Blood'n'vinegar, chaps! Eulaliiiiiiaaaaa!"

Kurda's sabre was upraised when suddenly there came
a huge booming answer, which she knew was no echo.

"Eulaliiiiiaaaaaa! We're coming! Eulaliiiiiiaaaaaa!"

Crashing through the shallows of the lakeshore, Sagax
came thundering towards Kurda, swinging his massive
battle-axe in one paw. On the bank alongside him, Log a
Log and Triss ran their hardest to keep up with him.

Kurda screeched to Vorto and Riggan, "Shtop dem,
quick!"

She had her back to Scarum. Swinging himself forward, he grabbed her around the back of her neck and
hung on grimly. Riggan turned to run away, but Log a
Log's rapier, hurled like a javelin, stopped her for good.

Triss put on a turn of speed, shouting at Sagax as she
passed him, "The white one's mine!"

Vorto's spear snapped like a twig as Sagax bulled him
into the lake. The battle-axe cleaved midair, water, and the
Ratguard Captain, all in one stroke.

Kurda was struggling wildly in Scarum's grip as Triss
went bounding by, leaping like an acrobat. Her sword
sheared the rope from the alder branch, dropping Scarum
onto Kurda. They both went down in a huddle, and the
sabre was knocked from Kurda's grasp. She reached for
it, only to find a footpaw resting heavily on the blade.
Scarum extricated himself and scrambled free.

Triss stepped away from the blade and stood over
Kurda. The squirrelmaid's voice shook with pent-up rage
as she grated at her foe, "Remember me, Princess? I used
to throw turnips up for you to practice on. I'm the escaped
slave who stole your ship. Well, you've chased me across
the great seas, and now you've found me. Pick up that
sabre, stand and face me!"

It was the first time in her life Kurda had faced a creature that was armed and ready for her. The others had
never been a problem. They were usually bound and helpless, and she had always been surrounded by Ratguards to

protect her. A chill of fear ran through the Pure Ferret. Rising slowly, Kurda picked up her sabre. Triss circled her, the point of Martin's sword weaving and flickering about her sworn enemy, taunting her.

"My father was Rocc Arrem, the greatest swordmaster in all the Northlands. He was slain by your family, with arrows, because they feared him. You slew his friend Drufo, who was old and weak. I watched you kill him. So now, let's see what murdering one old creature and chopping lots of turnips has taught you, coward!"

Triss deliberately lowered her sword. Kurda tried a swift sabre slash at her opponent's head. Like lightning Martin's sword came into play, whipping through the basket-hilted sabreguard and flicking the weapon out of Kurda's paw. Triss moved back a pace. "Pick it up and try again, turnip chopper!"

Kurda felt her paws shaking as she retrieved her sabre. This time Triss allowed her two thrusts before disarming her with a similar swift twist.

Log a Log murmured admiringly to Sagax, "Great seasons, I never saw anybeast that good with a blade!"

Kurda dived to grab back her sabre, panic-stricken. Triss slapped the flat of her blade across the Pure Ferret's rump, admonishing her like a clumsy novice. "I never told you to pick it up again. Tell me, how does it feel, being treated like a slave?"

Triss contemptuously turned her back and walked away. Kurda's anger at the way she was being treated overcame fear. She grabbed the heavy sabre with both paws and charged screeching at Triss's unprotected back. The squirrelmaid skipped to one side as the sabrepoint buried itself in the earth. Triss whirled and struck the blade with all her might. It was a sturdy sabre, but no match for the great sword of Martin the Warrior. There followed a loud metallic clang as the sabre snapped in two halves.

Kurda stood shocked, staring at the broken weapon in her paws. Then she ran for her life. Triss sped after her, yelling, "You can run, but there's nowhere you can hide, coward. I'll get you!"

Kurda looked back as she ran full pelt, to see Triss hot on her trail. It was a fatal mistake. The Pure Ferret tripped on a protruding tree root and slammed down heavily on the lake bank. She was lying curled up and still when Triss reached her. Triss saw the broken sabre blade, which was still held tight in both of her enemy's paws. Kurda had fallen onto the broken blade. She stared up at the squirrelmaid through dead eyes.

Sagax picked up the Crown of Sarengo from where it had fallen and gave it to Triss. "I think this belongs to you now."

Bitter tears welled in the squirrelmaid's eyes as she sat gazing at her slain foe. "She cheated me of my revenge!"

Log a Log gently removed the sword from her grasp. "No, she never, Trissy. You defeated 'er, fair'n'square!"

Grasping the shrew's paw, Triss pulled herself upright. "But she killed herself by accident."

Placing the sword back over Triss's shoulder, the Guosim Chieftain shook his head firmly. "Wot would ye 'ave done if'n you caught up with 'er, eh? Made Kurda fight on wid a broken blade? No, matey, that's not yore style. You couldn't slay a beast in cold blood, ain't that right, Sagax?"

"Aye, right, friend. Kurda lived and died like a coward: running away. Think about it, Triss, you wouldn't allow yourself to dishonour Martin's sword by using it to slay that gutless craven when she wasn't properly armed. You aren't a killer—there's a lot more to you than that. Martin chose you for the creature you are, right?"

Triss tucked the crown into her belt. "Thank you for your kind words, Sagax—you are right!"

Log a Log threw a paw about her shoulders. "Of course 'e is. Come on, let's go home, Trisscar Swordmaid."

Scarum came hopping up, rubbing a bruised forehead. "I say, chaps, would somebeast mind cuttin' this confounded rope off me footpaws? It's tight as blazes!"

Sagax took a mighty swing with his battle-axe. "Eulaliiiaaa!"

The hare closed his eyes and winced as the axe chopped clean through the ropes that bound his footpaws together. He tossed the rope ends huffily into the lake. "Great big showoff, y'nearly left me pawless. Oh, an' you, too, miss. Y'might have taken the trouble to cut a chap down properly. Leapin' about an' choppin' with that sword. Just look at this bloomin' wound on me bonce—I fell right on top of that vermin, she had a blinkin' skull like a rock. Oh, woe is me, chaps, only half a flamin' set o' whiskers an' my young good looks ruined by this enormous bump!"

Sagax caught Scarum, none too gently, by his ear. "I thought we left you to guard the Abbey. What are you doing out here in the middle of the woodlands?"

Scarum suddenly forgot his injuries. "What, er, oh that! Long an' complicated tale, had whacking great injustices done to me, y'know. Thought it best to relinquish command an' join me old comrades, couldn't let you lot face those vermin alone, wot!"

Sagax growled menacingly. "I hope you're telling the truth."

The incorrigible hare put on his noblest face. "Shame on you for thinkin' otherwise, sah! Oh, er, I say, Triss, you're a good-hearted type. Would you like to put in a word or two for me when we get back? Talk to the Abbot an' Memm, an' those other old fogeys. Tell 'em how I found you three strung up by the footpaws an' risked life'n'limb to rescue you. Pretty maid with an honest face, they'll believe you, I bet. But don't get too jolly fancy about it, just picture me as a modest type doin' me duty."

Triss could not help laughing at the horrified look on the face of Sagax. She winked reassuringly at Scarum. "Of course I will. And what about the three serpents you slew? Shall I mention them also?"

Scarum clapped Log a Log on the back cheerfully. "No no, old Log'll do that, won't you, me stout shrewchap. No need to go into detail, just mutter somethin' about me tyin' 'em up in knots an' pullin' their fangs out, that should do the trick. Er, Sagax, old pal of my Dibbun days, don't you say anything. Lips sealed, keep mum, nod's as good as a wink an' all that. Be a strong silent badger type, wot, don't say a blinkin' word!"

Both Triss and Log a Log nearly collapsed laughing. "Hohoho, don't say a blinkin' word, eh?"

"Heeheehee, he's speechless now. Just look at his face!"

Scarum did. "Huh, looks like a toad chokin' on a tadpole, if y'ask me. Yowchyow! Gerroff, y'big brute!"

Triss and Log a Log sat dabbling their paws at the lake edge. They watched Sagax chasing Scarum, aiming hefty kicks at his tailscut as the hare fled, complaining loudly.

"Wowch! Some pal you are, what've I done now? Woop! Where's your jolly old sense of humour, wot? Owch, gerroff!"

41

Extract from the journal of Malbun Grimp, Healer and Recorder of Redwall Abbey.

Joy and sorrow, sorrow and joy. There are times when the two go paw in paw. Sorrow for the goodbeasts we lost in battle, Redwallers and our friends, the Guosim shrews. There is always a price to be paid for peace. Though by Skipper's account, the vermin paid the heavier price—very few of them escaped to tell of their defeat. Yet the saddest picture that remains in my mind is that of Kroova, the otter who stayed behind to guard our Abbey. He and Shogg had become close friends. I was standing beside him on the walltops as Shogg marched off after the vermin. He waved to Shogg and shouted that he would ask Friar Gooch to make some shrimp'n'hotroot soup for them to share on his friend's return. Poor Kroova, when he saw Shogg's body being borne back on the shoulders of Skipper and Churk, my heart went out to him. Though Shogg was only a visitor to Redwall, that brave otter will be with us

always now, resting beneath a shady willow by the
pond. I awoke this morning and watched the sun
rise over Redwall. In that stillness I felt the joy that
peace brings. Our home, free from the threat of serpents and roving vermin bands. There is no feeling
on earth to equal it!

Now, let me tell you of some extraordinary
events. My friend, Abbot Apodemus, told me that
he is allowing Martin the Warrior's sword to leave
Redwall! I could see clearly that Apodemus had
been touched by the Warrior's spirit. He assured me
that one day the sword would come back—he was
quite positive of it in his quiet way. So here is what
will happen. Trisscar Swordmaid, accompanied by
Kroova, Sagax, that rascal Scarum, Log a Log,
Skipper and Mokug, together with a few chosen
others, are embarking on a voyage. Before the summer is out they will sail to that land called Riftgard
in the Northlands, far across the wide seas. Churk
the ottermaid, splendid young creature, is to take
Skipper's place at the Abbey. Her brother Rumbol
has recruited ten other otters, all huge trustworthy
beasts, to hold Redwall safe. These and a full regiment of Guosim shrews, commanded in Log a
Log's absence by Gulif, will stay with us until Skipper returns. I do not normally take to vermin, but
the sole captive whom Redwallers took is a jolly
fellow, and not at all unlikeable. His name is Grubbage. He is an excellent navigator, and will be going along on the voyage. Trisscar Swordmaid has
sworn to free every slave in Riftgard. She has the
bravest and best of companions to aid her. Good
fortune go with them all.

*Extract from the diary of Churk, ottermaid and Head
Scholar to Redwall Abbey:*

The feasting is done and our friends have departed.
But what feasting! Four nights and three days, the

food, the fun, the poems and the singing. Even the
Dibbuns will remember it for as long as they live.
Gulif and I accompanied the voyagers to the coast.
We rose quietly and left in the hours before dawn.
Uncle Skipper said that if we had not, it would have
taken another three days to say our goodbyes and
have even more supplies of food loaded onto the
travellers.

Gulif is the proudest Guosim shrew alive. Just up
the stream from where the ford crosses the path,
Triss uncovered the most beautifully crafted small
ship from its hiding place in a backwater. She presented it to the Guosim tribe, promoting Gulif to
captain. It now goes under a new name; the strange
writings have been blotted from its stern. Triss re-
named it with one single word: *Shogg!* We jour-
neyed down to the sand shores that fringe the wide
blue seas. Grubbage took us to where a huge vessel
was moored. We let Mokug rename it *Freedom*. So
much food went aboard that Scarum wanted it
called *Scofftub*. He was most disappointed not to be
made cook, but Sagax would not permit it. It took a
day to get the *Freedom* cleaned up and seaworthy
again. She sailed on the evening tide. Gulif and I
watched her go. We stood in the shallows and
waved until she was out of sight, sailing over the
deeps with a fiery setting sun turning her sails to
crimson. May the wind be at their backs and the
weather fair to speed them homeward one day.

*Taken from the writings of Merola, Badger Lady of Sala-
mandastron on the western shores of Mossflower territory:*

This very afternoon a huge vessel sailed into the
bay. Alarms were sounded; my husband, Lord
Hightor, and Colonel Whippscut turned out the
guard! Myself and the Colonel's good lady, Dunfreda, watched from an upper window of the moun-

tain. Imagine our surprise when our sons Sagaxus
and Bescarum came wading ashore at the head of a
very strange-looking crew! Well, we brought them
all to the banqueting hall and the cooks went to
work. Hightor and Whippscut kept pacing around
Scarum and Sagax, patting their backs, calling them
young rips, winking a lot, and enquiring about their
adventures. But they are not young rips any longer,
it is plain to see. In the space of a single season they
have become warriors. They seem to have grown—
even Dunfreda stopped wailing into her kerchief
long enough to remark on this. They stand
straighter, they even look perilous. My Sagax carries a battle-axe, of all things! I was astounded to
hear that Memm Flackery sends her best regards
and dearest wishes to me. We were the best of
friends. Oh dear, suddenly I feel quite old. But
proud also, like Lord Hightor, to think our son has
grown up as we wished he would: strong, honest,
and true to his friends. Do you know, I've even
taken a liking to that rascal Kroova Wavedog—he's
growing up nicely, too. Scarum's appetite hasn't
been affected, though he does look funny with half
a set of whiskers. The stories I heard him telling his
parents, he must be very, very brave! The pretty
squirrelmaid and that fine big otter, Skipper, sat up
almost all night, conferring with Sagax, Scarum,
my husband and Colonel Whippscut. Unfortunately
I had to take Dunfreda up to her room, as she was
wailing so much nobeasts could hear themselves
speak. She cried herself to sleep, saying it was because she was so happy. I fell asleep in the
Colonel's comfy armchair, overcome by the day's
events.

Next morning after breakfast, Hightor broke the
news to me. Sagaxus is sailing away again! After
being back home little more than a day, would you
scarce credit it? However, I heard the full story, and
I wish I was young enough to go with him. All those

poor creatures across the sea, forced to live in slavery. My son and his friends will soon put a stop to all that, believe me. Hightor immediately put extra provisions and twenty veteran Long Patrol fighting hares aboard the ship to accompany them. Quite rightly, too!

My paws still ache from waving them off. I had to tear up an old bedsheet for poor Dunfreda's tears—you know how she always weeps. Both our sons assured us they would be back, if not permanently, then at least once every two seasons for a longer visit. I am sad and happy at the same time— it is all very confusing. Dunfreda and I hugged and kissed them so much, we got our gowns wet, standing there in the shallows. Skipper is the dearest of otters—he would not let either of them aboard until they had said goodbye properly. I let Sagaxus go, because I felt I was embarrassing him in front of his friends. As the *Freedom* got under way, I had to borrow some of Dunfreda's bedsheet. I could not stop myself from weeping. Hightor's cheeks were damp, too, but he said it was seaspray. There they go, out onto the deeps, to who knows where. Goodbye, my son, I know you will make me even more proud of you than I am now. Sagaxus . . . Sagaxus . . .

Section from the log of the good ship Freedom, *written by Bescarum Lepuswold Whippscut, formerly of Salamandastron:*

Rotten bounders, the whole crew of 'em! Makin' me get my dainty young paws covered in blinkin' ink. I hate messin' about with quill pens, an' parchment an' ink. I'm a jolly good cook, y'know, but they won't let me near the galley, cads! Oh well, as my dear old ma always says, make do with what you've got an' weep a lot until they give you what you want, wot?

Right, here goes. We've been out at sea now for

exactly, er, a jolly long time. All the landlubbers
aboard have become pretty salty old dogs (which
means they're all done with bein' seasick). The
other mornin' I heard one of those Guosim types
yellin' out from the crows' nest (don't know why
they call it that, I've never seen a bloomin' crow sittin' up there)—anyhow, he woke me up with his
shoutin'. Somethin' about two points north an' a
tack west, an' all that nautical jimjam. What the
blighter meant was that he'd spotted an island.
Bloomin' great mountain o' greeny blue rock glim-
merin' away in the sunlight. Triss called it Peace Island. Had to agree with her, it's the hugest piece o'
rock I ever saw stickin' up out o' the briny, wot. We
didn't go ashore really, too many of us t'be clam-
berin' up a whoppin' great mountainside. But the
chaps who live there came t'see us. Sturdy-lookin'
bumpkins, big healthy hedgehog types. Spoke quite
oddly, I can tell you. Theein' an' thouin' an' thyin',
bit of a rum do, wot? But the scoff they brought
with them, great fur'n'frog feathers! I've never
clamped eye on fruit'n'vegetables so big an' plump
an' tasty. A good old mammy-type hog, name of
Downyrose, took a shine t'me an' fed yours truly
enough to stuff a tribe o' toads! I gave her a kiss an'
a hug (got the old paws prickled a bit, but well
worth it, I'd say).

   Whilst this all was goin' on, Triss is weepin' an'
kissin' a hogmaid she calls Welfo, an' another
young chap named Urtica, an' a big old daddy hog,
name o' Bistort. They did carry on, though, all
laughin' an' cryin' an' sayin', "Thou hast returned,
welcome to thee!" Nobeast seemed t'be payin'
much attention to the tuck, so I located a rhubarb-
'n'apple crumble, an' let 'em get on with it.

   Naturally there were lots more tears when Triss
gave 'em the sad news about poor Shogg, but when
she told Welfo and her friends about the pretty little
boat named after him, it cheered 'em up a touch.

D'you know, I can't stand that blinkin' Sagax, he
paces the deck with that flamin' great hatchet thing,
watchin' every mouthful I take. Keeps remindin' me
that there's others aboard, an' that we've got the rest
o' the voyage to complete, wot? As if I didn't jolly
well know. I told him if he didn't like it he could
swim behind the ship with his axe in his mouth,
keepin' an eye out for sharks the rest o' the way.
Good job he's a pal o' mine, or I might've tossed
him overboard myself!

*N.B. There is a space in the log here, also several stains
on the parchment, which look like blueberry juice, leek-
and-mushroom soup, and an unidentifiable pudding with
honey and nuts in it. Then the log continues on the following day.*

Life's flippin' rotten at times, ain't it! We've hardly
been here since last noon, an' it's furl the anchor,
lower the bilges, rattle your reef sails (an' all that
seagoin' codswallop). We're leavin'? All that wonderful scoff, those delectable dishes, that fabulous
fruit, those . . . (what's a word that begins with V?)
those very very nice vegetables, an' we're sailin'
off, leavin' the bloomin' lot behind! Miss Triss is
lookin' pretty edgy, I notice. Even old chubby-
cheeks Mokug has gone all pensive an' grim. I expect it's 'cos the next stop is Riftgard. Well, forward
the Buffs say I, true blue an' never fail. A perilous
hare like me should gain a few medals in the battle
to come, wot. I'll show 'em! Not a blot on me copy-
book an' covered in glory, that's how this young
hero will return. Wonder what the food's like on
Riftgard?

This ink gets everyflippin'where, I'll have to
change me name to Scarum Bluepaw. Righty ho,
then, ship's log finished for the day, gorgeous
smells waftin' from the galley. Good cooks, those
Guosim lads. Oh, that reminds me. Log a Log an'

Sagax want a word with me, something important
probably, wot. I hope they don't mention that
blueberry-an'-pear pudden missin' from the galley
last night. It wasn't me, I was never near the
place—this is ink on me paws, not blinkin' blueberry juice. Bet it was Skipper, I don't know where
he puts it. Must have a hollow rudder. Think I'll go
an' hide in the fruit locker for a bit—pleasant in
there, wot! Bescarum Lepuswold Whippscut, Es-
quire, signin' off.

42

The following is an eyewitness account by a sea otter-maid.

My name is Sleeve. I am a slave, born and bred in the fortress of King Agarnu at Riftgard. I know no other place. It is a hard and cruel life. My mother and father died here when I was very young. We bend our backs to the whips of Ratguards, working from before dawn until long after dusk. We are always hungry. I was taught to write by an old squirrel called Drufo, who is gone now, slain by a princess of the Royal Blood. It was he who used to recite "The Slave's Lot" to me. I can still recall the words as he spoke them:

Bend your back beneath the lash,
Straighten it and feel some more,
Sleep and wake, work and starve,
That is what a slave is for.
Speak in whispers, never smile,
Serve the masters, bow your head.

The only time a slave is free,
Is when that slave is dead.

Yet I can remember the first day I really smiled. The
day when three slaves stole a royal ship and escaped. My heart leapt within me to know that they
had gone from Riftgard and all its miseries. I
charged forward, with no weapon but my paws and
teeth, me and many others. We stopped the Ratguards from capturing those brave three. But then
we were outnumbered, Drufo was slain and I was
beaten senseless. They threw us in the dungeons beneath Riftgard and locked us there, starving for
many days. Yet we smiled, we laughed, because
three of our number had found liberty and lived.
Later, I was one of the group who carried food
aboard that monstrous Freebooter ship, the
Seascab. I saw the Princess screaming with rage,
vowing to bring the fugitives back and punish them.
I saw Riggan the slavecatcher come aboard with
Captain Riftun. I saw the wicked Prince Bladd join
the ship. My heart sank within me. How could three
half-starved slaves on a little vessel escape such a
dreadful force?
   But hope lives in every living thing, even a slave.
We would whisper together as we toiled all day beneath the whips, we would dream every night as we
were locked inside to sleep on stone floors. Where
were our three friends, Triss, Shogg and Welfo?
Had they really escaped? Were they living in some
sunny peaceful place? I would join them in my
dreams, wandering through summery green woodlands, singing and laughing, with plenty of good
food, and soft mossy banks where they could lie at
night. Gazing up at the stars in an open sky. Sleep
can be glorious freedom to a slave, if the dreams are
beautiful. But then the guards come, banging and
shouting. Then you are forced into a waking nightmare. We were put to work on the King's new idea:

a stone tower on the clifftops, where he could watch for the *Seascab*'s return. As we laboured, we watched also, hoping that it would never return, for then we would be sure the three had made good their bid for freedom. Our new captain, Hydrad, used his spearbutt instead of a whip. Anybeast caught gazing at the sea got badly beaten by him, yet still we took the chance to scan the horizon whenever we could.

Then one morning it happened. Small at first, a mere dot out in the dawn light, but as it drew nearer, every slave fell silent. That ship, the *Seascab,* like a great dark bird of ill omen, was returning. We were swiftly marched down to the pier and jetty by the fjord. Messengers were sent to the fortress. King Agarnu was carried out on a litter, for he has become too heavy to walk on that false leg of his. Captain Hydrad estimated that the *Seascab* would make land on the floodtide and sail up the fjord. Spear-carrying Ratguards, freshly uniformed, were lined up along the route to the fortress. We slaves were forced to kneel at the Fjord edge in rows. Instructions were given. It was our honour to receive a day off work, and we were told that when the *Seascab* docked, we were to keep chanting, "Hail Princess Kurda! Hail Prince Bladd! Hail Agarnu, King of all Riftgard!" What choice does a slave have? As soon as Hydrad laid about one or two with his spearbutt, we started the hateful chant.

The sandbars and shallows at the estuary were deep under the running floodtide. The *Seascab* sailed into the fjord smoothly. Some of the slaves were weeping openly. I felt a lead weight inside my chest. Mental images of the three escapers being dragged in chains from the ship invaded my mind. Then I saw Triss the squirrelmaid. She was holding a magnificent sword. She was actually smiling! The hairs on my rudder still stand up when I think of how she raised that sword and yelled, "Freedoooooooom!" The deck became suddenly alive with warriors. Not vermin, but hares, otters, shrews and a massive young badger holding a battle-axe. Triss swung over the side on a rope, shouting, "Agarnu, I am Trisscar Swordmaid, I have returned!" Then the warriors poured off the ship, which had the word *Freedom* painted in large letters along its side. Agarnu called to his guards to engage the newcomers.

Caught up in the fantastic moment, I found myself yelling "Freedom," and rushing the guards who stood over us with whips. Then something heavy hit the back of my neck and I went down. Captain Hydrad was standing over me with his spearpoint at my throat. I was going to die. Magic happened then. I saw Hydrad's eyes roll up to the whites as he gave a sigh, let go of the spear and fell across me. A sea otter like myself pushed Hydrad's body off me. He had the nicest smile as he held out his paw and said, "Sorry about that, miss. I meant 'im t'fall the other way. You stick by me, I'll see ye safe!"

That was how I met Kroova Wavedog.

The Warriors made short work of the King's Ratguards. The vermin were overwhelmed by hares and shrews, who gave no quarter and took no prisoners. I turned my face away from the guards with whips, who vanished beneath roaring crowds of slaves, each one wanting to get at them. Those guards paid the final price for their seasons of cruelty. But it was Agarnu who screamed loudest. The slaves who had been carrying his litter, groaning under the weight of their burden, waded into the fjord and set it afloat. It did not sail far before it sank into the deep icy waters. Agarnu was sobbing, "I cannot svim, I cannot svim!" I saw the badger holding Triss back, then the King of Riftgard went under and never came up.

We made a bonfire in the courtyard of the fortress. Whips, spears, uniforms and anything, including the throne, which had the royal symbol on it, were burned: cushions, drapes, scrolls, tables, chairs, beds, everything! Some slaves took a white silk bedsheet and painted on it, in green dye, the word *FREE-DOM!* in large bold capitals. Kroova and I hung it out on two spearpoles over the fortress gates.

Food, we found food! Large stocks of it locked away in storehouses and pantries. Food that slaves had grown in the fields of Riftgard's slopes. Our cooks put on an amazing banquet. I was sitting by the bonfire, between Kroova and Triss, eating and singing. My face was hurting from smiling and laughing. Log a Log, the Guosim Chieftain, and a funny hare called Scarum followed Sagax down to the dungeons belowstairs. I was told later that the badger demolished each cell door with a single blow from his big battle-axe. The prisoners had to be treated carefully, for they were very weak and puzzled. When I told them they were free, some of them could not stop crying. We had to stop one or two who wanted to go back to the cells, afraid of what would happen if they were caught outside.

Mokug the old hamster came up from the cells carrying a small bundle. It was a tiny mousebabe. Nobeast knew who he belonged to. Kroova and I took him, fed him and wrapped him in silk sheets. Triss could see we liked the little fellow very much. She asked what we were going to call him. Kroova never hesitated. "Freedom, that's wot he'll be called. Freedom!"

Triss took a golden crown and a gold pawring from under her cloak. Both were studded with jet-stones. She watched the baby's eyes shining in the firelight as he gurgled and reached out with his tiny paws for the shiny objects. Triss gave both the pawring and the crown to him. She patted his head and said, "Pretty toys, that's all they are, pretty toys for a babe to play with. If he gets tired of them, let him throw them in the sea, because they're no use to any other creature."

This account of what happened at Riftgard, I entrust to Skipper. He has promised to let others read it. I do this because I want to thank all those good friends across the seas whom I have never met. Without them I would still be a slave. The Badger Lord and Lady of Salamandastron, the kind hedgehogs of Peace Island, and the Abbot of Redwall, together with all the dear creatures who dwell at the Abbey. There must be others I do not know about, honest beasts, who in some way or other helped Triss to honour her vow and free the Northlands of tyranny. My thanks goes out to all of you. I hope the reading of my letter conveys the gratitude I owe to you. Drufo, Shogg, and many slaves who died so others could live in the sweet light of liberty, did not give their lives in vain. The memory of their courageous deeds will be with us always.

There are no more kings or rulers here; we live together as one great family, though everybeast seems to look to Kroova and Mokug for guidance, they having been out across the seas to other lands. Talking of families, with Mokug acting as grandfather to our mousebabe, and Kroova and I treating him as if we were his parents, we have our own little family, the four of us. We have a lot to learn, never having known parents of our own. But from what Kroova and Mokug experienced at Redwall, its way of life and kind treatment to all, I think between them they will make our home a happy place to live. Yes, Kroova is staying here with me. He is sorry to see his old friends sailing away, but glad to have finally made something of his own. Perchance we may meet again one day, who knows? I will often go to the sea. There I will gaze out over the deeps and think of you all. You, who have made us straighten our backs and smile. May your seasons be long and peaceful.

—Sleeve.

*Written personally into the Abbey Archives by Apodemus,
Father Abbot of Redwall in Mossflower Country:*

Autumn mists have given way to winter's first frost.
Our Abbey prospers in calm and safety. Normally I
would lie abed a little longer, now that the mornings
are cold and dark. But today I walked in my sleep!
That is something I have never done before. It must
have been the spirit of our Warrior, Martin. Just before dawn he led me up to the northeast walltop and
left me standing there in my nightgown. Crikulus
and Malbun joined me, having heard me pass by the
gatehouse door. Those two! They had been up all
night, studying the artefacts they gathered from
Brockhall after it had been cleared and cleaned up.
So we stood there in the silent grey fog, all three of
us. I told them how I came to be there. Crikulus said
that Martin had his reasons. We decided to stay and
find out what they were.

Dawn arrived with a pale sun piercing the
oatmeal-hued gloom. We heard creatures coming
down the path towards Redwall. They were marching, singing a song to keep their paws stepping in
time. I knew it was one of that rascally Scarum's
Salamandastron barrack-room ballads. He was
leading the singing:

> "Straighten up those shoulders,
> Keep your chins up, chaps,
> Step lively in the ranks there,
> Don't ye dare collapse.
> I know the road's been long, sah,
> We've all been far away,
> But smile, ye laggardly, dusty lot,
> We're comin' home today!
> Home! Home! Home!
> Wake up the fat ole cook.
> Home! Home! Home!
> You'll see it if ye look.

> We'll kiss the babes an' pretty ones,
> Ring out the welcome bell,
> An' if the grub is good enough,
> We'll kiss the cook as well!
> Hurrah! Hurrah!
> Salute the Colonel, sah,
> An' pin a medal on me chest,
> Three ribbons an' a bar . . . Hurrah!"

The noise ended abruptly, because Scarum marched through the mist and straight into the wall. They had to carry him in.

And so our friends returned. We rang the bells until I feared they would crack. The whole Abbey was immediately aroused. Sister Vernal, Memm Flackery, Gurdle Sprink, and a pack of squealing Dibbuns came running. They hurried the travellers inside, served them hot drinks, bathed their foot-paws in warm water and applied salves. I was not surprised to see that our Triss had come back. She presented me with Martin's sword and told me to hang it up in Great Hall. I am vastly relieved that should we ever have need of a Warrior, one lives right here. Trisscar Swordmaid! I think Sagax will stay, too, and Scarum also (if the kitchens can stand it). They said they will visit Salamandastron every spring, and arrange for their parents to visit our Abbey. I would like that.

Well, the feasting, the song, the stories they had to tell about their adventures! We did some laugh-ing, I can tell you. There were also a few tears shed, but that is life, sunshine and showers. The main thing is that they are all home safe and well. Scarum is furious; he allowed Log a Log to trim his right whiskers to match the left ones, which were chopped off short. Unfortunately, Log a Log is no expert with shears. He cut the right side whiskers too short. Now the poor hare has hardly a whisker on his snout, he looks like a bemused rabbit. But

they'll grow back—time heals all. Did I tell you
Malbun is retiring, Churk is to become our new
Recorder and Sister Vernal is taking over as Healer
and Herbalist? Ruggum and Bikkle are training as
bellringers. Dearie me, will we ever get used to being wakened for breakfast in the middle of the
night? They are so enthusiastic, bless them.

So, here we are, back together again, all the old
faces and one or two new ones. Looking forward to
resting up through the winter. Fires and storytelling
in Cavern Hole, wonderful aromas coming from the
kitchens. Harvest all in, October Ale not long bar-
relled up, and our Abbeybabes plump and healthy.
Who could ask for anything nicer? And remember,
guests are always welcome at Redwall Abbey, anytime. Here is your invitation.

ABOUT THE AUTHOR

The cheers and cries of Redwall bands and their adventures have been heard around the globe, as storyteller **Brian Jacques** has explored the many worlds of the Mossflower mouse kingdom. An actor, a dramatist, a commentator for the BBC, Jacques has long had a following in England. But it was the publication of *Redwall,* the first volume in the epic, that brought him and his story to the world's children.

In recent years, Jacques has formed a dramatic company who have created audio presentations of his books. The Nelvana Company presents weekly, on PBS stations across the United States, the now-famous epic. And Jacques has invented another series, as different and magical as the first, in *Castaways of the Flying Dutchman*, an epic about a boy and his dog who, having escaped an evil ship, are destined to walk the world in search and aid of goodness.

When not writing or performing or commentating, Brian Jacques enjoys cooking, singing, taking long walks with his dog, and spending time with his friends and family at his home in Liverpool, England.

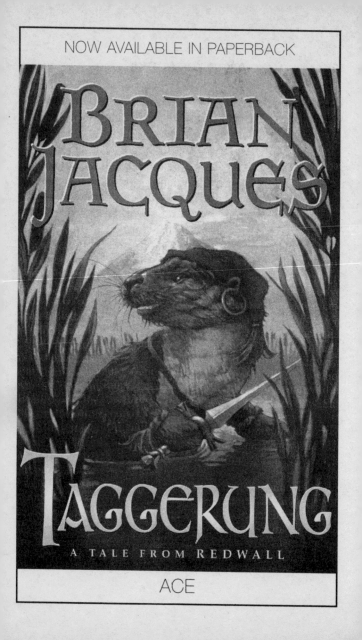

NOW AVAILABLE IN PAPERBACK

BRIAN JACQUES

TAGGERUNG

A TALE FROM REDWALL

ACE